THE SOLSTICE CIPHER

THE SOLSTICE CIPHER

BY
BRUCE HATTON BOYER

J. B. Lippincott Company
Philadelphia and New York

ST. PHILIPS COLLEGE LIBRARY

Copyright © 1979 by Bruce Hatton Boyer
All rights reserved
1 2 3 4 5 6 7 8 9
Printed in the United States of America

U.S. Library of Congress Cataloging in Publication Data

Boyer, Bruce Hatton,
The solstice cipher.

1. World War, 1939–1945—Fiction.   I. Title.
PZ4.B79226So [PS3552.O888]   813'.5'4   79-40
ISBN-0-397-01346-9

TO MY FATHER

Whose own experiences in World War II
were the unwitting source of this story

THE SOLSTICE CIPHER

1

The engines of the Army Air Force C-54 droned as it bounced down out of the gray storm clouds and leveled out over the dark earth. The whole craft rocked giddily in the gusts of wind as it descended. In a minute, it landed with a sharp clunk. The engines reversed, and the propellers grasped at the air, sending fine sprays of mist over Tim's window, obscuring his view.

When the plane finally came to a stop, Tim stared out through the beads of water over the bleak landscape before him. The stunted trees surrounding the military airfield stood naked against the October sky. Sheets of rain drummed onto the concrete runway; Tim could see that the storm had turned the grass field and dirt roads beyond it into furrows of mud. Someone at the front end of the C-54 opened the door. A burst of wind cut into the fetid atmosphere of the cabin. Tim breathed the wet air deeply. At long last he was in England.

The jeep ride was equally bleak. Tim grabbed onto the side panel to keep himself in his seat as the car lurched wildly into the swollen road. The American corporal at the wheel puffed on the cigarette dangling from his lips as he swung the wheel violently to maintain the jeep's course on the rutted highway. Through the sweeping gusts of rain Tim could vaguely make out quonset huts, ammunition dumps, and rows of vehicles stretching out across the fields, all covered with stringy nets of camouflage. There was an eerie stillness over everything, a stillness broken only by the patter of the rain.

"How far is it, corporal?"

"Bushey Park, sir? Just ahead."

"What can you tell me about it?"

The corporal looked at Tim quickly, then reset his eyes on the road. "You'll find out, sir."

Tim stared out through the flat windshield. He thought quickly of the hurried briefings he had gotten stateside and the quick shuttles between aircraft and trains. He remembered the terse smiles of the officers as they repeated what the corporal had just said. He rubbed his sleepy eyes and tried to ignore the uneasy feeling in the depth of his stomach.

The jeep pulled up to the guardhouse. Tim showed his papers to a sentry, and they continued on into the compound. Underneath the scattered trees were four wooden buildings, all one-story and all makeshift. Over them were tatters of camouflage. The corporal pulled the jeep over to one of them and slammed on the brakes.

"Here you are, sir. I'll take your duffel on over to your billet."

Tim grunted and got out of the jeep. "Thank you, corporal. Don't work too hard." The jeep belched noisily, spat mud from its tires, bounced in a wide circle, and went out the way it had entered.

Tim crossed a slatted sidewalk half sunk in mud and climbed wooden steps to the door. Inside, he walked over to the single desk in the cramped reception area. A British officer there was busy with stacks of papers.

"Sir?"

"Major Loftis, United States Army, reporting. I guess this is where I'm supposed to be."

The lieutenant rose. "Yes, Major Loftis. Glad to see you. Major Hardaway's been waiting for you quite some time now."

"The flight was late. Lousy weather."

"Of course, sir. At least you made it. Right this way, sir."

Tim followed him down a narrow hallway which extended along the entire side of the building. The lieutenant stopped at the third door and knocked. In the faint light provided by the windows and a few naked light bulbs hanging from their wires, Tim could barely make out a nameplate, which read, simply, MAJOR DAVID S. HARDAWAY.

A curt voice came from inside the office. The lieutenant opened the door a foot or so and put his head inside.

"Major Loftis is here, sir."

"Good. Send him in."

The lieutenant swung the door open all the way and stepped aside to allow Tim to enter.

In contrast to the hallway, the office was bathed with light. A large window admitted what was left of the dying afternoon. A ceiling fixture shed a warm glow over the room, aided by an antique rubbed-brass table lamp on the desk and a tall floor lamp standing next to a beat-up but comfortable-looking English club chair. In one corner stood the predictable file cabinet. On all four walls were hung maps and photographs, some of them pinned four or five deep. On the wall behind the desk was an elaborate map holder, with eight or ten metal arms which could be swung out to expose the maps beneath.

"Hello, major. Do come in." The British officer stood up and extended his hand, which Tim shook. "Sit down, by all means," he said, motioning to the club chair. Tim did so.

Major Hardaway sat down again behind the desk. He was of medium height, with graying hair brushed neatly back from a prominent widow's peak. He wore a thin mustache, neatly trimmed, and he gazed at Tim with cool, clear blue eyes. He had on a full field uniform, with a dark green tie tied precisely in a half-Windsor knot and framed exactly by starched collar points which sat perfectly on the shirt below them. The jacket held two rows of campaign ribbons. Tim thought he looked terribly English.

"Well, it's good finally to meet you, Major Loftis. I've just been reading your dossier. Most impressive."

"It's not that much."

"Don't be modest. A Ph.D. from Stanford University at your

age is quite an accomplishment." Hardaway leafed through a few papers in the open file before him. "I found your thesis title intriguing: 'Wave-Erosion Patterns and Their Influence on Berm Formation in the Salmon Creek, California, Quadrangle.' Bit beyond me, I'm afraid."

"It means that I spent a lot of time on the beach looking at the waves."

Hardaway chuckled lightly. "I'm sure you know a great deal more than you're letting on. At any rate, it's good to have you aboard."

"Where am I?"

Hardaway looked at him, one eye cocked quizzically. "You don't know?"

"Eight days ago I was in charge of beach security at Ford Ord, California. Then I got a message to see the C.O. Next thing I knew I was in Chicago, then Washington, then Newfoundland, then here. Nobody's told me anything."

"I'm sorry. Security and urgency account for that." Hardaway rose and walked over to the window. He pointed at the low buildings. "This, major, is part of COSSAC, office of the Chief of Staff to the Supreme Allied Commander. Main COSSAC headquarters is in London. Out here is the overflow. This is called Bushey Park."

"So this is a British base."

"Not exactly. It's an Allied post: combined British and American, with some Frenchmen and Canadians thrown in for good measure. Suffice it to say for now that every position at COSSAC is double-staffed, by both a British and an American officer. You and I, major, will be opposite numbers." Hardaway walked back to his desk, sat down in the swivel chair, leaned back, and slapped the map behind him with his hand. "Recognize this?"

"Coast of France," Tim replied. "From Normandy to the Belgian border."

"Correct. COSSAC is charged with making preliminary plans for a massive amphibious invasion somewhere along that coast by next summer at the latest. In a few months' time, a Supreme Commander will be named, COSSAC will be replaced by an organization known as SHAEF—Supreme Headquarters, Allied Expeditionary Force—and the attack will be launched.

"What we've been about for the last six months or so is laying out general strategies. Part of that process involved, naturally, detailed investigation of all the conditions along the projected invasion sites. I've been in charge of that. We've been combing every available topographic source for the entire hundred-and-twenty-mile coastal sector. And we've been poring through books, maps, travel brochures, and aerial recons, plus all the dispatches from the French underground, trying to find out everything we possibly can about man-made and natural features."

"That makes sense."

Hardaway shrugged. "Of course it does. Soon enough you'll see what we've gathered. However, it became apparent a while back that we were lacking reliable information on one critical area."

Tim chuckled. "Let me guess. The beaches."

"Precisely. We've learned a good deal about amphibious assault from operations in Africa and from some of the American operations in the Pacific. The technology is well-known." Hardaway paused. "You know about Dieppe, major?"

"A little bit."

"I believe it was the beaches that did us in there. It was an extremely costly lesson. We don't want another Dieppe."

"I can understand that."

Hardaway rose, took up a pointer leaning against the file cabinet, and started tracing along the map. "The primary areas under consideration are centered in two districts: here in Normandy and up here in the Pas-de-Calais. Each has advantages and disadvantages. Our research so far has shown that some of the ideal spots, at least at first glance, are also among the trickiest and least-charted beaches in the world. As I'm sure you know, tide levels and offshore shoal profiles are treacherous beyond description. About a month ago I began to insist at staff meetings that we bring on board someone who could do some hard inquiry into those beaches." Hardaway turned and smiled at Tim. "Luck would have it that the American army contained someone who could do just that."

"I'm beginning to get the picture."

"You're a trained geologist, and your specialty is waves and beaches. There aren't too many people like you, in or out of uniform."

"That's why I picked the field. Not a lot of competition."

Hardaway set the pointer aside and sat down. "What you'll do is provide COSSAC with as detailed a picture as you can put together of those geologic features. You'll have all the resources we can possibly furnish you. Here, take a glance at these."

Hardaway grabbed a thick file from the stack on his desk and pushed it over to Tim, who opened it. Inside were aerial reconnaissance photographs of part of the French coastline. Tim flipped through them, noting the data inked along the edge of each picture about date, place, height, and camera angle. He tossed the file back onto the desk.

"Those are nice photos, major, but I can't do much with them. They're all from ten thousand feet or more. I can't tell you any more from those pictures than any other reasonably intelligent person could. Sorry."

"I was afraid you would say that. And I appreciate your saying so. Ideally, you should walk along the beaches, or swim in the surf, or do whatever it is you geologists do. We've gotten hold of charts, but most of them are fifty or more years old. I'm told they're hopelessly out of date."

"For beach terrain as geologically unstable as Normandy's, I should think they would be."

Hardaway pursed his lips. "Nonetheless, major, we must make the effort. Or, rather, you must. The invasion of France will most likely be the pivotal event of the war. If it succeeds, we can bring Hitler to his knees. If it fails, the war could go into stalemate and leave all of Europe in the hands of the Germans. And we'll have only one chance."

"Well, I'll give it a try," Tim said without much conviction. The lack of sleep caused by the thirty-one-hour plane flight suddenly caught up with him, and he yawned. He looked up at Hardaway, who returned his gaze pensively.

"I know what you're thinking, Major Loftis. Here we are, each of us, doing things under conditions which make our doing them next to impossible. Yet somehow we're better equipped, or in better position, than the next chap, so we go ahead and do them. Praying the whole time." Hardaway rested his elbows on the arms of his chair and leaned back. The wooden chair gave out a mournful squeak. "We can only pray, I suppose, that we're guessing right, and that we're doing the proper thing. If we can believe that, we can hope that we'll finally win this war and be able to go back home and do whatever it is that we can really do, and do it well." He paused, then leaned back to the desk. "Tell me what you'll need to start with, and I'll do my best to get it."

Tim scratched his head. "First off, I want more pictures. I want you to figure out . . . oh, the top ten or eleven possibilities among the invasion sites and get me vertical and thirty-five-degree oblique recons from not higher than five thousand feet. Possible?"

Hardaway gave a low whistle. "We can try. It's a risky business, but perhaps we can get in a few sweeps some day when there's a low ceiling."

"Fine. Then I want all the charts you can get me, no matter how old."

"Those we have, as I mentioned, both here and up in London. They're fairly complete, but they're mostly in French. Do you read French?" Tim nodded. "Good."

"I want a large basement room, as free from vibrations as possible, and a carpenter skilled enough to make a wave channel."

"What's that?"

"A large tank, ten by twenty feet or so, and about two feet deep. Watertight, with glass sides, and a lot of sand. I'll make some sketches."

"Sounds fair enough. I'll ring up Staff Operations and see what I can do."

"Okay. And I want all the books in French, German, Dutch, and English that you can lay your hands on that describe the beaches and the entire coastal regions we're talking about."

"For that, the best wager is the British Museum. We have a research unit there, so you'll be able to move right in. I'd guess right now that you'll be out here for a week or two, and then get posted up to London so you can do your research there. Anything else?"

"A drink, a shave, and some sleep."

Hardaway pushed a button on his desk and smiled. "I'd imagine so. Lieutenant Nicoll will show you to your billet. Here." He opened his top desk drawer and removed a large envelope. "I've prepared a packet for you. Memos, operation orders, organizational charts, summaries, that sort of thing. Just to bring you up to where we are as of the present. There's a good deal of material, so you should be occupied for quite some time. Get a good night's sleep. I'd like to see you around oh-nine-hundred hours tomorrow so that I can introduce you to the rest of the staff."

The door opened, and the same officer who had shown Tim to Hardaway's office stepped in and saluted.

"Lieutenant, take Major Loftis to Clover Three and make sure his luggage hasn't been sent to North Africa. Major?" Hardaway rose and offered Tim his hand. Tim got up and shook it.

"Good night, sir." Tim left the room and Lieutenant Nicoll shut the door behind them. Tim started to go out the way he had come in, but Nicoll stopped him.

"This way, sir. Quicker out the back."

They went down the dim corridor and out the back door. It was evening, and the rain had stopped. A cruel wind bit into Tim.

He looked up. The heavy gray clouds were rolling overhead. From across the field came the low rumble of distant thunder. One hell of a storm was on its way.

The afternoon sun threw a pale yellow cast over the rim of the Dolomite Alps, deepening the cool green colors of the stands of pine trees and seeming to still the clear, rippling waters of Lake Garda. Under the shadow of the mountains, the little town of Gargnano spilled into the placid lake, the whitewashed fronts of the small houses along the water reflecting the dancing rims of light as sailboats put into the harbor after a brisk afternoon in the November sun. There was no evidence that a war was in progress 600 kilometers to the south except for the roadblocks at either end of the two principal entrances to the tiny resort town. At the roadblocks, sentries of the Waffen-SS stood guard by the colorful booths and wooden barriers. This village housed the headquarters of Army Group B of the Wehrmacht.

The black Horch with the small flags on the front fenders was waved quickly through the roadblock at the north end of town and proceeded down the Via Buozzi. Both in front of it and behind rode pairs of motorcyclists in black tunics, their bronzed helmets glistening in the clear Alpine sun.

Reaching the Piazza Maggiore, the limousine swept around the burbling, moss-covered fountain, its tires squealing slightly, and headed down the narrow street toward the Laterna, a centuries-old plaster lighthouse that might have inspired Stendhal had he known it. At the end of the street a gravel driveway led through thick Italian cypresses to a turnaround in front of a pale-ochre palace in the style of fifteenth-century Lombardy. The cortege came to a halt, and bare-headed German officers came streaming out of the front doors to fall into line.

The SS major who had been riding in the front seat of the Horch leaped out and snapped to attention by the car. From the front steps of the palace, a young colonel walked to the staff car and opened the door to the back seat. As the field marshal emerged from the automobile, twenty or so officers snapped to attention, their arms stiffened in the Nazi salute.

Erwin Rommel tapped his cap with his baton in acknowledgment and turned to the young officer who stood by the car door. Colonel Hans von Frickstein, aide to the Commander of Army Group B, slammed the door shut. *"Guten Abend, Herr Generalfeldmarschall.* We are pleased to see you safely back."

"Danke. The Italian sun feels good. It was very stormy at Berchtesgaden. Stormy in more ways than one." Rommel sighed. Time had not been kind to the former commander of the Afrika Korps. The two months he had spent in a military hospital in Semmering, following the final defeat at El Alamein and his recall from Africa, had not entirely erased the desert sores, nor had they allowed the husky timbre of the voice to return. Underneath the military field hat, the once-thin hair had completely disappeared, and Rommel appeared ten years older than the fifty-two he had become just a few days before, November 15. Still, as he crossed the gravel driveway and mounted the broad steps flanked by carved lions, the crisp military gait revealed glimpses of the determination and strength which had made him such a legend in the Fatherland.

Inside, Rommel walked down the corridor and turned left into an anteroom. The three staff officers who had been working busily at their desks rose and came to attention as he crossed the high-ceilinged chamber and went through the double French doors.

This formal dining room, which Rommel used as his private office, was immense, eight by seventeen meters, with French windows along two sides and a ceiling fresco representing the martyrdom of Saint Stephen done by Paolo Verocchino, from the workshop of Bellini. Rommel removed his field coat and hat and threw them over the Louis XIII love seat by the fireplace. Von Frickstein and the SS major followed closely after him. Taking his place behind the desk, which was set in the corner, where it commanded a splendid view of Lake Garda and the Alps beyond, Rommel glanced quickly through the papers stacked there and then looked up. "*Herr Oberst*, the Sturmbannführer is from the RSHA. See that he is given a bed, and tell the staff that I wish to see them tomorrow morning for a meeting at oh-six-hundred."

Von Frickstein clicked his heels and bowed his head slightly. "*Jawohl, Herr Generalfeldmarschall*. Most of the Command Staff anticipated your return today, and those who were at the front lines have returned. I will have the courier taken care of at once." He crossed to the doors leading to the anteroom and threw them open, issued a quick command, and stepped aside to allow the visitor to pass out of the office. Then he rejoined Rommel, who sat staring out of the windows.

"There are many sailboats today."

"We have had a regatta, *Herr Generalfeldmarschall*."

"A regatta? In the midst of a war? How curious that the German High Command should have time for such frivolities when Italy is being lost!"

"We . . . felt, *Herr Generalfeldmarschall*, that there was nothing to be done here until you came back from your conference with the Führer."

"Yes, I know," Rommel said. "Nothing ever gets done when the commanding officer goes to see the Führer. Everyone waits to see if he is still the commanding officer when he returns." When von Frickstein started to protest, Rommel held up his hand. "No, I am only joking." He raised his eyebrows. "Somewhat." He gazed at the handsome, aristocratic officer whom he had known and trusted since their days in Africa. Von Frickstein was the very model of the decent and honorable soldier.

A noise from outside turned Rommel's attention back to the window. Two SS officers were trying to navigate their pedal boat across the lake into its slip. They were obviously drunk; one of them waved an empty wine bottle. Three SS companions on the dock

[19]

were howling with laughter, redoubling their amusement whenever the boat crashed into the pier. The thick glass in the palace almost masked the sounds of their swearing and obscene jokes.

Finally, the Italian who owned the boat came running out onto the pier carrying a long gaff. He forced his way through the knot of officers standing on the pier, shouting angrily all the while in rapid-fire Italian as they stared at him. When he hooked the boat and started to draw it in to the slip, one of the SS officers stepped back and kicked him in the seat of the pants and all the soldiers burst into renewed gales of laughter.

"Look at them!" Rommel said, pointing to the officers, who were now punching the Italian. "The swine! This is what the Wehrmacht must bow down to! Their uniforms give the SS bravura and swagger they never had when they were begging their meals in the Marienplatz!" Rommel rose and walked away from the window. "It is a good thing I am leaving Italy. The Führer will soon cause us to lose Italy the same way he is causing us to lose Russia."

There was a pause. "Then it is true, *Herr Generalfeldmarschall*? The Führer has removed you completely from the Italian front?"

"I have been assigned to France. I will be in charge of strengthening the Atlantic defenses against the coming invasion." Rommel sat on the edge of his desk and crossed his arms. "I fear the Führer is going mad. When I walked into the room at Berchtesgaden, he was very cordial to me. At first. He smiled and shook my hand, asked me if my wounds had healed, and congratulated me on my strategies here in Italy.

"That was in the morning. Later in the afternoon the reports came in from Berlin and he went into a rage. It was a very good thing, he said, that he had decided to put me on the Atlantic seawall after my trip there last month, because it was my fault that Italy was being lost. Why, he screamed, was he surrounded by incompetents and cowards? His eyes bulged, and his arms shook with anger as he reminded me that it was my blundering that had lost Africa."

Rommel walked over to the window and absently fingered the swastika flag which hung on a gold standard near it. He sighed, then turned to von Frickstein.

"And now I am in charge of coastal defenses. I, the one general who truly understands the use of mobile forces, speed, the unconventional, the unusual . . ."

The sentence went unfinished as Rommel turned his attention to the view from the window. The sun was behind the mountains now, and the late afternoon had turned to evening. Along the lakefront, the warm glow of lights in the cafés and shops began to overtake the coolness of the night, casting a thousand reflections across the lapping water.

"When do we leave, *Herr Generalfeldmarschall?*"

Rommel turned. "Tomorrow. I have taken an old castle at La Roche-Guyon for my headquarters. You and I will go ahead of the rest of the staff. Please pass the order."

Von Frickstein clicked his heels, bowed, and went through the doors into the outer office. Rommel walked back to his desk. The piles of dispatches lay where von Frickstein had put them. Seeing them reminded Rommel of something. He walked over to the love seat and withdrew an envelope from one of the pockets of his field coat. Reading as he went back to the desk, he shook his head at the official order sending him to France.

Von Frickstein reappeared in the doorway. *"Entschuldigen Sie, Herr Generalfeldmarschall. Oberst* von Stauffenberg has just arrived from Berlin and wishes to speak with you."

Rommel walked to greet Colonel Claus Schenk, Count von Stauffenberg, as he came into the office. An intellectual like von Frickstein, he too had come from a family with a distinguished military history. Tall, incredibly handsome, he had been a superior horseman and a superb athlete. Rommel had not seen him since the battle of Kasserine Pass, where he had been wounded.

The change was horrifying. His clear face was now marred by a black patch where his left eye had been. His right hand was missing, and he extended his left one to Rommel, who gripped it warmly, only to notice that two fingers there were missing as well. The von Stauffenberg Rommel had known in Africa was good-humored, open, and brave; in contrast, here was a guarded, shadowy, maimed figure. Von Stauffenberg had once been what von Frickstein was now. Rommel shuddered at the thought that von Stauffenberg's fate might await all young and promising von Fricksteins.

"*Lieber* Stauffenberg! What an unexpected honor! Von Frickstein, bring coffee and cognac, *bitte*." Von Frickstein left. Von Stauffenberg removed his field hat with his left hand and tucked it under what had once been his right arm.

"It is good to see you again, *Herr Generalfeldmarschall*. It has been a while." Von Stauffenberg smiled grimly. "I am somewhat changed since last we met in Africa."

Rommel motioned for his visitor to sit in one of the side chairs by the fireplace. "*Ja*, I am sorry. I, too, have changed, not so violently perhaps, but almost as much!" So saying, he rubbed his hand over his bald head. The two men laughed. "What brings you here, to our lively little mountain village?"

"I have just come from Berlin. I was on my way to *Generalfeldmarschall* Kesselring's headquarters with new orders. My airplane developed engine trouble and was forced to land in Milan." Von Stauffenberg smiled. "I thought I would take advantage of the delay to come see my old commander."

Rommel returned the smile and waited. The urgency in von Stauffenberg's voice told him that this was more than a friendly social call.

Von Frickstein entered carrying a silver tray bearing a Florentine coffee urn, two cups, a bottle of V.S.O.P. cognac, and two snifters. He placed it on the table between the two generals and withdrew. Rommel poured cognac into the glasses and handed one to von Stauffenberg, who raised it in the obligatory toast: "To the Führer!" They drank.

Next Rommel poured the coffee. He handed a cup to von Stauffenberg, dropped a lump of sugar in his own, then sat back and stirred it slowly. There was a long silence, broken only by the gentle tinkling of the silver spoon against the delicate Danish bone china.

"The coffee feels good."

"Indeed, colonel. Winter is nearly upon us again."

"And how is the *Gnädige Frau* and your son?"

"Very well. I have not seen them for a few months now, but her letters suggest that things are going as well as can be expected."

Von Stauffenberg looked up quickly. "As well as expected, *Herr Generalfeldmarschall?*"

"The war. I refer only to that."

"Yes, of course. It is hard on all our families."

The room was dark now, as the last vestiges of twilight faded away. Only the small table lamps by the love seat and the desk lamp were turned on. They were like torches in a cavern, gently flicking the far corners of the large room with mysterious shadows.

"Tell me," Rommel said finally. "Why have you really come?"

Von Stauffenberg's smile vanished. "You are blunt." He set his cup gently on its saucer. "I too will be blunt." He took a deep breath. "I represent a group of concerned Germans."

"I trust we are all concerned Germans."

"Indeed. But our concerns are specific. I cannot say now how many we are, but we are numerous. Many of us are in the Wehrmacht, and others are in high positions elsewhere in the Reich."

Invisible fingers tickled the hairs on Rommel's neck. He had heard such introductions before, usually whispered in dark corners. "How specific?"

"We believe that the war cannot be won, and that we must act now and sue for peace."

"The thought is hardly a new one."

"I have been selected to talk with the major Wehrmacht officers in the West. If enough of us agree that the war will be lost, we will confront the Führer with these opinions. God willing, the Führer will realize that his major military strategists have seen the situation correctly and will bow to their judgment."

"I am trying to imagine the Führer ever conceding that his generals know more than he does. And I find I cannot imagine such a scene."

"*Generalfeldmarschall* von Kluge and *Generalmajor* Fromm have said they would support such a move. They are highly respected by the Führer."

"So are Keitel and Jodl. And those men would oppose any agreements with the Allies because they know, or they think they know, that the Führer would oppose them. Their support would be enough for him."

"And you, *Herr Generalfeldmarschall?*"

"What of me?"

"Would you oppose them?"

"Knowing that the war cannot be won and suggesting so to the Führer are two different things."

There was a silence. Rommel set his coffee cup onto the table and leaned against the love seat. He gave a long sigh. "Will you stay here tonight? It is a long way back to Milan."

"It depends on my airplane. You remember that it had engine trouble. That was why I was able to visit you."

"Yes, of course." Rommel smiled. "I hope you can stay, so we can have dinner together."

"It has been a long time since we have done that, *Herr Generalfeldmarschall.*"

"It would be enjoyable."

Von Stauffenberg reached for his cognac. "You have just been given command of the Atlantic Coast. Do you believe that you can keep the English and the Americans from landing in France?"

"Perhaps. Only perhaps. It will all depend on how quickly we can complete our fortifications there." He clicked his tongue softly. "If the invasion were to come tomorrow, no, we could not prevent them. If the invasion were to come in a year's time, yes. But since I feel that it will come in the late spring or early summer, I can only say perhaps."

"No doubt you will try to destroy them as they disembark?"

"In general, yes. That will be my strategy."

Von Stauffenberg fixed his eyes on Rommel, then spoke deliberately. "Will that make the war winnable?"

"No. It will only postpone things."

"Until when?"

"The Allies are sure to effect a landing in France. Sooner or later their air power will make that inevitable. Sooner or later the Russians are going to break through our lines on the Eastern Front." He paused, smiling slightly. "Sooner or later."

"Then what do we do? Continue to throw away the lives of our soldiers and our civilians in a useless struggle? Think about the casualties on the Eastern Front. Think about those!"

"Throw away lives, you say? That is what the Führer wants us to do, is it not?"

Von Stauffenberg rose quickly and walked into the darkness of the vast room. His boots clicked eerily on the floor as he went to one of the French windows. Rommel remained on the love seat, looking impassively at the coffee cups. "You know me well, *Herr Generalfeldmarschall.* You know that I am not a coward, and that I revere Germany." He paused. "If we cannot convince the Führer to make peace, I will carry out an alternative plan. I have applied myself for the last nine months to the problem of ending the war without being called a traitor to the *Vaterland.* And I have found no easy solutions. My life is of no importance, but my duty and my honor are sacrosanct. Yet I believe that even an act of cowardice would be preferable to the agony we are now going through! I am convinced that a few courageous officers must stage a *coup d'état* against the Führer."

Rommel had turned to look at von Stauffenberg but could not see him in the darkness. His pulse quickened and his hands trembled, but he managed to speak in a matter-of-fact voice. "What of Himmler? What of the SS?"

"We will deal with them as we must. If they wish bloodshed, the Wehrmacht will give it to them."

"And the Führer? What will happen to him?"

Von Stauffenberg walked back over to the love seat. The amber light threw a ghostly shadow on his fact. "The Führer has done much for Germany. We must stop him before his madness leads us all to ruin."

"Will you kill him?"

"Not unless we are forced to."

The room was silent. Rommel suddenly became aware of the clock ticking on the mantelpiece. Every beat of the pendulum seemed to crack like a rifle shot. He rose and walked over to the desk. "I must think about what you have said." He gathered up the unread dispatches, slid them into his briefcase, and snapped the lock shut. Von Stauffenberg remained standing by the love seat, a halo of light outlining his body. "There is much to consider. When can we talk again?"

"I think it is important that you talk with other people besides myself, whom you know and respect. They will contact you when they are able."

"One last question. What would be my part?"

Von Stauffenberg, who had been putting on his field coat, hesitated. "I cannot say. Others will speak to you."

Rommel nodded. "I shall wait, then."

After von Stauffenberg's departure, Rommel remained lost in thought. Across his mind flashed alternating images of the Führer yelling at him at Berchtesgaden and of von Stauffenberg's cool and thoughtful directness. As always, he couldn't force from his brain the images of death, of the dying and wounded, of young soldiers screaming, of civilians huddled in the underground shelters of Berlin, Köln, Hamburg, and München. They were the people who suffered most for the deranged decisions of the Führer and the OKW, the *Oberkommando der Wehrmacht*. And they were the people whose lives depended on a decision which he, Erwin Rommel, had to make all by himself.

As the sun had set on the blue waters of Lake Garda, so it set also on the cool frost-covered fields of Normandy. Jean-Claude Valberg rode his bicycle down the frozen roadway of National Route 13, which leads into the heart of Valognes.

Jean-Claude was a *courrier de la poste*, a mailman, in the town of Valognes, and he was glad to have finished his route for the day. The weak autumn sun, he thought, didn't bring much relief from the winds that howled in from the ocean. As he wearily pedaled his way up the last long slope into town, his breath became shorter and faster and the smoke from his nostrils trailed behind him. The wheels of the bicycle caught and grabbed in the frozen ruts formed by carts and motorcycles.

The bells of the great church tolled five o'clock as he entered the vast square in the center of Valognes. It had been a rough day, Jean-Claude thought, and a warm glass of wine would feel very good after pedaling so hard. He turned and headed down the Rue Delisle. Here the three-story stone buildings cast deep shadows over the street. Without the sun, it was even colder. Jean-Claude wound his way down the narrow street, stopped, dismounted, leaned his bicycle up against a wall, and went inside the café of the Hôtel de Toulouse.

Inside, the warm air of the cheery café made his face flush. In contrast to the cool loneliness of the country roads, the café was noisy, bustling, and filled with merry faces. Jean-Claude unwrapped the long beige muffler from around his face and neck and walked slowly through the room, smiling at the people who addressed him.

"*Bonjour, Jean-Claude! Il fait froid aujourd'hui, n'est-ce pas?*"

"*Très froid, Monsieur Picard!*" he answered cheerfully, and grinned.

Jean-Claude leaned against a pillar in the corner and sipped his wine, appreciating the warm glow which the red Brouilly caused in his limbs. His eyes darted about the room. One table of SS men in the front sat drinking their beer sullenly while the twenty or so villagers joked and laughed.

"*Bonjour, compère.*"

Jean-Claude looked up at the middle-aged man who had spoken to him.

"*Ça sera bientôt l'été, n'est-ce pas?*" It will be summer soon enough. The password of the Resistance.

Jean-Claude nodded. "*Oui, monsieur.*" He looked into the man's wrinkled, kindly face. Jean-Claude did not know his name. He knew only that he was a plumber from a nearby town, probably Sainte-Mère-Église, thirteen miles away, and that every Thursday he was at the Hôtel de Toulouse near the end of the day.

The man stood next to the pillar against which Jean-Claude was leaning. "Do you have news?"

"*Oui.*"

"What is it?"

"A man from a nearby farm was in Cherbourg this morning. He heard that we were soon to have visitors here."

"In Valognes?"

Jean-Claude nodded.

"What kind?"

"German officers. Very high ones. He said one was perhaps a field marshal."

"Where are they going?"

Jean-Claude took another sip of his wine and shot a sharp glance toward the SS men. They did not notice the quiet conversation. "The SS in Cherbourg is preparing security for him. He is the new commander of some sector. He will be going from Cherbourg down the coast. To see all the defenses."

"When?"

"In a few days."

The old man nodded slowly. Jean-Claude looked at his tired eyes as they stared thoughtfully at the timbered ceiling. "I will radio London tonight. Any more?"

Jean-Claude thought quickly of the gasoline bombs stored in the woods on a nearby farm. "Shall we—?"

"*Non.* We shall see first who it is." As the old man quietly walked away, Jean-Claude returned to his wine. He would be ready.

Ten miles away, the beaches of Normandy were ready, too. The gray, cold waters of the English Channel rolled and crashed on the forlorn stretches of sand, washing over pieces of driftwood, large pebbles, and black triangles of steel stuck in the ground. Up from the beaches in concrete bunkers, lonely eyes peered through binoculars, scanning the coastline in the fading twilight. Back and forth the glasses went, traversing the narrow field provided by the bunkers' horizontal slits. Day in and day out, hundreds of eyes did the same task, and the vigil kept up throughout the nights as well, as the Atlantic Wall waited for the invasion that was sure to come.

2

Tim cupped his hands together, blew into them, and put them back into his pockets. He shifted in the back seat of the jeep in a futile attempt to ward off the chill of the December morning. He turned to Hardaway. "Where are we?"

"Putney, I should think. Yes, here's the bridge." Tim looked out the scratched window that hung from the metal frame and banged against the sides of the jeep. Through the dull morning light he saw freshly fallen snow clinging to the bare trees and small rural houses. The jeep slowed for an intersection, then cruised across the bridge over the Thames. Upstream Tim saw a country river, with stark branches hanging into the water, their blackness outlined by the thin white lines of snow. He looked in the other direction. "That London, off there?"

"Chelsea, actually. Battersea to the south. All part of London." Hardaway stifled a yawn. "Half an hour and we'll be there."

Tim nodded glumly and looked back out the window. Across the river there were more houses, little scrubbed ones, once prim and tidy but now neglected. All of them had blackout curtains at the windows. "They look sad, for some reason."

Hardaway looked out. "Built to hold a family of four, and now fifteen people are living under the same roof."

"It's all hard to believe."

"It gets worse. Look over there."

Tim saw crumbled ruins of what had once been a handsome farmhouse with outbuildings. The charred timbers lay askew in the second story where the roof and flooring had caved in. The snow served to emphasize the blackness of soot and charcoal. There was an air of desertion and hopelessness, as if Armageddon had come and gone.

"My God."

"Even this far out you're not safe from the Germans." Hardaway leaned over to talk to the driver. "Up ahead you'll want to take off to the right, sergeant. Up Fulham Road." He settled back in his seat. "I'm afraid this won't be pretty to look at, any of it."

"I hope I'm ready for the worst."

"Ever been to England before?"

"Until three weeks ago, I'd never been east of Moline."

"Moline? Where the devil is that?"

"Moline, Illinois. It's on the Mississippi River."

"What on earth were you doing there?"

"I had an uncle who lived there. When I was a kid growing up in Nebraska, I used to visit him for a week every summer when I was . . . oh, six, seven years old. He was a river pilot."

Hardaway sighed. "Must be something to see, the Mississippi River. Nothing like it in Britain."

"My uncle would take me along sometimes when he would go aboard one of those large barges to pilot it through the islands and oxbows up around Savanna, Illinois. He'd point out all the land formations and tell me how the river had carved them out centuries before."

"That's why you became a geologist?"

Tim shrugged. "Might be."

Hardaway chuckled. "Funny thing, isn't it, how we get caught up in little things and they grow into obsessions. Or occupations, at any rate. From watching rivers to measuring beaches. . . . We're in town now, Loftis."

Tim stared at the blocks and blocks of burnt-out buildings. Rubble was lying everywhere except where it had been pushed into piles by the clean-up crews. Even though it was early on a Saturday morning, people were already out on the streets, walking toward shops which were just opening, oblivious to the devastation that surrounded them.

"Right up ahead, sergeant. That should take us to Marble Arch. You know your way from there, I presume?" The driver nodded.

Tim turned to Hardaway. "What did you do before the war?"

"Schoolteacher. Just like yourself."

"Where?"

"A boys' school in Somerset. You've never heard of it, so I won't bore you with the name." Hardaway reached inside his uniform jacket, pulled out a large envelope, and checked its contents. Satisfied, he put it back. "I taught classics."

"Classics?"

"That's correct, you needn't be so shocked. I taught little boys how to conjugate deponent verbs, why Greek has a middle voice and English doesn't, and why Vergil was the greatest poet who ever lived—according to some people, that is. Ever take Latin?"

"Couple of years in high school."

"Pity you didn't take more. So many people give up on the classics before they really find out how to enjoy them. Or learn from them." A concerned expression appeared on Hardaway's face. "Ever read Thucydides?"

"No."

"He was a truly brilliant man. Do you know what he says it was that started the Peloponnesian Wars?"

"Uh-uh."

Hardaway stared up at the flapping canvas roof of the jeep while he searched his memory. " 'What made war inevitable was the increase in Athenian power, and the great trembling which this caused in Sparta.' That's the reason right there: fear. If Athens hadn't built a strong army, Sparta would never have felt threatened."

"That's pretty depressing."

Hardaway smiled wryly. "What started *this* war, I wonder? Was it Hitler's armies or Chamberlain's trembling?"

"I don't know. I always thought it was Hitler's armies. He's the bad guy, isn't he?"

"There are no good guys and bad guys in the modern world, Loftis. Those kind of characters exist only in your Western movies."

"Wait a minute. You don't think Hitler's bad?"

"Of course I do. What I meant was that no one sets out to be bad. Hitler thinks he's right. And the technological war doesn't allow for good guys or bad guys. Or heroes or villains. Only for greater degrees of fools. . . . Good. Here we are."

The jeep stopped. Tim and Hardaway crawled out onto the sidewalk by the main gate of the British Museum. Hardaway leaned over and muttered instructions to the driver; then he straightened up and looked at his watch. "Good timing. It's just opened. Let's get inside where it's warm."

Together they trekked across the snow toward the imposing facade of the museum. Hardaway headed for a doorway which in turn led them to a small reception room. It was dark. Tim stood by the door while Hardaway stepped into an even smaller room off the reception area where a secretary and a British soldier were seated. He talked for a few minutes with them, producing the same envelope that Tim had seen him look at in the jeep. When he emerged from the room, he gave Tim a sheet of paper.

"Here you are, Loftis. Your pass and clearance authorization."

Tim put the sheet into his jacket. He followed Hardaway down a hallway and into the main reading room.

Even though the skies outside were leaden, daylight seemed to flood the room through the windows in the immense dome. Tim and Hardaway worked their way across the expanse of the room, shifting in and out between desks, dictionary stands, carts loaded with books, and musty-looking scholars who ambled along, muttering to themselves, oblivious to the fact that outside a cruel and desperate war was being fought and perhaps lost.

On the far side of the reading room, they plunged into a claustrophobic row of iron bookstacks only vaguely illuminated by yellowed light bulbs, turned left, went through a heavy metal door, bounded down metal steps that clanged and echoed under their boots, out through another metal door, and into a hallway that led them fifty or so feet to a blank wooden door. Seated next to the door was a British soldier, who rose to greet them.

"Good morning, corporal," Hardaway said. "This is Major Loftis of the American army. He'll be here quite a lot, so you might as well get used to seeing him."

"Yes, sir. Good to know you, major." Tim nodded in reply. Hardaway opened the door and they went inside.

The battleship-gray walls glistened dully from the rows of lights in the ceiling, for there were no windows. Pipes crisscrossed above their heads. Opposite the door was an alcove with tall stacks reaching to the ceiling. Tim recognized them as map drawers. Around the rest of the walls were bookcases, mostly filled. In the center of the room, an area twenty by forty feet, were four large tables. Some had maps laid on them, and all had stacks of books and photographs.

As they entered, the three soldiers working at various tables rose and came to attention.

Hardaway nodded to them as he started to pull off his trench coat. "At ease, gentlemen. This is Major Loftis of the American army, whom I told you about. He's our trained geologist, so do please be kind to him. He's the only one we have." Hardaway hung his coat up on one of the hooks by the door, and Tim did the same. "Loftis, this is Captain Gregory. Captain Stewart. And Lieutenant O'Donnell."

Tim nodded at them. They were all about his age, in their late twenties or early thirties. Gregory, a dark, serious-looking man of slight build, walked over.

Hardaway continued talking. "This is our little research hideaway, Loftis. We've been here ever since COSSAC started up. Captain Gregory is more or less in charge of things, so if you need anything, he's the one to talk to. Now, what we've done is fairly simple. Over there," he said, pointing to the map racks, "are all the charts, maps, large photographs, what-have-you that we've gathered, both from the museum collections and other places. Most of the books are from the collections. Over here"—he motioned toward three sets of shelves stacked with papers and magazines—"are all the periodicals and file sheets we've found on France. You'll find everything from agricultural reports to old Michelin guides. As you can see, there's a slide lantern in the event you want to project anything. We've access to the museum photo service, in case you want any work done. Anything top secret should be done at COSSAC HQ here in town. All the museum holdings are open to you, and Captain Gregory will check out any materials you want. Captain?"

"Thank you. We've done some of your work for you already, Major Loftis." Gregory walked over to one of the large tables, where a three-inch-thick pile of maps lay. Tim and Hardaway followed him. "Here are the main charts that we've used to date. As I'm sure Major Hardaway has explained, some of them are quite old, so I'm not sure just how useful they'll be. A great number of them are rather general—limited to climate, rainfall, that type of thing. I've prepared a short bibliography for you, as per the major's instructions. Most of the books aren't in English."

"I expected that."

"Yes. I suggest you go through these materials first, and then you'll be current with our thinking."

"You've got your work cut out for you, Loftis." Hardaway looked at his watch. "It's ten-thirty hours now, and I've got a meeting at Norfolk House. What do you say if I come back here at sixteen hundred and see how you're getting on?" Tim nodded. Hardaway opened the leather portfolio he was carrying and pulled

[35]

out several files. "Here are some of those aerial recons I promised you."

"That should get me started."

"Good. See you later this afternoon."

Tim was the only person in the room when Hardaway returned that evening. Tim heard him enter as he was leaning over a magnifying glass positioned over a large map. He stood up and groaned as his back muscles stretched out of their cramped state.

"Any luck?" Hardaway asked.

"Some. Look."

Hardaway bent over the glass and stared at the map. He looked from the glass to the aerial recons and back again. Then he stood up. "Doesn't say much to me, I'm afraid. What does it tell you?"

"It provides a check for our photos. I took the recons from the Bernières sector, and I've been going through the printed materials. They give a before-and-after comparison which should be useful in pinpointing how much the terrain has changed through the years."

"How old's this map?"

"This one's from the 1890s. Most of the ones we've got here, though, were published by the Comité National de Géographie in the early twenties. They were part of a large scheme after the last war to map every square inch of France's coastline in order to prepare defenses. Foch and his boys apparently decided that what France needed was a Maginot Line around the perimeter of the country, so they started this commission under the guise of a geological survey."

"Bloody lot of good it did the poor bastards."

"Right. But at least they were meticulous. The maps look pretty reliable, for anything this old."

"Then we're in luck."

"As far as they go."

"What does that mean? What do they tell you?"

Tim scratched his head. "Well, a lot and not much, all at the same time. Simple things I didn't know. Rainfall. During July the range is between fifty and seventy-five millimeters. In August, when the rainy season's heaviest, levels get up to two hundred millimeters. Taking into account the absorption levels of the terrain, I'd say offhand that our chances of finding good weather and dry beaches are about forty percent higher if we go before mid-July."

"Good to know."

"The beaches along most of Normandy, all the way over to Cabourg or Deauville, are sandy, all right. From here on east, the coast gets rocky. But there seems to be a tremendous variation in the depth of the sand, from six inches in some spots to over four feet in others. And, where the sand is thin, there's usually a lot of kaolinite."

"What's that?"

"Clay. If there's heavy rainfall preceding the operation it might be that the water will have been only partially absorbed into the groundwater table. The rest of it will puddle along the kaolinite surface, underneath the sand, and cause the whole beach to float."

"That would make a landing prohibitive, I should think."

"I don't know. I don't know anything about the tonnage we'll be putting ashore, so I can't tell yet. Now here"—Tim pulled a large colored map of Normandy from the Cotentin Peninsula to the Côte Fleurie—"is a nice map with the vegetation marked. There are some interesting things going on. Just inland from the beach we have what they call *pins sylvestres*—I assume that means scrub pine, jack pine, easy to knock over or cut down—which is an advantage. But I don't know yet how thick it is, so we can't count on it for cover. Also, until I get some data on the soil composition, I won't know how easily our tanks could bowl the trees over and uproot them. Or here," he said, tracing a section of yellow splotches, "are *pins maritimes en reboisement.* Okay, we know the forest has been replanted, but this map is dated 1925. In twenty years that sort of pine can grow pretty fast. If the trees are thick enough, they could stop our vehicles." Tim shrugged. "You win a few, you lose a few."

"What do the recons show?"

"Not enough. A photo from ten thousand feet doesn't have the resolution. That's why I want some sweeps from a lower altitude."

Hardaway nodded. His eyes went up and down the crucial topography, the narrow area where the beaches ended and the broad *bocage* country began. Hardaway had seen pictures of the *bocage* terrain—small farms surrounded by earthen embankments and thick hedgerows—which stretched all the way from Dieppe to Cherbourg. He pointed to the red areas in back of the pine interfaces. "What's this here?"

"*Prairie naturelle.* That should be fairly stable. I found a monograph on that." Tim rummaged through a stack of books, picked up a heavy volume, and opened it. "Here. *Bulletin des services de la carte géologique de la France* for 1929. A professor at the University of Louvain took a lot of cores in the areas just east of Fécamp which indicate a solid bed of sandstone and limestone conglomerate about six feet down. That should do a good job of soaking up rain while still keeping the topsoil compact. It should support any vehicles we might put on it."

"Or any vehicle the Jerries put on it."

Tim clicked his tongue. "Sure. That's the risk." There was a silence as both men stared at the colored specks on the map and tried mentally to translate them into actual fields and hills. "The maps are old, some are sloppy, some I don't trust. But they do have information which no recon can ever give us."

"The photos aren't reliable, is that what you're saying?"

"Well, Christ, any time you pass over with antiaircraft fire all around you, you don't have time to make sure your camera lens is perpendicular to within the tenth of a degree, do you?"

"Guess not. Sorry."

"They're good recons, but there are special problems with beaches. They're so flat that every inch of pilot error is critical. Fortunately, most of these maps were drawn by men who walked the beaches themselves. Between the two I should be able to extrapolate some guesses."

Hardaway bit his lip. "You all done?"

"For today."

"Good. I've got a billet for you."

"Where?"

"Grosvenor Square, with the American military liaison. I've had your duffel dropped off there, because I suppose that you'll be up here for some time. Anything else?"

"Yeah. Dinner and a drink."

It was good Scotch, and it more than made up for the gristly mutton and boiled potatoes that had passed for dinner. Tim took another swallow of whisky and looked around.

The St. Giles Tavern was a long, narrow restaurant which stretched from its front door on Regent Street into depths at the back that Tim couldn't even see through the smoke and the crowds of jabbering servicemen. It was an old Victorian building, judging by the gaslight fixtures along the wall, the heavy mahogany carvings around the booths, and the dark walls. Behind the bar were rows of bottles standing in front of patterned mirrors, most of them empty because of wartime restrictions but still displayed for decoration.

"Quite a place," Tim said.

Hardaway finished his drink, tilting his head back to get every last drop, and looked over toward the bar. Catching the bartender's eye, he waved two fingers. Then he looked back at Tim. "Best we can offer you on a Saturday night, I'm afraid."

"Feels good after the quiet at Bushey Park and the museum." Tim glanced at the crowd of soldiers, packed in the confines between the bar and the booths. Cigarette smoke hung in clouds, masking faces, making all figures anonymous, blending the dull uniforms together in the soft yellow light. "Who comes here?"

"COSSAC people, mostly. It's midway between St. James's Square, where COSSAC HQ is, and where you Yanks are. It's convenient."

"It feels good to unwind a bit."

"It does indeed." The bartender arrived with two more drinks. Hardaway pulled some bills from his pocket, gave them to the bartender, and waved him away. He clutched his drink with both hands and stared into it. After a moment he spoke quietly. "God, I'm tired of this whole business!"

"The war?"

"What other business do we have right now?" Hardaway stirred his drink absently with his finger. "Yes, Loftis, this bloody war. It's been going on for what . . . four years?" He took a long drink. "Four bloody years. Bombs. Bombs, day and night. More bombs. Everywhere you go, there are bombs. After a while you get used to them. You get so you don't notice them."

"I noticed those ruins this morning."

"Yes, you do in the beginning. The first time you see a house explode, and see bricks and mortar flying about, or see a fire lorry racing down a street, you think to yourself, How terrible! How like the cinema, or something. And here it is, happening to me, I'm in the midst of it. Quick! I must do something!"

He shook his head wearily.

"But after a while you get so you don't care. You walk along a street and you kick away the rubble and dust in front of you as if it were autumn leaves instead of the remains of someone's house. You hear the drone of the aircraft, or the whistle of the bombs falling, but after a while you don't even have to listen anymore. Experience tells you in a fraction of a second whether or not the Heinies are close enough to make you scramble for cover. The whole thing is . . . well, God, what is it? It's so damn tiring." The gray eyebrows rose. "Can you understand that?"

"I'm trying. It's hard. I've been so far away."

"You know, the blitz was a terrible time. It was really bloody awful. But, God forgive me for saying it, at least it was exciting! Or . . ." He threw up his hand in a vacant gesture. "Oh, Jesus God, I'm getting potted and can't even say what I'm thinking!"

"It should be over soon."

"What makes you say that?"

"I don't know. I just think the tide has turned."

"Perhaps. But there's a hell of a lot more fighting to be done."

"Everything I've seen or read tells me that the Germans are stretched thin. The Russians are beginning to push them back. Once we land in France, it should be short work."

"I doubt it's that simple, Loftis."

"A massive invasion should be a crippling blow."

"A sharp chop to the ribs, you mean?"

"Sonething like that."

"Snap! Bang! Crunch! And out go Hitler and his high-kicking generals?" Hardaway sighed. "Won't happen. That sort of thing was fine for Sir Walter Scott and Robin Hood, but it can't happen that way anymore.

"It's not that romantic, Loftis. Look at Dieppe. Good show for the home front, some good information on amphibious operations. But militarily? Useless."

"It was poorly executed."

"What if it had been well executed? What would have happened? We would have grabbed a foothold in France, but so what? We had no way of supporting that foothold. It's a long way from taking a beach to capturing Berlin.

"No, Loftis, simple quick thrusts don't happen in a war this big. There's too much inertia, too many people, too many machines, for any single operation to end the whole thing, no matter

[41]

how daring or bold it is. When we finally win this war, it's going to be because we had more ships, and more tanks, and more planes than Hitler had."

A bell rang in Tim's head. "You said something like that this morning. Something about there being no more heroes."

"I did? Well, of course, there are always heroic acts. If a heroic act makes a hero, then I guess we have heroes. But no single man is going to be the hero of this war. It's too big."

"That's discouraging."

"What is?"

"The idea that none of us can do anything."

"I didn't say that. We can all do something by doing what we can. There just won't be a Cincinnatus, or a Horatio, or any three hundred Spartans."

Tim finished his drink. "Another?"

Hardaway looked down at his half-empty glass. "Oh, God. Why not?"

Tim rose. "I'm going to the can. I'll get them on the way."

Slowly, laboriously, he started moving through the crowd. He had no idea how long it took him to get all the way to the back of the St. Giles. He shuffled between people, muttering soft apologies as he squeezed through the tightly packed mass.

It was right near the dark hallway all the way to the back that he saw her. He had just shouldered past two burly officers engrossed in a discussion about hunting dogs when he turned and almost ran her over. She looked up at him.

"Waiting for the loo?"

In the soft light Tim saw auburn hair tied neatly back above a white collar and a necktie, the rich tone of her skin, full, wide lips, and large brown eyes. He felt a deep stirring inside himself. It was as if he had just found something he had forgotten he had lost. He stared at her.

She smiled back, her lips widening sensuously. "Are you—oh,

I see; you're an American, aren't you? Well, are you waiting to use the . . . facilities?"

"No. No, I mean, yes, but you go right ahead." She nodded and entered the small hallway. Tim stared after her. Then he turned and leaned on the bar.

"Yes, sir?"

"Two whiskies, please. Little water in them."

"Very good, sir." Tim watched him walk away behind the bar. Suddenly the voices and noise in the pub became an irritating roar in his ears. He turned quickly to see the British woman walking out of the hallway. She caught sight of him out of the corner of her eye and smiled. Then she plunged back into the crowd and disappeared.

It took Tim another five minutes before he got back to the booth and set the drinks down. Hardaway looked up at him.

"Sorry, Loftis, if I got a bit morose back there. That happens."

"Sure, I understand."

"Bit tired, I guess."

A thought occurred to Tim. "Where's your wife?"

"Back home in Somerset. With the children. Why?"

"Just curious. Get to see her often?"

"Once a fortnight or so." Hardaway's eyes rolled with fatigue. "It's a bit rough." He looked at his watch. "See here, Loftis, it's twenty-one hundred hours. I've got some reading to do tonight, and I'm tired as well. Shall we push off?"

"I think I'll stay a bit, if that's all right. It's been a long time since I've seen this much activity."

"Suit yourself. Here." Hardaway pulled a paper from his pocket, scribbled on it, and handed it to Tim. "Here's the address of your billet and my telephone exchange. Ring me if you need me. Otherwise, I'll see you at the museum tomorrow." He rose and pulled on his trench coat. "Another long day, as you said yourself, so I would suggest you get some rest. And for God's sake, stay out of trouble! Good night."

[43]

For several minutes after Hardaway left, Tim sat in silence, slowly finishing his drink. The loud voices, the crowd, the foreign accents, the laughter, and the fuzziness of the liquor on his brain combined to make him feel very lonely. He realized, with a depressing harshness, how far away he was from all that he knew. How different England was from Nebraska, he thought, not only in its terrain but in its buildings, its customs, its people. He thought of Hardaway and his talk of weariness and suddenly felt very young, very naïve, and very unsure.

"Hello."

The voice above him snapped Tim back to the St. Giles. He looked up quickly. The brown eyes looked back at him. In his own sadness he had forgotten why he had stayed when Hardaway had left: the one small shred of hope that he would get a chance to talk with the pretty British officer. And there she was, standing at his booth.

"May I sit down?" she asked cheerfully.

"Uh, yes. Please do."

She settled in opposite Tim, and he took a longer look at her. Her face was expressive, with strong features, and she had an air of disarming grace. She wore very little makeup, which, along with her uniform, made her look austere. Yet the warmth of her rich smile was infectious. "You don't mind, do you? I'm so tired of standing about. I thought my legs were about to fall off."

"No, I'm glad you did. Would you like a drink?"

"Thank you, I have one." She laughed softly as she swirled the liquid around in her glass.

"Good. My name's Tim. Tim Loftis."

"Quite glad to meet you. Prudence Lapthorne."

"That's an odd name: Prudence. I've never known anyone with that name. Not in America, anyway."

"Really? It's common enough, I should have thought. But call me Pru. Cheers!"

"Cheers." They lifted their glasses. Tim took a swallow from the nearly depleted glass, then put it back on the table. "You're in the army, aren't you? Funny, I forgot that the British had put women in uniform."

"Well, there aren't awfully many of us." She laughed. "It's not an enviable lot. The military's been designed for men, and it's a bother having to queue up for the loo and so on. It isn't very often that a senior officer lets me go ahead of him."

Tim shrugged.

"What are you doing in London? Are you with the American army command over in Grosvenor House?"

"Sort of. Actually I'm with a group of British and American officers."

"Oh, are you with COSSAC?" she asked brightly. "Don't worry, so am I."

"You are? What do you do?"

"I'm in G-Two. Intelligence."

"Funny thing for an attractive woman to be in. Spies and stuff."

"Well, not really. We women can't go to the front lines, and we aren't schooled in strategy or operations or anything, so we end up doing desk work on the home front. The only reason I ended up doing something more interesting than typing is that I speak German."

"That's kind of strange, isn't it?"

"My father was in the Foreign Service, so I lived in Berlin when I was a girl. What do you do?"

"Me? I'm in G-Three." He chuckled. "I'm not sure what I do. I'm a geologist."

"A geologist? You mean, rocks and things? How exciting!"

"Not really. They just lie there. All I do is look at them."

Pru laughed. "I'm sure there's more to it than that. You're being modest!"

"I guess I am." Tim finished the watery drink and fought hard to find something to say. "Come here a lot?"

"Every so often. After duty we'll come around for a little cheer. It's so dreadful going back to the flat, especially now that it's getting dark so early."

At the mention of the word "we" Tim's eyes dropped to her left hand and saw the gold hammered wedding ring. "We?"

"Some of the other women in the office. Always noisy here. Keeps you from getting lonely."

"It's worse if you're an American. I don't know anyone."

"Who was that you were chatting with?"

"Him? Oh, he's my partner at COSSAC."

"Do you get along?"

"I guess we do. He's thirty years older than I am, so he's more like a father than a buddy. That makes it rough."

Pru gave him a coy smile. "I think I understand. He thinks you're brash. Correct?"

"Something like that. He's awfully serious."

"You don't like army life, I gather?"

"I'd rather be doing what I like to do. You know, rocks and things."

"I suppose all of us would rather be doing what we're best at." She looked directly at him, her eyes suddenly becoming clear and earnest. "But there's no choice, is there? There is a war, and we can't very well pretend it will go away if we ignore it, can we?"

"I guess not."

"Still, I imagine it must be difficult, being teamed up with a senior officer from another country."

"It has its problems. But I'm not really complaining. Just a little drunk and tired. And lonely."

"I suspected that." Just then two women officers stopped by the booth.

"Twenty-one-thirty, lieutenant. Time we're off," one of them said cheerlessly. Pru nodded. She finished her drink and rose. As she got her coat on, she looked at Tim.

"Thank you for the chat, major."

Tim stood up and faced her. "Look, lieutenant . . . uh, maybe I could see you again. I'll be around for a long time." He looked at the other two women, who remained expressionless. He turned back to Pru. "It'd be fun, you know. Talk, have a drink."

Pru finished buttoning her coat. She raised her head and stared at him. She smiled slightly. "I'd like that. Tuesday?"

"Here?" She nodded. "Nineteen hundred?"

"That would be fine. Good night."

Tim watched the three of them walk through the crowd and disappear toward the front door. He sat down. Then he motioned to the bartender for another drink. He didn't care now whether he stayed sober or not.

She was twenty minutes late. Tim had gotten to the St. Giles early, right after Hardaway had dropped him off at Grosvenor Square following a meeting with the "Martians," a group of intelligence analysts who worked in a basement office at Clive Steps near Whitehall. They had spent two hours at Clive Steps, poring over radio reports from the Resistance in France. It had been depressing for Tim, for while the Resistance had transmitted a wealth of detail about German troop placements and armaments, they had sent over little information about the beaches themselves.

"Tough luck on the Martians," Hardaway had said as Tim got off the jeep and stood in the frosty blizzard. "I thought they would have been more useful."

"That's life. Any other suggestions?"

"You might try G-Two at COSSAC. Brigadier Beauclerk. He's unorthodox, but he might have something. Will I see you tomorrow?"

"I'll be at the museum."

"I've a few appointments in the morning, but perhaps I can pop around in the afternoon. We'll have a drink."

"Good." Hardaway had driven off into the night, and Tim sat for forty minutes at the St. Giles, nursing several drinks and thinking about the beaches. Each blind alley, each dead end, each aborted attempt to uncover more data only increased his anxieties. The long stretches of sand were beginning to become part of his dreams. In his sleep, he had pictured each piece of the Normandy coastline—the harbor at Arromanches, the hundred-foot cliff at Pointe du Hoc, the lonely bathing areas near Sainte-Marie-du-Mont and Ravenoville. When he tired of thinking about the beaches, he looked nervously at his watch and wondered whether or not she would show up.

Finally she arrived. He watched her stand by the door while she took off her muffler. Her hair was loose, falling in long, gentle curves down to her shoulders. She shook off a light dusting of snow and looked around.

Tim waved until she noticed him and smiled. Then she worked her way slowly through the throng of people until she could sit down next to him.

"Good evening," she said breathlessly. "I'm sorry I'm late, but I was caught at the office. My, but it's nice and warm in here!"

"You got here just in time. I had trouble saving a seat for you."

"I'm glad you did." The bartender stopped by them. "Whisky, please."

"Make that two."

Pru took off her coat. "Well, now, major, tell me about yourself."

"Not much to tell. Major Timothy McKinley Loftis. Serial number 0900-214. Age: twenty-eight. Born and raised in North Platte, Nebraska. Graduated from the University of Nebraska in 1937 with a major in geology. Ph.D. from Stanford University in 1941. One half year of teaching until drafted into the United States Army. One and a half years of duty at Fort Ord, California, in charge of beach security. That's it."

"Nebraska? Isn't that the Wild West?"

"Some people say it is."

She laughed. "I'm sorry. Geography never was my subject.

When I hear the word Nebraska, I just think of Indians and wagon trains. I must have seen too many of your Western movies."

"It's part of the Great Plains."

"How did you ever become such an impressive scientist, then? My, my, you're a doctor!"

"Well, I went to Stanford because I got a fellowship. What that meant mostly was that I spent four years lying in the sun on the beaches. Studying wave erosion, of course. All in the name of science."

"It sounds as though you have a knack for finding the easy way out."

"When I have to." The bartender arrived with the drinks and Tim paid for them. "Cheers."

"Cheers."

"Now tell me about you."

Pru shrugged. "Not a great deal to tell either. My father was in the Foreign Service. He passed away four years ago. I was born in Hong Kong, although I can't remember it because he was posted to Berlin when I was two. Mum died when I was three. We stayed in Berlin for nine years. Finally he was promoted, or so they called it, and sent back to London."

"Why do you say that?"

"Apparently Papa thought Hitler was a good thing for Germany. And in 1929, he was. The whole country was depressed, there were no jobs, a monstrous inflation, the governments kept failing, everything was askew. Not that Papa liked Hitler. I'm sure he never even laid eyes on him. When he was transferred, Hitler was still just a Bavarian politician with a local following."

She sighed.

"Nonetheless, Papa thought that any unity for the Germans was better than none. And he said so to his superiors in London. There were all sorts of discussions which ended up with his being posted back here." Pru pursed her lips. "I went to English school in Berlin, but I grew up speaking German in the streets. When the war broke out, I contacted some of Papa's old chums and earned a commission in the WAAF. And into Intelligence. Rather simple, isn't it?"

"And your husband?" Pru gave him a startled look. "I noticed the ring. Very pretty."

"Thank you. It's hammered gold. The set belonged to my grandparents." She took a sip from her drink and slowly set the glass back down. "Ronald had its mate. He and I were married in 1940. He was a captain in the RAF. He disappeared on a bombing raid over Hamburg in 1942."

"I'm sorry."

"You needn't be. What's done is done. I don't really know if I've given up hope yet or not, deep inside of me." Nervously she finished her drink, then looked at Tim. "Would you mind awfully if we went somewhere else?"

"Why?"

"This place is so noisy. And . . . it's difficult to explain, really, but it's filled with military people. I see them all day long, and I was in the office for such a long time today, that I just thought it would be nicer to get away."

"Anything you say."

She smiled. "You're nice. You sound so different, I want to chat with you. Here I just feel hemmed in by the war."

"I understand that. So do I."

"I'm not being forward, am I?" Tim looked at her. "I really do mean just for a chat."

They walked together in the cold night, the snow blowing into their faces. The streets were pitch dark because of the blackout, and often they had to find their way by feeling the sides of buildings. After twenty minutes Tim's hands and feet were frozen. He was glad when Pru ducked down a small stairway toward a cellar door.

Inside it was warm again. They were in a small supper club, a cozy corner hidden away in Westminster near Oxford Street.

There were square tables with fresh white linen on them, a bar along one side, and soft lighting from the recesses built in along the beige masonry walls. The low ceiling made the club look longer than it really was, and the swirls of cigarette smoke which hung in the air like spiderwebs drew invisible curtains across the room. Tim didn't see a single uniform.

They sat at a table near an alcove by a hidden speaker through which the BBC was broadcasting soft music. When they had gotten their drinks, Pru closed her eyes and rested her elbows on the table. "Mmmm. Music sounds good."

"Sure does. I've been spending my days listening to the sounds of scratching pens in the British Museum."

"You're working in the museum?"

"It's like any other library. Very quiet and very dull."

"What are you working on?"

"Research. I can't say any more."

"I understand. Well, it isn't terribly exciting where I am either, you know. Paperwork is dull no matter where you find it."

Tim shrugged, then looked up to find Pru's glistening eyes focused on him.

"Did you ever study music?" He shook his head. "I did. Dance classes and the piano. When I was in Berlin we would go to concerts or the ballet every week. Sometimes twice a week. I heard Rachmaninoff play several times back in the twenties. I always thought it odd that such a quiet-looking man would write such sonorous romantic melodies."

"Isn't he the one that sounds like Gershwin?"

"Well, Gershwin sounds like him, but you're an American, so you can say that."

"I guess."

Pru stared at him. "You're quite unlike anyone I've ever met."

"Why do you say that?"

"I meant that endearingly. You're . . . well, I've never met anyone from Nebraska before. Come to think of it, I've met very few Americans. But I have this image of the American West from the cinema. Broad plains, miles and miles of nothing except the wind, and, in the middle of it all, handsome, silent cowboys living out in the open. You seem to fit that."

"That's how it is, in a lot of ways."

"Who's that American movie actor? Gary Cooper. Yes. You remind me of him."

Tim's eyes widened. "I remind you of Gary Cooper? You've had too much to drink!"

Pru laughed. "No, no, I mean, you don't look like him, particularly, but you have the same quality."

"Which is?"

"It's difficult to describe. Shy, perhaps. Thoughtful. The unsung hero."

"I don't feel like a hero."

"You might someday, then. I think it's there inside you. It's a wonderful quality. Very appealing." Tim shrugged, and she laughed. "That's it! That's what I mean."

"What?"

"You shrugged. Just like Gary Cooper." Her brown eyes glowed at him. "Have you ever been in love?"

Tim scratched his neck. "Couple of times."

"No, I mean really in love?"

"Well, maybe not, then. I don't know. Why?"

"I take it you're unmarried. How is it some pretty frontier woman hasn't snared you? Lassoed you. That's the word, isn't it?"

"What?"

"Lassoed?" Pru circled her right hand and threw an imaginary rope.

"Yeah, that's the word." Tim laughed. "I don't know why not. Never had time, I suppose."

"What on earth were you doing that you didn't have time to fall in love? That's the silliest answer I've ever heard!"

"School. Research. Stuff like that."

Pru shook her head. "Well, there's more to life than laboratories, major. I shall have to take you under my wing and show you some civilization while you're in London."

When they finally left, the icy cold of the December night slapped them in the face. By instinct Tim put his arm around Pru's shoulder to shield her from the blast.

"Tim."

He looked at her face, framed by the muffler, and the auburn hair flecked with snow. Her lips trembled as he kissed her. They kissed again, and her arms tightened around his neck. Her knees buckled as her body crushed against his. For long minutes they stood in the doorway kissing, oblivious to the cold. Finally Pru pushed herself away and tucked her head onto his chest. "Please, Tim," she said quietly. "Take me home."

It was chilly in the little flat on Chandos Place, down from Whitcomb Street, just off Piccadilly. The three twisting flights of stairs had been as cold as the outdoors. Pru shut the door behind them as they entered.

"Wait here," she said. "I'll stoke the fire and put on some water." In the darkness Tim heard her open the door to a coal stove and empty a scuttle of new fuel onto the dying embers. Sparks flew and the coals burst into flames. Pru slammed the iron door shut with a clank. Then she turned on a small wall lamp.

The flat was one small room. There was a pair of double windows covered with blackout curtains. The stove had been built into what was once a handsome wood fireplace. Along the mantel were books and old newspapers. Next to the fireplace was a square iron gas range upon which Pru set a kettle she had just filled at a small sink opposite it.

Striking a wooden match, she bent over and lit the flame as she turned on the gas jet. Tim looked over at the windows. In front of them was a wing chair, with a small table and lamp next to it. In the far corner was a bed, its covers rumpled, and above it was a line stretched with clothes thrown over it.

Pru took off her coat and muffler, throwing them over the chair. "It isn't much, is it?"

Tim put his coat over hers. "It serves its purpose, I guess."

Pru took down a teapot and two cups from the cabinet above the range. "It's rather comfy, actually. For one person. Sundays I like to sit over there in the chair and read while I listen to the BBC. I just finished *Sense and Sensibility*. Have you read it?"

"No. Who's it by?"

"Jane Austen, you silly boy." Pru looked over at him and realized that he hadn't been joking. "You've never heard of her?"

"Nope. I like rocks and things, remember?"

Pru reached beneath the sink and pulled up a porcelain cannister which she set next to the teapot. Without looking at Tim she continued talking. "Perhaps it is true what they say: that all Americans are barbarians. Anyhow, she soothes me. With this blackout and blitz and everything, it's nice to read about the eighteenth century when all anyone worried about was getting married to the right man."

Pru measured the tea, poured in the rest of the water, put the kettle back, and turned off the gas. Then she was next to him, her arms around his waist.

Tim kissed her. She broke away and regarded him coyly. "Well, I suppose 'rocks and things' must be interesting. In their own time and place."

She was warm under the covers, her smooth skin tingling under his touch. The sheer energy of her hot, aroused body made Tim ache with welcome pleasure. Their hands roamed desperately as their pent-up energies found release.

Soon the bed was no longer cold, and the loneliness which Tim had felt for so long disappeared under her ardent lovemaking. That night, for the first time in two weeks, Tim did not dream of beaches.

*   *   *

The little horse trap bounced along the road. It was all that Pierre Deschamps could do to keep it from overturning into one the snowbanks that lined the right-of-way. In the trap itself, Pierre's tools clanked and slammed against each other with every lurch.

Pierre was the plumber of Sainte-Mère-Église and was not particularly happy about having to travel so far to work on such a cold day. It was ten miles from his house on the west end of town to his destination that morning, and the chilly winds which came directly off of the English Channel blew through his woolen coat. All around him the *bocage* landscape of shrubs and hedgerows whistled as the fierce wind swept over the snow. Pierre glanced at the green sea, covered with whitecaps which glistened in the pale winter sun.

He stopped the trap. The small road he was following had ended in a barbed-wire gate. In front of it stood two German sentries, both of whom aimed their machine pistols at him.

"Halt! Eintritt verboten!" One of the sentries kept his gun aimed at Pierre while the other slung his weapon over his shoulder and walked toward the cart. *"Wohin gehen Sie?"*

"Voici mes papiers." Pierre handed the sentry his identification card and the pass which the Wehrmacht captain had issued to him the day before.

The sentry looked them over carefully, then glanced into the back of the wagon. Satisfied, he motioned to his comrade to open the gate.

Pierre smiled at him. *"Merci bien,"* he said.

With a flick of the reins, the horse and cart passed through the outer perimeter into the area of the great Atlantic Wall. Fifty yards down the pathway the road ended altogether. Pierre stopped the horse and, tying the reins to the wagon, jumped down from his seat. He struggled across twenty meters of frozen sand, holding his coat against the harsh wet winds, to the small iron door in the concrete bunker so cleverly hidden in the hillside. His knock echoed metallically thoroughout the structure. In a moment, the same captain who had given him the pass opened the door and beckoned him inside. The door clanged shut behind them.

Inside was barely warmer than outdoors. Pierre had never been in a blockhouse before. He crouched as he descended the narrow flight of steps, following the German officer. They emerged into the main battery room.

Dazzling light from the sea flooded through an open slit through which Pierre could see beach and surf. The light made the room seem almost pleasant despite the chalky starkness of the new concrete walls.

In front of the slit were mounted two guns on tripods. M.G. 34 7.92 air-cooled machine guns, Pierre noted, 250 rounds per minute. He smiled happily and carelessly at the captain, showing how incomprehensible his peasant's mind found all this equipment.

The captain pointed to a small steel door. Pierre looked through it. Inside he saw a small toilet with barely enough room for a man to sit, let alone stand. Pierre crawled into the niche. The toilet had overflowed and then frozen. The captain was jabbering something in German behind his back. Pierre turned his head and smiled again, as if to say that he understood what had to be done.

In an hour and a half Pierre had finished repairing the toilet in the bunker. During that time he had left twice to go back to his horse trap and get additional tools. Each time, as he groped across the sand, he forced into his memory all that he had seen: estimates of dimensions, distances from the shoreline, thicknesses of the walls and roof, number of doors, sizes of the ammunition storage rooms, and floor plan, including the location of the emergency exit right next to the toilet itself. He ran the estimates and observations over and over in his mind so that he would be sure to remember them accurately when he finally had a chance to write them down.

When the last bolts had been tightened he beamed proudly at the captain and pushed down the handle. The toilet worked perfectly. The German smiled, then motioned brusquely for Pierre to gather his tools and leave. Pierre smiled back.

That night Pierre went out at nine fifteen to go to his barn, as was his routine. He had always checked the livestock before going to bed, his neighbors knew, ever since he first took over his father's farm and house when the elder Deschamps died in 1934.

Tonight was no different. Pierre checked the two cows. One was very old, nearly twelve. Soon he would have to slaughter her. The chickens were quiet except for one or two hens which were beginning to lay. After he had poured feed into the trough, he set down his shovel and listened intently for a moment. There was no sound except the gentle moaning of the wind.

Pierre opened the stall where Agnes, his soon-to-be-slaughtered cow, stood munching. He scraped away at the dirt in the rear of the stall. In a second a bag appeared. As he had done a hundred times before, Pierre quickly hung the loose wires of the antenna to the rafters over his head. He looked at his watch: nine twenty-eight. In two minutes it would be his time. Quietly he turned the crank of the battery case to charge up the crystal. In three minutes he was ready. Deftly his fingers began tapping. "FC . . . FC . . . ROUGE 14 . . . ROUGE 14 . . ."

London was listening. From the dark December night the antennas picked up faint vibrations in the sky. The radio operator made his pencil dance across the page as the tiny clicks made by Pierre Deschamps's wireless were transformed into dots and dashes. In fifteen minutes the transmission was over. The operator routinely transcribed the dots and dashes into letters he could not read because they were in code.

Rising from his desk, he walked past the other six operators on duty that night and dropped the message into the decoding box.

By 2205 hours Pierre Deschamps's observations on the German bunker hidden on the lonely beach in Normandy were being typed in code and in French by a secretary onto four copies: one for the Martian files, one for MI-6, one for the War Ministry, and one for COSSAC G-2. She pulled the copies from her typewriter and laid them into the proper out boxes.

At 2330 hours the military attaché from Norfolk House arrived and gathered up the papers in one of the boxes. He put them into his briefcase and locked it. Signing the log, he handed the secretary a receipt and departed.

The next morning the Intelligence Officer at COSSAC G-2:Classification and Translation Division read Deschamps's dispatch and matched the translation to the original French. Then she shook her head. More specifications, Prudence Lapthorne thought. What her new boyfriend was after was hard data on the beaches themselves. The Resistance seemed to send over every little tidbit they happened to pick up. For once, she mused, I would like to see the Resistance send a message that had real meaning behind it.

3

Having been an inn ever since it was built in the twelfth century, the Hôtel de Toulouse had a small, cobblestoned inner courtyard which was reached through an angular archway directly facing on the Rue Delisle. In earlier days it had been the custom to shut the courtyard gate at sundown and allow the horses to feed and sleep in the open space.

This evening the horses were replaced by gray-coated sentries who paced across the courtyard past the great silent Horch parked there.

From outside came the noise of motorcycles, their blasting exhausts echoing in the narrow streets. At the sound, the sentries rapidly opened the gates and two motorcyclists entered, followed by a Mercedes staff car, which was in turn followed by two more motorcyclists. Like the black Horch, the Mercedes had small flags fluttering on the bumpers.

The sentries snapped to attention as the car pulled alongside the Horch. The driver cut the motor, leaped out of the front seat, and opened the rear door to allow a slight, graying Wehrmacht general with an austere face to alight. General Ludwig Beck motioned to his aides, and they both fell in behind him as he strode across the courtyard, the military boots giving off cold clicks as they struck the uneven brick pavement.

Inside it was warmer. The lobby of the Hôtel de Toulouse was long, narrow, and cheery, largely illuminated by a giant masonry fireplace opposite the main desk. Beck and his aides crossed the lobby quickly, oblivious to the single local resident who sat reading a week-old copy of *Le Figaro*. Reaching the stairs, they climbed to the second floor, turned left, and walked down the dim corridor.

Outside Room 28, which faced onto the courtyard, two Wehrmacht soldiers stood guard. When they saw Beck, they came to attention and delivered the Nazi salute. Beck nodded perfunctorily, knocked lightly on the door, and went in.

Rommel was seated on the bed, his uniform coat off. About him on the bed and floor were strewn dispatches and reports. On hearing the door open, he looked up to see Beck. Then he rose.

"*Herr Generaloberst, guten Abend!* What a joy to see you! *Herr Oberst,*" he said quickly to von Frickstein, who was sitting by the window at a small secretary writing out the orders for the next day's travel, "find the concierge and have him send up coffee."

Von Frickstein rose and bowed graciously, his heels snapping together, and left the room swiftly.

Rommel motioned to the small chair in the corner by the bidet. "Please sit down. It is not much, but it is all that I have."

"Thank you, *Herr Generalfeldmarschall.* I hope I do not disturb you."

"No, nothing. Reports, proposals, statistics. The same thing as always when you receive a new command. There is always so much to catch up on."

Beck smiled cordially. "You are in charge now of the coastal defenses. I heard that. Good. We will be in the same theater of operations."

"Yes, that pleases me."

"You will enjoy working with von Rundstedt."

"I will, I know. No doubt it was he who sent you?"

"No. I come on the request of *Oberst* von Stauffenberg."

"I see," Rommel said in a quiet voice. "We must be swift, then. Say what you have come to say."

"I received a cable from him last night. He said that he had talked with you in Gargnano and asked me to speak with you as soon as you arrived in Normandy."

"We had a pleasant chat, yes."

"He said that you have certain sympathies. Sympathies a number of us share."

"Sympathies, yes. But perhaps little else."

"Which means, *Herr Generalfeldmarschall?*"

"Which means, *Herr Generaloberst,* that you should say what you have come here to say."

Beck drew in his breath. "It has become clear to many of us in the western sectors that we cannot hope to forestall a successful Allied invasion of France. Even if the British and American forces are repelled once, it is clear that they will eventually secure a foothold. We hope, therefore, to negotiate a peace with the Western Allies. We feel they must be as eager as we are to avoid unnecessary bloodshed."

"And who is this 'we' you speak of?"

Beck lowered his head. "There are many of us. I cannot name their names."

A long silence followed. "But you must! For such a plan to work, you must have the entire Wehrmacht behind you."

Beck wearily rubbed his eyes, then looked up at Rommel. "*Generalfeldmarschall* von Kluge is among us. And *Generalleutnant* von Steulpnagel. And so is *Generalfeldmarschall* von Rundstedt."

Rommel rose and walked over to the sink. Turning on the cold tap, he splashed cold water over his face. He turned off the water and wiped his face slowly with a towel. He faced Beck. "Von Rundstedt, you say? He counts very much. What does he think?"

"He thinks as we do, that the war is lost. He feels your aid is crucial."

"In what way?"

"You are popular with the people. When we act in the West, we must arrest the Führer. You are the only officer in the Wehrmacht who has enough sympathy among the German people to be able to withstand the counterattack from the SS." Beck paused. "You, *Herr Generalfeldmarschall,* will be the new Führer."

Rommel threw the towel into the sink. "I do not wish to be Führer!"

"You would be so only for a while. Until we could make peace with the British and the Americans."

"Then what?"

Beck shrugged. "Then, we do not know for sure. Some of us favor restoring the Republic. Others favor a monarchy. In either case, we would move quickly to destroy the Nazi Party."

Rommel thought for a moment. "And the Führer?"

"As I mentioned, he will be arrested and tried before the Volksgerichtshof. Only such a public trial in the People's Court would convince the Allies that the Wehrmacht was acting sincerely."

"And if he resists arrest? Or if Reichsführer Himmler intervenes?"

"They will be killed," Beck said softly.

Rommel nodded, then walked over to the bed and sat down. He sank his head into his hands for a minute before looking up. "How will we negotiate with the Allies?"

"We must establish contact with the Allies before the *coup d'état*. We must know that the Allies will consider us, and not the SS, the rightful government of Germany. If they recognize us and offer peace terms, the German people will have no choice but to follow."

"You still have not answered my question. I asked you how we are to establish contact with the Allies. We can hardly call them on the telephone and arrange a luncheon, can we?" Beck laughed. "Our consulates are under von Ribbentrop's control, so there is no chance of arranging for a truce that way. We control no transmitters, and the borders are sealed by the SS. We are watched night and day by the Gestapo. How do we let the Allies know what is on our minds?"

"I have given much thought to that problem, *Herr Generalfeldmarschall*, and I believe I have come up with a solution. Since we cannot use any official channels of communication, we must use our only unofficial one."

Rommel looked puzzled. "Which is?"

"The French Resistance." Rommel's puzzled look changed to a deep frown. "I see your doubts. You are thinking that the Resistance is too disorganized for such a task. You are right. It is their very disorganization that will be the key to our success."

Rommel's head shook slowly. "How?"

"The Resistance in France daily sends hundreds of messages to the Allied intelligence forces in England. We monitor them at OB West. There are many small bands of partisans, some of them with only two or three members. They all operate independently. That is why the Gestapo and the Sipo are having so much difficulty breaking up the operation."

"I am still confused."

Beck rose and paced the tiny room, his hands clasped behind his back. "Each of these bands reports information to the Allies: troop movements, fortification data, anything. It is not their task to interpret information. Their sole job is to send on to London anything that comes to their attention."

The door suddenly swung open and von Frickstein entered with a tray of coffee. Beck, startled, walked to the window and looked out as von Frickstein placed the tray on the table.

Rommel walked over to it. *"Danke, Herr Oberst."* Von Frickstein left. Rommel poured coffee and milk into two cups. He handed one to Beck, then took up his own. "I am still unable to follow your reasoning, *Herr Generaloberst.*"

"It is simplicity itself. We ourselves will feed information to the Resistance: piece by piece, drop by drop, all over France. Each partisan will see only that part which he himself transmits. They can never discover our strategy." Beck paused to let his idea sink in. "And, what is more important, there can be no danger that the Sipo will discover our plan, even if they arrest any of the Resistance transmitters."

"It is a jigsaw puzzle."

"Exactly, *Herr Generalfeldmarschall.*"

Rommel looked at Beck. "If the request for contact is so hidden, what assurance do we have that the Allies will find it?"

Beck sat in the chair. "That is a risk, I confess. We cannot be completely sure. But there are several factors in our favor.

"First, they have established a single command post, the so-called COSSAC, which means that they must have a centralized intelligence operation. We have learned that messages from the French are collected in one office, part of the British MI-Six. One group of officers, then, will see all the French dispatches.

"If the Allies assemble enough reports in one place, and if there are similar markings in enough of them, someone will notice that fact and investigate." Beck stirred a lump of sugar into his *café au lait.* "One thing more. The British and American cryptographers are the finest in the world. If anyone can find such a tiny needle in a haystack, it will be they."

"And when our request gets through, what then?"

"The Allies broadcast continually to Europe on open frequencies, sending coded messages to the Resistance. We know what they are doing even if we do not know what they are saying. If the Allies do find our request, they can reply on the BCC and we will be able to pick out their answer. The Sipo will suspect nothing. We can always say that we are looking for clues as to when the invasion will take place."

"And then?"

"And then"—Beck drew a sharp breath—"then we must arrange a rendezvous."

"To what end?"

"To surrender the Western Front. To yield to the Allies so that they will join us in the fight to stop Bolshevism."

"And there is only one person who could represent our side?"

"*Ja, Herr Generalfeldmarschall,*" Beck said. "It must be you."

Rommel looked out of the window, but the darkness of the

night and the light of the room were such that the window only reflected back his pale image.

What an image it was, he thought. Without his uniform jacket on, he looked old and wasted. The arms, once bronzed by the desert sun, were gray and flabby. The flaring pants, which looked so smart tucked inside the military boots and topped with the tailored field jacket, flopped absurdly at his sides, like pants a schoolboy wears that really belong to his older brother. It was not a pleasant sight. Rommel looked back to Beck.

"You are right, my friend. I will act with you."

Beck smiled. "I am happy indeed, *Herr Generalfeldmarschall!* For the first time in over a year, I feel that the honor of Germany will be saved!"

The sentries snapped to attention as Beck emerged from Room 28 of the Hôtel de Toulouse. The two aides, who had waited in the hallway, smoking cigarettes, followed their commander as he strode down the corridor and descended the steps.

In the lobby the desk clerk was polishing the hammered pewter wall sconces above the main desk. He followed the German soldiers with his eyes as they crossed the foyer, opened the wooden door, and walked into the cold night. The clerk then turned his attention to the sole other person in the room, the figure reading the copy of *Le Figaro*. The newspaper was lowered and the man shook his head.

The clerk went back to his polishing as the sound of the marching boots faded into the night.

The darkened room was quiet except for the *pish-pish-pish* of the small paddle lapping the water surface in the large tank. As small wavelets produced by the paddle traveled down the twenty-foot length of the shallow tank, a large floodlight at the side of the tank threw their shadows onto the ceiling.

White lines danced across the plaster until they hit the place where the ceiling and the wall joined. There they rebounded, to travel backward, passing through the waves which had been transmitted behind them. Where the waves overlapped, the light flashed brightly on the ceiling. Then the advancing and receding waves parted, traveling in their respective directions. The reflected patterns marched onward, rhythmically, magically, like so many ghosts dancing across Halloween gravestones on a moonless night.

Tim turned the rheostat up another point. Instantly, the quiet hum of the small electric motor that drove the paddle grew slightly higher in pitch. The paddle beat the water's surface slightly faster, and the wave reflections sliding across the ceiling followed suit.

Tim checked his watch. After a minute, he stopped the motor. Putting down his clipboard, he walked over and snapped on the overhead lights. Hardaway winced at the sudden burst of light.

"Well, what do you think?" Tim asked.

"Very impressive, Loftis, I must say." Hardaway cocked an eyebrow. "I can't say that I follow it all, but you seem sure enough of your calculations, and that's good enough for me."

Tim shrugged. "Well, let's just say that I'm pretty sure of my margin of error."

Hardaway rose from his metal chair. "That will satisfy them up at SHAEF, I should think. How soon can you get all this data written up so we can send it to General Morgan?"

"Hold on a minute," Tim said. "There's a lot I haven't done."

"Such as?"

"Well, checking over at G-Two for one thing. The figures I'm working with are the ones I've pulled from the tank and the recons. There might be some hard facts over there."

"What else?"

"Well, I've got to finish drawing up my profiles, and I've got to make my predictions."

"That's not our department, Loftis."

"I'm not talking about military predictions. I'm talking about predicting what these ocean bottoms will look like in six months."

"Why should they be any different from what they are now?"

Tim gave him an exasperated glance. Hardaway's like all humanists, he thought. He doesn't know how uncertain science really is. "Beaches change all the time. They're never stable. What I've done here is to establish a reasonable profile for all twelve of the principal beaches. Winter profiles."

Hardaway frowned. "So?"

"They're completely different from the summer ones. And I'm afraid," he said, as he unplugged the electric motor, "that I'm operating in an area that is still unexplored. Scientifically, I mean."

"I don't follow you."

Tim held up his index finger. "Okay. A quick little lesson. Berms, the name for beaches in the scientific world, are created by the surf. The surf also creates underwater bars. The beach part of a berm formation is only a small part of the total picture."

"Like an iceberg."

"Yes, like an iceberg. We know that during winter months the surf tends to be heavier. The action on the sand is therefore stronger. Tides are more violent.

"Now, what the surf does is to pick up sand from the exposed berms and pull it out under the water to form offshore bars."

"That much I understand."

"It's more complicated than that, actually, and there's a lot of math involved, but that's the general idea. Now, when the season changes, the mild summer surf takes over. That's around April. That will tend to lift these underwater bars and deposit them onto the exposed berm. The wave vortexes reverse." Tim looked at Hardaway, who nodded. "So, what was a short berm with a lot of underwater bars in the winter will become a long berm with few or no bars in the summer. That's the theory, anyway. Real life is never that smooth and simple."

"Well, so much the better for us. Fewer obstacles for landing craft to get hung up on."

"Right. But much wider beaches for the troops to cross under fire."

Hardaway nodded. "I see what you're driving at, Loftis. The summer beaches could be fifty feet wider."

"In some places they'll be a hell of a lot wider than that. Look at this."

Tim walked over to the wall opposite the wave tank where a large drafting table had been set up. On it, and on the large table next to it, rolls of paper were piled. Hardaway crossed over to the table and watched while Tim danced a pointer across the paper pinned down on the tilted surface.

"Here's my profile for Ravenoville Beach. You can see how flat it is: almost a straight line dipping into the Atlantic Ocean. If you remember that I've drawn the slope in a one-to-five exaggeration just to make it easier to work with, you can guess how flat it really is. My current guess is that even a mile out the water might be only twelve or thirteen feet deep.

"Here," he went on, "are the bunkers. Right now, it's about four hundred and fifty feet from the edge of the surf to the bunkers. That measurement is based on my latest recons, dated December twenty-first. Winter solstice.

"Now, in the summer, with all this sand shifted around, that beach might be seven hundred feet wider"—Hardaway's brows arched in amazement—"eleven or twelve hundred feet in all. And worse, I don't know how deep the water will be at low tide. This beach might get so flat that the landing craft wouldn't even be able to hit dry land. Our troops might have to jump in and wade the last fifty feet."

Hardaway looked at the diagram and slowly shook his head. "That's too damn far. Fifty feet in the surf, twelve hundred across the sand." He exhaled deeply. "Our lads would never make it."

"Well, as you said, that's not our department. Some of the other beaches are narrower and steeper, but that only makes the likelihood of permanent submerged sandbars higher." Tim reached under the drafting table and pulled out another roll of paper, seemingly at random. He flattened it on the table and quickly tacked down the corners. "Here. This is the profile at Grandcamp, thirteen miles down the coast from Ravenoville. Here the beach is only about two hundred feet wide, but the recons show some strange wave patterns offshore, strange even for December."

"Meaning?"

Tim shrugged. "I don't know. Perhaps some particularly large winter bars, perhaps rocks. Perhaps even a few submerged wrecks. There might be stuff out there which could really hang us up, come spring. I just don't know."

Hardaway stared at the profile a moment longer, then walked over to the tank and looked down into it. Idly he put his finger into the water and made little splashes on the rippled surface. He turned back to face Tim. "Good enough, Loftis. It's all a bit stickier than I had imagined. I guess your days in the museum and with this little tank here have paid off. I'm convinced."

A compliment from Hardaway was rare. "You're the one who keeps saying it's a technological war!"

"So I am." Hardaway chuckled. "How much more time will you need?"

"I've pretty much finished up with the wave tank. It'll take three or four days to draw up the rest of the profiles. Today's the twenty-fourth. With a day off for Christmas"—Tim thought for a second—"the thirty-first."

Hardaway gave a low whistle. "That doesn't leave much time. The big meeting at SHAEF is scheduled for January eighteenth. That only gives COSSAC a fortnight to finish the final report."

"It'll take me that long to do a thorough job."

Hardaway was silent for a moment. "Good enough, Loftis. We can always put in a further report later if something unexpected comes up."

Tim took off his lab coat, threw it casually over the drawing table, and rolled down his sleeves. He put on his overcoat and stuffed more papers into his briefcase, looking around the room to see if he was leaving anything behind.

The two men went into the hallway. Tim snapped off the overhead lights, shut the door, and locked it. They walked down the institutional corridor that constituted the cellar of Grosvenor House. Then they went up the steps to the ground floor, turned, walked down the main hallway, saluted the guards at the side door, and signed out.

It was a cold, sunny afternoon. Tim stopped for a moment on the steps. "Hardly seems like Christmas Eve, does it?"

Hardaway shook his head. "No, hardly." He walked down the steps away from Tim, then stopped and turned. "Loftis?"

"Yes?"

"Busy for Christmas?"

"Well . . . uh, yes, I am. Why?"

Hardaway smiled. "I thought if you weren't, being a stranger and all, you might want to come up to Somerset for the day. It won't be fancy, but it will be festive enough."

Tim was flattered by the invitation. "Yes, it sounds like fun, but another time. Thanks."

Tim had barely finished apologizing when Pru came racing around the corner. She waved at him. Hardaway turned his head just in time to see her trip up the steps and kiss Tim quickly. Tim looked at Hardaway. "Previous engagement."

Hardaway chuckled. "So I see. Merry Christmas." He turned and walked briskly away.

The 5:43 from Waterloo was only ten minutes behind schedule as it chugged peacefully through the twilight and the wooded countryside of Kent. Tim looked out at the passing landscape of hedgerows and thatched farmhouses, the papers strewn over his lap forgotten. "Hardly know there was a war going on, would you?"

Pru looked up from her book, distracted. "Mmmm?"

"Hardly know there was a war going on. It's all so peaceful. It's what I always imagined England would look like when I was a kid."

Pru looked out of the window at the snow-covered cottages. "Yes, it is lovely, isn't it?" She set her book upside down on her lap and sank back in her seat. A wistful smile crept across her face. "What a relief to get away from London!"

Tim looked at his watch. "Where are we, do you know?"

"That last town was Sevenoaks, I believe. We should be there any minute." She gazed at him as he sat opposite her in the small compartment, then laughed softly. "My God, you Americans are a queer lot!"

Tim looked at her. "What's wrong?"

"You're always in such a hurry! Here we are, with a day's liberty, barely thirty-six hours, and you can't wait for the time to fly by!"

In twenty minutes, they were at Tunbridge Wells. The twilight had turned to a deep, crisp December night. Grabbing their bags, they started down High Street.

It was cold, but not windy. They talked very little. The only sound was the crunching of feet on the frozen snow of the roadway. Perhaps, if the tranquillity of the night or the spirit of Christmas had not so infected them, they would have heard the crunching of the feet that followed them.

The Rose and Crown was a very old inn. The facade dated from the early eighteenth century, but the beamed interiors with the mahogany Jacobean paneling attested to its truer origins in the seventeenth century, when it had housed the nobles who sought the cure at the nearby spas.

They sat in the corner of the pub, surrounded by celebrating locals. It was a far different crowd from the one at the St. Giles, Tim noticed. The only uniforms belonged to the local constables and two air raid wardens who were standing in the corner, laughing heartily and leading the singing of "Good King Wenceslas."

He looked at Pru. The warm light of the pub danced off her eyes as she caught his glance and returned it. He leaned over and kissed her softly on the neck. "Got much work with you, lieutenant?"

She laughed and shook her head. "Not much. Translating, mostly." She sighed. "Laborious and dull."

"Anything I can see?"

With her right hand Pru pushed Tim's head up and looked at him with amusement. "You can help me with it! Your French is better than mine." The kissable smile flashed at him. "And later, Major Loftis. Christmas Eve is not the time to worry about intelligence reports!"

In the lobby, a kind-looking gentleman in a tweed jacket was quite worried about intelligence reports. The flickering light from the fireplace glinted off his wire spectacles and his high, smooth forehead. He slowly turned the pages of *Country Life,* glancing every so often at the doorway to the pub. He read sporadically as his mind wandered. Some of the paragraphs in the article on beekeeping in the Cotswolds he had to read twice, partly because his attention strayed, partly because the English colloquialisms were sometimes mystifying to him, as they always are in a language other than one's native tongue.

The Westminster clock on the corner cabinet alongside the blue and white Staffordshire pottery chimed. He glanced at the face. It was ten fifteen. In a few minutes, he thought, it would be last call, and then the festivities would be over.

He had just finished the beekeeping article and started reading one on trout angling when the couple he had been assigned to follow came out of the pub. He watched them carefully out of the corner of his eye: The young American officer slid his arm around the British lieutenant and kissed her quickly.

When they had gone upstairs, he waited for a minute and then shut the magazine. Tucking it under his arm, he walked across the spacious lobby, wished the two couples having tea in the corner the salutations of the season, silently crossed the foyer, and started up the steps. Following the faint voices, he went down a corridor and stopped before rounding a corner. Peering around the edge of the wall, he was just in time to see the two officers disappear into a room halfway along another passageway. When their door had shut, he sauntered past it, not even pausing as he noticed the number of the room into which the couple had just disappeared.

Then he turned around and walked briskly back, descended the stairs, and crossed the lobby to the main desk.

"Excuse me, please."

The drowsy-looking clerk looked up from his ledger. "Yes, sir?"

"I've been expecting friends all evening. I was to get a lift back to London, but I've just telephoned and the motorcar has broken down." The man with the wire spectacles smiled meekly. "So it appears I shall have to spend the night. Do you have something?"

"We do have some rooms, yes, sir." The clerk looked down at the blotter. "Will there be just yourself, sir?"

"Yes, that's all."

"Any preferences, sir?"

"Well, yes, actually, if I have a choice"—he coughed quickly —"I should like to be in the rear. I'm a terribly light sleeper, and I do need quiet."

The clerk smiled appreciatively and ran his finger down the large sheet before him.

"Actually, I've stayed here before, a number of years ago, and I had a delightful room then."

"Do you remember the number, sir? Perhaps it's open."

"It was number thirteen, I believe."

The clerk shook his head. "Sorry, sir, number thirteen's booked. Number twelve is available, however."

The man smiled. It was a stroke of luck that the room next door to where his targets had retired was open. "That would be fine, I'm sure."

"If you would be so kind, sir, and I'll fetch the key," said the clerk, turning the registration blotter toward the man.

As the clerk turned his back, the man quickly ran his finger down the columns and cursed to himself; the name of the American major and his "wife" had been smeared by the blotter. He looked up at the clerk, returning with the key.

"Bottom line, sir. I'll fill in the rest." The man smiled and then wrote in a round script, *Mr. Charles Houghton, 15 Portland Square, London N.W.2.*

The clerk handed him the key and looked at the signature. "Yes, Mr.—Houghton. If you don't mind, sir," he said apologetically, "I'll need identification. Wartime regulations. Home Office requires us to be on the lookout for spies."

"Certainly. I understand." He handed over a Canadian passport. The clerk examined it quickly, then gave it back.

"Very good, sir. Breakfast service at nine tomorrow, sir. Hour later than usual. Due to Christmas."

Mr. Houghton nodded and replaced the passport in his pocket. He crossed the lobby and gathered up his coat and small suitcase from where he had left them. Turning quickly, he headed for the stairs.

Inside the room, he shut the door, shot the bolt, then walked to the small Georgian writing table beneath the window. He set the suitcase on it, released the snap, and opened it. Rummaging quickly through the clothing, he found the stethoscope and quietly moved the small chair at the desk next to the wall which separated his room from number 13. Placing the two arms of the instrument around his neck and into his ears, he set the rubber end against the wall to listen.

"Good, God, is this the sort of stuff you rummage through all day long?"

Pru looked at Tim while she finished unbuttoning her blouse. "Such as?"

"Number of bottles of wine sold by a vintner in Dieppe." He shuffled to the next sheet. "Number of chickens foraged by a German patrol from a farm near Fontaine-le-Bourg. Where the hell is that?"

"Just north of Rouen, I think. I forget."

Tim flipped casually through the pile of dispatches. "No wonder there's no security on this stuff. It's useless junk."

Pru hung up her blouse and military jacket and put them into the small wardrobe. "It's not useless if you have enough of it. You can tell where the German troops are thickest, and that's something." She undid the buttons on her skirt and let it fall to the floor. Stepping out of it, she leaned over, picked it up, and hung it in the wardrobe. "Sometimes I see gun figures and so on, but I don't know very many technical things, so I send those on. The Resistance can't get very close to the guns, after all, so there aren't very many of them anyway."

Tim grunted. "Must be tiresome."

"It often is. There are times when I think that we keep in contact with the Resistance only to keep their morale up." She pulled her slip up over her head and draped it lazily over the back of the small chair by the desk. "I don't know. I don't see much, you know. Remember, major." She walked behind Tim, slid her arms around his neck, and leaned over and kissed him playfully on the cheek. "I'm only a poor lieutenant."

"Yeah, I know." He turned his attention back to the papers. He held up a dispatch. " 'On the solstice the weather was heavier than usual.' There's a vital piece of information!" Laughing, he turned his head and kissed Pru. Her lips were warm and soft, and Tim suddenly realized how good it felt, being here alone with Pru, with nothing to do but make love all night and all morning. She kissed him back, then sat down on the bed and started removing her stockings.

"It's funny," she said absently. "We've had a lot of those types of dispatches."

"What type?"

"About the weather. And the solstice. Moonrise times. I can't remember them all." She waved one of her stockings in the air, then let it float to the floor. "I thought it a bit queer at the time."

Tim rose and took off his jacket. "Not too surprising, dear." He stopped. A distant little bell rang in the back of his mind. Where had he heard that before? It had been just that afternoon, when he had been talking with Hardaway about the winter beach profiles. What had he said about them? Something about calculating the profile at Ravenoville at the time of the solstice. He shrugged. It wasn't important. He undid his tie and started unbuttoning his shirt. He looked at Pru, dressed only in her lingerie, brushing her hair in the mirror. She caught his reflected glance.

"What are you thinking?"

Tim shook his head. "Nothing much. Something I came across today."

Pru turned in her chair. "The beaches?"

Tim smiled wearily as he pulled his shirt off. "Yeah, the beaches."

"They never go away, do they?"

He looked at her. The room was silent. Pru gazed at him, her lips tightened, a questioning look in her eyes. Then she turned and went back to brushing her hair.

After a moment, she spoke. "What is the solstice, anyway, Mr. Scientist?"

"Sun's greatest declination from the equator. The two days when the solar year reverses. Winter solstice was three days ago."

Pru's brush crackled as it slid through her hair. "Rather poetic, isn't it?"

"What?"

"Shortest day of the year. Turning point. You know what I mean." She sighed. "It just struck me as being rather poetic."

"I guess so." Tim shrugged as he threw his shirt on the chair. "Funny, though, you should get messages about it."

"And that, my friend," said Pru, taking the dispatches and putting them on her suitcase, "is that!" She grabbed Tim and pulled him down beside her on the bed. Their arms wrapped around each other and their lips met. They finished undressing each other tenderly and soon were naked between the sheets.

The man with the stethoscope listened for a moment, then looked disgusted and yanked the rubber cap away from the wall. Dropping it in the suitcase, he prepared to retire. Even eavesdropping had its limits.

4

It was December twenty-ninth. Hoping to get his material to Hardaway at least a day early, Tim left Grosvenor House and went over to Norfolk House for one last sweep through the Resistance dispatches, one last chance to find some small scrap of information which might make a difference in his final report. He had remembered Hardaway's tip about going over to G-2 and seeing Brigadier Beauclerk.

A saltier man than Brigadier James Beauclerk, aide to General P. G. Whitefoord, Director of G-2 for COSSAC, Tim had never met. He was a tall, fiftyish Scot, with a sallow complexion and a leathery face. He smoked incessantly, even while he talked in his half-swallowed Highland brogue. Once Beauclerk had been a redhead. Now advancing age and natural graying had turned him into a dishwater blond. His face was lined with wrinkles and crow's-feet. Above all, his eyes flicked everywhere with an amused twinkle while he rambled on about any topic at hand or took one of his long, whistling draws on his Senior Service cigarettes. With his rumpled uniform and his angular six-and-a-half foot frame, he exuded brashness and wit. Maybe that was why Hardaway had called him unorthodox.

For two hours Tim and Pru had been sorting through dispatches in a bare room on the third floor of Norfolk House while Beauclerk had looked in at intervals between his various meetings. It was a gray, blustery day, and the two large windows which opened onto St. James's Square let in the leaden afternoon.

All intelligence from the Martians at Clive Steps which had been sent to G-2:C&T had been assembled into large blue folders, each one representing a different sector in the northwestern part of France. There were over three hundred in Normandy and the Somme. There were some seventy sectors along the coastline alone from Dieppe to Cherbourg. The single long table pushed up against the wall was filled with stacks and stacks of blue folders.

Tim looked at them and sighed. In two hours he had only read twelve.

Pru threw a packet on the table and looked over at him. "How's it going?"

"Slowly."

At that moment they heard Beauclerk's raspy voice booming down the corridor. The door opened and he strode in. "Well, major," he said, his wrinkled eyes twinkling, "have you found anything yet?"

"Not much. At this point, I guess that's a good sign."

Beauclerk sprawled his giant frame into a totally inadequate straight chair, his legs thrust out from under him. "No surprises, you mean?"

Tim nodded. He threw the folder he had just finished reading onto the small stack of reports on the floor. "God, that's a lot of data!"

Beauclerk nodded. "Too bloody much, if you ask me. Most of it doesn't tell us a damn thing."

There was silence in the room. Tim picked up another folder, thumbed it for a minute, then shook his head slowly.

Beauclerk stared at him with one eye cocked. "What is it, lad?"

Tim felt sheepish. "Nothing. Just frustrated, I guess."

"Well, what about?" Tim shrugged. Beauclerk leaned forward in his chair. "Listen, lad, this is a frustrating business. Something's on your mind. I want to know what it is."

"Well, sir, there's only one thing about all this that seems strange."

"And that is?"

"The weather messages."

Pru let out an exasperated groan. "For heaven's sake, Tim, I told you! Weather reports are common."

Tim looked at her, then at Beauclerk. The brigadier shrugged comically, then flicked his cigarette ash onto the floor. "They're common, all right." His ragged eyebrow arched. "Why do they seem strange to you?"

The expression on Beauclerk's face caught Tim off guard. He got up and walked to the window. Leaning against the frame, he looked down at the buses and pedestrians scurrying around St. James's Square. The bustle of activity seemed to stir his mind. "They're strange because they don't have anything to do with what we want. What the hell does the December weather have to do with plans for a spring invasion?" He turned and faced them.

"And . . . ?" Beauclerk said.

"Not 'and,' but 'why'?" Tim said. "Why is the Resistance sending over hundreds of messages about the weather?"

Pru spoke up. "You yourself said that winter storms were what changed the beach profiles."

"Sure, but the Resistance doesn't know that. Only a geologist knows or cares. Besides, they don't even know that we're interested in beach profiles at all, do they?"

Pru and Beauclerk exchanged glances. Pru spoke. "The sources are probably chitchatting with us. They do that, you know. Even if they don't have any substantial information when their transmission time comes around, they'll send a message through anyway, just to maintain contact. We've gotten so that if we don't hear from them, we assume they've been captured."

"They all talk about the weather?"

"What else is there to talk about, for heaven's sake?" Pru said.

"What do you talk about when you're at a function and don't know anyone? I've been reading dispatches for six months now, and I've read all sorts of things: you know, color of shrubbery, the wine is better than ever before, I can't remember them all. They're silly, perhaps, but it's standard procedure."

Beauclerk stirred in his chair and waved his cigarette at Pru. "That's true enough, lieutenant." He turned to Tim. "But keep talking, major. Nobody's combed these reports as thoroughly as you have, and you think you're on to something. I want to hear about it."

Tim got up and walked to the table where the folders lay. "I've read twelve folders today. I'd say that ten of them, at least, describe the weather in the sectors for the three days before Christmas. Look."

He grabbed one and flipped it open. "Creuilly sector. There are three dispatches from the period of the twentieth to the twenty-third. None of them have anything to do with fortifications or troop movements or anything even remotely military. One is about the sale of three hundred pounds of flour to the Germans, and two are about the weather." He threw the folder down and picked up another. "Doudeville sector. Nine reports during the same period. One describes the arrival of some new German tanks. That's fine; that makes sense. One talks about how a German platoon on liberty got drunk and tried to rape a farm girl. Three others, all from the same operator, tell about sentry postings. But there are four reports about the weather." Tim looked up at the other two. "Four! Four reports when one would almost have been too many."

Pru shrugged. "So what?"

Tim shook his hand. "I don't know what, dammit! But for a three-day period the volume of reports about the weather is double what it usually is. You don't think something funny's going on?"

Beauclerk took another long draw on his cigarette and ex-

[81]

haled. "Keep talking, lad. I'm with you. But remember that so far you've only got coincidence."

"When does coincidence become a pattern?"

Beauclerk smiled impishly. "When it does, and not before."

"Hell, I'm probably all wet," he said. "You people are the intelligence group—"

"We're in charge of that, yes," Beauclerk broke in, "but that probably only means we don't know what the hell we're doing. I don't know about you, major, but I think that experts are the stupidest lot of all. In any field." He smiled his toothy grin again. "Our real job is to keep our ears open, so keep talking. I want to know what it is you think these reports suggest."

Tim shrugged helplessly. "That's tough to say exactly. Suddenly, for no reason, the Resistance starts talking about the weather. They start talking about the weather a lot. I've got a creepy feeling that there's something in those messages we're missing. Could these transmissions be from Resistance members who've been captured and are being forced to transmit?"

Beauclerk took out his cigarettes, offered the pack around, then lit one for himself. "There's a chance of that. Always is. But it's not very likely in this case."

"The first thing every spy learns," Pru said, "is to always make the same deliberate encoding mistake when he transcribes for transmission. It's his signature. In case he's captured and forced to transmit, or in case the Germans capture the code sheet, the deliberate mistake won't appear, and we'll know what's afoot."

"Well, has that happened?"

Beauclerk smiled. "Ask Lieutenant Lapthorne."

"Not that we've seen."

The room fell quiet. Tim leaned against the table and cracked his knuckles. Then he asked, half musing, of no one in particular, "Doesn't all that repetition about the weather strike you as odd?"

"Frankly, yes." Beauclerk replied. "But you've got to ask

yourself, lad, what it is they could be wanting to tell us? Behind every code there's always an intention. What is it here?" Tim threw up his hands in ignorance. "Well, let's consider it and see if we can find it."

Beauclerk rose, walked over to the table near where Tim was standing, and sat on the edge.

"First, the mere existence of lots of weather reports could be simply fortuitous. It's not the job of the Resistance to interpret what they say. They just bang things along to us in the hopes that we can use it. Now, perhaps all these operatives might be thinking that storm conditions are useful to us." Beauclerk looked at Pru and Tim as if waiting for an answer.

"Do you think that, sir?" Pru asked.

"No, I don't, lieutenant. I'm inclined to go along with Major Loftis here, at least for another step." He waved his cigarette to emphasize his point. "What could they want to conceal? They can't be using the weather to suggest that the Germans are harassing them any more than usual. You know," he said, grinning. "Stormy weather, and all that rot!"

"Why not?" Tim asked.

"Well, why not come right out and say it? Why not say that the Heinies have been taking more hostages than usual, or that Code Blue Twelve has gone over, or whatever? After all, lad, if they're captured, they're shot no matter what they've said, so why bother to be confusing? Correct?"

Tim nodded.

Beauclerk rose and paced the room. "The other possibility—besides a metaphor, I mean—is remote, but a possibility nonetheless. That is of a code within a code. Perhaps some of the chaps over there are hiding messages that they don't want us to see."

An amazed expression hit Pru's face. "Why on earth should they wish to do that, sir?"

"I don't know," Beauclerk said. "But let's consider it." He

[83]

stopped pacing and rubbed his chin. "All messages from France are cleared through the Martians at Clive Steps. Some go to the Deuxième Bureau. It could be that the Resistance is trying to send messages to their fellow Frenchmen and to keep them from us."

That was a good idea, Tim thought. "What could they want to tell them?"

Beauclerk winced. "There's the rub, lad. I don't know. Something about internal French politics, perhaps. Information about Frenchmen in the Vichy government who have doubled over to the Germans. Something along those lines."

"Why wouldn't they want the British and the Americans to know such things?" Pru asked.

"That's the major question in that theory, lieutenant. French pride could account for it. They feel badly enough that their old enemies, the British, are having to come to the rescue of *la patrie*. Perhaps they want to set their own house in order."

Beauclerk paused, looked at both of them, then shook his head.

"The problem with that theory is that it won't hold enough water. Some, but not enough. It won't explain why an elaborate code has been established. And who, in God's name, ordered it?"

"Why is that a problem?" Tim asked.

"Because we control the transmitters. Our connections with the Resistance are basically one-way affairs. They transmit, we receive. If we want to tell them anything we do it over the regular transmissions from the BBC."

"Could the Free French have their own transmitter?"

Pru shook her head. "No. The Royal Signal Corps would have noticed any new signals."

"Any other way the French here could send over a code?"

Beauclerk grimaced. "Not very likely. If it didn't go over on the BBC, it would have to be sent via airdrop. The Resistance is compartmentalized, major. Few agents know the identity of many others. And they would have had to have sent over elaborate instructions on when to use any new code. No, major, it won't do, I'm afraid. You've a good notion, but there's no pattern."

Beauclerk was sitting deep in thought on the edge of the table, feet dangling and arms folded across his chest, when Tim asked quietly, "What would it take to convince you?"

Beauclerk started, then stared at Tim. "Proof."

"In what form?"

"Enough of a pattern. Enough numbers to justify putting a few cryptologists to work—cryptologists we don't have to spare, I'm afraid, unless we know that we've latched on to a sure thing. We're spread dreadfully thin around here."

"If I give you those numbers, would you do it?"

Beauclerk's blue eyes focused on Tim. Pru rose from her chair, alarmed. She walked over to Tim and took hold of his arm. "Tim, for heaven's sake, why are you so insistent?"

"Never mind, damn it. I've got a hunch I'm on to something!"

Pru frowned at him. After a moment of leaden silence, she turned to Beauclerk. "Excuse me, brigadier, I have other work to do." Quickly, she gathered up her papers and her purse and rushed out of the room. The door slammed behind her.

Tim gazed after her. Beauclerk took a puff of his cigarette and chuckled quietly as he exhaled. "Well, lad, you've done it now."

"Oh, Christ, I'm sorry, sir. I—"

Beauclerk waved his hand. "Don't be sorry. Those bloody English can't take rough going."

"But you, sir—"

Beauclerk rose from the table, straightening himself out to his full height. His eyes danced. "I'm a Scot! And don't you forget it! You're a good lad, major," Beauclerk added. "You've got to learn to mind your tongue, but that was what they always told me, too. I'm proud to say I never have." He chuckled. "Tell me, what did you do before the war?"

"I was—I mean, I am a geologist. You know, rocks and things." He watched Beauclerk throw his cigarette on the floor and mash it out with his foot. "It's funny," Tim said.

"What is?"

"All my life I've followed my hunches. I've gotten some crazy ideas that everybody laughed at, said I was crazy for even considering such wild schemes. Sometimes they even worked out."

"A scientist with hunches?"

"That's all science is, sir," Tim said. "You get a hunch and see where it leads you."

Beauclerk nodded his head slowly, a pensive look on his craggy face. "What are you involved in at G-Three?"

"I'm finishing up a report on the proposed landing sites. Tides, water levels, ground water. I just came over here today to see if there were any odds and ends in these folders."

Beauclerk was serious. "When will you be finished?"

"Day after tomorrow is my due date."

"And after that?"

"I don't know."

"Well, major, I think your hunch is a good one." He grinned. "I've been in intelligence work most of my military career. Thirty-two years. I only know one thing, and that is that you've always got your fat rear end parked right on top of what you're looking for. There's no reason why every idea about intelligence has to come from an intelligence officer." Beauclerk snorted contemptuously. "God, they're the biggest bloody fools of all! Anyhow, ring me when you're finished over there, and I'll have you transferred over to G-Two."

It was a tempting offer, a chance to get away from Hardaway and be near Pru, but Tim knew he couldn't accept it. "I appreciate that, sir. I . . . um . . . I think I ought to stay over there, though. I'm their only beach expert, and, besides, that's what I really know."

Beauclerk gave him a long glance, his left eyebrow arching in an expression of doubt. "Fair enough, major. I don't hold much with experts, as you know, but I suppose there are such things. But if you want to come over, ring me. And if you have some spare time and you want to go through these reports in search of that pattern, do it."

"Do you mean that, sir?"

"Sure as you're born, lad. Come around when you're able. If there's any trouble, I'll clear it. Who's your opposite?"

"Hardaway, sir. Major David Hardaway."

Beauclerk searched his memory. "Gray hair, always combed?"

"That's the one."

"And do you get along with him, lad?"

"Well enough, I guess."

Beauclerk sighed. "You're a better man than I. Well, it's sixteen hundred hours, and I've got to run." He headed for the door, opened it, then paused and looked back at Tim. "Will I see you soon?"

"I always play a hunch."

Beauclerk smiled and left.

Two hours later, Tim was walking briskly down South Audley Street, deep in his own thoughts. He had rushed back to Grosvenor House to finish up the drafts of the report and to give them to the stenographic staff. Now he had to see Pru. The events of the afternoon had upset him. He wished that he hadn't offended her. You never know the value of a relationship, he thought, until its survival is threatened. Then it becomes a gnawing ache right in the gut.

He came to Curzon Street and turned left. He was walking faster now, anxious to see her, to explain himself. He dodged the other pedestrians, keeping his hands firmly planted in his trench coat pockets as he strode swiftly across the wet pavements.

Suddenly he had the sensation that he was being followed. It was a feeling at his back, as if two eyes were literally boring into his spine. At Queen Street, he stopped to let a bus go by. He turned around quickly. There was nothing behind him except the normal flow of people rushing home before night fell and the streets became too dark to see. Or was there? Had he seen something disappear into a doorway, a flash of coat, a sudden movement?

The feeling didn't go away. Tim looked at the traffic, then darted across Curzon Street to the south side. The odd feeling persisted. He stopped and whirled around. The street was empty. He walked more briskly. A block behind him, the man in the wire spectacles who had spent Christmas Eve in the hotel room at Tunbridge Wells resumed walking, too.

Tim reached Piccadilly and turned left. The sidewalks were full now. Civilians held their coats shut against the chill December wind. Men hurried home from work. Women carried small bags of groceries. There was nothing unusual. At the corner of Regent Street, he stopped to buy an *Observer,* folding the paper carefully and tucking it under his arm, sticking his already cold hands back into his pockets. He looked up again. There it was, he thought, another flash of clothing disappearing into a doorway. It was the same color as the last time, too. Or was it?

Tim plunged into Piccadilly Circus. His steps were faster now, almost a trot, as he skipped past the cars and headed up Coventry Street. His breath was coming in spurts. Panic seized him. Am I going mad, he thought? Am I close to cracking or something, that I imagine people are following me? Once again he looked behind him and saw nothing. He reached St. Martin's Lane and raced around the corner, toward Chandos Place and the safety of Pru's apartment.

The American major was difficult to shadow. It was impossible that he had been spotted, the man with the wire spectacles thought. There had been close calls, to be sure, when the American had looked around suddenly, and only alertness and instinctive reactions had sent him leaping into doorways just in time.

The man quickened his pace. A large lorry had barreled out of Oxenden Street onto Coventry at a bad moment. When the lorry had passed, the American had disappeared. The man started to run.

At Whitcomb Street he stopped. He looked down the avenue. Only a few people were walking, a woman on the far side and a young British soldier with his arm around his girl coming toward him. The American must be going to see the Englishwoman at the address in Chandos Place, he thought.

He started walking again. Halfway down the street, Chandos Place appeared. The man stopped and looked at his watch. Slowly his eyes panned up and down the street. Satisfied that no one was watching him, he peered around the corner. Chandos Place was empty.

The man leaned against the building. His breath gave off white clouds as he thought for a minute. No doubt the American would stay at her flat for a while. There would probably not be any more chance for contact tonight. He cursed to himself. For a week he had been following Mrs. Lapthorne and her mysterious friend without discovering his identity. The blurred name on the registry at the Rose and Crown had been particularly vexing.

The man with the wire spectacles looked about him and then headed down Whitcomb Street toward Pall Mall. From there, he zigzagged over to Trafalgar Square and into the tube. He had to transmit a report that night, and his lack of progress would anger his superiors in Berlin. Impatient, they would no doubt order him to confront the woman now.

But he knew better. He knew that the power he held over Mrs. Lapthorne could perhaps get crucial information from her, but it would be wiser to wait until he was sure she knew the secrets the bureau in Berlin had ordered him to get at any cost, to wait until it would be too late for the Allies to alter their invasion plans.

As the train ground to a halt and he stepped aboard, he knew that the romantic affair with the American had spoiled the otherwise splendid isolation in which most war widows live. The American was an unfortunate complication that would have to be dealt with when the time came. One way or another.

5

Tim was in the same blank room on the third floor of Norfolk House by nine the next morning. The folders of the seventy-six sectors along the French coast from Normandy to the Pas-de-Calais lay on the table before him. It promised to be a long project, sorting out all those dispatches, but Tim attacked it with the sort of perverse vigor he always managed to muster when confronted with a thorny new problem. Slowly he moved up the coast.

Saint-Laurent-sur-Mer: three dispatches, none about the weather. Sainte-Honorine: one dispatch, reporting heavy seas. Tim copied the message on a tablet. Port-en-Bessin: no transmissions. Arromanches: nine reports, including one which said that the longest night of the year had been cold. Courseulles: five transmissions, including two which mentioned the damage of the heavy surf on the night of the twenty-first. Saint-Aubin: two reports, neither about the weather. Bénouville: seven dispatches, none about the weather. Varaville: six reports, one of which mentioned that the moonrise on the twenty-second had been late but beautiful. And on it went.

By eleven o'clock Tim had compiled statistics on the coast of France. In seventy-six sectors, there had been 386 transmissions. Of these, 83 had been about the weather: 22 percent. That's either a big coincidence or a small pattern, Tim thought. He felt discouraged. Maybe Pru had been right. Maybe the Resistance operators had just been chitchatting, keeping their avenues of contact with England open and nothing more.

Tim tried again, this time with the fifty-eight sectors which were directly inland from the coastal sectors. Bayeux: nine trans-

[91]

missions, three about the moonrise. That encouraged him. Three people in the same town talking about the lateness of the moonrise couldn't be just coincidence, he thought. On the other hand, if the moon had been as late as they all had said, it could be pure chance. He continued. Caen: twelve messages, three about the cold temperature on the night of the twenty-first. Arromanches had talked about that, Tim remembered. Could there be a connection, he wondered? Dozulé: two transmissions, one about the lack of moonlight on the twenty-first of December. Tim began to get excited. Annebault: seven messages, none about the weather. Tim's excitement faltered. Beuzeville: two reports, one about how the strong winds on the twenty-first had blown a tree down and blocked the driveway of a house which a German Wehrmacht officer had confiscated for his residence. Pont-Audemer: three dispatches, one about how the moon had not appeared until 1:00 A.M. on the twenty-first. Bourneville: one transmission about the rain on the morning of the twenty-second. After another hour and a half, Tim compiled his totals. In fifty-six sectors, there had been 212 transmissions, of which 51 had been about the weather. That gave him a figure of 24 percent, about the same as the coastal districts had yielded.

He tried again with the thirty-seven districts stretching from Granville on the Atlantic Coast to Rouen. Granville: eleven messages, none about the weather. Beauchamps: six, none about the weather. Montbray: four, none about the weather. Saint-Lô: fourteen dispatches, none about the weather. Saint-Martin-des-Besaces: four transmissions, all four of which mentioned how late the moon had risen. Le Mesnil-Auzouf, three miles away, had furnished four transmissions, none about the weather. Villers-Bocage: one transmission about a hostage being taken. The thirty-seven districts had sent a total of 115 messages, of which 27 had concerned themselves with the weather: 23 percent. So far, Tim had no pattern.

The forty-four sectors between Vire and Évreux yielded 131

transmissions, with 33, or 25 percent, concerning themselves with the weather. The sixteen districts in the triangle between Louviers, Neufchatel, and Beauvais, excluding Rouen, furnished 49 messages, of which ten, or 20 percent, were about the weather.

Tim threw his pencil down and sat with his head cocked into his left hand, the fingers of his right hand drumming the table in frustration. He had spent six hours plodding through the folders. He had come up with 204 dispatches which had discussed the weather out of 893 messages sent. He had gotten figures of 22, 24, 23, 25, and 20 percent. He shook his head. Those were square numbers, suggesting that the bell-shaped curve of normal probability was hard at work producing coincidence and nothing more. But still, Tim thought, I've got 204 weather dispatches, and that seems like a lot. What was the normal percentage of weather reports, of what Pru called the "chitchat," he wondered?

He slumped in his chair and stared at the large map of France on the wall. In his mind's eye he tried to supply a picture for every village. He saw stone huts, streams, streets, people running back and forth. The question, he thought, what was it? As Beauclerk had said, there must be a motive. If there is a motive, there will inevitably be a pattern. Tim tried to draw motives from the French peasants who scurried around the landscapes of his mind.

There was a knock on the door. Tim looked up, startled. "Come in."

Beauclerk entered and shut the door behind him. He grinned at Tim. "Any luck, lad?"

"Afraid not. I've run a lot of these folders through the hopper and there's nothing. Here."

Tim picked up his tally sheet and handed it to Beauclerk, who read it through, his head bobbing back and forth as he muttered under his breath.

"Pretty discouraging, huh?"

"Not necessarily," Beauclerk said, stroking his chin thoughtfully. "Not at all. The first thing to remember in intelligence work is that the whole point of it is secrecy. If a code is easily broken, then secrecy is vulnerable, and the code is no bloody good. You can never expect to break a code, or find one, or track down a spy network the first time out."

Beauclerk sat down in the heavy wooden armchair across the room from Tim. He lit a cigarette, exhaled, then looked at Tim.

"Your statistics are awfully square, though, lad. Not much handle on them." He rolled his tongue pensively in his cheek, then took another drag of his cigarette.

"I've been thinking since yesterday," he said finally. "I don't know if twenty-three percent is high or low for weather reports, but the total output, what was it?"

"Two hundred four dispatches, sir."

"Yes. Well, that's a bloody lot of talk about the weather in absolute terms. Bloody lot. How many days does that cover?"

"Three. December nineteenth through the twenty-second."

"Why those dates?"

"That's more or less when the weather reports started coming thick and fast."

"Well, as I said, I've been thinking since yesterday. I was, and I still am, impressed by the amount of weather reports. I'm with you on that score.

"But" he went on, "codes don't operate on content, they operate on letter arrangement. All that talk about the weather might merely be someone's way of getting our attention. If so, our real clue lies within the messages."

"Like times and dates?"

"I mean that something, somewhere, in those two hundred and whatever dispatches should be a cipher key. That key would be the way to unlock the rest of the message. It could be a number or a date. Often is. But it might be a phrase or a word. Have a look at those messages you've copied. Is there anything that repeats itself a lot?"

It came in an electric flash.

"Solstice."

"Eh?"

"Solstice. Most of the weather reports are about the solstice." Tim's eyes shot down the pages. "Listen here, sir. Courseulles reports, 'Heavy surf on the solstice. *Todt* not on the beach.' And another, 'Solstice storm floods German supply shed.' Later on, it's Varaville, which says, 'Moon on solstice at one thirteen but still beautiful.' There are lots of these!"

"How many?"

After a quick count, Tim turned to Beauclerk. "Seventy-six, sir. That's it, isn't it? Doesn't it make sense?"

"Easy, lad. We're a long way from home yet. You've counted all those repetitions in the translations. If it's really a cipher key, we'll have to find it in the clear texts." Beauclerk stood up slightly, grabbed his chair, and scooted over to the table next to Tim. "Give me some paper. You take half of the stack, I'll take the other. I want the messages that use the word 'solstice' in the decoded original French, and I want the date and place of transmission."

It was dark by the time they finished. Tim had covered the coastal districts, and Beauclerk the interior ones. In the 83 coastal dispatches about the weather, 51 had mentioned the date of the solstice specifically in the translation, but only 19 had used the word itself in the original French. The 51 transmissions from the first string of interior towns gave a total of 9 messages with the word "solstice" in the original text. Of the original 115 messages in the sectors from Granville to Rouen, 27 had mentioned the weather, 16 had referred to the day of the twenty-first, but only 4 mentioned the word "solstice." The remaining sixty districts, which had given 41 messages about the weather, mentioned the twenty-first 10 times and used the word "solstice" twice.

Tim added up the totals. He read them to Beauclerk, who sat exhausted with his right arm leaning on the table, drumming his head with a pencil and humming "Annie Laurie" very, very softly.

"Here it is. Two hundred and thirty-one sectors sent eight

hundred and ninety-three dispatches, of which thirty-four used the word 'solstice' proper. Not very good, is it?"

"What's the percentage?"

Tim pushed his pencil. "Three point seven percent. Good or bad?"

"Neither. If we're right, it's sufficient. If we're wrong, it's not enough." Beauclerk chewed on his pencil for a moment. "Three point seven percent, you say? How common a word is 'solstice'?"

"Not that common."

"How common is it around the time of the solstice?"

Tim frowned. "Still not that common."

"What's solstice in French?"

"Solstice."

"How common is it?"

"About the same as in English, I'd guess."

It started to rain outside, one of those freezing, icy rains that London is famous for. The large, half-frozen drops clattered against the windowpanes and echoed in the bare room. Beauclerk sighed. He sunk his chin into his cupped hands.

"We're still in the realm of coincidence, I'm afraid." He shook his head wearily. "I don't believe it, though. I think you're bang on, lad." He lifted tired eyes to look at Tim from inside wrinkled, sunken, lined sockets. "But there's still no pattern. And no motive."

Tim clasped his hands behind his neck and stretched his cramped muscles. He looked across the room to the map of France. "Maybe I should plot the solstice messages on the map with those tacks?"

"Good idea! That might yield something."

Of the sixty sectors the farthest inland, six messages had used the word "solstice" and all of them had come from Rouen. Of the four messages which had used the word from the thirty-seven sectors between Granville and Rouen, three had come from Lisieux. Of the nine messages from the fifty-eight districts just inland from the coast, three were from Bayeux, three from Caen, and three from Abbeville. Along the coast, there were three pins in Sainte-Mère-Église, two in Courseulles, seven in Deauville, five in Le Havre, and two in Fécamp. The thirty-four messages had come from only eleven towns.

Tim felt his heart starting to pound. He'd been right. "There it is, sir. The pattern."

Beauclerk peered over at Tim. "It may be. And it may not be. It's a hundred and sixty miles from Sainte-Mère-Église on the west to Abbeville on the east. There's still a great deal of room for coincidence. However," he said, with a faint trace of a smile, "the fact that only one town sent one message, and only two sent two, is curious. All the other towns sent at least three. Check the folders again, lad. Did the towns that sent three send them all on the same day?"

Tim looked at Sainte-Mère-Église, Bayeux, Caen, Lisieux, and Abbeville. In each instance the three transmissions had been on the night of the twenty-first and the morning of the twenty-second. They had all been within twelve hours of one another during the thirty-six-hour period Tim had staked out.

Beauclerk smiled. "Major, we are steadily marching from the gloomy forest of coincidence into the bright highland meadow of pattern!" The numbers were beginning to tell their secrets. Grinning, Tim looked back at the map. Le Havre, Rouen, and Deauville would make or break the pattern. Of the seven reports from Deauville, four had come from the evening of the twenty-first, and three on the evening of the twenty-second. All four of Rouen's messages had come on the twenty-first. And four of the five from Le Havre had come on the same day, the twenty-first. "That's it," Tim said triumphantly. "We've got our pattern."

Beauclerk sat down on the window sill and lit his forty-second cigarette of the day. "Yes, there's our pattern. But that's all we've got."

"What do you mean, that's all we've got? We've got the cipher key to a code!"

"But where are the messages in that code? There haven't been any dispatches that we haven't been able to decipher with our present books. All we've got is a code word with no code."

"Maybe the messages haven't been sent yet."

Beauclerk nodded. "That's what we should pray for. I'm hoping that someone, whoever it is, is alerting us that they're about to send over something valuable, and that they want us to be prepared when it comes."

Tim thrust his hands into his pockets and slumped in his chair. His stomach rumbled loudly as he did, and he remembered that he had eaten nothing since breakfast.

Beauclerk chuckled. "Don't be so glum, lad. Come on, it's late, and we've neither of us eaten." He got up from the window, walked over to Tim, and slapped him on the back. "We need a good stiff drink or two as well."

Tim got up and reached for his jacket, which lay flung across the table. As he put it on, he said resolutely, "We'll get them. I just know we will."

Beauclerk nodded wearily. "I hope you're right, lad."

It was late February, over a month later, when the messages finally came.

The three black Gestapo vans slowed as they cruised down the Boulevard Louis Pasteur. One by one the ominous vehicles passed through the Gothic archway into the Matignon courtyard of the Palais de Justice. As the last one passed, SS guards swung shut the massive wooden gates which sealed off the courtyard whenever new prisoners were being delivered to the Sipo garrison in the town of Lisieux.

The vans came to a stop alongside one wall of the ancient building. The black doors of the first one opened and a squad of black-shirted Sipo officers emerged. Swiftly they moved to the second van. While two of them raised their machine pistols, the remaining officers opened the back doors of the van. Seven handcuffed prisoners stumbled out of the windowless van and stood on the cobblestones, blinking at the gray morning light.

Another detachment of SS soldiers had emerged from the Palais, followed by the lieutenant who commanded the detail. The detachment opened the doors of the third van and herded the five prisoners from it over to where the first seven stood. Motioning with their machine pistols, the policemen lined the prisoners up. The sergeant who had led the squad in the first van walked over to the lieutenant and saluted. Then he presented a sheaf of papers to his superior, who looked through them, glancing up every so often at the prisoners. He handed the papers back to the first man, who started reading names. As each prisoner responded, he was pushed to one side. When nine names had been read, the soldiers with machine pistols fell in alongside the men. They marched briskly across the courtyard.

Father Jean-Baptiste Saurel stared after them. The handcuffs bit cruelly into his wrists and he felt dizzy, having been pulled from his bed in the parish house of Église Sainte-Catherine at three in the morning and forced to squat in a police van for four hours while the Sipo had swept Lisieux making additional arrests. Father Saurel watched as the men were led past a chilling sight: a three-meter row of sandbags with three wooden posts embedded in the cobblestones in front of it. How convenient, he thought to himself, to have a place of execution so close by the courtrooms, so there might be no delays in the administration of justice.

"Saurel!" He turned his head, the wind blowing his gray hair as he did. The SS leader was facing him. "Father Jean-Baptiste Saurel?"

"Oui?"

"Inside. You are to be questioned."

He began to tremble only as he and his guards marched up the grand staircase in the main lobby of the building, following the leader's gestured commands. He had often contemplated arrest, but now that it was upon him, a sickness grew in his stomach. He tried to imagine what lay in store for him. There would first be the questioning. Then the questioning would become more intense. Then, he knew, there would be torture if the Gestapo had not learned what it wanted to know from him. Father Saurel had seen too many victims of Hitler's secret police to imagine for a minute that his calling would spare him a gram of their cruelty if they decided to take that course with him. He wondered, as they reached the top of the steps and turned down one of the corridors, how much he could tell his captors and still not betray himself or his operations.

They stopped at a door. The lieutenant turned sharply and knocked. *"Herein!"* said a voice from within. He opened the door, jerking his head to indicate that they should enter. The guards pushed Father Saurel ahead of them into the middle of the room. The lieutenant shut the door, stepped in front of the desk, and snapped the Nazi salute.

"Heil Hitler! Herr Sturmbannführer, wir haben den Gefangenen."

Major Josef Kreitzl rose and walked out from behind the desk. He looked at the French prisoner for a minute, then waved at the three Gestapo men. *"Raus."*

The officers snapped salutes and left.

Kreitzl motioned to the chair by the desk. *"Asseyez-vous,* Father, this is merely a routine inquiry. I will ask you a few questions. If you cooperate, you will be free soon. Cigarette?" He extended a pack of Gitanes. Father Saurel shook his head. Kreitzl lit one and returned to his chair. He sat in it, paused for a moment, then looked back at Father Saurel. "Father, do you know a man named Maurice Boudreau?"

Father Saurel shook his head. "I have never heard of him."

"Jacques Plibot?" Again the headshake. "Roland Lavier?" Another shake. The German officer stared at him. "Come, Father, if you do not know these men, why have you been communicating with them by radio?"

Father Saurel managed a wan smile. "I am sorry, but I am sure there has been a mistake. My loyalty to the Reich is well known."

Kreitzl reached for a stack of folders which lay on his desk. He took the top one, put it in front of him, and opened it. "We already know much about you. Father Jean-Baptiste Saurel. Age: Fifty-two. Born in Soissons. Educated at the Jesuit Seminary in Reims. Priest at Église Saint-Catherine in Lisieux since 1934. That is you?"

Father Saurel nodded.

The German officer looked through the other papers in the file slowly, occasionally glancing at the clergyman. Then he shut the folder and leaned back in his chair, inhaling on the cigarette. Finally he spoke. "Father Saurel, spying is a serious crime. It is punishable by death. You know that?"

Father Saurel nodded.

"We know that you are a radio operator for the Resistance. At the very least. For that alone you can be shot." He looked at Father Saurel. "However, shooting people is not a desirable thing, in my view. It arouses anger among the citizens, for one thing. In addition, it deprives me of information valuable to the Reich. So I have found it best to negotiate with people who come within my jurisdiction. Do you understand me?"

"I am sorry, monsieur, but I am ignorant—"

"Quiet! I have no desire to listen to claims of innocence! If you confess, I will be lenient. Your cooperation is all that stands between you and a firing squad." He paused. "I will promise you one thing. If you furnish me with a list of the Resistance operatives in your cell, you will go free."

"I can tell you nothing about something of which I am ignorant."

The SS officer buzzed for the guards. "I give you twenty-four hours, Father Saurel. Then we will not be gentle. *Raus!*"

The guards marched Father Saurel downstairs to the small row of cells in the cellar directly below the great courtroom in the northwest wing of the building. The Gestapo jailer swiftly opened the wooden door with the small barred window in it, and the guards removed Father Saurel's handcuffs and roughly shoved him in the dark room. The door shut behind him. He heard the steel bolt being thrown.

He looked around. In the corner stood a battered steel bucket that served as a toilet. In the opposite corner lay a tattered army blanket. Otherwise, the cell was bare. Father Saurel sat down on the blanket. After a minute, his nerves calmed somewhat, and he lay down. Despite the coldness of the rough floor and the anxiety in his mind, he fell into a fitful sleep.

The daylight had disappeared from the small window at the top of his cell when he heard the clicking bootsteps down the corridor. They stopped in front of his door. The bolt slammed back. The door opened and the same SS man who had arrested him earlier in the day stepped into the room.

"*Los, französiches Schwein!*" Father Saurel followed him into the corridor, where guards put handcuffs back onto his sore wrists. He knew what was next. He had heard the stories. He would be taken outside, tied to one of the posts facing a firing squad, and told to tell all he knew. It was a prized tactic of the Gestapo to frighten information out of French citizens.

They marched down the corridor, the lieutenant in the lead, followed by the French priest and the guards. They went up the narrow wooden steps to the first floor, passed through another security checkpoint, then turned into the main lobby.

From the marble staircase, the same one he had climbed that morning right after his arrest, came the sound of voices. Father Saurel strained to hear what they were saying, but the cavernous lobby made the voices echo madly. Between the acoustics and his limited German, the priest could only gather that two men were arguing over the jurisdiction of a prisoner. After a few minutes, the voices stopped, and a blond Wehrmacht colonel came rapidly down the steps. When he reached the lobby, he looked at Father Saurel and then at the SS guards who surrounded him.

"*Alles in Ordnung. Den Gefangenen loslassen! Er kommt mit uns.*" Father Saurel felt the guards release their tight grip on his arms. Three Wehrmacht soldiers who had been standing in the shadows marched over to him. One drew his machine pistol and shoved it harshly into Father Saurel's ribs. The colonel motioned with his hand. The soldier jammed the gun harder into his side, and they walked toward the doors. The other two soldiers held the double doors open as they stepped outside into the night.

In the courtyard was a Mercedes staff car with the convertible top up. The soldiers roughly pushed Father Saurel into the rear seat. They climbed in after him, one sitting on each side. The third soldier got behind the wheel while the colonel sat in the front passenger seat. The driver started the car and, crunching it into gear, screeched out of the courtyard. One of the soldiers withdrew a black hood from his field coat and slipped it over Father Saurel's head.

Father Saurel estimated that it must have been at least an hour before the car slowed down appreciably. It made a sharp right turn, proceeded for what seemed like two or three kilometers down a very bumpy road, and then stopped. He could hear muffled conversation through the heavy hood before the car started up again. He guessed that they had just gone through a checkpoint. In another few minutes, the car stopped again. The guards at his side leaped out. Without a word, they pulled him from the back seat and, grasping him by either arm, half led and half dragged him through a door which clanged shut behind him.

They descended a narrow staircase, one guard in front and one guard behind. The walls were cold and bare to the touch, and Father Saurel felt he was underground. At the bottom of the staircase, they turned sharply to the left.

The hood flew off. Father Saurel squinted at naked light bulbs illuminating a bare concrete room with no windows. The colonel motioned for the soldiers to leave. They did, shutting the heavy steel door behind them.

As his eyes grew accustomed to the light, the Frenchman saw his crystal set, his code sheet, and a pile of papers spread out on a table. He looked at the colonel, who responded by walking over to him, unlocking his handcuffs, and motioning for him to sit down.

The German walked back to the far side of the table. He sat down, resting his hands on the table surface, and then spoke in flawless French. "Father Saurel, I am Colonel von Frickstein. The Gestapo has unmasked you as a Resistance operative. These items were found this morning during a search of your parish office." He paused. "The Gestapo has demanded a firing squad for you.

"But," continued von Frickstein, "we are not the Gestapo. You can be far more useful to your country if we can persuade you to cooperate with us." Von Frickstein paused again.

"I am listening."

"I offer you a simple choice. You can continue your broadcasts to London under our guidance, or you can be returned to the Gestapo."

"That is a choice?"

"I understand your bravery and contempt," von Frickstein answered firmly. "I applaud them, Father Saurel. I will tell you very little, of course. Although I wish you could trust me, I know there can never be trust between us. If you continue your transmissions, sending messages which we will prepare for you, I promise you your

[104]

life. Even more than that, I promise you that you will be helping to end the war far more rapidly than you can possibly imagine."

"A familiar argument, one I heard from the Gestapo this morning."

"I imagine you did. You do not wish to transmit for us. That is natural. Will it change your mind if I tell you that you have been doing so for the last two months?"

For the first time since his arrest Father Saurel became angry. "*Cochon!*"

Von Frickstein dropped a sheaf of papers on the table in front of the priest, who looked through them quickly. It was a transmission log. The German was not lying. It was all there.

"Some of these broadcasts, of course, Father Saurel, were legitimate ones: pieces of information which your Resistance friends picked up and sent to you. However, on December fourteenth, we arrested Alain Guinet. You did not know him by that name, of course. You knew him only as Évêque Treize of Orléans."

Von Frickstein read the expression on Father Saurel's face.

"You have been duped. You have already sent to the Allies certain key messages which, even as you transmitted them, you did not know the importance of. We could have continued the deception indefinitely, but our plans are not that simple. What we are after is not to deceive the Allies but to inform them. For that, we need your help."

"What do you want me to do?"

"Continue your broadcasts. From here. You will use your standard procedures and codes. From time to time we will give you a special message to encode and transmit."

"How will you know if I am cooperating? I might send a totally different message than one you give me."

"That is a risk worth taking."

Father Saurel had spent thirteen hours in a cold cell and felt totally drained. He stared dazedly at the German, trying to compose himself. "I will think about it," he said flatly.

"Very well. You will be imprisoned here until your normal time to transmit to London tomorrow night at six o'clock. I will want your answer by then." He gathered up the radio and dispatches from the table and left the room quickly. The door closed behind him. The last thing Father Saurel heard was the turning of the lock. Then he slumped to the floor, asleep.

6

Tim and Hardaway were at Bushey Park when the call came. They were being briefed on the landing craft which the U.S. Navy had designed for the amphibious assaults. Tim was there to look at films of the Pacific landings to see how the craft behaved in surf. There were many questions about the surf in the English Channel, most of them raised by American officers recently transferred to SHAEF from the Pacific Theater of Operations. How strong would the English surf be? Were there many side currents? What about the possibility of riptides?

The American lieutenant commander who was running the meeting was talking dryly about naval firepower. Tim shifted restlessly in his chair and looked around at the new faces. They're all navy men, he said to himself, you can tell that much. Smooth-faced gentlemen who aren't afraid to show how much they miss their mahogany wardrooms. His eyes fell on Hardaway, who yawned slightly and then glanced sheepishly at Tim for having done so. Hardaway liked the U.S. Navy personnel, the ones Tim found arrogant. "They know their stuff, Loftis, so we can't afford not to listen," he had said once.

A British sergeant came into the room and handed a slip of paper to the lieutenant commander. He looked up. "Major Loftis here?" Tim rose from his seat. "Telephone call for you, Major. Most urgent."

Tim followed the sergeant. They walked down the hallway of the small country house into an office. The sergeant pointed to the telephone lying on a desk by a window. "Right here, sir."

"Thanks, sergeant." Tim picked up the receiver. "Major Loftis."

"Beauclerk here. How are things going down there?"

"Well enough, I guess."

"Good, that means they can do without you. I'd like you to come up to London as soon as possible. When can you make it?"

Tim looked at his watch: fourteen hundred hours. "Well, sir, I'm in a meeting now. I don't imagine it'll be over much before sixteen—"

"Good. I'll see you at seventeen hundred in my office."

"What's up, sir? If I may ask."

"They've come in, lad."

"What, sir?"

"The messages. They've come in, so don't dally about. See you then." The phone clicked off.

Tim slowly set the receiver down in its cradle, a slow smile spreading across his face. "Mrs. Anderson," he said to the secretary, "would you please call Lieutenant Matthews of Motor Pool and order a jeep for me. Sixteen hundred hours today."

"Certainly, major."

Tim strode out of the office, back down the hallway, and into the conference room. The lights were off, and the assembled officers were watching films of tanks and trucks being unloaded onto the beaches of Salamaua in New Guinea. He slipped into his seat next to Hardaway, who turned slightly toward him and whispered, "What's up?"

"Nothing much. Some new info at G-Two."

"More of your supersleuth?" Hardaway's contempt was apparent. Tim did not answer, but focused his attention on the screen instead.

The meeting was over at the time Tim had guessed. As they walked out of the room, Hardaway exhaled deeply and shook his head. "That was a bloody bore, if you ask me. Shall we pop over for a drink?"

Tim shook his head. "I have to be off."

"Where to?"

"London. I've got a car waiting."

"Look here, Loftis. There's still one hell of a lot of work to be done here. You can't go running off to London every time some tidbit comes in."

"Why not? That's my job, isn't it?"

"You job is to advise the General Staff on the geologic factors in the invasion. Period. End of quote. You can't advise them if you're always scooting off to London!"

They were at the front door now. Tim stopped to look at Hardaway. "I think I'm on to something."

"Well, if you are, tell me what it is instead of snooping around here like a second former with a slingshot!"

"I can't. Not yet."

"Listen, Loftis, you know damn well that I can't do my job without your cooperation, and you can't do yours without mine. Now, either we level with one another and make it all cricket, or we don't, in which case I'll put in for a replacement for you!"

"Look, it's only a hunch. I'll know more in a few days."

"You've said that before."

"Then I'll tell you everything," Tim said reassuringly. "I've really got to go." Before Hardaway could say another word, Tim bounded down the steps and into the waiting jeep.

It was 1715 hours when Tim walked into the familiar bare room on the third floor. Beauclerk was waiting for him, as were Pru and another officer, whom Tim didn't recognize.

"Ah, there you are, major! You know Lieutenant Lapthorne, of course. This is Captain O'Neill-Butler, from General Strong's office." Tim shook hands with a tall, slim, handsome man of almost corrosive stiffness. "All right, lad, have a seat. Captain?"

O'Neill-Butler walked over to the desk and set down his briefcase. "The brigadier here told me about the research both of you did on some of the transmissions from France," the captain explained to Tim. "When was that, brigadier?"

"Middle of January."

"Yes, that's right. It sounded rather flimsy to me, major, I don't mind telling you that, but you learn in intelligence never to discard anything. I said as much to the brigadier and told him to get back to me if anything else developed. He called me this morning." O'Neill-Butler cast a sidelong glance at Beauclerk, who nodded.

Tim sensed by the somber expressions on all three faces that there was some problem. "What about the messages?" Tim asked. "Didn't you say some came in?"

"That I did, lad. Captain?"

"You see, major, if these new messages do have any content —or I should say, rather, if they have any significant implications —your presence puts us in a bit of a squeeze. Officially speaking."

"What the captain is saying, major," said Beauclerk, casting an irritated glance at the impervious officer, "is that you know more than you should. Being from G-Three. For us to keep you in on this, we'll need a higher clearance."

"Thank you, brigadier. Major Loftis, I talked with General Strong after the brigadier rang me this morning. He had only one question, really? Are you a 'Bigot,' Major Loftis?"

Tim nodded. Bigot meant that he was privy to the actual plans for Operation Overlord, the cross-channel invasion. O'Neill-Butler smiled slightly. "Very good. The general had no objections to your continuing with us at least one step further, so long as you're Bigot-ed. I must warn you, though, that G-Two might at any time refuse you further access to this work."

"That makes sense."

Beauclerk clapped his hands together. "Good! That's out of the way. Lieutenant, bring the major up to date."

Pru glanced at her pad. "Two days ago we received a dispatch from an operative in Bernay. When our staff cryptologist in C and

T tried to put it into plaintext, it wouldn't go. He tried all the current ciphers and it still garbled. The cryptologist followed the routine procedures. He rechecked the transcription, verified it, and then gave the message to another cryptologist. Quite often one code expert gets tired and keeps making the same mental mistakes," she explained. "When the second man couldn't break it, he put it into the tray to be filed. And he made a note of it. That's also standard procedure. Sometimes things just won't give and they're not worth worrying over.

"Yesterday," she continued, "the morning dispatches contained eight new messages which wouldn't break out either. Ordinarily, that many non-breaks would cause a stir, but as luck would have it, each of the messages was handled by a different officer in C and T. Each thought he only had one non-break, and so the frequency went unreported."

Beauclerk chuckled. "Amazing, isn't it?"

Pru smiled. "This morning, there were eight more dispatches that wouldn't break. The people in my section who had handled the messages yesterday recognized the coincidence. We got together and checked the logs, and I called up Brigadier Beauclerk."

Beauclerk picked up his cue. "The first message was from Bernay, the one town that had sent a single 'solstice' message. One town, one 'solstice,' one message."

Tim's eyes widened.

"I thought you would be interested." Beauclerk's eyes twinkled. "The eight messages yesterday were from Sainte-Mère-Église, Bayeux, Caen, Lisieux, Deauville, Le Havre, Rouen, and Abbeville. The same eight towns that sent three or more 'solstice' messages last month. And the clincher is that the eight messages this morning came from those same eight towns."

"That's it!"

Beauclerk held up his right hand. "Don't be premature, lad. Captain, your show."

"Thank you, brigadier." O'Neill-Butler sat down at the table next to Tim and started removing papers from his briefcase. "He's right, major, excitement is premature. I'm afraid there's nothing to proceed with at this point, cryptographically speaking. Here, look at these."

He spread the papers across the table. Each of them had a SHAEF:G-2:C&T letterhead, with boxes for such information as dates, times, places of transmissions, initials of radio operators, cryptanalysts, translators. In the white expanses on each sheet were typed single lines of ciphertext. Tim stared at the first one:

EWPSEHWPCQRAWDHKAWJEWPDSHGWKIIR
HFCDIKDLSKFIQPZMSKSIOORYHDNFIAPABAUIAIA
OJPGLHIBJFKFIQMHMGJFIFJDNDKSPBSWARSD
PALSOFMAOWUGMAODKMKZIAM
OALQPOOGUDDALUIFGJBAI
YGHFIDJSIZOAMWKDIDOSLAPSMFHXIAMFHOGAKDLGNNZ
WTSGDIFOALLPZMZDSHSLFIGODM,LIEIDJCPMKLIPOMDJAWAZZCNIM
ZDZGDLOOSRDEVJFMXI

"Do you know anything about cryptography, major?"

"Well, we used to have a secret code when I was in junior high school in Nebraska, but this is probably a little more complicated."

"Yes, major, it is," O'Neill-Butler said dryly. "These messages, if they are indeed from the Resistance, are most likely enciphered in what we call an alphabetic substitution. The key word is used to scramble the letters of the code alphabet in a relatively simple fashion. By way of demonstration, let us assume as key word the one which you and the brigadier suggested." O'Neill-Butler began to write on a blank sheet of paper:

SOLTICEABDFGHJKMNPQRUVWXYZ
ABCDEFGHIJKLMNOPQRSTUVWXYZ

"The top line is the code alphabet. Notice that the key word begins it. Since the S is repeated in the key word, it would stand for two letters at the same time if it were repeated in the code alphabet, so SOLSTICE must become SOLTICE. To encode a message, we obviously substitute a letter from the top line for each one on the bottom. This is the simplest type of encipherment. It's called monoalphabetic substitution."

"It's like the one we had back in Nebraska."

"The advantages of such a code are numerous. First, it is easy to remember, so there is no need for code books, one-time pads, or machines. Second, it is easily changed by substituting another key word. The chief disadvantage is, naturally, that it is not very secure.

"Now we use these types of ciphers with the Resistance because security is far less important than clarity and accuracy. We are dealing with amateurs, after all, and no one expects them to spend a great deal of effort transcribing messages. If the Germans really wished to crack these messages, it wouldn't be too difficult. The reason they don't is that there are too many of them. What's more important to the enemy is finding the transmitters and putting them out of business."

O'Neill-Butler looked at Tim to see if he understood. When Tim nodded, he continued.

"The sure way to crack a code such as this is by frequency. The brigadier tells me that you're a geologist by training, so you must know probability theory." Tim nodded again. "The frequency patterns for the letters of the alphabet in all languages have been carefully established, and they all follow the bell-shaped curve. You naturally know, major, that the bell-shaped curve only appears when the sample has passed a critical threshold in size."

"What I guess you're trying to tell me," Tim said, "is that you don't have enough messages here to crack the code."

"You are quite perceptive, major. Although we have several hundred letters, the messages appear to be in different ciphers, or at the very least in variations of the same cipher."

"How do you know that?"

"It is governed by mathematics. There is a complicated formula I shan't bore you with at this time, but it involves multiplying the number of characters in each code text by two coefficients known as K-sub-r and K-sub-p to determine the recurrence patterns. The resulting superimposition products are different for each message. What that means in effect is that we have eight different ciphers in front of us, with between twenty-one and forty-three characters in each cipher. That's below our threshold for frequency tables.

"Furthermore, these might or might not be polyalphabetic ciphers, meaning that more than one code text is used in each message. Our coefficients can't tell us the difference between monos and polys, unfortunately. For that, we employ something known as the phi test. That involves multiplying each character's frequency by the frequency number minus one and then finding the sum of the products and comparing that sum to the expected sum based on known behavior characteristics of monoalphabetic and polyalphabetic ciphers. Are you still with me?"

"I understand the math involved, if that's what you mean."

"Very good. It is pleasant to be around a scientist who appreciates numbers." O'Neill-Butler gave Tim a faint smile again. "Since again the samples are so small, the phi text gave us muddled results. It appears that lines one, three, four, five, and seven on that page"—he pointed to the sheet Tim held in his hand—"are polys, which is what the penciled-in P stands for. However, I would not swear to it."

Beauclerk shot out a loud breath of cigarette smoke. "What does all this mean?"

O'Neill-Butler turned in his chair to face the craggy Scot. "What it means is that with fragmented messages such as these we simply don't have enough material to use our standard techniques. We'll have to wait for more transmissions."

Tim continued to stare at the sheets. "How many more, captain?"

"Well, if they're all of this length, if the cipher variations continue, and if there remain the same number of transmission points, I would say . . . forty at the very least."

Tim sighed loudly and got up. He put the sheets back on the table, thrust his hands into his pockets, and started to pace the room. Beauclerk broke the silence. "You've tried all the mechanisms?" he asked O'Neill-Butler.

"All the mechanisms currently in use in France, sir."

"Are there any other mechanisms available, captain?" Pru asked.

"I shouldn't think so. There are more complicated ones, but we're dealing with the underground, not the Germans. We could try some others, but it would take a great deal of staff time which I'm afraid SHAEF can't spare right now."

Tim sighed. "Tell me frankly, captain, what do you think about all this?"

O'Neill-Butler rose. "Frankly, major? Frankly, I don't know. All the internal evidence, the sheerly cryptological evidence, suggests that these messages are rather ordinary. They came over normal channels in a normal fashion. The only thing extraordinary about this is that we can't crack them, but that's happened before and will again, I dare say.

"However," he continued, "the fact that you predicted the arrival of the messages a month ago, that you said which towns would send them, and that you estimated the transmission sequences gives pause for thought."

"It's not a problem of cryptography, is what you're saying. It's a detective hunt."

O'Neill-Butler nodded. "The key to these messages is external. I don't imagine the codes themselves are complicated. It's a matter of finding the key."

"And that will happen if we get more clues," Beauclerk said. O'Neill-Butler nodded again. "Thank you, captain. We shall let you know when something develops."

O'Neill-Butler replaced the papers in his briefcase, snapped it shut, saluted, and left.

For a long moment after the door shut, no one moved.

"Well, major, another dead end?"

"Not yet. We're way past the point of coincidence now. An unknown code coming from the eight towns we guessed it would come from over a month ago? No, sir, we've just got more digging to do."

"That's the spirit, lad!"

"Where do we go from here, sir?" Pru asked.

Beauclerk whistled under his breath. "That's a good question. We can wait for more messages and hope that the captain and his men can crack the code without more clues." He looked at Tim and Pru. "*If*, that is, we get more messages. and *if*, God help us, we're not too late."

"Too late for what, sir?" Pru asked.

"I don't know. That's the big question. Always is. This whole affair might be very important, or it might be just a prank. We can't know until we crack those messages."

"What choice do we have?" Tim asked.

Beauclerk leaned against the window frame. "Not much, I'm afraid, except to keep our ears open and wait for a break. I've got a hunch that we're near to something very big. Eight towns is a big number, and even bigger if you consider that they're spread out over a hundred and fifty miles. There must be something very important happening in France that we don't know about. All our other dispatches are normal. Whatever it is that we've hit upon must be very grand and very secret."

Then he added, thoughtfully, "And very frightening."

It was during the first week in March that Tim went to Norfolk House in response to a phone message from Pru, on a blustery spring day filled with wind and sporadic rain. Ominous clouds rolled across the London sky.

Tim climbed the familiar steps slowly to the third floor and walked down the corridor to Pru's office. The twelve desks in the Classification and Translation Division were filled with busy workers. Dreary weather or not, the Resistance kept up the steady stream of information and G-2 had to digest it. Pru's desk was the third from the rear on the side next to the windows. She looked up when he walked in. Her eyes widened. She stood up, gathered a small stack of papers from her desk, and started toward Tim. As he watched her full round body swaying between the desks, he felt a sudden urge to take her home and make love to her, to drown his melancholy in the pleasures of her body and forget all the headaches pounding inside his skull. She smiled when she reached him.

"Good news, major. Come along to Brigadier Beauclerk's office."

Beauclerk was in a flinty mood himself. He wore the persecuted, fit-to-be-tied look of someone for whom everything has gone haywire all day long. But when he saw Tim, the craggy grin split his face. "Ah, Loftis, there you are! More messages finally."

Although he should have been excited, Tim slouched in the easy chair that stood by Beauclerk's desk. "Whoopee."

"Look here, buck up! Don't let the weather get you down. If you think this is grim, you should go to Scotland sometime." Beauclerk turned to Pru. "All right, lieutenant, let's have it."

"Last night we received eight more messages from the same towns." Tim looked at her and perked up a bit. "Not only were they from the same towns, they were the same messages."

"There's no doubt anymore, lad. We're on to something. And the fact that we've been sent the same messages again means that we're not too late."

"How do we know the messages were sent to us?"

"We don't entirely," Beauclerk replied. "But I'm fairly certain that whomever the cipher is intended for hasn't deciphered it yet."

"How do you know that?"

"That's the only explanation for repeating the same messages. It tells us two things. First, that we haven't figured it out yet and that someone wants us to. And second, that the messages require some sort of reply. They haven't received a reply, which is why they have repeated themselves."

"What do we do now? Doesn't this leave us in exactly the same place?"

Beauclerk grimaced. "Not entirely, I think. It gives us some more information about their intentions." He sat down on the edge of his desk. "It's clear that those messages don't contain simple information. There would be no need to repeat them."

"As you said before, sir," Pru interjected, "they've asked a question."

Beauclerk nodded. "Or they've made a request and wish to have a confirmation."

"What kind of request could that be?" Tim asked.

"Usually it's for supplies. Guns, dynamite, disguises. Forged papers especially. Usually we just send the request right over to Special Operations Executive, which is in charge of all that." Beauclerk paused. "That's obviously not the case here, though. If they had an urgent request, their prime consideration would be speed, not secrecy. It wouldn't be in their interest to muck about with new ciphers."

"Hell, there's another objection," Tim said. "You said before, when we first started working on this, that the Resistance is compartmentalized. We're dealing with a hundred-and-fifty-mile stretch and at least eight agents, if not more. They couldn't all have the same request. Even if they did, they wouldn't all ask it in the same way. That'd be too much coincidence."

"For that matter," Pru offered, "we don't even know that these messages are in the same code. We only know that they're not in any of ours."

They had reached an impasse. The three sat in silence. It was a big merry-go-round, Tim thought. The minute you came up with one solution, you ran smack into the tail end of an objection you'd just raised two minutes before in connection with another point. All the while the whole problem kept revolving, kept you moving, yet kept you on the same spot. Each answer had its built-in nonanswer. There was simply no explanation as to why the Resistance would suddenly adopt a new code, stick to it, and not tell anyone about it. Unless it wasn't the Resistance at all.

"Hey," Tim exclaimed, startling the other two out of their thoughts. "Does it have to be the Resistance?"

Pru sighed. "Who else could it be? Except perhaps for Vichy?"

"What about the Germans?"

Beauclerk shrugged. "It's possible. What you're saying is that the Germans have turned eight agents over to their side and are trying to make us swallow some hugh scheme?"

"Something like that. Why not?"

Beauclerk scratched his chin for a moment. "Well, it could be. They could invent a new code and get us all excited. You know how it is. We feel so bloody full of ourselves that we go blundering in somewhere and get kicked in the teeth. It might be, lad. I don't know."

"There's one trouble with that," Pru said. "All the agents are sending their normal broadcasts as well."

"You mean, in addition to those in the solstice cipher?"

"That's right."

"Are their codes intact? No sign they're being coerced?"

"Not that we've noticed."

Tim spoke. "Could it be that the Germans have gotten hold of eight or nine transmitters and are sending us messages directly, pretending that they're Resistance agents?"

Beauclerk frowned. "Not likely. Our chaps have been monitoring these broadcasts with powerful equipment, capable of picking up every nuance. They would have noticed any changes in transmission style. I doubt the Gestapo is good enough to fool *all* our experts."

"What if it weren't the Gestapo?"

"Well, Jesus Christ, lad, who else could it be? The German army?"

Tim shrugged. "Why not? The war's going badly. The Russians are about to break through any day, and the Italian front is crumbling. They know we're going to invade France in the near future. All right, then, any general with half a brain in his head knows that the invasion is going to be a big battle, one he'll eventually lose. Wouldn't it make sense to open negotiations with us now?"

Beauclerk raised a finger. "Fair enough. But why the code?"

The answer suddenly jumped in Tim's brain. "How else can they contact us except with a code? The SS and the Gestapo are patroling all the fronts. The Wehrmacht couldn't talk to us if they wanted to. They'd be shot."

Beauclerk paused, then cocked his left eye. "Go on, lad. Keep going!"

"It fits all the patterns. It explains how eight agents, supposedly independent from one another, can send related messages at the same time in an area a hundred and fifty miles wide. The Germans are the only people in France who are organized over such large distances. And it explains the repetition. We can't understand why the Resistance would want a reply to a secret message, but I can sure as hell see why the Germans would. Presto! We have the intention!"

Beauclerk smiled wryly but said nothing. Tim turned to Pru for her reaction.

"It doesn't explain why the code won't break," she said quietly.

That set off another explosion in Tim's mind, a bolt from the blue. He laughed softly, then sat down in the empty chair by the table.

"Tim, what's so funny?"

"The code. Do you know what mistake we've been making all along?"

Beauclerk stiffened. "What?"

"We've been assuming that the master language of that code was French."

It took Captain O'Neill-Butler ten minutes to get up to the third floor of Norfolk House from his office in the basement. When he opened the door and saluted in his usual polite manner, Beauclerk roared at him to come in and sit. O'Neill-Butler looked genuinely stunned at the tone in the Scot's voice, but he did as he was told. He looks, Tim thought, like the person at a party who is sent out of the room and has to guess some big secret when he returns.

"Brigadier, I must apologize—"

"Quiet! Sorry, captain, I'm not angry. Quite the opposite. Tell me, what language have you been trying to crack that code with?"

O'Neill-Butler was completely confused. "Why, French, of course."

Beauclerk played with him like a cat plays with a mouse before eating it. "Try German."

"I can't do that here. I'll need my charts."

"No, you won't." O'Neill-Butler turned to Tim, who smiled at him, walked over to the desk, picked up the solstice file O'Neill-Butler had brought along, and dropped it in his lap.

"The French word for solstice is *solstice*. The word in German is *Sonnenwende*," Tim said.

A beatific smile slowly spread across O'Neill-Butler's face. "Thank you, major," he said quietly. "I think we might just have it this time."

In five minutes it was over. The British captain decoded the first message, the lone transmission that had started the entire wild-goose chase, the seemingly impossible search for the needle in the gigantic haystack, and handed the transcription to Tim. Impatiently, Beauclerk leaned over Tim's shoulder at the incomprehensible German in front of him. "Well, for God's sake, lad, what does it say?"

Tim leaned over the desk and wrote out the translation. He gave the paper to Beauclerk, who read:

THE EAGLE HAS FLOWN. THE STORM IS COMING.

7

From his office in the old Ministry of Finance in the Louvre, SS Colonel Helmut Knochen, director of the Sicherheitspolizei, the Sipo, for the occupied territory of France, could see out over the gardens of the Tuileries, past the Seine, the dome of the Invalides and the Eiffel Tower if he cared to. It was a large office in the southwest corner of the third floor, with tall French windows all along two sides. The only furniture was a pair of elegant sofas facing each other near the windows on the short wall, and the massive Louis XIV writing table, festooned with gilt, at which Knochen now sat, reading the thick report which had just arrived from Berlin and the office of *Reichsführer* Himmler.

In January the Gestapo had arrested hundreds of German traitors who had been plotting against the Führer. He read of their executions. More important to Knochen was the news that the Abwehr, the intelligence arm of the Wehrmacht, had been liquidated, and that its leader, Admiral Wilhelm Canaris, had been imprisoned and was about to be executed for high crimes against the Reich. It was high time, Knochen reflected, that the den of half-hearts and liars was wiped out and its function as chief intelligence-gathering agency assigned to the Ausland Sicherheitsdienst, the intelligence branch of the SS, led by Walter Schellenberg. It had been these developments in Berlin, all a part of the Führer's growing mistrust of the Wehrmacht and the OKW, that had been responsible for Knochen's new office in the Louvre.

The SS now ruled Germany and its timid generals. It was Knochen's job to tighten the grip on France and to utterly destroy the weaklings whose hesitations were delaying the ultimate victory of the Reich.

There was a soft knock at the door. *"Herein!"* Knochen said, folding up the thick report and setting it on his desk. The captain who served as Knochen's aide entered the room.

"Herr Standartenführer, the district commandants are here to give their reports."

"Send them in."

The meeting lasted over two hours. In turn each major had given Knochen a report and summarized its contents verbally for his compatriots. The reports had been disturbing. Sabotage was rampant: trains derailed at Nantes; factories bombed in Bordeaux, Lyon, and Orléans; assassinations of local Nazi Party officials in Toulon, Clermont-Ferrand, Besançon; bridges of crucial military importance blown up near Dijon, Étienne, Troyes, and Nancy. The growing military strength of the Resistance in the Poitou, Touraine, and Bourbonnais regions was alarming, as Allied planes made almost nightly drops of arms and ammunition. Only three such drops had been intercepted, the district commandant from Poitiers had reported, and there had been only seven raids on arms caches. Seventeen Frenchmen had been shot.

That was not good enough, Knochen had reprimanded them. The will of the French peasantry to resist must be broken, no matter how many shootings it took. Disregard the populace, Knochen had said. If they complain, a few hangings would silence them. Scarce food was desperately needed by the loyal troops of the Führer, who were on the verge of the most crucial battles of the entire war.

All in all, Knochen had not been pleased by the results of the meeting, and he had told the commandants so. The current situation was the result of the negligence and incompetence of the Feldsicherheitsdienst, the Army Intelligence Service, but the commandants would have to produce immediate results or they would be replaced.

As they left the office, one of the officers dawdled behind. "*Herr Standartenführer*, a word, if you please?"

"Yes, *Herr Sturmbannführer*, what is it?" Knochen had been impressed with the report of Josef Kreitzl, commandant of Wehrkreis Frankreich VII: Normandie.

"There have been many problems in my sector, as I reported. Most of them can be solved if I am given the additional staff I requested."

Knochen nodded as he shuffled through papers on his desk. "I will do what I can. You have a crucial sector."

Kreitzl looked uncomfortable. "*Herr Standartenführer*, my major problem in Sector VII I felt unable to mention in my report."

Knochen looked up warily. "And that is?"

"The Wehrmacht, *Herr Standartenführer*. They have refused to relinquish their controls over counterespionage activities."

"Tell them that the Führer has specifically ordered the SS to control those functions."

"It is not that easy, *Herr Standartenführer*, when you are dealing with two *Generalfeldmarschalls*." Knochen straightened up and looked at Kreitzl.

"I appreciate that. Which *Generalfeldmarschalls* are you referring to?"

"Von Rundstedt and Rommel, *Herr Standartenführer*."

Knochen paused for a moment. Such famous and glorified generals must be intimidating, whatever the Führer may have ordered from Berlin. Especially Rommel, whose loyalty to the Führer Knochen had doubted ever since the coward of El Alamein had been assigned to France. There had been reports about him. Rommel had been making frequent trips back to his home in Herrlingen. There had been reports that Rommel had talked with Colonel von Stauffenberg, a good friend of Count von Moltke, who had just been executed for treason. And Knochen had read about a mysterious meeting with General Beck in a small hotel in Valognes, far away from both Rommel's headquarters in La Roche-Guyon and OB West in Saint-Germain-en-Laye.

"Can you name specific incidents, *Herr Sturmbannführer?*"

Kreitzl zipped open his leather pouch, searched for a minute among the papers, withdrew some, and laid them on the desk so that Knochen could read them. "In the last two months, the Wehrmacht has arrested at least ten radio operators from among the French underground. They are maintaining custody of the men and have refused to let the Sipo interrogate them. It is all in that report I have just given you. The captured agents were from Bernay, Sainte-Mère-Église, Bayeux, Caen, Lisieux, Deauville, Le Havre, Rouen, and Abbeville."

"Le Havre, Rouen, and Abbeville are not in your district."

Kreitzl stiffened to attention. "I know, but *Sturmbannführer* Liebmann thought I should submit the problems in his sector to you along with my own."

"Very well, *Herr Sturmbannführer*, I will read your report." Knochen flipped through the pages of the folder and threw it onto a pile at the front of the desk.

Kreitzl bit his lip. *"Herr Standartenführer,* we feel this matter is urgent. We feel there is possible treason in the Wehrmacht."

Knochen rose and walked around the desk. He stood in the middle of the room, hands clasped behind his back. "That is a serious charge. Do you have proof, or merely suspicion?"

"Suspicion only, but it is strong. With your permission, I will furnish an example."

"Yes, proceed."

"Six weeks ago we arrested one of the chief radio spies in the coastal part of Normandy. He was captured in Lisieux, where I was then Operations Director. This spy was the center of a large ring. Before we could interrogate him thoroughly, a courier arrived from *Generalfeldmarschall* Rommel's headquarters. He carried orders for us to surrender the prisoner. I argued, but the order had been countersigned by *Generalfeldmarschall* von Rundstedt, so there was little I could do but comply."

"What of it?"

"I have reason to believe that the prisoner was neither interrogated nor shot."

"What would the Wehrmacht want with him, then?"

"I believe they are using him to broadcast to the Allies."

Knochen nodded. The ins and outs of espionage take a long time to master, and Kreitzl had a way to go yet. "I appreciate your concern. I will check into the matter as soon as I am able. In the meantime, you are to do everything you can to confirm if these suspicious activities are indeed taking place. Report to me at once if you find anything."

Kreitzl stood passively for a moment, then snapped a salute and left the room.

Knochen went back to his desk. He would investigate the accusations in a few days. It may be nothing, he thought, but it was certainly worth looking into. The loyalty of all the Wehrmacht commanders at OB West was far less than perfect. The reports on Rommel were particularly alarming. It was up to him, *Standartenführer* Helmut Knochen, to hunt down the traitors to the Reich and destroy them, completely and ruthlessly. Knochen knew, as did everyone else on the Western Front, that time was running out.

Life was becoming unbearable at G-3, Tim told Beauclerk, ever since G-2 had thrown a security screen around the Solstice cipher.

"Can't be helped, lad," Beauclerk said to Tim sympathetically. "Until some final decision is made on how to proceed, I don't want anyone at Operations to know what we're about."

They were sitting in their favorite haunt, the bare room on the third floor of Norfolk House.

"When'll that decision be made?"

"I don't know. Soon, I should hope. I'll be talking with General Strong today or tomorrow. If he's in favor of launching an operation, we can proceed to devise a plan."

"What kind of operation?"

"That's what I want to ask you." Beauclerk squinted at Tim. "You're from Operations, you know. Look sharp, now. These are the final messages. Since you've already seen them in coded form and know they exist, I think I can show you the final version."

The decoded and translated messages were spread across the table. What faced Tim was very disappointing. "The seventeen messages," Beauclerk was saying, "turned out to be only five. That's how many repetitions and variations they used. They don't tell us a great deal, do they?"

Tim read them and sighed:

THE EAGLE HAS FLOWN. THE STORM IS COMING.

THE EAGLE IS OVER THE SEA.

THE WOLF IS AT BAY.

THE EAGLE MUST HEAR THE FALCON.

THE FALCON MUST CAPTURE THE EAGLE.

"What do they say to you, sir?"

"Well, they're from the Germans, all right. No doubt about that. A few things are easy enough to guess. 'The eagle must hear the falcon' is an obvious call for a reply. We must be the falcon. They, whoever 'they' is, must be the eagle."

"Could it be the Nazi Party?"

Beauclerk shrugged. "Possibly. All those blasted eagles they've got on their uniforms. I shouldn't think so, but we have to bear that in mind. Anyhow, the wolf is also fairly obvious. That's Hitler."

"How do you know?"

"That's Hitler's favorite nickname for himself. His headquarters in East Prussia is known as the Wolf's Lair. Now, I'm not sure what they mean when they say the eagle has flown. The logical guess is that they're referring to the war situation in general. You know, retreat. Or, they could be referring just to the Russian front, which is rapidly deteriorating. Or"—Beauclerk clicked his tongue thoughtfully—"they could be referring to some sort of political development within the German government.

"Our spies have told us a few things. There was a huge spy ring rounded up last month in Germany. Some of them escaped to Switzerland and got in touch with your OSS. The ring consisted mostly of Germans who had been trying to contact the West through the German embassy in Turkey. The SS found out, and they're probably all dead by now, poor chaps.

"That means more and more power is going to Himmler and the SS. Which could mean two things: Either the generals are running scared and want peace now, or the SS is about to overthrow the government."

"They're not mutually exclusive," Tim said.

"No, they're not. If the army has sent these messages, the wolf being at bay would mean that the army has somehow neutralized Hitler."

"Mutiny? Assassination?"

Beauclerk nodded. "All possible. Anyhow, the part about the storm coming seems fairly clear. That's a reference to our little landing party, which they certainly expect. But that's the end of what I know. The rest of the messages are damned vague. The part about the eagle being over the sea confuses me. Does it mean that a few generals or diplomats are going to do what Hess did—steal an airplane and fly to England?"

"Not very likely. If that's what they're planning, why tell us? Why not just go ahead and do it?"

"Exactly. Or are they being metaphorical? Do they mean 'over the sea' not as in 'above the sea' but as in 'across the sea'?"

"Both. The word *über* in German means both those things."

"That's what Captain O'Neill-Butler told me. If the Germans mean 'over' as 'across,' and that's where the eagle is, it seems clear the eagle is the German command on the Atlantic Wall. That means we're talking about Rommel, since he's in command there now. And perhaps von Rundstedt."

"Wouldn't the other fronts have noticed something?"

"Right you are, lad. But they haven't. Italy and Greece have been pretty much knocked out of the war, so there's nothing there. The Danish and the Dutch undergrounds are acting up, but the Nazi grip is still pretty strong, so our connections with them are tenuous. That leaves us pretty much alone. If there is a conspiracy in the Wehrmacht, it's well hidden, and we're not likely to find out anything about it that the conspirators themselves don't tell us. That makes Solstice doubly important and doubly doubtful all at the same time."

"That doesn't follow. There would have to be some action on the other fronts. If the German army wants to end the war, they'd have to send out lots of feelers."

"That's just what makes me believe that we've gotten on to the real thing. The fighting between the Germans and the Russians has been pretty savage. Some stories have leaked out to us, and the atrocities have been horrifying. If and when the Germans surrender to Stalin, they'll be letting themselves in for a terrible bloodbath. They're hoping, I think, that they can end the war with Britain and America so they can concentrate their strength in the East.

"But to get back to Solstice," Beauclerk went on. "We still have one message which we haven't discussed, and that's the most crucial one. 'The falcon must capture the eagle.' That's our cue for action, and I'm stymied by it, I don't mind admitting. Are they being metaphorical again? Do they mean that the falcon must 'overtake' the eagle, in the sense of catch up to, or do they mean that we must literally capture Rommel and his cronies?" Beauclerk sat on the window ledge and lit another cigarette.

"Let's consider the other interpretation," Tim said. "The metaphorical one. I don't know much about falcons except what I've seen in movies, but it's always a bird of prey that you let loose to track down its victim in midair. Could they be asking for a secret meeting?"

Beauclerk thought for a moment. "Could be. If you consider the sentence 'The eagle is over the sea,' and think about what a falcon does, they might be referring to a meeting somewhere between here and France. On a boat in the Channel, perhaps?"

"It seems to me that the trick with falcons is to release them on the ground and let them fly over the victim's territory, where they snatch the prey. Right?"

Beauclerk looked up, his eyes wide. "Good enough, lad! They want us to send someone over there." The excitement faded. "But who? And for what purpose? If they want to talk about terms of surrender, that someone would have to be high-ranking. I don't think that SHAEF General Staff would leap at that idea. And if we did drop someone in, how can we be sure that he'd get to the right people and not just get shunted into a POW camp?"

Beauclerk opened the window, threw his cigarette out, and shut it again. He turned to Tim.

"Stickiest of all, how do we get him back?"

"Maybe they'll tell us how later."

"I doubt that. Whoever is sending these messages—let's assume it's Rommel—is living on borrowed time already. He can't afford a lot of chatter back and forth, lest the Gestapo find him out. That's why these messages are so ambiguous. No, lad, we can't hope for any more messages other than a few yeses or noes."

"How can we set anything up with them, then?"

"All we have to do is send messages about eagles and falcons over the regular BBC channels. We can count on Rommel's hearing them. So there's no problem replying to their messages. If they can manage to tell us 'yes' or 'no' on any given message, we can arrange something. It's a bit like talking to a mute. It takes longer, but you can eventually get through."

Beauclerk paused to light another cigarette and started pacing restlessly. "There's no doubt in my mind that we actually have to talk with Rommel. Face to face. That in itself is a big risk. The bigger question is timing," he added emphatically. "A mission before the invasion would be suicidal, I fear. The Germans could take our man and wrench the crucial information from him. To send somebody in after the invasion would be after the fact, so to speak. We would already be ashore, hopefully lodged and ready to stay, and the casualties of the first assault waves wouldn't have been avoided."

He paced for a minute longer, then stopped. "But a meeting *during* the invasion would have a chance. If we could get them to capitulate by sending a man in just before Overlord hit, we could still surprise them and soften the blow."

"That's cutting it awfully close, isn't it?"

"Perhaps, but that's the name of the game. If we could drop in a man a few hours before the airborne assault begins, and have him meet Rommel, it might be possible to speed up the surrender. It would save us a few hours of fighting, but a few hours of fighting early on D-Day means a bloody lot of lives saved. On both sides. If, that is, we're really talking with Rommel, if the drop goes perfectly, and if the messages aren't a trap."

"Lots of 'ifs.' "

"Yes, there are. But it seems to be our only course, eh, lad?"

"Hell, I don't know! One minute it all makes sense, and the next it seems so damned cockeyed, I think we should both be sent to the funny farm."

"You're right. It is a bit dotty, isn't it?" Beauclerk grinned broadly. "Good. We'll do it!" Then he shrugged. "Now, how do I sell it to General Strong?"

"Tell them we don't have much to lose. Maybe one or two men, at most an airplane. That's not much of a gamble, is it? Compared to the possible returns?"

"No, except that the man we send in has to be high enough in rank so that the Germans will know he speaks for Eisenhower."

"How high is that? A general?"

"Pretty close, I should think. And he's got to be sufficiently informed of the plans for Overlord. Only someone who knows the invasion plans could guide the Germans as to how and where to lay down their arms so that the whole thing looked good. That's the point they'll hit us on."

"What point?"

"Sending over someone who's privy to Overlord. You know how tight security is around here on it. Supreme Headquarters will turn purple when we ask them to waltz a chap into German hands who knows all about it."

"But if the attack is coming right away, what's the risk?"

"We can't be sure when the invasion is coming. What if the attack is postponed, even for a day? Bad weather, or a sudden German troop movement which calls for a shift in our assault plans? Our man could be in German hands, and the attack could be called off. Four or five hours' advance notice wouldn't give the Germans much chance to change their positions, but twenty-four or forty-eight hours sure as hell would. And, believe me, lad, if this whole caper is a trap and the Gestapo gets hold of him, he's finished."

There was a knock on the door.

"Come," Beauclerk said. The door opened, and Pru entered. "Oh, hello, lieutenant."

"I've got the figures."

"Good." Beauclerk sprawled into a chair. "Let's have them."

"I've run checks on all eight operatives in France who have been sending in the Solstice cipher. The number of their regular transmissions is down a bit, after all. The average is eight point two percent. One of them, Purple Six in Lisieux, is down fourteen percent. Daffodil seven in Caen is only off four percent."

"That says something, I should think. It doesn't mean for certain they've been picked up, though."

"That would be my view as well, sir," Pru said. She flipped to the next sheet. "The coding and transmission accuracy is a little more difficult to measure. Purple Six omitted his signature six times in thirty opportunities in fourteen messages. Scarlet Fourteen in Sainte-Marie-du-Mont was letter-perfect, on the other hand. He's never been that way in the nine months we've been in contact with him."

"Christ Almighty!" said Beauclerk after a pause. "We're back mucking about in the same mess again! Is it coincidence or is it pattern? What was the first one you gave me, lieutenant?"

"Purple Six, Lisieux, sir. Six omissions in thirty opportunities in fourteen messages."

"How's he been before?"

"Better than that, sir. Once, in November, he had a perfect week, but usually he's about eleven percent on signatures."

Beauclerk rose and walked over to the window. He looked out of it for a minute. "Damn it!" he said, turning to face Tim and Pru. "It's these bloody amateurs! What's your opinion, lieutenant? Have the Germans picked them up?"

"I should think not, sir. Eight-point-two percent isn't conclusive."

Beauclerk nodded wearily, as if he had expected such a grim prognosis. "I'm afraid you may be right. Loftis, what do you think?"

"Jesus, I don't know."

"Common sense, lad! Have the Germans picked them up or not? And remember, if they haven't been picked up, a lot of our case goes right out the window."

Tim took a deep breath. "I think they have. That's got to be what's happened. The pattern of those transmissions, the German key word, the messages in German. The fact that we called the messages before they came in. It's all too strong to be offset by faulty code signatures."

Beauclerk paused, as if expecting final arguments before sending the case to the jury in the back of his mind.

"All right, we'll go," he said finally. "I'll get up a report tonight and send it to General Strong tomorrow morning first thing. Loftis?"

"Yes, sir?"

"Put in for transfer over to G-Two. I want you over here as soon as you've finished your beach reconnaissance at G-Three. You'll need all the time we can give you."

"Time?" Tim was confused. "What for, sir?"

"Training, lad. I want you to make the jump."

Tim drove Pru home from Norfolk House. It was a fresh April day, moist from spring showers yet sunny and warm, prompting Tim to take the canvas top off the jeep. They didn't talk until he pulled up in Chandos Place, shifted into neutral, and turned to face her.

She looked at him brightly. "Coming up?"

"Can't. Got to be at Bushey Park tonight."

Disappointment showed. "When will you be back next?"

"Tomorrow, I hope. I'm almost done. I'll ship a lot of my stuff over to the stenographic pool in the morning. Then I'll talk to Hardaway."

"What do you think he'll say?"

"Well, he won't like it."

Pru gave him a searching look. The soft wind blew the few strands of her auburn hair which weren't tied back. They drifted across her face, and she brushed them away lightly with her hand. "And you? Do you like it?"

"You mean the mission?"

"That's precisely what I mean."

"I don't know. I don't know any more than what I told you. I don't know what I'm in for." Tim didn't want to think about the mission now. He leaned over and kissed her. "We'll talk about it tomorrow, okay? I've gotta run. Night, dear."

Pru kissed him, shot one questioning glance at him, and then climbed out onto the sidewalk. "Don't walk me up. I'll make it," she said, a touch of exasperation in her voice. She walked through the front door without looking back. He watched her go in, then put the car into first and drove off.

Pru's footsteps echoed in the bare hallway. They grew fainter and fainter as she reached the third floor. There was a moment of silence, the faint rattling of keys, a clunking sound as she turned the lock, and finally the slamming of the door.

A few minutes later the man with the wire spectacles emerged from beneath the stairwell. After a quick look through the small window in the front door to make sure that the American had left, he swiftly mounted the steps.

His right hand slid noiselessly along the rickety banister while his left hand probed the pocket of his trench coat for the hammered gold wedding band he had brought with him as ammunition. At the second floor he paused to listen. From inside one of the flats came the sounds of pans rattling. Someone was preparing dinner, he thought. Otherwise, the bleak stairwell was ghostly quiet.

He moved up the stairs, past the landing, and onto the threshold of the flat he had watched carefully for over three months. As he raised his hand to knock, he reflected to himself that the crucial moment had come. Then his fist descended and struck the door with a single loud rap.

8

"Have you gone out of your mind, Loftis? The answer is no, no again, and a thousand times no!" Hardaway slammed the file he had been holding in his hands down onto the desk and looked at Tim. For the first time since Tim had known him, the major's hair was askew, his eyes livid, his temper gone. "Listen here, Loftis! I've had enough of this, do you hear? For two months you've been corkscrewing your way around, sticking your nose everywhere except where it belongs! I warned you when you engineered that phony special assignment over at G-Two that my patience was about gone. And now you expect me to approve this transfer request!"

"Look, I know you've got a good reason—"

"A good reason! Look here, Loftis." Hardaway came out from behind his desk and faced Tim. "There's work to be done on those beaches and you know it! The General Staff has been waiting for your report. Here it is April, over two months since the invasion sites were staked out, and they still don't have your final predictions on the beach conditions. And I've got a good reason, you say! My God, that's the understatement of the century!" He shook his head in anger, checked himself, and walked over to the map of Normandy which hung on the wall next to his desk.

"You know as well as I do why I haven't gotten those reports in," Tim said.

"You mean all that nonsense you've been feeding me about waiting until the ice breaks up?"

"That's exactly what I mean! Those beaches were covered two weeks ago, and I didn't have the proper aerial recons until last week, so don't blame me for the lack of reports! Tell it to the Army Air Corps! Besides, I don't know what the hell the staff wants with more beach profiles. They've already decided on the targets."

"That's not your business! Your job is to give them anything they ask for. This is the military, Loftis, not a smoking club! When you're given an order, you obey it."

"I'm not questioning my orders, I'm just trying to help get this war over as quickly as possible. I'd be a hell of a lot more useful on this mission than I would be drawing more beach profiles, that's all I'm saying!"

Hardaway snorted. "This mission! This half-baked parachute idea? Good God, Loftis, when are you going to knock those schoolboy notions out of your head? We're supposed to be operating as a team, not a bunch of would-be Robin Hoods! You take care of the beaches and leave intelligence to the boys over at Intelligence. Your request is denied." Hardaway walked back over to his chair and sat down. He gripped the arms tightly and swiveled back and forth nervously. "I warn you, if you try and transfer without my approval, I'll fight it!"

"Why? What's your big stake in all this? I'd think you'd be happy to see me go!"

Hardaway fumed. "You're missing my point. It's not just that you're our only real geologist. That's reason enough to keep you here, of course. It's just that—well, damn it, it's not done that way! If we had everybody running around trying to do everybody else's job, SHAEF'd be in a fine mess and we'd never get into France at all." He stopped swiveling and stared at Tim. "This wouldn't have happened if it weren't for your little friend in G-Two."

"You mean Pru?"

"Yes, that's who I mean!"

"Oh, now I get it! My sex life is sinking this invasion?"

Hardaway looked up at Tim. "Watch yourself, Loftis!"

"I am. Now listen to me!" Tim leaned over the desk, resting

on his hands, and looked Hardaway straight in the eye. "You always accuse me of skimping on my job. Loftis, the pleasure boy! Well, damn it, I did what I was assigned to do, and now that job is done. I need a new assignment, and I've managed to find one because I didn't mind my own business. If it hadn't been for me, this whole business in France would have been passed right over. So I'm going ahead and do what I can to help end this goddam war, and then you can go back to your boys in Somerset and I can go back to my beaches in California!" Tim straightened himself up. With the outburst, his anger passed. "Oh, Christ, can't you see what I'm after? This is a chance to do something, to take a risk, and maybe shorten the war by six months. It's my risk. Why are you so opposed to it?"

Hardaway regarded him coolly. "Because you're acting like a damn fool. In fact, you are a damn fool. You still think that soldiering is lovely, with heroes, medals, brass bands, and the whole charade. Well, it isn't!" Hardaway picked up a pencil from his blotter and drummed with it nervously. "Loftis, you've never seen combat. And God knows you've never been a spy! You're a trained specialist. We can't go throwing people like you into the arms of the Nazis simply because you want a little glamour."

"But—"

"No 'buts' about it! If G-Two thinks this mission is so important, why don't they send one of their own men?"

"That's easy. They don't have one." Hardaway turned away in disgust. "It's true. They need someone who knows the terrain thoroughly, who's been privy to the whole cipher affair, and who speaks French and German. That's me. I'm here, I'm free, I'm ready to go, and they want to use me."

"That's what you say. I'm inclined to doubt it. We'll see what happens when you put in your request and General Strong has to pass on it. He's not going to risk sending a top officer of SHAEF who's privy to all the invasion plans into France so that he can have tea and chat with a couple of disgruntled German officers, I'll wager!"

The disadvantage of having left Hardaway in the dark about the true significance and content of the Solstice cipher was now apparent. "It's more complicated than you think. That's all I can say."

"You'll have to say more than that to General Bull if you want him to sanction this lunacy, whatever it is! He's your superior, after all." Hardaway looked at Tim pleadingly. "Can't you see what *I'm* trying to do, Loftis? This is a gigantic operation. Coordination and planning are the only things that will keep it all from going up in flames." His eyes softened. "And I'm trying to save your damn fool neck! I like you, Loftis, I like you immensely. I may get peeved at you at times, but that doesn't mean there's animosity. Heaven knows, quite the opposite. You want a Bronze Star to wear on your uniform? I can only tell you that it won't do you a damn bit of good if you're dead!"

Tim felt a sudden choke in his throat. Hardaway had melted him. He realized in a flash how close he was to Hardaway after all, this strange man old enough to be his father. "Okay, okay. I'll think about it. Keep that transfer request in your desk. I have to go up to London tonight, and I should be back day after tomorrow. We can talk more about it then."

Tim was already leaving the room when Hardaway's voice stopped him.

"Sorry about the tantrum. Pressure's getting to me, I think."

Tim turned and looked back. The British major was sitting at the desk, as he had when they first met six months before. The same maps were on the wall, the same family photograph on the file cabinet. It was all the same except that it was immeasurably and irrevocably different.

That evening Tim lay on his back in bed while Pru playfully walked her fingers up and down his stomach and chest. The night seemed deathly quiet as they lay relaxed after their lovemaking. From far off came the sounds of sirens as trucks raced to the scene of a bomb explosion, but it was suspended in the silence of the room, eerily, as if it came from another planet.

"Pru?"

"Mmmmm?" She tucked her head even tighter underneath his arm.

"Had a fight with Hardaway. Over the mission."

"Oh, Hardaway! He infuriates me."

"How can he infuriate you? You've never met him."

She laughed softly and kissed him on the chest. "Because he infuriates you, darling." She pulled herself up slightly and kissed him fully on the mouth. Then she laughed again. "What did you fight about?"

"He doesn't want me to go. He says I'm needed at SHAEF."

"What did you tell him?"

"That I had to go. It wasn't a question of choice. I just had to go."

"What did he reply?"

"He said that my job was beaches and not spying."

"And you told him your duty was to drop into France regardless of what your job was!"

"How'd you guess?"

Pru leaned her chin into the palms of her clasped hands so that she was looking down at him. "Because I know you so well, Mr. Rocks and Things, major, sir!"

"In what way?"

"Well, if you must know, it's because despite your flippant attitude, and your characterization of yourself as a brash young upstart, underneath you're an idealist and far too serious for your own good. You sit about tearing yourself down in front of other people, protesting your ignorance or your incompetence at one thing or another, when in reality you are fantastically brilliant and incredibly hard-working."

"So?"

"So, your protests about military life are in vain, Major Loftis. You produced those stunning reports on the beaches, which were far more detailed than anyone at G-Two imagined possible. Then you spotted the cipher when O'Neill-Butler and his chaps were too stupid to notice it and everyone else was too busy to pay attention. And now you want to go to France." Pru tickled his chin lightly. "Can't you see why I know Hardaway doesn't have a ghost of a chance of stopping you?"

Tim laughed. "You've made your point, lieutenant. Only I think he convinced me that I should stay here." Pru was silent. "What's the matter?"

"Nothing," she said. "Thinking."

"What about?"

"Nothing." Silence again.

"Do you think I shouldn't go?"

Pru sighed, raised her head from off of her hands, and, with a great heave, rolled over on her side facing away from Tim. "It's not for me to say, is it, now?"

Tim sat up in bed suddenly and leaned over her. He rolled her over so that she faced him. In the soft light from the dying fire in the coal stove he saw that her eyes were moist. "What does that mean?"

Pru shook her head. Her lips quivered, and a tear appeared on her cheek. Tim felt her body tighten under his hand. "It means that you'll do whatever you feel like doing, regardless of what I tell you."

She was crying now. Her trembling hand reached out. Slowly it went up his arm, slid around his neck, and pulled him to her. He wrapped his arms around her and kissed her. He could feel her take shuddering breaths beneath him, and the choking in her throat reverberated through him as she spoke into his ear.

"I don't think I could go through it all again!"

Tim pulled her even more closely to him. "Through what?"

"Through seeing a man I love fly off over Europe and not come back!" Pru's body stiffened and her arms squeezed him desperately. They lay there awhile, as Pru cried and Tim's mind raced. They rarely talked about the future because they both knew there was no future they could count on. For a second the bright golden sands of California beaches danced across his imagination: the mecca of his carelessness and independence.

Then Tim sat up slightly and looked at Pru. "If he is alive, what will you do?"

"I don't know." Her crying had stopped, although her eyes were still wet. "We hardly knew each other, really. We were both in the service when we got married, and Ronald was gone so often. It had only been a year and three months when his plane was shot down over Hamburg." She sniffled and then managed a small laugh. "I don't think I'd know him, after what he'd have been through." Her voice trailed off slightly. "Would he still want me after this?"

"What do I say now?"

Pru smiled. "There's not a great deal to say, I should think. I couldn't choose today even—" Pru stopped and looked away. A dark cloud seemed to pass over her mind as Tim watched her. "Even if I were forced to."

She reached up and pulled him down on top of her. Her tears were gone and her breathing regular, although Tim could feel her heart pumping furiously. Slowly she slid her hands up and down his back, over his hips, and between his legs. She kissed him, and as he curled his arms around her back, her tongue touched his ear. "I love you so much!"

"I love you, too," Tim said. France was a long, long way from the warm bed in Chandos Place.

A few meters below the level fields of France, Lieutenant Colonel Hellmuth Meyer was confused. As head intelligence officer for the Fifteenth Army under General Hans von Salmuth,

Meyer had drawn the unenviable job of monitoring all radio broadcasts between the Allied forces and the French underground. With a team of thirty operators working around the clock in the radio-filled bunker, Meyer listened to the Allied open-band transmissions.

What confused him that night was a new series of broadcasts from England, quite different from any that had gone before. As Meyer sat in his office, a four-by-eight-meter cubicle just off of the central radio reception room, he stared at the messages and wondered what they portended. THE FALCON WILL FLY AFTER THE EAGLE had been received six times in the last two weeks, having been broadcast in English, French, German, Dutch, and Danish. Usually the broadcasts from England were in English and perhaps in French. Was this it, he thought, the general alert to the underground that the great invasion was about to begin?

Meyer scratched his head. No. Intelligence reports from the Abwehr were emphatic that the code alert for the invasion would be a two-part message consisting of the first lines of a poem by the French poet Paul Verlaine called "Chanson d'Automne." What, then, was the meaning of this curious message about eagles and falcons?

Meyer was a young officer, in his late thirties, with thin hair which he brushed back from his prominent forehead. The thin-framed glasses he wore made him seem owlish and bookish, which he was. He took his job very seriously, because he knew that the Allies would transmit their intentions to the French peasants and that therefore he, Hellmuth Meyer, would be the first German to know when the invasion was being launched.

Meyer focused his attention back to the page before him. The message read: THE FALCON SWOOPS TO THE SAND. This dispatch had been received six times also, but within the last four days. It had been broadcast in French, German, and Dutch only. There had been rumors sent down to the Fifteenth Wehrmacht Group headquarters from OKW in Berlin that the Allies were planning an airborne attack in central Belgium as part of the invasion. The image of the falcon, especially as it swooped from the sky, did suggest to him a paratroop operation. If the Belgian airdrop rumors were true, it would only make sense to alert the peasants of Belgium by talking to them in the three languages of that country. As Meyer contemplated his choices, the telephone rang and he picked it up.

"*Ja, hier Oberstleutnant Meyer.*"

"*Herr Oberstleutnant, Standartenführer Knochen ist hier und muss mit Sie sprechen.*" Knochen again, Meyer thought. What a bother!

"*Sehr gut. Bringen Sie ihn herein.*"

Meyer rose and walked into the principal radio reception room. It was a bare concrete chamber, six meters wide by ten long. At either end the steel-shuttered ventilation ducts hummed as the air from the cool night above was pumped in. Along one of the walls was a table-bench loaded with radios. Meyer was proud of this installation, for the reception equipment was highly sophisticated and infinitely sensitive. The five slender twenty-meter towers which rose above the bunker in the French-Belgian border area ten kilometers west of Tournai commanded a range of 650 kilometers, from Groningen on the northwest coast of the Netherlands to the tip of the Cherbourg peninsula. The entire Atlantic Wall was thus under Meyer's close personal surveillance.

From the small tunnel at the far end of the room Meyer heard the echoing click of boots. Turning his head, he saw the crouched figures of three soldiers in black uniforms as they negotiated the narrow passageway. They entered the radio reception room and snapped the Nazi salute. Meyer returned it. One of the SS men was Knochen. The other two Meyer did not recognize.

"*Herr Oberstleutnant, Heil Hitler!*" Knochen said. Meyer bowed his head by way of greeting and motioned for the three officers to step into his office.

[145]

Inside the room Meyer shut the door. Knochen introduced the other visitors. One, a young auburn-haired major named Kreitzl, seemed pleasant enough. But the other one, called Sammstag, was distant and cold.

When they were seated, Knochen opened his briefcase and talked while he removed some papers. *"Herr Oberstleutnant,* we have come to you concerning a matter of some mystery and delicacy. *Sturmbannführer* Kreitzl is the Wehrkreis commandant for the Normandy sector. *Sturmbannführer* Sammstag has come here from the *Reichsführer's* office in Berlin."

"Yes, *Herr Standartenführer?"*

Knochen laid a file on Meyer's desk. "In late January, the Feldsicherheitsdienst arrested a number of Resistance operators. Their names and places and dates of arrest are there." Knochen pointed to the file. "Please, look."

Meyer opened the folder. It contained a stack of Sipo arrest reports. Each one listed a separate Frenchman and had a small photograph stapled to the upper right-hand corner. Meyer thumbed through the sheets. Absentmindedly he looked at the data. Dates: 14 January, 22 January, 19 January, 8 January. The places were familiar but not of much consequence: Abbeville, Le Havre, Rouen, Courseulles.

"I am confused, *Herr Standartenführer.* What am I supposed to make of these reports?"

Knochen glanced at each of the two SS officers, then returned his gaze to Meyer. "You do not know?" he asked.

A small tingle formed at the base of Meyer's neck. He shook his head. "No, *Herr Standartenführer."*

Knochen nodded slowly. "You have been monitoring the broadcasts of the radio operatives in France since last year, have you not?" Meyer nodded. "Where are they kept?"

"In the next bunker, *Herr Standartenführer.* They are all there, if you wish to see them. I have sent copies to the Sipo."

"Only since the Sipo took over the responsibility for the internal security of France from the FSD. That was in March. I am interested in earlier reports. *Herr Sturmbannführer,*" he said, looking over his shoulder at Sammstag, "go and retrieve the dispatches in question. You know which ones we are after."

"*Hauptmann* Kunzer will show you, *Herr Sturmbannführer,*" Meyer said. "He is my aide. He is in the next room."

Sammstag left, shutting the door behind him. Knochen was playing absently with the pen which Meyer had left lying on the table. He looked up. "*Herr Oberstleutnant,* I will be frank. The Sipo has reason to suspect that certain members of the Wehrmacht have been attempting to contact the Allies in London. Each of the men in that file was arrested by the FSD or was taken from the custody of the Sipo. As far as I know, none of them have been interrogated or incarcerated. Indeed," Knochen said, his eyes narrowing as he stared right at Meyer, "they have all disappeared."

"Where to, *Herr Standartenführer?*"

"A good question. I was about to ask you that."

"*Herr Standartenführer,* you must know that I have nothing to do with spies or traitors. Nothing whatever. It is my job to monitor broadcasts and to pass transcriptions on to the proper bureaus. That is all."

Knochen frowned impatiently. "I know that, *Herr Oberstleutnant.* I am not accusing you of sheltering these French pigs. I am here only to see that your office has surpressed nothing. We will wait for *Sturmbannführer* Sammstag to return."

It was half an hour before he did. Knochen stayed in his chair the whole time, lazily smoking cigarettes in his ivory holder. Meyer sat quietly, listening to the sounds of the radios. Occasionally he glanced at Knochen, who invariably smiled back at him. Finally they heard footsteps in the other room, the door opened, and Sammstag entered carrying a sheaf of papers. He looked blankly at

Meyer while he handed the papers to Knochen. Knochen flipped through them and then handed them to Meyer. "Do you recognize these transmissions?"

Meyer looked at them. They were still in code. There was neither plaintext nor German translation on any of them. Meyer looked at the dates and the identification numbers. He frowned and shook his head. "No, *Herr Standartenführer.* That means little, however. There are hundreds, even thousands, of messages which come through here every day."

"I understand. Why have these not been decoded?"

"Obviously because we do not have the cipher for them."

"Has there been an attempt to crack the cipher?"

Meyer scanned the bottoms of the sheets where the receiving, transcribing, and decoding officers were required to place their initials. "An attempt was made, *Herr Standartenführer,* but only a limited one."

"Why?"

"There were probably not enough messages. There were only these seventeen, if the logs are correct. We would have needed twice as many to even begin an analysis."

"Who attempted to break the cipher?"

"*Hauptmann* Bäuml, of my staff."

"I want to speak with him."

"I am sorry, *Herr Standartenführer.* He was borrowed by *Generalfeldmarschall* Rommel a few weeks ago for some special decoding work at Army Group B. They are very short on staff there, I understand."

Knochen looked at Sammstag as if they had expected such a development. He turned back to Meyer. *"Herr Oberstleutnant,* these are the messages which we suspect were sent to the Allies by certain members of the Wehrmacht. Last week we arrested a key radio operator in Le Havre. Rather than face the rope, he produced a ledger of transmissions which he said had been given to him for safekeeping by an operative in Caen. The radio operative in Caen disappeared shortly after he had given this log to our prisoner. These transmissions were logged in that book. They were the only ones the Sipo did not know of. Apparently they are in a cipher which we, or you, do not know. Our task, then, seems obvious. We must crack the cipher."

"I will do what I can, *Herr Standartenführer,* but I am understaffed myself. The invasion seems to be at hand, and the radio traffic is quite heavy."

"You will do what you are ordered to do, *Herr Oberstleutnant!*" The anger in Knochen's voice was unmistakable. "I want this cipher broken as soon as possible!"

Meyer looked at Knochen with amazement. "Do you think this cipher will help tell us about the invasion?"

For the first time Sammstag spoke. "We cannot tell, *Herr Oberstleutnant.* Our agents have contacted someone with British Intelligence in London. They have extracted some information from her. We have no way of knowing how accurate it is, but it does seem that a special cipher has been the object of much attention recently at Allied headquarters."

The news flabbergasted Meyer. "And you think this is that cipher?"

Knochen stood up abruptly. "We hope it is. It would make things quite convenient if it were." Looking quickly through his briefcase, he withdrew a small photograph and handed it to Meyer. "Have you ever seen this man?"

Meyer studied the picture. It was a blond man of about thirty-five in a Wehrmacht uniform. By the flashings on his collar Meyer could tell that he was a colonel. Meyer shook his head.

"Look again, *Herr Oberstleutnant.* This is a picture of *Oberst* Hans von Frickstein, aide to *Generalfeldmarschall* Rommel."

Meyer looked at the photograph again, then shrugged. "Perhaps I have seen him on the few occasions I have been at La Roche-Guyon, but I don't remember him."

"Last January fourteenth, on specific orders from *Generalfeldmarschall* Rommel, *Oberst* von Frickstein took custody of an arrested French operative from the Sipo garrison in Lisieux. *Sturmbannführer* Kreitzl here was the officer in charge. That operative has disappeared like all the others. Yet, *Herr Oberstleutnant*"— Knochen paused to leaf through the dispatches Sammstag had brought with him; he picked one out and held it up so that Meyer could see it—"yet, on January twentieth this same operative transmitted this message. The captured radio log identified this transmission. What do you have to say about that?"

Meyer looked helplessly at Knochen. "Nothing, *Herr Standartenführer*. I know nothing of the whole affair."

Knochen continued to gaze at Meyer for another extremely long minute. "Very good, *Herr Oberstleutnant.* Your answers have satisfied me." He started gathering the dispatches and files from the table, putting them into his briefcase. "You are to say nothing of what I have said to anyone. And you are to report anything suspicious or out of the ordinary to me at once. Personally." Knochen snapped the briefcase shut and straightened up. "There is grave danger all around us. *Heil Hitler, Herr Oberstleutnant.*"

It was then that Meyer remembered. During the whole interview his fear had made him forget, and only the relief he felt at having passed Knochen's scrutiny allowed him to remember. *"Herr Standartenführer,* a moment."

Knochen, who was nearly through the door of Meyer's office, stopped and looked back.

"There is something, perhaps. It may be nothing."

"What is that, *Herr Oberstleutnant?*"

"Some messages which we have transcribed from the Allied broadcasts. They are a bit unusual."

Knochen glanced quickly at Sammstag, then set his briefcase back down on the desk. "Continue, *Herr Oberstleutnant.*"

"Over the past two weeks we have received these." Meyer shuffled through the papers on his desk and picked up the two transmissions he had been mulling over before the arrival of the SS men. "Here, *Herr Standartenführer.* These two messages."

He handed them to Knochen, who looked at them, then passed them to Sammstag, who also examined them carefully and deliberately. "They were transmitted in French, German, and Dutch. The first was also sent in English and Danish."

Sammstag finished studying the documents. He looked at Meyer. "What do you make of them?"

"Very little as yet. I was, in fact, studying them when you arrived."

"Whom have you told about them?" Knochen asked sharply.

"No one, *Herr Standartenführer.* I was about to pass them on to Sipo and OB West."

"You will not do that, *Herr Oberstleutnant!* OB West must not be allowed to see these. Have copies made for me at once."

Meyer nodded. In ten minutes the copies had been typed by the staff sergeant, and Knochen had stuffed them into his thick case.

Knochen looked at Meyer. "Just remember, *Herr Oberstleutnant.* You are to say nothing of these transmissions, or of the cipher. This is a matter of the highest security."

The three SS men headed for the small doorway which led to the tunnel and the earth's surface. Meyer watched them go, then turned to the radio bench. Satisfied that matters there were well under control, he returned to his office and shut the door. He sat at his desk for a moment, staring at the reports and dispatches. Then he reached for the telephone.

As he hung up the telephone, Hans von Frickstein felt the adrenaline quicken his system. He stood for a moment by the desk where he had taken the call, before he turned and left the room.

He walked down the paneled hallway on the ground floor of

the château of La Roche-Guyon, the old ruined tower which commanded a sweeping view of the little town fifty kilometers west of Paris. At the end of the corridor he stopped at a door, knocked, opened it, and walked into a large bare room, to the desk where Rommel sat writing.

"*Herr Generalfeldmarschall*, I have just taken a call from *Oberstleutnant* Meyer, intelligence officer for the Fifteenth Army."

"Yes?"

"The Sipo has been to see him. They have found out our plan."

Rommel looked up quickly. His face was frozen. Only the sound of the curtain rustling in the warm spring winds disturbed the silence. "What did he say?" he finally asked.

"The Sipo traced the dispatches of last January. They suspect treason in the Wehrmacht, but they are not sure yet where to look next."

Rommel exhaled softly. "Then there is still time."

"Yes, *Herr Generalfeldmarschall.* And no. They showed Meyer a photograph of me."

Rommel rose and intently paced the creaking wooden floor. "What else did he say?"

"They have not yet cracked the cipher. *Standartenführer* Knochen ordered the *Oberstleutnant* to intensify his efforts at breaking it. Fortunately, *Hauptmann* Bäuml is here, as you requested."

Rommel gave von Frickstein a wry smile. "Yes, that is fortunate, isn't it?" Rommel stopped pacing. "What did you tell him? The *Oberstleutnant?*"

"That I thought the Sipo was crazy. And that I had never heard of such-and-such a cipher."

"Did he tell you why they showed him your photograph?"

"I was identified by the *Wehrkreis* commandant in Lisieux as the man who had taken the French radio operative from him."

"As I feared, *Herr Oberst.* What did you say then?"

"I told him that I had taken the prisoner, of course. I told him that we had crossed the agent to our side, and that he had transmitted for us for a few weeks until the British had suspected what had happened and cut off communication. Then we had him shot."

Rommel looked at von Frickstein with alert eyes. "And did he believe you, *Herr Oberst?*"

"I think so, *Herr Generalfeldmarschall.*"

Rommel sank into the small sofa beneath a Gobelin tapestry and buried his face in his hands. He rubbed his face briskly as if trying to shake out the fatigue which showed so vividly on him. The last two months had been filled with twenty-four-hour days for Rommel, days of furious inspections of the wall itself, of conferences with the field commanders, of heated telephone arguments with OKW in which he demanded more troops and matériel in vain.

"We still have time," he said finally. "If and when the Sipo breaks the cipher, they will still have no way of knowing what it means or what our plans are."

"But, *Herr Generalfeldmarschall,* don't forget—"

"Yes, I know. We still have one more message to send. Did you hear anything about new transmissions from London?"

"Yes, *Herr Generalfeldmarschall.* I asked the *Oberstleutnant* what kind of messages he was referring to. He read me the last two transmissions, just to show me what nonsense they were."

Rommel managed a small smile. "Very good, *Herr Oberst!* What were they?"

" 'The falcon will fly after the eagle' and 'The falcon swoops to the sand.' "

"Then they have agreed!" Rommel clenched his fists with excitement. "Good! They will drop the messenger by air. To the sand, you say?"

"Yes, *Herr Generalfeldmarschall.*"

Rommel walked to the large map of the northwestern coast of France which lay on his desk. He looked at it and thought. "The sand? There is sand everywhere." He looked at the map again, his eyes slowly tracing the jagged lines of the coast. "But there is one sector along the coast that is sandy. Only one. The area here." He moved his finger between Ouistreham and Grandcamp. *"Herr Oberst,* they will land him in Normandy."

"Yes, *Herr Generalfeldmarschall,* I thought the same thing."

Rommel walked around his desk, where he grasped the small water carafe, poured some into a glass, and took a swallow. "So far our plan is working. So far. As long as the cipher remains unbroken, it will be difficult for the Sipo to even know what it is they are looking for."

"The cipher will not stand for long, *Herr Generalfeldmarschall.* Time is against us."

"I know that. The Sipo will break it eventually, with or without *Hauptmann* Bäuml. Unfortunately that part of the affair is completely out of our control."

Rommel stopped pacing and looked up, his face wearing a quizzical expression. "Today is May twenty-seventh. If the invasion does not come by the end of the month, I think that it will not come before the fifteenth of June. That is my guess. We will be leaving for Herrlingen on June fourth. There will be ample time to get to Herrlingen and return before the Allies land. If the invasion comes before we leave, the trip will naturally be called off. But I fear that if I cancel the trip now, the Sipo's suspicions would only increase."

"What about the Allied messenger?"

Rommel shrugged. "I hope we can meet him next week. Before the invasion and before I leave. We can do nothing, however. It is up to the Allies to name the date. If they set a time which conflicts with the trip to Herrlingen, we will cross that bridge when we have to." He paused. "The message, *Herr Oberst.* Have it transmitted at once."

Von Frickstein turned and left. Rommel stared after him for a moment, then walked to the desk and sat down. He opened a drawer and removed a sheet of paper. He scrawled across the page with his pen. When he had finished, he reread what he had written, folded the sheet, placed it in an envelope, and sealed it. He reached for the telephone and clicked the small button to arouse the operator. The voice crackled on the other end.

"Ja?"

"Rommel." The drowsy voice on the other end suddenly woke up. "I must speak with *Oberstleutnant* Reinhardt at once. In my office."

"Jawohl, Herr Generalfeldmarschall!" The phone clicked off, and Rommel replaced the receiver. He sat back in his chair, folded his arms in front of him, and waited for his Feldsicherheitsdienst commander to arrive.

Von Frickstein went back to his office. He unlocked the door, flipped on the light, entered, shut the door, and locked it. He went to the desk. Unlocking the center drawer, he pulled it out a few inches to clear the locking mechanism on the side drawers. Removing the bottom drawer all the way, he reached into the shallow well created by the slide supports. Lifting out a thin sheet of wood , he reached in and removed a folded piece of paper. He opened the paper, read it, then put it into his pocket. Quickly, von Frickstein replaced the wood, put the drawer back into its well, closed it, shut the middle drawer, locked the desk, and was about to leave when the phone rang.

Von Frickstein's heart leaped into his throat as he looked at the clanging instrument on his desk. Gingerly he picked up the receiver. His voice was dry. *"Ja?"*

"Herr Oberst von Frickstein?"

"Ja."

"This is Sipo headquarters in Paris." Von Frickstein's palms sweated as he unconsciously thrust his hand into his pocket and clutched the scrap of paper which he had just put there.

"*Ja.* Your business, please."

"I have a question about a report which you have filed with us. *Ach,* where is it? It was right in front of me, and now it's gone. *Augenblick, bitte, Herr Oberst.*"

Von Frickstein tried to laugh even though his tensed neck muscles made the sound seem more like a croak. "*Ja,* take your time!"

"Ah, I have found it! *Generalfeldmarschall* Rommel is going to Herrlingen on June the fifth, *ja?*"

Von Frickstein could not understand what the Sipo was after. "No, we will be leaving on the fourth."

The voice seemed surprised. "Very good, *Herr Oberst.* I was simply preparing the orders for the motorcycle escort. *Danke. Auf Wiedersehen.*"

"*Auf Wiedersehen.*" The line went dead. Von Frickstein set the receiver down and breathed deeply. Two phone calls in the same night had shaken him. He would be glad, he thought, when the rendezvous had been made and the tension was past. He opened the door, turned off the lights, shut and locked the door, and strode down the corridor.

In a minute he was in the cellar of the old fortress. He passed the sentry at the entrance to the jail wing and stepped into the small cubicle which served as an office of sorts for the jailer. The sergeant sprang to his feet and snapped a salute as von Frickstein entered.

"*Heil Hitler!*"

"*Heil Hitler!* I must speak with Number Twenty-four, *bitte.*" The jailer, a beefy red-faced Thuringian of forty-five or so, nodded. He led von Frickstein down a short hallway, where they descended five steps and stopped before a wooden door. The jailer shot the heavy bolts back.

A hot dank rush of moldy air hit von Frickstein's nostrils as the door opened. They walked down the dingy hall. La Roche-Guyon had been built in the fourteenth century, and its dungeons showed their age. Small doors on either side of the corridor were barely visible in the light given off by the string of naked bulbs which had been hung at the highest part of the barrel-vaulted roof. They groped along in the passage and finally stopped in front of a cell door. The jailer pulled back the bolt, pulled the door open, and von Frickstein entered.

Father Saurel had changed remarkably after five months of inactivity and confinement. The tanned face had grown pale, and the once groomed hair with the dashing flecks of gray at the temples was long, untidy, and brushed roughly back.

"Time," von Frickstein said quietly. Father Saurel set his book down and rose. He followed the officer out into the passageway and into a small empty cell a few meters away. Von Frickstein turned on the light, revealing a wooden table on which lay eight crystal sets. The priest sat down on the stool by the table and picked up his radio. As he made ready to transmit, von Frickstein took the piece of paper out of his pocket and handed it to Father Saurel. He smiled briefly at it, put on his head phones, opened and closed his fist vigorously several times to limber up his fingers, shook his hand, and started to transmit.

Von Frickstein watched as the tiny clicks sounded from the heavy nickel key. He had learned to trust the holy man fron Lisieux. He no longer required that a radio expert be present when he transmitted. In a minute, the message had been sent twice. Von Frickstein asked if London had acknowledged receipt. Father Saurel nodded slowly.

Then from the far end of the corridor they heard loud voices and stamping feet. Von Frickstein stepped into the corridor in time to see a detachment of Wehrmacht guards swarm into the prison, shouting out numbers. A sergeant stopped in front of cell 24, saw that the door was open, and turned to Von Frickstein.

"*Herr Oberst, Nummer vierundzwanzig—ist er da drin?*" he asked, pointing to the room where the priest sat.

"*Ja, er ist da. Warum?*" Ignoring von Frickstein's question, the sergeant motioned to two soldiers, who came down the hallway and went into the transmitting room. They picked the priest up roughly and handcuffed him.

It was odd, von Frickstein suddenly thought, that the *Generalfeldmarschall* had not informed him of transfer plans. He looked at Father Saurel, who stood between the two guards, his hands painfully chained behind his back, and felt a sudden seizure of panic. He turned and walked rapidly down the corridor, stormed out of the jail, rushed up the flights of stairs, and in a minute was knocking on the *Generalfeldmarschall*'s door. When he burst in, he saw Rommel standing at the tall windows behind his desk.

Upon hearing him enter, Rommel turned. "You have sent the message?"

"*Ja, Herr Generalfeldmarschall.* I—" Rommel held up his hand to silence him. Slowly he looked back into the courtyard of the old castle. Von Frickstein rushed to the window.

In the courtyard spotlights he could see eight men being marched to the stone and mortar walls of the fortress. Two trucks were backing up toward them. Two soldiers sat in the back of each truck, one manning the machine guns mounted there. Dazed by the flood of lights which shone in their eyes, the bewildered prisoners kept their heads bowed to block out the bright rays. Von Frickstein could see Father Saurel, with whom he had been speaking cordially only five minutes before, looking about him, unable to understand what was happening.

In a burst of disgust and anger, von Frickstein turned from the window just as the multiple reports of the machine guns shattered the quiet spring night. The shrieking volleys boomed in the courtyard, and the echoes careened madly into the air before finally dying out. Von Frickstein heard the trucks starting up and a few voices shouting commands.

He turned and looked at Rommel. The field marshal stood staring sadly at the scene below him. Slowly he turned and saw von Frickstein staring at him. "We had no choice, my friend. The Sipo would have been heartless with them." He paused and added very quietly, "They will be even more heartless with us if we fail."

9

SOE, Special Operations Executive, was located on the second floor of a low building in northwest London, on Baker Street, and for the months of April and May it replaced the beaches of Normandy in Tim's nightmares.

Six days a week for two hours every day Tim was closeted with a French exile in a small room on Baker Street and forced to converse in French. After learning the street idioms, the slang, and the curious twists of Norman regional dialects, he began to think in French and even to imagine himself a French citizen. He knew French currency, French train schedules, French village government, French food, French wine, French provincial architecture, French identification cards, French passports, and French ration cards.

During the first two weeks Tim also had intensive training in coding and decoding procedures. For three hours a day he had studied single and double columnar encipherments, mono- and polyalphabetical substitutions, reversed vowel and consonant methods, and Beaufort ciphers. He had memorized whole sections from Hitt's *Manual for the Solution of Military Ciphers*. He had been given messages in English plaintext and been told to translate them into French and then encipher them, all the time racing a stopwatch. He had been assigned to reduce code texts to English plaintext while an instructor beat out the seconds and minutes with a walking stick. At the end of two weeks, Tim had been able to translate and encode a twenty-word message in two minutes. He was told that he would have to halve that time. It had taken another week to accomplish that. His principal instructor, one of

O'Neill-Butler's cryptologists whom Beauclerk had assigned to SOE in order to minimize the number of people who knew about Tim's mission, had told Tim that his work was adequate for a two-day mission but for no longer.

He had been taught to disassemble, clean, and reassemble three different types of shortwave crystal radio sets. He had learned where every part went and what it did. After a week he had been able to do that in five minutes for each set. His instructor had then blindfolded Tim. It had taken another week before Tim had gotten his time back down to five minutes again. He had been shown how to conceal radio transmitters in coffee cans, shoes, hats, coats, milk bottles, ration packets, books, and even bouquets of roses. He had been taught how to set and reset the crystals for different frequencies, and he had memorized the thirty-seven frequencies used by the French underground in the Normandy sectors. As a boy scout in North Platte, Tim had learned Morse code. Now he relearned it and its variations: American, international, and cable codes. He had been pushed by his teachers to the point where he could recognize and transcribe transmissions clicking at the rate of twenty-four words a minute.

Even his painstaking work on the beaches had not prepared Tim for the detailed knowledge of the French countryside which was now being forced upon him. Names of villages, highway numbers, distances between towns, names of hotels, shops, mayors, local government officials were all relentlessly pounded into his head.

Each day Tim was confronted with four or five men who mercilessly interrogated him for two or more hours in French. The questions flew at him, until his head started to swim as he groped for the correct answers. Occasionally one of the men shot a quick question at him in English. It took immense mental effort for Tim to learn not to respond at all. A French peasant, it was explained, would understand little if any English, so Tim could not know it.

In five weeks he was expected to totally suppress twenty-five years of speaking his native tongue.

Slowly, an identity began to emerge. Tim was slowly becoming Jean Robichon, twenty-seven, *serrurier,* or locksmith, in Caen. The small fuzz which had barely sprouted under his nose had in four weeks become a healthy mustache. Tim had never grown his facial hair before, and the mustache tickled him. Couldn't he please shave it off? he had pleaded with Beauclerk. No, had been the reply, it makes you look more French.

A married Frenchman at that, for Jean Robichon, it turned out, had a wife named Françoise and a small two-year-old girl named Louise.

The crucial events in Jean Robichon's life had become established. Born in Toulouse in 1917, his mother had died when Jean was four, and his father had moved first to Rennes, then to Caen. His father had died when Jean was eighteen, and Jean had gone to work for a locksmith in Caen by the name of Louis Pellegrin. His wife had come from the small Cotentin village of Saint-Vaast-la-Hougue, which explained why Jean often traveled along the coast in Normandy, sometimes late at night. His daughter had polio and often went to stay with her grandparents while Jean was busy being an itinerant journeyman. The polio had been Beauclerk's idea. His eyes had twinkled when he had told Tim about it. "Most of the Germans are just like you and me, lad. They have a strain of pity."

By the end of the fourth week Tim was free enough from his classroom duties to spend three days a week at the SHAEF army training center at St. Paul's School in Hammersmith. He was there first for obstacle drills and field exercises, the same sort of thing he had done in 1942 at advanced infantry school. Twice he went to the group headquarters of AEAF, the Allied Expeditionary Air Force, near Uxbridge, to refresh his parachute training. By the seventh week, he was sent to Fershfield, the secluded RAF airbase in Suffolk, where he took four practice jumps. He was then sent to Woolacombe, the SHAEF Assault Training Center on the north coast of Devonshire on the Bristol Channel. There the American, British, Canadian, and French troops slated to land at Normandy had been in training. For the first time Tim actually saw landing craft in operation, and he was glad he wouldn't have to ride in one.

In the third week of May, Tim had spent five days at Woolacombe learning tactics from the same British commandos who had raided Dieppe: knife fighting and basic jujitsu and the rudiments of assault methods, how to sneak up on a sentry and cut his throat before he can give an alarm. He refreshed his target shooting using a .45-caliber Colt automatic pistol. Then he went back to London for more practice with the French linguists, more quizzing, and the final cementing of his identy as Jean Robichon. For three hours one hot day in May, SOE officials interrogated and crossexamined him, asking him every detail about his life, his trade, his identification numbers, and the history of France. When it was all over, the senior official, a pleasant bookish-looking colonel from the Free French Second Corps whom Tim knew only as Michel, smiled at him. It would do, he said. If Tim's luck held.

Norfolk House became a haunted mansion as officers either went to Bushey Park or to join units up and down the coast. The halls which had hummed with human activity for so long were now deserted. It reminded Tim, as he walked down the third-floor corridor toward Beauclerk's office, of when school let out for the summer. One day, suddenly, the halls became empty except for a few teachers and a janitor or two. All the noise and pranks which filled the days during the winter vanished as everyone went home to the farms for the summer, to help hay and herd the cattle which dotted the plains of western Nebraska.

Beauclerk was sitting in his swivel chair, his feet up on the window ledge, as he looked out the open window. The breeze ruffled his baggy uniform as it rolled over him. Tim chuckled. The craggy angular profile was more craggy and more angular than ever today. Beauclerk looked up.

"Oh, Loftis, there you are! Good. Have a seat." Tim sat in the chair next to the desk, where he always sat. Beauclerk pulled his feet down with a grunt, sat upright, and gave Tim a wink. "Like a snort?"

"Sure. Got some?"

Beauclerk laughed, opened the bottom drawer of his desk, and removed a bottle of Pinch. Setting it on the desk, he pulled out two glasses and started pouring.

"Where the hell did you get that?" Tim asked.

Beauclerk chuckled merrily as the golden liquor gurgled into the glasses. "From home. It's been in my cellar since before the war. I brought it down last month. After next week, I'll use it either to toast our great victory or to get myself so potted I slide down a gutter and out of sight forever. Cheers, lad!"

Beauclerk opened his middle desk drawer and threw a large brown envelope across the blotter to Tim. "There you are, major. There's Jean Robichon."

Tim looked through the papers in the envelope. The passbook, weathered and aged, with hundreds of creases across each page, looked absolutely authentic except for the picture of Tim stapled to it. Tim chuckled to see himself in the mustache, with a rough linen shirt collar at his neck and a small *paysan* cap on his head. "Good job," he said. "Looks real."

"It is real." Tim looked up. "Except for the picture and some of the information that we shifted about to fit you. Our boys in the workshop know their stuff."

Tim looked at the other papers. The ration card was perfect, as was the identification card used by the city of Caen, which allowed one Jean Robichon to draw his weekly quotas of meat and bread. There were other items. There was a photograph of Françoise and Louise, his "wife" and his "daughter." It was perfect, he thought, the whole thing was perfect.

Beauclerk read his mind. "Pretty, aren't they?"

Tim smiled. "Yeah. Who are they?"

[164]

"Wife and child of a chap I know over at G-Four." The toothy grin spread across the leathery face. "All the other stuff you should look over and become familiar with. There's a work permit and a union card, a few other family-type photographs, and some money. We've issued you five thousand francs. I'd advise you to keep only a thousand or so out in the open. Hide the rest in your shoe. I'm working on getting some other props for you: newspapers, cigarettes, that sort of thing. If we can't get them over here, you'll have to get them on your own."

"It's like a play, isn't it?"

"Yes, that's what it's like. Only for keeps." Beauclerk let his words sink in, then lit a cigarette. "Any questions?"

"Just one. When?"

"Target date for D-Day is June fifth at oh-six-hundred hours. That means you'll take off at twenty-one-thirty hours on the fourth. We're sending a rendezvous time to the Germans tonight."

"How'll it work?"

"It's been arranged. You'll get a full rundown when you get your sealed orders as you board the plane, but, roughly, it goes like this." Beauclerk took a long draw on his Senior Service. "You'll be dropped near Ravenoville around twenty-three-hundred hours on June fourth. The pathfinders of the U.S. Eighty-second Airborne will be coming in right after you, so you'll have to work fast. The French will have a drop zone all staked out and an agent set to meet you. You two will hightail it inland and start for Sainte-Marie-du-Mont. Once you get past there, you'll be 'arrested' by a Wehrmacht patrol about two miles east of town. Your French contact will know where. This patrol will take you to headquarters, and there you'll talk with Rommel."

"That's it?"

"That's it, lad. I ought to warn you that there are about seven thousand things that can go wrong. From the moment you step out of that plane, it's up to you to use your judgment and your training to get to Rommel. That's the important thing. Get to Rommel, no matter what you have to do or who you have to kill."

"What about the Gestapo?"

"That's a risk. So far as we know, the main Gestapo headquarters is in Caen and they're undermanned, so things should be a bit loose up around Sainte-Marie-du-Mont. The only SS in the area is a Waffen-SS Panzergrenadier Division, located just west of Lisieux. You'll be at least thirty-five miles from them, so you shouldn't have any worries unless they move. But it's all a matter for Providence. Here you go, lad, have another." Beauclerk started to pour more Scotch into the glasses.

"No, thanks."

"What's wrong, lad? You've always been a good one for the stuff."

"Tired, I guess."

Beauclerk set the bottle back down on the desk and looked at Tim. "There's more than that, isn't there?" Tim jerked his head up, startled. "I know you well enough by now to tell that much. It's the lieutenant, isn't it?"

"What makes you say that?"

"Because I've been around the course a few times." Beauclerk gave the glass a slight shove toward Tim. "Tell me about it."

Tim sighed. "I guess it's the invasion. And the mission. We're tired and tense, and things just don't seem to be that hot. That's all."

"There's more than that."

Tim gazed at Beauclerk and caught a sudden feeling of urgency from him. "What do you mean?"

"Without prying where I don't belong, lad, I think there's something gone wrong. More than a love affair, more than the normal pressure. I wish you'd tell me what it is."

"Then you've noticed it?" Beauclerk nodded. Tim reached over and took the drink. "I went to see her last night about twenty-one hundred, right after I left SOE. She didn't answer the door when I knocked, so I just went in. She was lying on the bed, crying. I asked her what was wrong, but she just shook her head."

"What did she say?"

"Nothing. Said I wouldn't understand. Something like that. She said we could talk about it after I got back from France."

"That's all?"

"We haven't been talking too much lately." Tim swallowed the rest of the Scotch. "She doesn't want me to go."

"Can't blame her for that. She's in love with you." Beauclerk thought for a moment, then slapped his palm on the desk. "Well, maybe you're right. Maybe it is all this business, and she's just worried, and everything will be fine once we kick those Heinie bastards square in the tail. We'll all be better then."

Tim laughed nervously and set the glass back down. "I guess so."

Beauclerk rose. "Good enough, lad. I'll see you here at fourteen hundred hours on June fourth. I'll take you up to Thetford and give you your final briefing. Keep the spirits up!" He extended his hand. They both laughed as they shook.

As Tim was about to leave Norfolk House by the east door, he heard a familiar voice echoing down the hallway. As the figure walked beneath the lights in the ceiling, the green-clad officer alternately passed from shadow into light and back again into the shadow. When he was thirty feet away Tim finally recognized Hardaway. He hadn't recognized the gait before because it had lacked the clipped military precision that Tim had come to associate with his old partner.

In a moment Hardaway was next to him. "Thought that was you, Loftis." The tired eyes shifted nervously. "How've you been?"

"Busy. But no complaints. You?"

Hardaway shrugged. "Same routine. Meetings and more meetings. You know how it is!" He laughed hollowly.

"Yeah. What're you doing here?"

"Oh, I had to drop off some material at G-One. I was on my way out to dinner. Have you had some?"

Tim shook his head. "No, but . . . uh, I have an appointment. Thanks."

"Next time. After the big day?"

Tim nodded. As the two former partners regarded each other, Tim was conscious that he wanted to say something but didn't know what it was exactly. Hardaway must have felt the same way, because he hemmed and hawed before he spoke again.

"Well, it certainly looks like good weather." He looked directly at Tim. "Awfully glad spring is here."

"So am I. The calm before the storm."

"Yes, I suppose you're right. You . . . enjoying your work at G-Two?"

"So far."

"Your mission. Still on?" Tim nodded. "Good luck, Loftis. And remember, we have a date after the invasion to go up to Somerset. Ever done much trout fishing?"

"Some. I kind of like it."

"You'll love it in Somerset. Fattest trout known to man. Well"—Hardaway extended his hand—"give them hell, Loftis."

Tim clasped the hand. "Thank you, sir. You, too."

Then Hardaway was off, down the steps, through the door, and into the street. Tim stared after him, almost wanting to call him back.

The message had been unbelievable. It had come over the radio at 12:48 A.M. British Double Summer Time, and Hans von Frickstein had heard it as he had been completing preparations for the departure of Field Marshall Rommel at seven that same morning, 4 June 1944. He had been in his office going through the daily summaries of troop deployments, logistical deliveries, and munitions transfers when the clear, crisp voice of the BBC announcer had said it.

"The falcon captures the eagle at two on the fifth." Von Frickstein's English was not terribly fluent, so he had managed only to catch the few key words. "Eagle" he knew was the English word for *Adler*, and "falcon" in English meant *Falke*.

He had instantly telephoned the radio communications officer at his office on the second floor of the château of La Roche-Guyon. The Allies are broadcasting strange messages, he had told him. I must have full transcriptions and translations for the *Generalfeldmarschall* by 500 hours. *Ja*, he had been told, I will listen to them. The *Generalfeldmarschall* must have these summaries before he leaves, von Frickstein had continued, so that he can cancel his trip if the messages seem to presage the invasion.

At oh-four-hundred hours von Frickstein walked down the hallway to the field marshal's quarters. He strode in and crossed the room to the door which led to Römmel's bedroom. A slight rap produced no response. Von Frickstein knocked again, then opened the door.

Rommel was asleep, which was unusual for him. Von Frickstein walked to the bed and gently shook his shoulder. The eyes fluttered opened and looked at von Frickstein.

"*Ja, Herr Oberst?*"

"The message, *Herr Generalfeldmarschall*. The final message has come."

In an instant Rommel was out of bed and silently dressing himself. Stripping off his silk pajamas, he stepped into his gray field jodhpurs. He looked up at von Frickstein as he finished buttoning his uniform blouse. "Tell me. What do the Allies say?"

Von Frickstein held out the piece of paper with the vital transcription. Rommel took it and read it. He looked at the paper, then chuckled lightly. "They have much nerve, the Allies, to broadcast a message so openly." He handed the paper back to von Frickstein. "Tomorrow morning, then. Have you telephoned the *Generaloberst?*"

"No, *Herr Generalfeldmarschall*. I thought it best to wait

until I had talked with you. Besides, a call to Saint-Germain-en-Laye this early in the morning might attract undue attention."

Rommel nodded. Caution was imperative in this, the last stage of the conspiracy. In Saint-Germain-en-Laye, General Beck stood ready at the control center of the Atlantic Wall to issue orders for the Wehrmacht to lay down their arms. There was no need as yet to alert the panzer troops or Berlin. But Beck must know at once what had happened.

"You are correct, *Herr Oberst.* The question now is what to do."

"What do you mean, *Herr Generalfeldmarschall?*"

"Our choice seems simple." Rommel had buttoned his uniform coat by this time and was sitting on the small stool at the foot of the bed, pulling on his boots. "We either go to Herrlingen or we stay here."

"But, *Herr Generalfeldmarschall,* we have no choice! We must attempt the rendezvous. There is no chance to depart for Herrlingen!"

Rommel stood up and stamped his feet quickly to get his feet adjusted in the boots. He flashed von Frickstein a small smile. "I know that, my friend. What I meant was, Do we stay here, or do we pretend to go to Herrlingen? Which will be less suspicious?"

"I don't know, *Herr Generalfeldmarschall.*"

"What have you heard from the Sipo in Paris?"

"Nothing in the last week."

"And from the *Oberstleutnant*—what was his name?—at the Fifteenth Wermacht Group?"

"Also nothing."

Rommel stood for a moment, thinking. Silence was worse than an adverse report. He walked to the dresser opposite the bed and picked up the Iron Cross which lay there, tangled in the folds of the colorful ribbon. Carefully he looped it over his neck and adjusted it at the collar of his jacket.

"Whom have you told about my trip to Herrlingen?"

"I sent a report to OB West the day before yesterday, *Herr Generalfeldmarschall*. I said in it that since we did not expect the invasion before the fifteenth of June, you were going to Herrlingen for a few days, and that you could continue from there to Berchtesgaden in order to talk with the Führer." Then he remembered something. "I nearly forgot, *Herr Generalfeldmarschall*. The Sipo has already arranged for a motorcycle escort for you."

"That is inconvenient. But I think we can turn it to advantage." Rommel became pensive. "Call Sipo headquarters in Paris at once and tell them that I am still going to Herrlingen despite the bad weather. Ask them if they have any important messages which I should transmit to the Führer."

"Yes, *Herr Generalfeldmarschall.*"

"Telephone *Generalleutnant* Speidel. He is one of us. Tell him to prepare at once to leave for Germany and to speak with no one. I will give him further instructions later.

"And then telephone *Generalleutnant* Reichert. Tell him to be prepared for special maneuvers in connection with the upcoming war games."

Rommel walked to the window and pulled back the brocaded draperies. It was still dark, but the moon which lit the sky despite the growing cloudbanks illuminated the puddles and streams of water which the incessant rains of the last day had caused. "It is still raining, *Herr Oberst*. That is good. The invasion cannot come in weather such as this, which means that there will be little traffic on the roads. And," he said, turning to face von Frickstein, "few SS men on the prowl."

"It will make the airdrop all the more difficult, *Herr Generalfeldmarschall.*"

"That is the Allies' problem, not ours." With a motion of the finger, Rommel dismissed von Frickstein, who turned smartly and left the room.

Rommel looked out of the window again. For a second, as he stared out at the small splashes caused by the drops of rain in the puddle directly beneath his window in that chilly June morning, he felt a strange pang of remorse. What has happened to it, the grand dream? How funny fate is to us, he thought, that I should be here, now, at this moment, about to do something which might cost me my life and certainly my honor.

Erwin Rommel let the draperies fall back to cover the windows. He sighed. He had crossed the Rubicon.

Lieutenant Colonel Hellmuth Meyer was beginning to get nervous, and that was not good for his digestion. All day long his stomach had been growling and churning, and the milk he had been drinking in order to calm it hadn't helped. Worse still, he couldn't explain where the nervousness was coming from. Everything was under control in his radio bunker near Tournai, and the Allies had not yet broadcast the second part of the Verlaine poem which would signal the beginning of the invasion. The first phrase —*"Les sanglots longs des violons de l'automne"*—had been broadcast three days earlier, on 1 June. Its reception had caused Meyer's tension to increase considerably. Perhaps that was the source of his current uneasiness, he thought. Or perhaps it was the strain of trying to crack the mysterious cipher which was wearing him down. Not that he had had time to try very hard, but he had spent every spare moment on it without success.

He threw his pencil down, got up, and strolled into the radio reception room to look at the clock. It was fifteen hundred hours, although it was always midnight, it seemed, in the bunker. The long days underground were beginning to show on Meyer. His face was pale, and he felt as if he were living in a perpetual dream, an eerie twilight underscored by the whirring of the ventilator and the fugal melodies given out by the radios. It had been four days since he had seen the sun. Maybe that was the cause of the indigestion, he speculated. He walked over to the table where Staff Sergeant Reichling had just taken off his earphones and set them down.

"Feldwebel Reichling, was gibt's Neues?"

"Nichts, Herr Oberstleutnant." Reichling reached for the rewind button on his wire recorder. He flicked it, and the tiny metal spools hummed as the thin gray wire whizzed past the miniature recording heads, occasionally glinting when it caught one of the lights. "The BBC newscast from this noon, *Herr Oberstleutnant.* I have not yet had a chance to listen to it." After a minute, Reichling stopped the machine and pressed the play switch. From the small tinny speaker on the wall above their heads came a voice speaking in crisp English.

Meyer sat in a chair by the table and leaned toward the speaker. Perhaps, he thought, this newscast will give me a clue to that damned cipher.

"Weather is predicted cloudy and stormy over all of England for the rest of the day and tonight," the voice was saying. "Hurricane-force winds will be felt along the southern coastland perhaps as far north as Yarmouth."

Meyer smiled at Reichling. "No invasion tonight, I think. Not with weather such as that!"

"Ja, Herr Oberstleutnant. Schon richtig!" Reichling's English wasn't very fluent, so he hadn't picked up every word in the broadcast, but he had understood enough to know that the weather was very bad. "No invasion tonight."

The tinny voice continued. "This is the BBC. And now, a few personal messages." Meyer tensed in his chair. The coded messages to the Resistance were beginning. *"C'est la mer rouge quand il saigne.* Trees of summer are the logs of winter. *Nel mezzo del cammin di nostra vita."* Meyer smiled and shook his head. Dante. What will they think of next? *"Les oiseaux ne mangent pas de beurre. Le tigre n'étudie pas le ciel. La tristesse se changera demain en joi. Blessent mon coeur d'une langeur monotone."*

Meyer's head shot up. He pointed his finger at the machine. Reichling stopped it. Meyer made a small circle with his index finger, and Reichling understood. He rewound the wire and started the machine again. "—*se changera demain en joi. Blessent mon coeur d'une langeur monotone.* The—"

Reichling snapped the machine off and looked at Meyer. His eyes bulged. "*Herr Oberstleutnant,* the message!" he said breathlessly. Meyer was quivering with excitement. The second part of the poem had been transmitted. If the Abwehr's information had been correct, it meant that the invasion would begin within twenty-four hours.

"*Feldwebel,* call up *General* von Salmuth at once!" Reichling leaped to his feet and ran into Meyer's office.

Meyer looked back at the machine. Slowly he rewound the wire by hand and pushed the play button. I must hear it one more time, he thought. It is unbelievable that I have actually heard what I have waited for six months to hear.

The tinny speaker crackled again. "*—demain en joi. Blessent mon coeur d'une langeur monotone.* The falcon—" Meyer mechanically turned the machine off.

Then he paused. What was that I heard? he wondered. With his index finger he revolved the spools backward once more. Once again he turned the machine on.

"*Blessent mon coeur d'une langeur monotone.* The falcon captures the eagle at two on the fifth."

Meyer shut off the wire recorder. For a week, there had been none of the mysterious messages about eagles and falcons. He remembered how puzzling they had been, and the interest that Colonel Knochen had shown in them. One final time Meyer rewound the wire and listened. Yes, he thought, my English is not perfect, but I have not made a mistake.

The fact that another mysterious message had been transmitted right after the signal for the invasion alarmed Meyer. Knochen had been correct. There was perhaps a connection between the unsolved cipher and the dispatches about the eagle. What could it be, Meyer asked himself?

Reichling's head appeared in the doorway of Meyer's office.

"*Herr Oberstleutnant*, the call is through." Meyer got up, walked into his office, and took the phone.

"What is all this uproar?" Meyer recognized the voice of Lieutenant General Rudolf Hofman, Chief of Staff to General von Salmuth.

"*Herr Generalleutnant*, the invasion is coming! We have intercepted the crucial message!"

There was a pause at the other end of the line. "*Herr Oberstleutnant*, have you gone mad?"

"No, *Herr General*—"

"There is no invasion! You have been in your bunker too long. You should take a look outside at the weather!"

"But, *Herr Generalleutnant*, my reports are that—"

"Never mind, *Herr Oberstleutnant!* I will tell the General when he finishes his bridge game." The phone clicked and went dead. Meyer slowly hung up the receiver. He looked up and saw Reichling standing expectantly in the doorway. Meyer shrugged.

"I have told them, but they do not believe me." Reichling stared at him. "Go back to your desk, *Feldwebel*, and finish your transcriptions."

Reichling left and Meyer collapsed in his chair. Emotionally he vacillated between excitement and dejection. The Verlaine lines had been predicted too accurately not to be true, and that excited him. The eagles and falcons had gone undeciphered too long, and the Wehrmacht staff would not listen to him, all of which depressed him.

He looked down at the dispatch in front of him, the first in the series which he had not decoded:

EWPS EHWP ITQQ EWJD SHGW JBRP WJ

For days Meyer had stared at the message, not knowing where to begin. Certain things did seem clear to him. The code text w was most likely the letter E. There were five w's, and E had the highest frequency of any letter in French. The message was too short to rely absolutely on frequency patterns, Meyer knew, but substituting E for W was at least a starting point. E nearly always follows a consonant, and one of the most common in French was L, because both *le* and *les* started that way. Here again Meyer became stuck. W in the code text was followed by E, H, G, and P. Unless the cipher used a sliding substitution, one of those letters could be plaintext L, but not all of them. And Meyer knew that the codes used between the Allies and the Resistance were so simple that a sliding substitution was unlikely.

He glanced at his notes. There were three E's, P's, and J's in the message, two H's, Q's, and S's, and one each of B, D, G, I, K, and T. Thirteen letters—A, C, F, L, M, N, O, R, U, V, X, Y, and Z—were completely absent. It was frustrating. In a twenty-six-letter message, only thirteen letters appeared, and one of those appeared five times. He shook his head. There was no pattern.

Meyer thought some more. If his hunch was right, the words *eagle* and *falcon* had to appear somewhere. He went back to his worksheet and rewrote the message:

EWPSEHWPITQQEWJDSHGWJBRPWJ

Something did seem unusual. E and W were clustered together three times: EWP, EHWP, and EWJ. If indeed E stood for plaintext L, the EWP and EWJ clusters could be variations for *les,* the plural definite article. But he knew no word, and no construction, in French that substituted another consonant between L and an E. He paused. All of the English messages had referred to *the* eagle and *the* falcon. If this message was related to the mysterious Allied broadcasts, as Meyer was virtually certain it was, the key words would be singular and not plural. Thus, *les* or *des* would not be in the message at all. Meyer sighed. If only this were in German, he said to himself, it would be easy.

Then it struck him. If indeed these messages were from members of the Wehrmacht, they would most likely be in German. His pencil hovered above the page. The most common words in German were *der*, *die*, and *das*. *Der* contained an E surrounded by two consonants, even when it declined down the cases to *des*, *dem*, and *den*. Under the EWP and the EWJ he cautiously wrote the letters DER and DEN.

The moment he had done so, another idea came into his head. *Adler* and *Falke* were both masculine words. They both took *der*. Meyer pushed his pencil across the page and looked at his work:

    EWPSEHWPITQQEWJDSHGWJBRPWJ
    DERADLER   DENFALKEN

Meyer's heart beat faster as he substituted the repeated letters throughout the message:

    EWPSEHWPITQQEWJDSHGWJBRPWJ
    DERADLER   DENFALKEN   REN

It seemed too simple, yet something deep inside Meyer's subconscious told him he was correct. He feverishly shuffled through the papers on his desk until he found the transcriptions of the Allied broadcasts. He read them again: "The falcon will fly after the eagle" and "The falcon swoops to the sand." The new message, the one he had just heard, had said, "The falcon captures the eagle at two on the fifth." Meyer pondered the messages. All of them were about eagles and falcons. Birds? he asked. Why birds? He remembered his earlier thinking that the messages suggested an airdrop. An airdrop meant a rendezvous. A rendezvous meant the establishment of a time and a place. He looked back at the coded message and the answer became blindingly clear. He wrote out the final words:

    EWPSEHWPITQQEWJDSHGWJBRPWJ
    DERADLERMUSSDENFALKENHOREN

Meyer then separated the words:

DER ADLER MUSS DEN FALKEN HOREN

The eagle must hear the falcon. Meyer thought for a moment. That was what the English broadcasts were about. The eagle must be the conspirators in the Wehrmacht, asking the Allies, who must be the falcon, to name a time and place for a meeting.

Meyer picked up the phone. As the switchboard operator put through his call, he chuckled. It had been child's play. The code had not been designed to remain hidden, the way most codes are, but instead to be discovered. Yet he would never have deciphered the message if the Allies hadn't repeated their part of the conversation right after the poetry by Verlaine.

Finally, a voice came on the other end of the phone. Meyer muttered something to him. In a moment, someone else picked up the phone and offered a disinterested salutation. Meyer's voice crackled as he spoke.

"This is Meyer. Good news, *Herr Standartenführer!* I have cracked the cipher!"

10

Sunday the fourth of June was a foul day. In midafternoon, Tim headed for Norfolk House in a hard-driving rain. The streets of London filled as the gutters clogged with dirty water. The sky echoed with low, rolling peals of thunder, and massive blue-gray swirls of clouds raced across the sky, dumping their unwelcome loads of rain the same way that the huge Allied bombers had been sweeping over the towns of France and Germany. Although it was only fourteen hundred hours, it was dark enough to have been night. Tim pulled his soaked trench coat more tightly around himself as he emerged from Duke of York Street into St. James's Square, turned right, and headed for the doors of Norfolk House.

Beauclerk was waiting for him just inside. He wore his full uniform and a mackintosh. In each hand he carried a fat briefcase. "There you are, lad. We'll be late if we aren't off right away."

Tim shook the water from his eyes and looked around. The halls were empty. The whole building had the eerie atmosphere of a hotel late at night, or of a summer resort in September when all the paying guests have gone home. "We still on?"

Beauclerk looked through the panes in the doors at the sheets of water which rolled off the cornices of Norfolk House and crashed on the pavement. "The landings have been postponed, lad. Word just came down a few hours ago."

"Until when?"

Beauclerk looked at Tim. "The sixth, hopefully. The orders have gone out to the ships."

"What do we do?"

"We go. There's no time to change the rendezvous. You'll have to use your wits and improvise." He glanced at Tim. "Well, it never was supposed to be a picnic, eh? Come on. Take this."

Beauclerk handed Tim one of the briefcases. He opened the door and pointed to the jeep idling at the curb, sending dense white clouds of exhaust into the wet air. "That's ours, lad. Dash for it."

Tim ran across the pavement and leaped into the back seat. Beauclerk followed him. He shut the flimsy metal door and plopped the briefcase onto the floor. "All right, sergeant."

"Wait a minute."

Beauclerk turned to Tim, puzzled. "What's wrong? Forgotten something?"

"You might say." Tim didn't know how to phrase his request. "I wondered if . . . uh . . . well, sir, if we might make a quick stop along the way."

"Where?"

"Chandos Place. It's not far from here."

Beauclerk turned and waved to the driver. "Out of the question. All right, driver."

Tim impulsively put his hand on Beauclerk's arm. "Please. It'll only take a minute, and it's awfully important."

Beauclerk motioned to the driver, who shifted the jeep back into neutral. He turned and looked at Tim harshly. "You want to see your friend, don't you?"

"Yeah, I thought it might be kind of a good idea."

"Don't, major." Beauclerk was serious, and his voice was full of warning. "Take my word for it. Don't."

"I haven't seen her in two days—"

"Loftis." Beauclerk stared at him. Tim had never seen him so solemn. "We can't go there."

There was something in his voice that clicked in Tim's mind. "Why not?"

Beauclerk turned quickly and waved at the driver. "Go on, sergeant!" He was getting impatient.

As the driver put the car into gear and started off, Tim looked directly at Beauclerk, who avoided his stare. "What is it? Something's happened. What?"

For a long moment Beauclerk said nothing. Then he turned slowly to Tim and said very quietly, as if to calm him, "You don't want to know, lad." His eyes pleaded with Tim not to pursue the matter. "You don't want to know, so don't ask me."

"The hell I don't! What's happened to her? Goddammit!" Tim grabbed the back of the front seat and whipped his body around so that he faced Beauclerk. "What's happened?"

Beauclerk regarded him for a moment, then turned to the driver. He spoke quietly. "Chandos Place, please, sergeant."

The driver veered off St. James's Square and shot up Charles II Street. Tim looked at Beauclerk. He seemed to be made of stone.

The jeep turned left up Haymarket, then zigzagged onto Orange Street. Tim looked at the water washing across the windows. It caught the green afternoon light and seemed to swirl in his eyes, increasing the rhythm of his already rapid heartbeats. At Whitcomb Street, the driver turned left, then turned left quickly again into Chandos Place. He stopped the jeep and dropped it into neutral.

Beauclerk looked at Tim blankly. "I wasn't going to tell you, lad. But maybe it's better you know."

Tim looked frantically out of the front window. The tiny street was empty except for a large black van at the curb in front of the doorway to Pru's flat. Three bobbies stood near the truck, shivering under their ponchos.

Tim grabbed for the door handle, flung it up, pushed the door open, and jumped onto the pavement. Images of Pru raced through his mind as his stomach knotted. His feet suddenly weighed a thousand pounds each as he tried to sprint down the slippery sidewalk. He saw her again in his mind's eye, that quick smile at the St. Giles the night they met, the snow dusting her hair when he'd first kissed her standing on those cold basement steps, her laughter, her lovely brown eyes, the warmth of her body clinging to him. The rain crept under his coat, chilling him and increasing his panic.

In a minute he was at the door. One of the bobbies held out his arm. "Sorry, sir, you can't go in."

Tim tried to push past the arm as if it were a turnstile. The bobby grabbed him with both hands, and one of the other policemen ran over to help restrain him. "What is it? What's happened?" Tim asked.

The bobby gave him a mechanical smile. "Nothing, sir. Routine investigation, that's all."

Tim shook his head frantically, oblivious of the water which poured down the back of his neck. From behind him came Beauclerk's voice, cool and deliberate.

"It's all right, officer. I'm Brigadier Beauclerk from Allied Intelligence." There was a pause. "Are we too late?"

There was no need for the bobby to answer. The door opened and two civilians emerged. Tim knew at once that they were detectives. One of them held the door while a bobby emerged, his right arm handcuffed to a man who followed him. The man wore no expression, his blue eyes staring straight ahead from behind wire spectacles.

After them emerged another bobby, handcuffed to Pru. With a shout of anguish Tim tried to break past the bobbies, but they held him firmly. Her face was ashen. Her eyes were glazed. Her jaw was clenched. When she saw Tim, her lips parted and a choked, sobbing sound emerged. She shut her eyes and turned her head over her left shoulder to avoid his gaze.

The bobby gently pulled her along the sidewalk toward the van.

"Pru!" Tim yelled. She didn't look at him. "Christ, Pru, what is it?" He turned to the policemen who held him. Their expressions were blank. He looked back at the van, just in time to see Pru step into the back. She took one resigned look at him and mounted the steps. The plainclothes policemen climbed in after her. The third bobby locked the doors and walked around to the driver's seat.

"There, sir, it's all right, sir. Merely routine it is, sir." Tim felt their grips loosen slightly. When they realized he was not going to interfere, they let go completely and got into the van. In a moment it started up and pulled away.

Tim stood there in the rain and stared after them. He felt ill and faint. He looked at Beauclerk, about fifteen feet behind him, smoking a cigarette and completely ignoring the rain that rolled off his cap and onto his shoulders. Weakness overcame Tim, and he wanted to vomit. He closed his eyes and breathed deeply a few times. When he opened them, he saw Beauclerk staring at him. The Scot exhaled a cloud of blue smoke and spoke calmly. "Ready, lad?"

Tim shook his head a few times. "What? What was that?"

"She's a spy."

The words hit Tim like a sledgehammer. "She's what?"

"A spy. For the Germans." Beauclerk flicked his cigarette into the gutter where the stream of rushing water picked it up and floated it rapidly along the curbside until it was out of sight. "Come along."

Tim shuffled slowly toward the jeep which had pulled up where the van had been standing. He climbed in, still shaking his head slowly. Beauclerk walked around to the other side of the vehicle and got in. He leaned over the front seat, whispered something to the driver, and sat back. The jeep took off.

After a long minute Beauclerk spoke. "I only found out myself yesterday. I didn't tell you. I didn't want to because of everything you had to worry about. As luck would have it, her rendezvous with her contact was at the same time as our departure." He looked out of the window and sighed. "Sorry you had to see it."

Tim sat frozen in the back seat. "What's she done?"

"Counterintelligence and Scotland Yard have been tracing that chap you just saw for a couple of months. He's a German agent. Name of Nils van der Moorge. Actually he's Dutch, but that doesn't matter. He was airdropped into Scotland last winter, and we've only now caught up with his circle of contacts."

For the first time since Tim had known him, Beauclerk's sense of humor was completely absent. He reached nervously for another cigarette and lit it, spat out the smoke, and coughed. "Did you know she was married?"

Tim nodded.

"Well, at least she told the truth part of the time." He took another draw on his cigarette. "Her husband's alive, apparently, in a POW camp in Poland. German Intelligence found out somehow that she worked with us. Van der Moorge's job was to blackmail her. Information about the invasion in exchange for her husband's life. Nasty business."

"How do you know?"

"We picked up one of van der Moorge's men yesterday. He talked quite a bit."

Tim's anger burst and he slammed his fist against the metal side of the jeep. Beauclerk watched him do it. "All right, lad. I know how you feel."

"How the hell could you? You haven't just been kicked in the balls by a traitor!"

"Wait a minute, lad. We don't know much yet. All we know is that van der Moorge's been to see her a few times. She may not have told him a thing. She may be innocent."

"That makes me feel a lot better!"

Beauclerk rolled his tongue in his cheek. "I know, it hurts. Always does." He glanced at Tim and saw that he was still sitting rigidly in the seat. "So far the only evidence against her is that she didn't report it when van der Moorge first contacted her. She may have led him a dance, you know."

Tim grunted. "Yeah, she might've. She's good at that." He shifted in his seat, withdrew his left hand from his pocket, and wiped the water from his face. His mind was a whirl. He thought of Pru, then suddenly remembered his meeting with Hardaway a few days before. "Christ, you never know, do you? Some people turn out to be okay, and some turn out to be heels. What'll they do to her?"

Beauclerk shrugged. "That depends on a great many things. If she fed him wrong information, she'll be up for a severe reprimand and a discharge, I'd imagine. If she's lucky. She would have done the right thing the wrong way. If she fed him crucial information . . ."

"Then what?"

"She'll hang." Beauclerk stared at Tim. "A lot depends on what I say, lad. If I tell the judge that she only used bad judgment under stress, that may save her."

"Christ, what does it matter?"

"It matters a great deal. We'll see what she says and what she admits to. You know, it's not just a matter of justice. There's more than that at stake."

"Like what? The honor of Merrie Olde England?"

"Don't be so bloody cantankerous!" Beauclerk shouted. "You're a fine one to be flippant! What will you do if she's told them about Solstice?"

Tim looked up quickly. He hadn't thought about that.

"You see the problem, then?"

"What do we do now?"

"I'll ask you that question. Do you want to cancel?"

Tim frowned. "God, I can't do that! Not after all we've done, and what it might mean."

"If she's told them, you'll be a sitting duck. If the Gestapo gets hold of you, they won't be gentle. And if they get you to tell the Overlord plans, the whole operation will go up in flames."

"What if she's already told the Germans about Overlord?"

Beauclerk nodded grimly. "There's no evidence yet that she

[185]

has. No troop movements, not yet. Let's pray the Germans aren't setting a bloody good trap."

They were out of downtown London by this time, heading northeast toward Harlow. The stiff winds and rain kept their speed down to forty miles an hour. Tim and Beauclerk fell silent in the back seat. Tim's thoughts whirled but kept returning to Pru. Was she truly caught in the middle, had she lied to the Dutchman, and, most important of all, had she told the Germans about Solstice?

"Well, lad, what do you think?"

"About what?"

"The drop. Do you still make it?"

"Sure. No other way."

"Good boy. I think so, too." He winked. "How do you feel?"

"Like hell."

"I mean about the drop?"

"Christ, I'll only know it's really happening when the plane starts roaring down the runway. And that's when I'll get scared."

In a moment Beauclerk spoke. "You're right, lad. It's only when it's on you that you know what you're made of. I'll be scared as well. Not in the same way, perhaps, but I'll be scared."

Tim thought for a minute of the troops who would hit the beaches and of the fear that must grip them when the flat fronts of the landing craft dropped and they rushed right into the face of machine-gun fire. "We'll all be scared."

The procession of black Mercedes 170 staff cars advanced slowly through the crowded village streets. The large headlights stared like gigantic eyes as they caught the falling rain. The cars went through on the main road from Évreux, then turned up the long driveway lined by linden trees that led to the château of La Roche-Guyon.

The three cars circled slowly in the outer courtyard. They

came to a stop opposite the double oaken doors that led to the main hallway of the old castle. Simultaneously all the doors on the cars opened.

As he alighted and drew his trench coat tightly around himself to protect himself from the pelting rain, Major Josef Kreitzl motioned sharply to the ten black-shirted Sipo officers. They followed Kreitzl up the stone steps of the building, steps worn down by centuries of suppliant feet which had come to beg audience with the Dukes of la Rochefoucauld. Kreitzl motioned to one of the lieutenants. He grabbed the wrought iron handles on the doors and flung them open.

The surprised sentries who had been sitting casually at the heavy tables set against the dank gray walls of the gloomy hallway leaped to their feet. Kreitzl walked over to both of them.

"*Sicherheitspolizei! Wir mussen mit dem Generalfeldmarschall reden!*"

The terrified officer of the watch, a young, pimpled Wehrmacht master sergeant who could barely have reached the age of twenty, shook his head helplessly. "The *Generalfeldmarschall* has left for Herrlingen, *Herr Sturmbannführer.*"

"When?"

The master sergeant licked his lips nervously. "This morning, *Herr Sturmbannführer.* At seven."

Kreitzl stared at the soldiers, then stepped back from them. He looked down the hallway. Although it was only late afternoon, the offices of the castle appeared deserted. Perhaps it was only his own anxiety, but Kreitzl thought that everything seemed suspiciously quiet.

When the phone call from Knochen in Paris had reached Kreitzl an hour before, he had been in his office in Caen, going over the daily reports of the Resistance activity. The news that the Wehrmacht Command Post of the Fifteenth Army had finally broken the mysterious cipher had been welcome news indeed.

Kreitzl had felt a flush of eagerness as Knochen had read the messages to him.

Knochen's orders had been specific. Kreitzl turned to the young master sergeant. "*Herr Oberst* von Frickstein?"

"In Herrlingen also, *Herr Sturmbannführer.*"

Kreitzl grunted. He had expected as much. He turned to the men he had brought with him. "*Herr Obersturmführer,* seize the transmission records. *Herr Hauptsturmführer,* gather the remaining high-ranking officers together. I wish to speak with them." Kreitzl watched the group of Sipo officers as they marched down the hallway.

Kreitzl turned back to the master sergeant and pointed to the telephone. "Get Herrlingen on the line, *bitte.*" The young soldier picked up the phone and nervously talked with the operator.

Kreitzl turned and walked to the front doors, which remained flung open. He looked up at the stormy skies. It is impossible, he thought, that the Allies would attempt an airdrop in such weather. He had examined the Luftwaffe weather reports before leaving Caen, and a maximum ceiling of only 200 meters was predicted throughout the night.

The master sergeant muttered something in a soft voice. Kreitzl turned and walked to the phone.

"*Ja? Wer spricht?*" he said.

From the other end of the line came a woman's voice, "*Hier spricht Frau Rommel. Wer ist da?*"

"*Sicherheitspolizei!*" There was a silence on the other end. Kreitzl strained to hear any trace of fear in the woman's voice as he asked to speak with her husband. He is not here now, she explained, he has gone hunting. Kreitzl paused upon hearing that, and then told her to have the field marshal telephone his headquarters as soon as he returned. She promised she would, and Kreitzl hung up.

He picked up the phone again. The operator clicked on.

"*Sicherheitspolizei Hauptquartier in Caen, bitte!*" The phone clicked, then clicked again. In a moment Kreitzl heard the dull whirring as the phone rang repeatedly at his office 135 kilometers away. Finally a voice answered.
"*Hier Sturmbannführer Kreitzl.*"
The tired voice at the other end came alive. "*Ja, Herr Sturmbannführer?*"
"New orders from Sipo in Paris. Round up the suspected Resistance wireless operatives in all the coastal sectors."
There was surprise in the voice. "That means many arrests, *Herr Sturmbannführer*. How soon?"
"At once!" Kreitzl barked. "Detain them at the Sipo bureau in Carentan. We have much information to obtain."

It was after 1700 hours when the jeep turned down the long dirt road which led to Fershfield. The rain still came down, but patches of white light showed through the purple and gray storm clouds.
They stopped at the guardhouse. There was no sound except for the low rumble of the engine, the slapping of the windshield wipers, and the patter of rain on the canvas roof. The guard looked in, and the driver showed him the identity cards and the orders. The jeep started up again and continued down the muddy, rutted road until it stopped at the low shed that served as a terminal.
Beauclerk and Tim climbed out of the jeep and grabbed their briefcases. They ran inside, slipping on the caked mud which filled the areas in front of the main doors. Inside it was wet and chilly. Dim bare bulbs strung along two pipes hanging from the ceiling gave the only illumination. Tables and benches strewn about the main room were empty. Only a few personal items lying about— magazines, ponchos, cigarettes, hats—gave any evidence that human beings used the desolate shack.

Desolate, except for one figure sitting at the far end of the room who now got up and walked toward them. As his face emerged from the shadows, Tim recognized Captain O'Neill-Butler, and Beauclerk flashed him a smile. "Hello, captain. Been here long?"

"A few hours, that's all, sir. Do you have everything?"

"Right here." Beauclerk patted the briefcase in his hand.

"Very good, sir. Major Southerne has said that we could use his office. This way, sir. Hello, Major Loftis," he added, almost as an afterthought. "All set?"

"Yeah, guess so."

From outside came the sound of an airplane engine coming to life. It sputtered, then whined, and Tim could hear the dull thumping as the blades cut into the gusty winds. Another engine started. As Tim walked past a small window, he stopped to look out. Through the beads of water the plane's lights gleamed, and dim shadows scurried about. In a minute, the plane wheeled and bounced away from Tim. At the far end of the runway, it turned, hesitated, and started revving up. The beating of the propellers grew louder. Then Tim saw the lights heading toward the hut. It seemed as though the plane were going to crash right through the wooden building when it gently rose. In a second it passed overhead with a tremendous roar and then flew off into the wet night.

"Loftis?" Tim turned and saw Beauclerk standing in the doorway to a small room at one end of the building.

"Coming." Tim grabbed his briefcase and crossed the room. As he got near the small doorway, the double doors which led to the runway opened and, amid a blast of wind, three men in rain suits came rushing in, dripping wet. They were lucky, Tim thought. They had to go out in the rain only a few times an hour. He would be out in it all night.

He entered what was obviously an officer's hideaway. Maps

dotted the walls, and a small blackboard stood in one corner. The large desk set in the middle of the room was strewn with maps, flight plans, logs, graphs, and manuals. A small Union Jack on a wooden stand was in use on the desk as a paperweight.

Beauclerk sat on the edge of the desk, emptying his briefcase. O'Neill-Butler was at a small table pushed up against the far wall. On it was another open case and next to it, on the floor, was a large knapsack. Beauclerk looked up at Tim, then motioned for him to sit down on the falling-apart upholstered chair set opposite the desk.

"All right, lad. Here we are—your passbook and other identifying papers." He handed Tim the same brown envelope which he had thumbed through a week earlier at Norfolk House. "And here's your watch." It was an old round-faced watch which appeared to be at least fifty years old. A LeCoultre.

"What's this for?"

"Part of your cover. Can't very well go in wearing a Bulova, can you?" Tim nodded and stripped off his own watch. He gave it to Beauclerk, who threw it into the briefcase.

"One thing about this watch." Beauclerk snapped open the back. Nestled in among the gears and mainspring was a white pill. "Potassium cyanide. One hard chomp and it will be all over." Tim took the watch, stared at the harmless-looking pellet for a moment, then snapped the back shut and strapped the watch on his wrist.

Turning to O'Neill-Butler, Beauclerk said, "Captain?"

O'Neill-Butler walked over to Tim's chair. "Thank you, sir. Major, here are your ciphers. There are three of them. The first, marked Chelsea, you will use when you make contact with the Resistance. It's not to be used after oh-six-hundred hours on D-Day morning. The second, marked Wimbledon, is to be used only after you make definite verbal contact with the German officers. The third, which is called Bloomsbury, is to be used for all other messages. Is that clear?"

"Simple reason for that, lad," Beauclerk said. "Chelsea's simple, and it's fast. That will be an asset in the dark and when you're rushed. But it's similar to some of our field codes, and we don't want to confuse our receivers when we're in full battle."

O'Neill-Butler went on. "Wimbledon is double-process and takes more time, but if you get to Rommel, you should have time enough to use it. If we get a message in it, we'll assume you've made contact no matter what the message says. Bloomsbury's also double-process, but it belongs to you alone. If we get a message in it before oh-six-hundred day after tomorrow morning, or after we've gotten any in Wimbledon, we'll know you've been caught.

"Now, if you're in a pinch, use the appropriate code, but sign off with one of the other code names. It won't matter which one. If you transmit in Chelsea, and say that you're Bloomsbury, we'll know you're caught.

"It would be best, major," O'Neill-Butler added, "if you memorize the ciphers as quickly as possible and destroy these cards."

O'Neill-Butler walked over to the table and returned with the knapsack. He set it on the desk and opened it. "In here are your civilian clothes. When you land, wait half an hour before changing into them. You're not a spy until you're out of uniform. There are two changes here. One consists of a pair of new wool pants with a bright red-checked shirt. Wear that one first. In case of a delay, in which case a description of you may be broadcast, switch to the other, which is more nondescript. You have toiletries as well, including this." He withdrew a straight-edge razor. "Know how to handle one of these?"

"Well, I tried one once."

"I don't have to tell you to be careful, then," O'Neill-Butler said. "If a description of you does go out, shave your mustache."

Beauclerk held up a finger. "Don't forget the razor, lad. It makes a good weapon."

"Now, major, we've given you two radios. The first is buried underneath the clothes in the knapsack. The second is smaller and is inside a doorknob mechanism in the tool kit we placed in the outside pocket of the sack. After all, you are a locksmith."

Beauclerk grunted, then smiled wryly. O'Neill-Butler glanced at him quickly, then continued with his monotone delivery. "Also at the bottom of the knapsack is a Colt .45, Belgian manufacture, automatic, with five clips of ammunition and a double-edged commando knife.

"I think that's all, brigadier," he said to Beauclerk and then turned back to Tim. "I suggest, major, that you go through this material before takeoff."

"Thank you, captain," Beauclerk said. "Put your papers in the red-checked shirt, lad, and the money in the pants pocket. Save you searching for them in the dark. Here." He reached into the briefcase and withdrew a large brown envelope with a bright purple seal on the flap. "Here are your orders. You'll open these after you're on the airplane and not before. Destroy them after you've read them. They contain the passwords you'll use with the Resistance as well as with the U.S. Eighty-second and Hundred and first Airborne divisions. They'll be coming into your sector tomorrow night, so you might run across them. Don't reveal yourself to them unless you absolutely have to, or if you're with Rommel. Finally, there's a schedule of your transmission times. We'll expect to hear from you at those times if at all possible. Any questions?" Tim shook his head. "All right, lad, we've done all we can. Your plane is scheduled to take off at twenty-one forty-five hours. Your drop time is in your orders. It's eighteen thirty-five hours now. Captain, see what you can do about getting us something to eat."

O'Neill-Butler nodded and left the room. Tim watched him go, then turned to Beauclerk, feeling anxious and disoriented. "What do we do now?" he said with a boyish grin.

Beauclerk got up, pulled the small table in front of where Tim sat, took the chair from behind the desk, set it on the far side of the table, reached into his briefcase, pulled out a deck of cards and a cribbage board, sat down, and started to deal.

"We wait."

The wind was howling furiously outside the stone farmhouse near Saint-Sauveur-le-Vicomte, and the fire in the elaborate Norman fireplace did little to kill the chilly dampness which seemed to seep into the building through the chinks in the walls.

It mattered little to Jacques Boisseau what the temperature inside his farmhouse was like. What mattered more was what the fierce rain and winds would do to the scheduled airdrop that his orders from his Resistance *réseau* had told him to meet. As he poked the fire underneath the heavy cast-iron pot which contained the supper for him and his wife, Jacques's mind was on little else but his late-night rendezvous.

His stomach felt heavy as he sat down at the table opposite Marie-Louise, his wife of twenty-four years. He had no appetite for the *ragoût d'agneau* before him. There was little conversation between Jacques and Marie-Louise as they ate their small repast. The only sound in the darkened farmhouse kitchen was the clunking of the wooden spoons against the dishes.

A faint tinkling came from the next room. Jacques looked up, then pulled out his pocket watch to check the time. Yes, he thought, it is nine o'clock. In an hour he would have to leave, for it would take all of another hour for him to bicycle the twenty or so kilometers to the drop site between Sainte-Mère-Église and the beach at Ravenoville. It would be a long ride to get to such a desolate place, although Jacques fully understood the necessity for such isolation. He could think of no more lonely or unimportant stretch of coastline than Ravenoville. There would be little chance for the Germans to see the flares he would stake out so that the parachutist could see where he was going.

Jacques finished his wine and walked over to the woodbin near which lay his knapsack containing his crystal set and some flares. That would be all he would need. He went to the cupboard near the stove and took out a small bottle of Calvados, intending to stuff it into the sack. After a long lonely drop from the skies, his contact would probably need something to warm him up.

Headlights appeared against the thick bottle-glass panes in the windows of the Boisseau farm. They swung in patterns across the ceiling. Jacques went to the window and looked out. He uttered a short cry and dropped the brandy bottle, which smashed on the stone floor. The brown liquid bubbled as it flowed along the chinks and cracks. Marie-Louise rose when she heard the slamming of car doors and the sounds of running feet heading toward the house.

In another instant the door burst open. Silhouetted against the doorway by the headlights, as the curtain of rain falling behind him danced in the refractions of light, stood a German officer. He glanced quickly around the room.

"Jacques Boisseau?" he said in gutteral French. Jacques nodded. The officer barked out commands in German. Two black-shirted Gestapo soldiers pushed past their commander into the kitchen. They grabbed Jacques and roughly put handcuffs on him.

Marie-Louise screamed. The SS lieutenant gave her a contemptuous look. When she screamed again, he strode across the room to deliver a sharp slap with the back of his hand. She moaned and put her hand to her mouth, to stop the flow of blood that trickled from her lips. The officer turned back and motioned to the soldiers to remove Jacques. As they passed him, he walked over to the woodbin where Jacques had been standing, picked up the knapsack, and quickly examined the contents. The soft light of the fire caught his smile as he removed the bundle of flares. He grunted, then put them back into the knapsack and slung it over his shoulder. He walked to the front door, with a quick glance at Marie-Louise, and left, slamming the door behind him.

Cowering, her knees buckling, Marie-Louise could hear his

footsteps crunch across the gravel. She heard a few more muffled commands in German, car doors slamming, and a crunch as the car pulled away. As when it had arrived, the headlights of the car careened across the beamed ceiling of the farmhouse and disappeared into the night.

Then there was no sound except for the ticking of the clock over the mantel in the living room, the patter of the rain, and the crackle of the logs. And the sound of Marie-Louise falling in a faint to the cold stone floor.

11

These have been the longest three hours I've ever spent, Tim thought, as he pegged off six points on the cribbage board. He picked up the loose pack of cards and threw them down on the table in front of Beauclerk. "Here, your deal."

Beauclerk picked up the cards and shuffled them. "Ten points and you're out. I've got some work to do."

Tim smiled wearily. As he picked up his cards, he looked at the electric clock on the wall. It read nine thirty.

"Nervous?"

Tim turned to Beauclerk. "Huh? Oh, no, Christ, no. Bored." He threw his two cards into the crib and stretched. Through the open door he heard voices and the stamping of feet in the flight room. The double doors slammed a few times. Maybe they're getting my plane ready, he thought. He played his cards absentmindedly. When the time to count came, he looked at his hand for the first time. Fifteen-two, fifteen-four. O'Neill-Butler's head popped through the door.

"We're ready for you, major."

Tim looked up. There it was: the word. He stood up, pulled on his knapsack, and walked over to the chair in the corner to get his poncho.

Beauclerk, who had put on his trench coat and cap, lit a cigarette. "You'll be off in a minute, lad. I don't know what to say to you. Words seem pointless now." He put his hand on Tim's shoulder. "We've had a lot of fun on this caper. Outwitted the rest of G-Two. That alone'll make me happy to my dying day." Beauclerk's eyes twinkled, the prankish schoolboy once again. "Keep your spirits up and don't panic. Keep your wits. And remember." Beauclerk's eyes narrowed as he took a long draw on his cigarette and the smoke curled up into his nostrils. "There's some more of that Pinch waiting in my desk. With your name on it."

Tim suppressed a fleeting urge to cry. He bit his lip instead.

Beauclerk threw both arms around Tim's shoulders and hugged him. Then he headed for the door. "Come on, it's time."

The wind cut into their faces as they walked toward the waiting RAF Halifax. The floodlights from the hut only lit the ground twenty feet from the building. Tim and Beauclerk had to make their way in the dark, through the last ninety feet of mud to the plane. O'Neill-Butler was waiting for them by the door. Tim walked up the three metal steps and clambered aboard. Beauclerk climbed in after him.

Inside, the plane was bare. Two benches ran along either side, and the cockpit was cordoned off with cloth. That was the limit of decor. A small bulb glimmered in the fuselage. Tim drew off his poncho and slipped out of his knapsack. Beauclerk walked up to the cockpit, talked with someone through the curtain for a minute, then walked back to Tim. At that moment an RAF officer stepped into the plane carrying a small canvas valise with him. He looked up at Tim and smiled. "Hello, major. I'm Captain MacDonald."

Tim shook his hand. "Glad to meet you. This is—"

MacDonald's swarthy face broke into a smile. "Brigadier Beauclerk and I are old friends."

"We grew up together in Glasgow. I wouldn't pick anything but the best for you this trip," Beauclerk said to Tim affectionately. "Have everything?"

"Guess so." With a loud crack, one of the right engines of the Halifax burst into life. The whole plane vibrated as the engine revved up. Beauclerk held out his hand.

"Good luck, lad." Then he was gone.

The other engines conked to life, one by one. The field crew pulled away the metal steps and shut the door. Tim sat down on the long bench and fastened his belt. The engines returned to idling speed, then slowly started revving again. The plane moved slowly, then bumped and jerked its way to the end of the runway. It turned and paused. As Tim looked out one of the small portholes and saw the lights of the building through the rain, the engines whined loudly, the plane lurched forward, and in a few seconds they were airborne. Tim leaned back in his seat and rested his head against one of the fuselage struts. In a minute he was asleep.

It was an hour later when MacDonald's gentle shaking roused Tim. "Major, we're getting near the coast of France. Better get set." Tim rubbed his eyes, then started. The aircraft lurched violently as it cut its way through the rain.

"Thank you, captain." Tim shook his head to clear the sleepiness out. He got up and was almost immediately thrown against the wall by a sudden dip of the plane. He leaned down to look out of a porthole, but he could see nothing but rain streaks on the glass. "Christ," he muttered, "how are we going to see a drop zone in this stuff?"

"If it's lit, we'll see it."

"What time is it?"

"Twenty-three thirty hours, sir. About fifteen minutes."

"Thanks." MacDonald walked up the bucking fuselage and disappeared behind the curtain. Tim took his parachute and stepped into it. As he fastened the straps and buckles, he started thinking about what he would do if his contact didn't show up.

Tim finished adjusting the parachute and pulled on his knapsack so that it fit across his chest. He reached into the pocket of his uniform and withdrew the now-crumpled letter which Beauclerk had given him. He ripped it open. The orders said nothing new. He looked down the list of passwords. There were twelve in all, four for the Resistance and eight for the Allied forces. Some of them amused Tim. The 82nd Airborne was to be greeted with Indianapolis, countered with Brooklyn, and counter-countered with DiMaggio. Finally Tim noted his transmission times: 0800,

1200, 1900, and 2400 hours. In addition he was to contact England as soon as he rendezvoused with the Resistance, or to signal that the rendezvous had not been kept, no later than 0300 hours on June 5. Tim glanced back over the orders, memorized the passwords, closed his eyes, recited the passwords, and checked himself. Then he ripped the letter into small strips and let them flutter down to the tin floor of the airplane.

MacDonald looked back from the cockpit. "Six minutes until the drop, major."

"Thanks." Tim said, as he clipped his cord to the pull line of the airplane. The plane hit another pocket of turbulence and bounced jerkily. Tim grabbed an overhead strut and swayed as the plane lurched through the cold air. MacDonald popped his head back through the curtains.

"We're at eleven hundred feet, major, and we should be seeing the flares."

Tim looked out of the window. "I can't see them."

"Neither can I. That's what worries me." The engines of the Halifax suddenly roared with new life and the plane shot upward. Tim was thrown against the wall as the first puffs of antiaircraft fire flashed outside. The plane kept climbing, then sharply banked to port and started hurtling toward the ground. It leveled off somewhat while it kept swinging in a large lazy circle to the left.

MacDonald's head reappeared. "One minute, major. I'm circling now. I'll go through the DZ at nine hundred feet and give you the light."

"Good enough." Tim watched as the bomb bay doors of the Halifax slowly opened near his feet. Through them he could see the ground dimly. The coast of France was a ghostly mass, without form or definition. In the distance he saw a vague cluster of lights. That must be Valognes, he thought. In a second, I'll be leaving this plane and dropping into God-knows-what. The plane suddenly seemed warm, even though he'd been freezing ever since they left Fershfield, because the night outside through the bomb bay doors seemed much colder. Another burst of flak appeared below and to the right of the plane. Tim stepped up to the edge of the doors and quickly went over his parachute rig and his drag line. He looked up at the small red light above the doors and sucked in his breath. His heart was pounding as he waited. The plane lurched down, the engines whined, and the light went out.

In an instant Tim was hurtling through the rain-soaked skies over Utah Beach.

The metal door to the bunker swung open. The Wehrmacht corporal who had opened it came to attention, his right arm stiffened in front of him as two officers came down the narrow steps into the Main Observation Post of the 711th Wehrmacht Division.

Field Marshal Rommel looked around quickly as he took off his drenched field coat. The Main Observation Post was a series of Type 636 shelters built into the Atlantic coast right at the mouth of the River Orne, near Cabourg. The main plotting room where Rommel stood was four and a half meters square, with a low ceiling scarcely two meters high. Along the wall next to him was built a long trestle table on which lay maps, compasses, a few logbooks, and a half-eaten Kaisertorte left over from a birthday celebration that afternoon. In the middle of the room were two architects' drafting tables, converted for use as plotting boards. Despite the dense atmosphere of the bunker, he could hear ever so slightly the sounds of the storm outside as they swept in through the slits in the bunker walls.

Rommel handed his field coat to the corporal, then turned to Colonel von Frickstein. "Well, *Herr Oberst*, we have made it."

"*Ja, Herr Generalfeldmarschall.* It has been a long day."

Rommel smiled weakly and returned his attention to the bunker. Now that he was here, he could breathe a little easier. There were no SS men to plague him and no Sipo motorcycle escorts.

June 4 had been a dangerous day for the field marshal. They had left La Roche-Guyon right on schedule at 0700 hours. Rommel and von Frickstein had made certain that everyone in the garrison had seen them climb into the black Horch together, along with Colonel von Tempelhof and Lang, Rommel's personal chauffeur. Everyone had also seen General Hans Speidel enter the second car in the procession. The three-car motorcade had pulled out of the castle and headed for Paris, just as the itinerary had noted. At Mantes the Sipo escort had met them, two pairs of motorcyclists. As the cars had made their way through the dank morning, with the rain drumming on the metal roof of the Horch, Rommel had watched the guards on their machines, the tires chewing and spitting mud as if it were lentil soup. The Sipo motorcyclists had been the biggest worry of Rommel's plan to slip away to the Atlantic Wall for the rendezvous with the Allied officer.

Everything had gone smoothly. The switch had been made in the forests near Fontainebleau. As the procession had left Melun for Fontainebleau along Route Nationale 5, they had entered the legendary forests. The rain and fog had shrouded the oak and wild pine trees, giving them a supernatural air. Much as the rains had made the roads nearly impassable, Rommel had been thankful for them. The fog had helped to conceal the crucial moment.

It had been swift. At the intersection of Route Nationale 5 and the Route des Hauteurs de la Solle, the Sipo motorcyclists had peeled off to return to Versailles. They had reached the boundaries of their district, and as usual their orders had been to return at once to headquarters. In the few kilometers between that intersection and the château of Fontainebleau, the motorcade was unescorted.

The Horch had suddenly pulled alongside the roadway and come to a stop. The other cars stopped behind it. Lang had leaped out of the car and raised the hood. The other drivers and military attachés had gathered around. It is all very mysterious, Lang had said, but the engine just died. Suddenly. Rommel had reprimanded Lang for being so careless. After a few moments Lang had discovered the problem. The engine was flooded. They would have to wait for ten minutes for the carburators to drain themselves. It was the cursed weather, Lang had said, which had forced him to choke the engines to keep them from dying. Instead, he lamented, this has happened.

Rommel had ordered the motorcade to proceed to Fontainebleau. As an afterthought, he had motioned to General Speidel to stay with him, for he had some important matters to discuss concerning the Atlantic Wall fortifications.

After the last sounds of the two staff cars had faded into the gray fog, a rumble had come from the woods. A ghostly black Mercedes had appeared from the small side road which led toward the Gorges de Franchard. In a moment Rommel and von Frickstein had swung into the back seat, replacing two Wehrmacht soldiers from the staff of General Beck who were dressed in long field coats and one of whom carried the black and gold staff of the field marshal.

From that point it had been relatively easy. To avoid the checkpoints of the Île de France, the Mercedes had gone through Orléans to Châteaudun, Le Mans, Alençon, Argentan, Falaise, and then straight through the heart of Caen. It had passed right below the Château de Caen, where the Sipo garrison was headquartered. From Caen they had driven to Varaville and then Cabourg, finally turning west from Cabourg down the small country roads which led to the bunkers.

As Rommel walked into the officers' quarters, he looked at his watch. It was now five minutes before midnight. Five minutes before 5 June 1944. The day of the rendezvous and perhaps the end of the war in the West.

The sound of von Frickstein entering the room caused Rommel to turn and face him. "Shut the door, *Herr Oberst.* Then show me the dispatches."

Von Frickstein closed the steel door with a clank. The room became unearthly quiet. He pulled a chair close to Rommel, who had just sat down on the bed to remove his boots.

"*Herr Generalfeldmarschall,* bad news. The Sicherheitspolizei have been to La Roche-Guyon today looking for us."

"What did they want?"

"They did not say. They telephoned Herrlingen and spoke with Frau Rommel."

Rommel sighed. It seem so far away, the pleasant little village in the narrow valley, the small white houses with the red-tiled roofs and the window boxes filled with geraniums. And his house, the stone and brick building on the hilltop with the spacious library and the garden, Rommel's pride and joy. It was so peaceful there, he thought.

"You have been requested to telephone your headquarters and Sipo headquarters in Caen."

"What did my wife say to them?"

"That you were out hunting, and that you would call as soon as you returned."

Rommel smiled slightly. Perhaps his wife's little lie had purchased them enough time to complete the rendezvous. "Very good. And what news of the patrol?"

"I telephoned *Generalleutnant* Reichert. The patrols have been sent out in all sectors. His aide assured me that the assignments were made strictly according to the requests which *Generaloberst* Beck sent yesterday."

Rommel nodded his head. "If the Resistance does their part well, the rendezvous should be made."

"*Ja, Herr Generalfeldmarschall,* I think so too."

Rommel looked at his watch. It was now nearly half past twelve. The patrol headed by Captain Schmeling should make contact with the falcon in an hour or so. Rommel stretched out on the cot. It felt good to lie down after all those hours in the car. He turned to von Frickstein. "There is nothing to do now but sleep. And wait."

The drop was a terrifying experience. The pelting rain so stung Tim's face that he was forced to close his eyes most of the way down. Worse, the high winds had pulled and tugged at him, causing him to spin deliriously at times. He felt himself being blown far off course.

The landing was a shock. As his boots sank into the mud at the bottom of a flooded field somewhere inland from Ravenoville beach, Tim struggled desperately to gather in his chute before it got soaking wet and too heavy to handle.

He succeeded to a degree. Pulling ferociously on the rough cords he managed to drag in the drenched silk. It took five minutes of hand-over-hand grasping until the tangle of lines and cloth floated in a circle around him. Tim paused to catch his breath and look around him.

He had no idea where he was. He had memorized the terrain of the drop site well enough to know that he had missed it. The small beams of moonlight which struggled from behind the thick storm clouds furnished only enough light for Tim to see that he was standing knee deep in water that stretched for a vast distance across an unknown field.

He tried to turn around so that he could see what lay behind him, but his feet were so mired that all he could manage was a twisted glance over his shoulder. There seemed to be high ground with a crest of trees to his left, although he couldn't judge how far away it was. As nearly as he could determine by the position of the moon, the ridge lay inland, so he decided to head in that direction. After a moment's thought, he started to stow his chute in the water. In ten minutes he had squeezed the last air bubble out of it, and he watched in the dim light as the red and white silk slowly disappeared.

It took twenty tortured minutes for Tim to reach dry ground. With each agonized step he felt the slime suck at the heavy soaked leather of his boots. Each time he pulled on one foot to take a step, he felt the other one sink even deeper. The water became a swirling enemy, soaking his pants, filling his boots, and making each leg weigh a ton. In one particularly oozy spot Tim struggled desperately to keep from sinking up to his waist. For a few panic-stricken moments he thought that he would drown or, worse, be spotted by a German patrol and machine-gunned to death while he stood helplessly in the mire.

When he finally reached dry ground, Tim dragged himself up to the ridge toward the line of trees. Groaning with exhaustion, he pulled his way underneath a cluster of pine trees. He dropped his knapsack and collapsed, panting, onto the ground, his body immobile.

In a few minutes he felt better. The trees sheltered him from the bite of the driving rain. He looked at his watch. It was 0030 hours. It had been half an hour since he had stepped out of the Halifax. Pulling himself up to a sitting position, Tim opened the knapsack and withdrew the .45. He checked the clip, then set the pistol back inside the knapsack where it would stay dry and still be easy to grasp in a hurry. Next he squeezed the water out of his pants as best he could, and then removed his boots. What seemed like a quart of water cascaded from each one. He found a small tree branch and used it to scrape away a large part of the mud that covered the tops and sides of the boots.

It occurred to Tim that his rendezvous had not been kept. He looked at his watch again, then swore to himself. It was nearly 0100 hours. He had been on the ground for an hour, and there was no sign of his contact. Something was terribly wrong. Tim was torn between staying up in the shelter and concealment of the trees, and going down into the field where he was more likely to be spotted. He thought glumly that the hard rain made any sort of visibility impossible, and that without the flares there was no way for him to find out where he was before daybreak, much less where he should go. He thought back to his orders. He had to signal London that his contact had been made or broken by 0300 hours.

He had four hours to get to Rommel.

By 0130 hours Tim's clothes were completely soaked. His limbs began to ache from fatigue and the cold. He reached inside his knapsack and withdrew the one piece of food he had brought with him, a Van Houten orange milk chocolate bar. He ripped off the paper wrapper and bit into the candy. The sweet flavor seemed to dispel the chill. He finished it slowly, savoring each creamy section.

He looked back at his watch. It was 0215 hours. Tim decided that his rendezvous would not be kept, and that it was time to contact London. He leaned back to his sack and reached underneath the clothing to the bottom. The soft dry wool felt appealing to his wet hands. He touched something cold and hard. Gingerly he withdrew the crystal set.

In a few minutes he had hung the antenna wire from two low-hanging branches and charged up the crystal. As he got ready to transmit he noticed that his fingers were so cold and numb that he could barely feel the metal key. In his mind he ran through the Chelsea encipherment. He closed his eyes as plaintext letters appeared in his mind, and mentally he transcribed them into code. In a few moments he had formulated his message. He pressed the key and heard the first clicks.

He was done in five minutes. If nothing else had gone right, at least he had told London as much. He pulled down the antenna wire and gathered the crystal set together. Carefully he stowed it back in the knapsack. He pulled out the dry clothing and started to strip. The wool pants and bright red-checked *paysan* shirt felt warm next to his drenched skin, even though he knew that in twenty minutes they would be as soaked as his uniform had been. As he adjusted the wool cap on his head, he felt a little shiver. He had crossed over a thin line. He was now a spy.

In another few minutes he had ditched his uniform under a clump of underbrush, swung the knapsack over his back, and scrambled down the slope to the water's edge again. Taking a quick glance at the moon, he estimated as well as he could which way was westward. Skirting the pond he began his long trek toward the nearest village.

The sharp pain from the boot which had just kicked him in the small of the back woke Tim up. Dazed and tired, he opened his eyes slightly. Even though he was lying on his stomach, his head buried in hay, he could tell that daylight had arrived. He grunted.

There was another sharp kick. Tim rolled over quickly onto his back and froze.

Silhouetted against the open barn door, through which Tim could see the stormy sky and the dripping rain, was a sturdy middle-aged French farmer. His face was tanned and lined; his hair hung down in a graying shock over his forehead, matching the bushy mustache which covered his lips. All of that Tim noticed later. What held his attention right away was the pitchfork which the farmer held with both hands, the long pole wavering as he clutched it. The tines were about six inches from Tim's neck.

Tim looked at the man for a minute. The farmer's lips were quivering and his entire body shook with tension, which caused the pitchfork to waver even more. He finally spoke.

"*Qui êtes-vous?*"

Tim hesitated for a moment, then started to raise his hand to assuage the farmer. As he did, the man crouched slightly. Tim stopped. He realized that the farmer was ready to plunge the pitchfork into Tim as if he were little more than a clump of fodder.

"*Arrêtez!*"

Tim remained frozen.

Again the farmer hesitated, then spoke, his thin gravelly voice barely audible above the sound of the rain on the wood and tarpaper roof. "*Qui êtes-vous?*"

"*Il fait mauvais aujourd'hui,*" Tim said, looking intently into the man's eyes, "*mais ça sera bientôt l'été.*"

The gamble with the password paid off. For an instant the farmer stared at Tim, but then he pulled the pitchfork away and stepped back. Tim pulled himself up slightly in the wet mass of hay until he was resting on his elbows. He remembered where he was.

It had been a long and difficult hike through the dark and flooded *bocage* country. The rain had turned most of the fields to mush, those which the Germans hadn't already flooded as protection against airborne assaults. Tim had seen some of the booby traps in the night: tall stakes with sharpened tips, or stakes with trip wires connected to hidden land mines. They had sent shudders through him. What the flooding hadn't done to twist his progress, the hedgerows and isolated farmhouses had. Tim had been forced to walk miles out of his way to cross securely through the wooded stretches of land, rather than be seen going through a farmyard.

The sky had begun to lighten before 0400 hours. Welcome as the daylight had been to Tim after two hours of stumbling through the darkness, brushing into tree branches and tripping in the underbrush, it had brought with it new problems. His mind had rolled with alternative courses of action. In the end he knew he could do one thing, now that the contact had been missed: nothing. Lacking a real knowledge of Resistance *réseaux*, he could only lie low for a day and then meet with the Allied troops when they got inland. With all the rain, Tim knew that it would be a simple matter to keep to the woods during the day and find a dry barn to spend the night in. He had remembered Beauclerk's offer to let him drop out of the mission when they had discovered about Pru. "With no prejudice," he had said.

But that idea rankled. The fact that somewhere nearby a German field marshal was waiting to surrender an entire army and save thousands of lives and shorten the war, if not end it, was too compelling.

It had been just as the daylight was strong enough to define the individual trees along the roadside that Tim had seen the farmhouse. The rain had slackened, but the wind still blew strongly enough to whip his clothes around his wet skin. The farmhouse was on the east side of the road, a low stone and mortar building with wooden shutters drawn tightly over the windows. Rough beams stuck out from beneath the red-tiled roof. Near the main building was a small barn and, farther away, two ancient and broken-down chicken houses. A stone wall ran jaggedly around the perimeter of the small compound.

Tim sat up. The farmer, who was still holding the pitchfork with both hands, was now standing by the doorway, looking out onto the road. At the sound of Tim's movement, he turned around sharply.

"Je m'appelle Jean Robichon," Tim said. The expression on the man's face did not change. *"Je suis de Caen."*

"Que faites-vous ici?"

Tim told him the whole story. He, Jean Robichon, had been to Saint-Vaast-la-Hougue where his wife and crippled daughter were staying with his mother-in-law. It was always difficult for him to get away from Caen, and he often had to make the trip at night. He had gotten a ride from Saint-Vaast-la-Hougue the night before, with a farmer who lived a little past Valognes. He had tried to walk to Sainte-Mère-Église in search of an empty hotel room, but had become too fatigued and cold. He had needed a place to sleep but knew no one. He had found this barn and intended to sleep only a little while and be on his way before anyone awakened.

Tim guessed that the farmer bought the story. *"Voilà,"* Tim said, reaching into his shirt pocket and withdrawing his ancient leather wallet. *"Les photographies de ma famille."* He threw down the pictures Beauclerk had given him onto the dirt floor of the barn.

The farmer walked over and picked them up. Tim noticed that, although the farmer seemed to be in his late fifties, his movements were strong and quick. He looked at the pictures, then back at Tim. Again his face was inscrutable. Tim pulled out his ration and identification cards. The man's eyes flicked up from the cards and pictures. *"Qui est le maire de Sainte-Mère-Église? Connaissez-vous?"*

"Alexandre Renaud," Tim replied without a pause.

The farmer nodded slightly, then smiled. He threw the cards back down onto the dirt. *"Bien, monsieur. Levez-vous."*

Tim gathered in the cards and put them back into his wallet, then replaced it in his shirt. He rose. His joints ached with the chill of the raw morning. He leaned over, grabbed his knapsack, and slung one of the straps over his shoulder.

"Vous avez faim?" the peasant asked. Tim nodded and followed him out of the barn.

The interior of the farmhouse was dark. Tim could make out a few tables and chairs by the dim light of the fire which burned in the stone fireplace at one end of the rectangular building. As he put his knapsack against the wall by the front door, the farmer went around to each wall, throwing the shutters back. The green light flooded in.

The house was one large room. The beams which had extended from underneath the roof on the outside stretched across its width. They were blackened oak, a foot thick, and supported a ceiling of wood that had once been whitewashed. The walls were of the same mortar and stone Tim had noticed from the outside. Their textured surfaces seemed to drip with the moisture of the storm outside.

Near the fireplace was a trestle table. Behind it on the long wall near the fireplace was the kitchen, which was nothing more than a few cupboards, an iron stove, and a counter with a metal sink built into it. There were a few chairs and one hard-backed bench with a cushion on it in corners of the room, along with hurricane lamps set on the tables and in sconces. At the end opposite the kitchen was a ship's companionway which led up to a hole in the ceiling.

The farmer walked to the fireplace and, after stoking the coals with a poker, put on a fresh supply of wood. The fire leaped to life, the fresh wood crackling and giving off a pungent aroma. Then he turned and faced Tim. With his left hand he motioned silently to the table. Tim walked over and sat on one of the stools. The man placed before him a hot mug of café au lait and a few damp croissants.

The steaming liquid gave Tim shudders as it raced down his throat. He devoured the croissants, each bite reawakening his stomach, which had contracted after so many hours in the cold. The farmer watched Tim eat in silence, then took the plate and returned from the cupboards with three more croissants for Tim. They, too, were quickly consumed.

Tim smiled as he finished the last of the bread and coffee. *"Les matins sont très froids."*

The farmer nodded agreement that, yes, the mornings had been cold recently. His eyes continued to study Tim.

Tim had been in the farmhouse for fifteen minutes when he heard footsteps above his head. His eyes shot up to the ceiling and followed the steps as they walked across the wooden floor toward the ladder. Tim looked at his companion, who smiled very slightly, then turned back on his stool so that he could see who was descending the steps.

She was beautiful. She couldn't have been more than eighteen, with long, fine, dark brown hair that hung in tangled swirls nearly to her waist. She wore a russet wool skirt which was wrapped around her waist, fastened with a brown leather belt. Her blouse was of the same heavy woven material. It laced up the front, and where it was open at the neck, Tim could see her finely formed neck and the tops of her round breasts. Her face was long, highlighted by a delicately sculptured nose. Her dark skin set off the whites of her flashing brown eyes.

She stopped at the foot of the stairway when she saw Tim, her eyes huge. Then she ran over to where the farmer sat and put her hands on his shoulders, asking him in her rapid French, Papa, who is this strange man? The man replied that he had been sleeping in the barn and seemed to be a friend.

The French girl glanced at Tim, who noticed how much her eyes resembled those of her father. He grinned at her, trying to release the hold which her icy stare had upon him. *"Bonjour, mademoiselle. Je m'appelle Jean Robichon. Je réside à Caen. Ce matin, je dormais dans la grange de votre père depuis quelques heures, quand—"*

Tim was cut off by the suddenly resonant voice of the farmer. "Tell us, *monsieur*, who you really are."

Josef Kreitzl shifted in his seat and told the driver to go faster. He looked out the car window at the rain-soaked fields. Time was of the essence, and this cursed rainstorm made driving slow and treacherous.

SS Major Kreitzl had been up all night. The entire SS staff in the Normandy district, including the Sipo, had been up all night as well, on his orders. There had been massive roundups of suspected Resistance agents. The phones had clanged for hours, reporting arrests and missing Frenchmen who had somehow managed to slip the traps sent for them. The SS interrogators had been working hard to break the secret of the mysterious code.

Kreitzl himself did not know what to make of the cipher. There was agreement among everyone that it suggested an airdrop.

That in itself meant little. There were airdrops all the time into France, and especially in Normandy, much to Kreitzl's embarrassment, since he had been unable to stop them. All messages between the Resistance and England suggested that this airdrop was, for some reason, special.

The black Mercedes entered the town of Carentan, cruised down the Boulevard de Verdun, and went out again on the northwest edge of the city. The town was quiet. Even though it was raining heavily, the absence of any townspeople on the streets on a Monday, normally a market day, alarmed Kreitzl. His fatigue made him see hobgoblins everywhere.

Two kilometers out of Carentan the Mercedes turned into a gravel driveway which led to a Norman villa set back nearly a kilometer from the highway. A formal courtyard opened onto the woods behind it. The walls and roofs were covered with vines that hung over the windows the way Spanish moss hangs over trees in southern climates.

La Mouette was the headquarters for a unit of the Wirtschaftsverwaltunghauptamt, the Administrative Control of the SS. It was the interrogation center for Normandy.

Kreitzl ran from the car to the entrance door, holding his hat tightly to shield himself from the rain. Inside he proceeded quickly toward the main salon at the rear of the château. The second lieutenant seated at the desk near the closed double doors leading to the salon stood when he saw Kreitzl approach. He tapped lightly on one of the doors and opened it a few inches. He stuck his head inside the room, then withdrew it. Pushing the doors open with both hands, he stood aside with an efficient *"Treten sie bitte ein"* to Kreitzl.

Kreitzl walked into the room and directly over to the desk, behind which sat Heinrich Sammstag, who looked up at him wearily.

"What results, *Herr Sturmbannführer?*" Kreitzl asked.

"There's little to report, I'm afraid. Sit, please." Kreitzl pulled up a chair while Sammstag continued. "We have been interrogating prisoners all night. We are very tired."

"I appreciate that, *Herr Sturmbannführer.*"

"Several of the arrested Frenchmen confessed under torture to being members of the Resistance. They have already been shot. Several more men and women are clearly Resistance operatives, although they have not confessed. About twenty-eight or twenty-nine in number, I think. They are still being questioned. I believe that we will select nine or ten of them and force the others to watch when we shoot them." Sammstag smiled slightly. "However, we have discovered nothing about your code."

"You have used the code words?"

"*Jawohl, Herr Sturmbannführer.* All of them. None of the prisoners have recognized them. Even faintly. I think none of the operatives here will recognize them, either. There have been no messages in the cipher for some time. I do not think that any of these prisoners have used it."

"But what about the messages we intercepted from the Allies?"

"Remember, *Herr Sturmbannführer,* that those messages need not be directed at the same Frenchmen who sent the original messages." Kreitzl nodded glumly. "However, I have some hope to offer you. We arrested one operative last night who had signal flares in his traveling kit."

"What has he said?"

"Little. He unfortunately fainted when we first questioned him. I have been waiting for you before beginning again."

The cellars of La Mouette were dank and moldy. They consisted of a long series of brick archways, perhaps ten feet high at the top. The two German officers stumbled on the lumpy earthen floor. At one intersection Kreitzl heard voices. Down the corridor were bolted wooden doors leading to further vaults that were the cells. A putrid smell hung in the air. As the two men walked down a flight of wooden steps into a large cavernous room lit only by bare light bulbs strung around the walls, Kreitzl noticed other odors: the acrid smell of burnt hair and human sweat.

The room was almost empty. There were two long tables on one side, on which lay papers and file folders. At one of them sat a young enlisted SS man, pen in hand, ready to record confessions. At the other end of the room were a small triangular wooden bench about two feet high and a large bathtub with a hose attached to an ancient faucet on the wall. From the ceiling hung a long chain which was connected over a pulley to an electric motor near the bench.

On the dirt floor next to the bathtub lay a naked man, his hands cuffed behind his back, his body glistening from the cold water which caused him to shiver violently.

The five Sipo agents in the room were smoking cigarettes and chatting. When Sammstag entered, they stood and saluted. Sammstag returned the salute, then spoke softly to the officer who commanded the group. The officer grabbed the naked man and rolled him over so that Kreitzl could see his face.

The large circles around the man's eyes gave him a gaunt, crazed look. He stumbled as the officers picked him up and carried him over to the bench. One of the other soldiers walked over to the group. The Frenchman moaned. The first officer hit him sharply across the mouth.

The soldiers forced the man to his knees, then made him lie face down over the bench. They took the end of the chain and fastened it to the handcuffs. Sammstag knelt before the frightened man's face and talked to him sharply in French. The man shook his head.

Kreitzl stared blankly when the winch yanked the man up by his wrists, his arms straining in their sockets. His screams rocketed over the brick walls, mingling with the whine of the motor. Then the motor stopped and the man fell with a crash back onto the bench. Again the machine whined, and again the screams came. They died eerily.

Kreitzl watched Sammstag grab the man by the back of the neck and shout at him in French, his face only a few inches away from that of the Frenchman. Kreitzl heard what he supposed was a familiar litany of questions: name, occupation, age, position with the Resistance, names of the leaders of *réseaux*. The man gurgled out short answers, most of them followed by blows to the back of his skull by a rubber truncheon.

It took half an hour for the Sipo men to learn what they wanted to know. When it was over, Sammstag stood up and brushed the dirt from the knees of his uniform. The bloodied Frenchman was unhooked from the chain and hauled to his feet. Sammstag looked directly at the dazed man.

"Shoot him."

The rain had stopped for a while when Sammstag and Kreitzl returned to the office in the main salon. Sammstag reviewed the Frenchman's information. There had indeed been an airdrop the night before, somewhere in the vicinity of Ravenoville beach. The Frenchman could not say who the parachutist was to have been, whether he was a civilian or not, or what his mission was. Despite the heavy blows inflicted on the poor man's head and face, he had known nothing more than the fact that he was to have met an airdrop at midnight, and that another rendezvous had been planned for five o'clock in the morning with an unknown party somewhere near Sainte-Marie-du-Mont.

Sammstag went to a large map of Normandy on the wall and picked up a small drawing compass from a table next to it. "Our problem seems clear, *Herr Sturmbannführer,*" he said, enscribing a small circle around Ravenoville. "The Allied agent dropped near here at midnight. Ten hours ago." He drew another circle with the center at Sainte-Mère-Église. "The nearest town is Sainte-Mère-Église, and it would take him at least four hours to reach it in the darkness." Sammstag drew a final circle around Sainte-Marie-du-

Mont. "And here is the area of the second rendezvous. The ultimate goal of the agent must be Sainte-Marie-du-Mont."

Kreitzl looked at the map. The three overlapping circles covered a territory not much larger than ten square kilometers.

Sammstag turned to Kreitzl. "Somewhere in that area is an Allied agent with the answers to many of our questions. We have only one task before us, as I see it."

Kreitzl nodded glumly. "Find him."

12

General Ludwig Beck's hands were shaking as he replaced the phone in the cradle.

It had been a long night for him, and the fatigue contributed to his sense of uneasiness. He had made certain that he was to have been the senior officer on duty at OB West in Saint-Germain-en-Laye on the crucial night, the fifth of June. It had been part of the careful planning that he would be at the headquarters, near the telephone and wireless lines, so that he could intercept any messages from the Western Wall.

It was now 1100 hours. Beck had been awake since 0600 hours the morning before. Twenty-nine hours without sleep had taken their toll. His eyes were glazed, and dark circles ringed them. His hands continued to tremble as he stared bleakly at the blotter on the desk in front of him. The phone call from Colonel von Frickstein had just confirmed Beck's worst fears: the rendezvous had not been kept.

Beck rose from his desk and walked into the situation room. It was relatively quiet. Officers sat at their desks or walked swiftly but silently from one desk to another, or to the gigantic maps on the wall, posting the latest intelligence reports. A few phones rang. Beck looked at the scene. It was almost too quiet, he thought.

He walked over to the largest map of northwestern France, the one that covered the entire north wall of the ground floor in the three-story blockhouse buried into the hill behind the school building at 20 Boulevard Victor Hugo. His heart pounded as he surveyed the territory in front of him. With the rendezvous broken,

Beck knew that the entire conspiracy hung in a precarious balance. Every passing minute gave the Sipo more time to break the cipher and discover the plot. Time, which before had been the ally of Beck, von Stauffenberg, and Rommel, had now become their enemy.

Beck knew that it was up to him to stabilize the front and devise alternative actions. He had to find a secure place for the field marshal and his aide while he, Beck, tried to contact the Resistance and find out what had gone wrong. The 711th Division bunkers at Cabourg, where Rommel and von Frickstein were now asleep, were not safe. They were too close to Caen and Sipo headquarters. For similar reasons the 716th Division garrison on the coast near Langrune was out of the question.

He eliminated the 84th Corps headquarters at Saint-Lô and the 67th Panzer Corps headquarters at Neubourg. There were too many officers at those posts, and hence too many tongues that might waggle in the direction of the Sipo. Besides, Beck thought, as he scratched his unshaven chin, they were both too far inland. That left the 709th Division at Valognes, the 91st Air Landing Division near Carentan, and the 352nd Division near Vierville. Beck paused. He had visited the fortifications at Vierville the month before. They were lonely bunkers, built into the sandy dunes immediately behind the sharp bluffs of the Pointe du Hoc. The forward batteries were particularly isolated, located just up from the empty beaches.

Beck returned to his office. He shut the door quietly, drowning out the murmured voices from the situation room, and picked up the telephone. *"Generalleutnant Kraiss, bitte."*

"Der Generalleutnant ist nicht hier," came the faint voice of the officer's aide.

"Wo ist er?"

"Zum Manöver, Herr Generaloberst."

"Danke." Beck hung up. So, he thought, Kraiss has joined the

other commanders of the Seventh Army at the war games being held at Rennes. He realized the advantage the games would give to his plan. He picked up the telephone again.

It was quickly arranged. Beck had remembered the young colonel who was in command of the forward batteries at Vierville. He had seemed a cooperative and eager sort when Beck had toured the installations. He had been correct. The young colonel was glad that some of the special operations connected with the war games were being held in his fortifications. It would break the monotony. Beck had been explicit in telling him that he would soon receive a German commander and his aide, and that he was to tell no one of their presence there. It was all part of a test of the communications network on the Atlantic Wall, Beck had said, and the colonel had understood completely.

Beck had only one more call to make. His mouth went dry as he waited for the answer at the other end of the line in Paris. His heart started pounding again as the voice answered.

"*Herr Standartenführer! Generaloberst Beck.*"

"*Guten Morgen, Herr Generaloberst,*" Helmut Knochen replied.

"I have received an alarming report, *Herr Standartenführer.* It says that the Allies have landed a man along the coast of France last night. It says that the purpose of the mission was to contact treasonous officers in the Wehrmacht."

There was a pause at the other end of the line. "*Ja, Herr Generaloberst,* I know of the reports. What of them?"

"*Sehr gut, Herr Standartenführer.* I have received calls here from one of our installations. It has reported a parachute drop in its sector. You must investigate at once!"

"*Jawohl, Herr Generaloberst.* Where?"

"Lion-sur-Mer," Beck said calmly, then hung up. He sighed. Lion-sur-Mer was seventy-five kilometers down the coast from Vierville.

*   *   *

The time had passed slowly in the farmhouse of Marcel Vuillard. Tim lay on the fur-covered bed in the dim sleeping loft, listening to the cascading water as it rumbled down the sloping eaves and landed noisily on the muddy ground outside. He had managed to sleep again, although the small wooden bed with the prickly goose-feather mattress was barely large enough to accommodate him.

He rolled over and pulled one of the blankets up to his chin. From below he heard slight sounds of Anne-Thérèse doing her chores. Vuillard himself had left the farm just before Tim had gone to sleep. The farmer had known the key phrase of the Resistance —*"Ça sera bientôt l'été"*—and the two passwords that Tim had been given in his orders the night before. He seemed to be at least a sympathizer with the Resistance, so Tim had told him that he was from SOE.

The sleep had helped Tim to recover his senses. He pondered what to do next. With luck old Vuillard could put him in touch with a *réseau* which could either get him to Rommel or keep him undercover until the invasion began. He glanced out the window at the end of the loft. The storm showed little sign of abating. The invasion had been postponed once already. It might be postponed again. That would leave him stuck behind enemy lines. It was only a matter of time before the Germans discovered his uniform and parachute. It would be a tight squeeze. Tim rose from the bed. As he carefully smoothed the blankets and fur back into place, he heard above the clatter of the rain the sound of a car. He walked quickly to one of the dormer windows which looked out onto the road. Advancing slowly up Route Nationale 13 from the direction of Sainte-Mère-Église were two German soldiers in a black car.

In an instant Tim was bounding down the steps of the companionway. His hands were shaking as he looked at Anne-Thérèse. She was standing near a window, broom in hand. She turned to face Tim, put her finger calmly to her pursed lips, and motioned toward the loft. Her brown eyes were alert but absolutely without panic.

My God, Tim thought, at the age of eighteen she is already a veteran of terror.

Once upstairs, Tim looked quickly around for a hiding place. The spare loft, filled only with beds, bureaus, and a few trunks, offered little refuge. His eyes fell on a wooden armoire which stood against the upright end wall near the companionway, next to the thick-paned window. Tim grabbed his knapsack. Quickly he strode over to the armoire and crept inside, taking the sack with him. As he closed the doors behind him as best he could, he heard the sounds of the car driving up and stopping by the farmhouse.

Tim's heart raced. From below he heard pounding on the front door. Fighting through the clothes which hung from the metal crossbar, he slipped his hand down to his knapsack. Gingerly he opened the top and withdrew the .45. As noiselessly as possible he felt to see that the clip was in place, then cocked a shell into the chamber. He tucked the pistol into his belt.

As he reached back into the sack, he heard loud voices from below. The clothes which hung next to his ears muffled everything, but he managed to catch snatches of both German and French. He heard the sound of boots stomping on the brick floor.

His hand finally found the commando knife. He tugged at it, but it remained caught in the clothing at the bottom of the sack. He gritted his teeth and pulled again. The knife came free, but as it did, Tim's elbow knocked against the armoire door and sent it flying open.

"*Augenblick!*" The sounds of footsteps from below stopped. Breathing furiously, Tim reached for the door and slowly started to close it. When it was nearly shut, the humidity-soaked wooden door gave out a mournful squeak.

Tim froze. He heard a few more words in German, then the sound of boots rushing across the floor to the foot of the companionway.

"*Nach oben?*"

"*Ja. Schnell!*" The adrenaline pumped through Tim's body.

[223]

His heart pounded like a stamping press as he heard the boots ascend the steps one at a time. In what seemed like hours, Tim heard the feet stop at the head of the stairs. The German was not more than eight feet away.

There was a long pause. Tim tried to stop breathing, fearing that he must sound like a locomotive. Any moment he expected the German soldier to empty his machine pistol into the cabinet.

Finally there were a few tentative steps into the loft. Tim listened as the leather soles ground into the wooden floor; the German must be turning slowly around, checking each corner of the room. The grinding stopped. He must have spotted the armoire, Tim thought, as his fingers clenched and unclenched nervously around the tape-wound handle of the knife. After another eternity there were a few quick steps. The German was now directly in front of the armoire. The door started to open.

The German's eyes widened in fear as Tim slammed the door wide open and simultaneously buried his knife in the German's stomach. Tim wrenched his right arm back, withdrawing the knife, and the soldier started to crumple over in slow motion, his hands flailing as he drew them to his lacerated abdomen.

In a second Tim was on top of him, his hand over the man's mouth, knife at his throat. With one quick slice, Tim severed his neck. The blue blade sank into the pink flesh and in an instant, blood gushed outward like water from behind a collapsing dam. The German gurgled blood and saliva into Tim's left hand, choking; Tim could hear spasmodic wheezing as the air escaped from the severed windpipe. Then the German's body jerked violently beneath Tim and they crashed to the floor.

Tim leaped to his feet as he heard the other German racing to the stairway, shouting in confusion. Anne-Thérèse screamed loudly, which caused the German, who by this time was halfway up the companionway, to pause and look in her direction for an instant.

It was all the time Tim needed. He tumbled into the opening

where the ladderway entered the loft and raised his .45 with both hands. The German heard the noise and turned quickly to face Tim.

A black hole appeared in his left cheek as the gun roared in Tim's hands. The German snapped upward. In another moment his face was covered with blood. He stumbled on the stairs, and his right hand jerked as his machine pistol fired a few quick bursts into the ceiling.

Tim's second shot slammed into the German's back as he twisted against the railing. The body shuddered, and then the legs collapsed and he slid down the stairs, his left leg buckling under his heavy trunk like a rag doll. His head hit each successive step, sending streamlets of blood into the air. Then he crashed to the bottom, where he lay still, his head resting on the second step.

The silence was terrifying. Tim stood up at the top of the steps, his frame shaking violently. He looked at his hands. Both of them were red and sticky. He grabbed his right wrist with his left hand, in a vain effort to stop the palsy. The veins throbbed in his forehead, and his breath came in staccato gasps.

Tim started to descend the companionway. He groped with each shaky leg for his footing. Halfway down, his head began to swim and he fell.

The jolt of landing on the corpse brought Tim back to consciousness. He rolled onto the wooden floor and rose shakily to his knees. He raised the .45 and aimed it at the German's head. Only then did he look at the body.

The twisted head lay in a grotesque death frenzy, blood all over the cheek and neck and dripping onto the back collar. The neck was exposed by the sharp tilt of the head. The eyes were wide open, staring blankly at the stone wall. The tongue stuck out of the mouth, clamped between the teeth in a ferocious death grip.

Tim stared at the dead German for a long time. His lightheadedness continued, and suddenly he felt a growling in his stomach which crept up his throat. He breathed sharply, got to his feet, flung the front door open, and sank to his knees in front of the house, heaving his breakfast into the small bushes along the wall. For the longest time afterward Tim knelt there, oblivious to the water pouring off the roof onto his head and shoulders. Its wetness cooled him, and the cold air stung his nostrils. His stomach pumped furiously for a full five minutes until it finally subsided.

Inside again, Anne-Thérèse handed him a glass of red wine. "*Buvez,*" she said quietly, pointing to the glass. It felt good as it trickled down Tim's throat, quieting his empty stomach. The flush it brought was welcome. Tim sat back on the hard-backed bench and breathed deeply. He took another swallow of wine. Anne-Thérèse remained motionless by the front door.

Finally Tim looked up. She smiled grimly. "*Ils sont morts, monsieur,*" she said. "*Bien fait.*"

Tim nodded. Anne-Thérèse walked over to the German at the foot of the steps and efficiently began searching through his pockets. She withdrew every item and threw them all on the floor: a wallet, cigarettes, matches, a key ring, loose coins, two pens, and some papers. She unfolded the papers when she was through, looked at them quickly, then turned to Tim.

"*Vous parlez allemand, n'est-ce pas?*" Tim nodded. Anne-Thérèse rose and brought the papers over to Tim. The German was complicated, and Tim had difficulty making out some of the words. There was no doubt that they were from Sipo headquarters in Caen and that they said something about searching the vicinity of Carentan and Sainte-Mère-Église for a suspected Allied agent. So, Tim thought, they do know I'm here. There was no description in the orders, which gave Tim some small comfort. Nonetheless, he realized how dangerous the situation was—two German soldiers combing the area of his drop scarcely twelve hours after he had landed in France, after the rendezvous had been broken. For an instant his mind flashed back twenty-four hours, to the scene on Chandos Place. The Germans were operating on suspicions, not facts. She didn't tell them, Tim said to himself with relief. She didn't betray me.

There was no time to worry about possibilities like that now. Anne-Thérèse motioned to the body she had been searching. Tim got up and walked over to the foot of the stairs. Together they pulled the corpse so that it lay sprawled on the floor, the face still frozen in its macabre death grin. Anne-Thérèse went to the wooden bin near the sink and returned with a bundle of rough rags. Without words they wrapped the rags around the head of the SS man, then tied the scraps of cloth in place with ropes.

Anne-Thérèse looked at Tim when they had finished. *"Nous devons mettre les cadavres dans la voiture et les cacher dans le bois. Pour l'instant mettez-les près la porte."* Tim nodded. She bent over and grabbed one of the German's legs. She motioned with her head for Tim to take the other one. Together they dragged the body to a spot near the front door.

They went upstairs. The first German to die was even messier than the second. The entire front of the black tunic was sticky with blood. Tim could see the severed vessels in the gaping neck. Anne-Thérèse closed her eyes and jerked her head away when she saw him. Tim gently reached out and laid his hand on her shoulder.

They wrapped more rags around his head and neck, then slowly lifted him to the hatchway and awkwardly eased him down the ladder. The rags were quickly soaked through, and blood trailed down the wooden treads after them. When they got him to the floor, they dragged him over to the body of his companion.

Tim opened the front door and stepped out. The rain continued to thunder down, providing veils of water which obscured the road. He dashed out to the car, climbed in, and studied the panel. In a minute he had figured out the controls and started the engine. He pulled the car up to the front door.

With Anne-Thérèse's help, Tim struggled to fit the two corpses in the small back seat. To get both bodies in, they were forced to bend and twist the limbs into awkward angles. It seemed to Tim as if rigor mortis were already setting in as he finally managed to cram the last leg behind the driver's seat.

Anne-Thérèse went inside the farmhouse, came out with a wooden bucket, and walked past the house to the pump. As if drawing water to cook Sunday dinner rather than to wash off blood after a murder, she filled the pail and returned inside. Tim watched her as she started the grim task of cleaning up.

"*Où puis-je cacher la voiture?*"

"*À deux cent metres d'ici, à droite, il y a un sentier. Par là.*" She pointed quickly.

Tim got back into the car. He backed it down the gravel driveway onto the highway. Pushing the shift into first, he swung the car onto the road and proceeded slowly toward Sainte-Mère-Église. As promised, the small cart road appeared a few hundred feet off to the right. Tim stopped. The road was filled with water. Tim raced the engine and released the clutch. In a spray of water the car bounced down the road. As it lurched, Tim looked for a hiding place. Three hundred feet in, he saw a clearing. He swung the car suddenly and careened it into a small pine tree. The front end crunched and the hood popped up. Tim got out. It was not the perfect spot, but it would have to do.

When he returned, Anne-Thérèse had finished her chores and was stoking the fire in the cast-iron stove. On top of the stove sat a large pot. Tim took a quick look at the floor and the companionway. The blood was gone. It was as though the killings had never taken place.

They ate the soup in silence. Tim had two more glasses of wine and his body began to relax. He looked at his watch. It was 1210 hours.

"Your father," he asked after a pause. "Where has he gone?"

"*Dans le village.*" Tim must have looked worried, for Anne-Thérèse stopped eating and looked over at him. "Be comforted, *monsieur*. He is a member of the Resistance."

"Anne-Thérèse, we must go."

She gazed at him. He explained the danger of being found by another German patrol. She understood. She rose and quietly removed the dishes from the trestle table. Placing them on the counter near the sink, she walked quickly to the stairway and disappeared into the loft.

Tim remembered the crystal sets in the knapsack. He wondered if there was any chance of using them to contact some operative who might just know about the planned contact with Rommel. He rejected the idea. If the Germans were already combing the area for him, they would probably be listening for any suspicious new radio activity. He realized that he had no choice but to follow Anne-Thérèse and to trust her completely. If he was to contact the underground, it would have to be through her. At the very least she would be able to keep him one step ahead of the Germans, at least until the paratroopers started coming in.

He rose and walked over to the sink. The commando knife was lying on the counter next to the soup dishes. He picked it up and stared at it. Anne-Thérèse had washed it off, and it was still wet. Tim wiped it dry on his pants, then stuck it in his belt. He picked up the two Walther .38s which Anne-Thérèse had stripped off the bodies of the dead Germans. He tucked one in his belt and hid the other one beneath the rags in the wooden bin next to him. After thinking again, he also put the loot from the German's pockets in with the gun.

Anne-Thérèse came back downstairs, wearing a long woolen overcoat with a hood on it. She carried his knapsack. Tim walked over to her and handed her the Walther. She regarded it for a moment, then tucked it into the lining of her coat. Tim opened the knapsack. His .45 lay on top, where she had obviously put it during the cleanup. He put the knife back in the sack, withdrew the pistol, stuck it in his belt behind his back where his peasant coat would cover it, and closed the sack.

Tim looked at Anne-Thérèse and started to speak. Her eyes caught his. They stared at each other, then Anne-Thérèse put her hands on his shoulders, stood on her toes, and brushed her cheek lightly along his. *"Vous êtes brave, monsieur."* She leaned away from him and their eyes caught again, for only a moment. Then Anne-Thérèse turned and opened the door.

"Venez, monsieur," she said. *"Vite!"*

The roadblock appeared in the misty afternoon as the Mercedes 170 crept along the lonely stretch of Route 814. Off to the left of the car lay shallow valleys, trees, and the *bocage* country. To the right were bluffs fifty meters high which swept down to the deserted beaches of Colleville.

Rommel scanned the tops of the bluffs as the car began to slow down for the security check. He could not see the bunkers that had been built along the lower edges of the wooded area, but he knew they were there. The heavy storm was causing the surf to pound mercilessly along the beaches, and Rommel could hear booming as the waves crashed over the pale yellow sands.

Colonel von Frickstein turned to his commander, who sat next to him in the front seat of the car. *"Herr Generalfeldmarschall,* the checkpoint is here."

Rommel nodded and looked through the swinging arc patterns of the windshield wipers. From the small house on the side of the road he saw two Waffen-SS soldiers appear, rain pouring off their helmets and the muzzles of their machine pistols.

The car stopped at the wooden barrier. One of the SS men walked to the driver's window and tapped it. Von Frickstein rolled it down.

"Sicherheitsamtkontrolle! Ihre Papiere, bitte!" Von Frickstein motioned toward Rommel with a quick flip of his head. The SS man bent over so that he could see Rommel. *"Herr Generalfeldmarschall, ich muss Ihre Papiere sehen!"*

Rommel looked at von Frickstein, who opened his briefcase

and withdrew the proper papers. He handed them to the master sergeant, who examined them carefully while von Frickstein shot a nervous glance toward Rommel, who sat impassively in his seat.

"*Danke, Herr Generalfeldmarschall.*" He handed the papers back to von Frickstein. He stepped away from the car and waved to his companion. The barrier rose slowly.

Von Frickstein put the car into gear and jerked it through the gate. He rolled up his window. The car continued along the road, the fog lights glaring off the banks of mist. "You seem very calm, *Herr Generalfeldmarschall.*"

"There is nothing to be gained by panic. We must wait until *Generalleutnant* Speidel returns from Herrlingen. And we must hope that the Sipo does not discover that we are here and not there." He smiled wryly. "It is cat and mouse, no?"

"I do not enjoy being the mouse, *Herr Generalfeldmarschall.*"

"Nor I. But we have no choice."

The SS sergeant shook the rain from his coat as he returned to the sentry house. He removed his helmet and set it down near his machine pistol; the water ran off it in streams and formed a small puddle on the table. He sat down at his desk to finish making out his report on the day's troop movements. There had been little activity in the Colleville sector, but then there rarely was much. There had been only the two duty shifts for the bunkers, the ordnance truck taking ammunition to the half-completed gun installations on the top of Pointe du Hoc, and the field marshal and his aide.

The corporal who shared watch with him came inside from locking down the barrier gate. He removed his helmet and poncho, shook the water off, then hung them on the wall hook. He exhaled with relief. "Terrible weather, no?"

The sergeant looked up. "It has one advantage, though. The Allies will not dare to try any landings in it." The corporal nodded. He sat down in the chair by the back window and picked up the newspaper. The sergeant worked for some more minutes in silence, then put down his pen.

"The movement reports are finished." He turned to his companion. "You can take them to Sipo now."

The corporal looked up. By the expression on his face, the sergeant could tell that he was not anxious to go back out into the rain and drive his motorcycle fifty kilometers to Caen. That was understandable, but the orders from Kreitzl had been quite specific: All reports were to be filed at Sipo headquarters by 1800 hours every day.

He looked back at the papers. It did seem foolish to send his only assistant on a two-hour trip to deliver such a puny report, especially with the weather making an invasion impossible. "*Augenblick, Scharführer.* Perhaps I can telephone the report in. That will save time as well as a case of pneumonia."

It was irregular, said Kreitzl's aide in response to his report, but understandable. You can file the actual papers with your report tomorrow, he said, but make sure that you do so, or I will get into big trouble. It was a friendly conversation, and a lengthy one. Major Kreitzl is very worried about something, the aide told him. He didn't know much about it, but it appeared that a spy had been dropped in the vicinity of Carentan the night before and there were roadblocks being set up that very moment. Yes, he continued, as a matter of fact, I was about to call up the Colleville SAK station and tell you to be on the lookout for any possible Allied agent. I know it is absurd to expect an agent on the beaches of Colleville, but you never can tell. Yes, yes, of course, I will tell the major right away about your report. Two duty shifts, an ordnance truck, and a lieutenant general and his aide. No, you say, it was a field marshal. *Entschuldigen Sie mich,* I must not have heard you correctly.

As soon as the aide hung up the phone he regretted having excused the SAK from submitting their report. It was clearly against orders, but to make that poor man drive so far on a motorcycle was out of the question. As long as the papers went into the file, it wouldn't matter when they were turned in.

Josef Kreitzl stood staring out of his fifth-story window in the ancient Château de Caen. From it his vision swept down over the fifteenth-century ramparts, over the Porte des Champs and across the hill which descended into the heart of Caen. The green clouds rumbled in from the west. Distant thunder echoed across the landscape, and the rain battered at the seams in the leaded window. The storm is getting even worse, he thought.

He looked at his watch. The troop movement reports would not be in for another two hours. They will be crucial, he knew. If indeed the agent was to have made contact with a member of the Wehrmacht, the troop movement reports would show just which officers had crossed into new sectors. Kreitzl knew that the war games scheduled for the next day at Rennes would account for much of that movement. His guess was that the rendezvous had been set up for just such a time and place in order to confuse the Sipo.

There was a knock on the door. *"Herein!"* Kreitzl said. His aide saluted as he entered. He was tall and pudgy, with the beginnings of a stomach sticking out over his belt, and a droopy auburn mustache. Kreitzl always thought that the mustache made him look even stupider than Kreitzl thought he was. He had been a medical student once but had been thrown out of the University of Köln because he had preferred beer and late nights to books. How he had ever made it through training for the SS, and why he was ever assigned to Kreitzl, Kreitzl could only guess.

"What is it, *Herr Hauptsturmführer?*"

"Letters and documents for your signature, *Herr Sturmbannführer.*" He set the stack onto the desk.

"Have any of the troop movement reports come in yet?' "

The aide hesitated. *"Nein, Herr Sturmbannführer.* But I have

[233]

reminded the sector checkpoints that the written reports must be here on time."

"*Gut.*" Kreitzl turned his attention to the letters. Now he knew he had to play a waiting game.

The bell was tolling a melancholy four o'clock from the tower of the Norman church on the Place d'Église when Tim and Anne-Thérèse arrived at the center of Sainte-Mère-Église. The rain had slackened to a drizzle, but the ominous clouds and distant thunder which echoed over the soaked fields promised that the respite was to be short-lived.

As the last peals of the church bell died in the gloomy afternoon, Anne-Thérèse did not hesitate. They crossed the Place d'Église and walked past the row of brick and mortar houses until they reached the front of the Auberge Lion d'Or. The main room was small and dark, with a flight of steps going up to the right of the front door and a small desk directly ahead. To the left a large portal made of wooden beams and covered with lathing led into a dining room.

Anne-Thérèse went straight to the desk, where a heavy, matronly woman of sixty was writing in a large ledger. She had gray hair which curled around her massive face. Double chins cascaded from her jaw, covering the neckline of her purple and black print dress which she wore under a heavy woolen sweater. Tim stopped behind Anne-Thérèse.

"*Bonjour.*"

"*Bonjour, Madame Pellesier. Roger est là?*"

The woman's searching eyes gave Tim a rapid but thorough scrutiny. She looked back at Anne-Thérèse, who took Tim's arm.

"*Madame, c'est Jean. L'oiseau bleu chante aujourd'hui.*"

Quietly the portly lady came out from behind the desk. Dropping the bar leaf behind her, she jerked her head as an indication for them to follow. They climbed up the uneven wooden steps to a narrow whitewashed corridor on the first floor. Leading them to a door at the end of the hallway, Madame Pellesier knocked lightly three times. When a man's voice answered faintly, she opened the door, swung it back, allowed Tim and Anne-Thérèse to pass, and shut the door behind them. Tim could hear her heavy footsteps in the hallway as she went back downstairs.

Inside the cozy room two men sat at a small wooden table set beneath the leaded window that looked out over the orchard and garden behind the Auberge Lion d'Or. They rose quietly from their chairs. On the table was a bottle of red wine and two glasses, and nearby an ashtray, from which smoke curled lazily from a French cigarette.

One of the men was much older than the other, perhaps fifty-five. He wore a threadbare black suit with a necktie which was loosened above the collar of the rumpled shirt beneath it. Graying temples gave him a distinguished look, and Tim guessed by the black bag at his feet on the floor that he was a doctor.

The other man was younger, in his thirties, with black hair and a full beard that hid most of his features. He wore rough woolen clothes, and a heavy coat was pulled over what Tim could tell were brawny shoulders. It was his eyes that arrested Tim: jet-black and piercing, they fixed him with a penetrating gaze.

"*Roger, c'est Jean,*" Anne-Thérèse said.

The young man called Roger glanced at her, then back to Tim. "*Qui est-ce?*"

"*L'oiseau blue chante aujourd'hui.*"

"*Les corbeaux sont allés à la guerre,*" Tim added.

Roger's eyes flashed. "*Qui l'a dit?*"

"*Le grand à Londres.*"

"*Bien!*" Roger smiled, his teeth gleaming as he did. He reached over to the bureau which stood in the far corner of the room, next to the brass bed with the faded blue quilt on it, and took down two more wine glasses, set them on the table, and filled them each halfway from the green bottle. With his hand he motioned for them to drink. Tim and Anne-Thérèse took the glasses as Roger picked up the burning cigarette and puffed on it. He looked down at the man who had resumed his seat at the table.

"*Voici mon ami Jean, Monsieur Raymond Glise.*" The grayed man smiled weakly at the two newcomers. His lined face and prominent Gallic nose gave him a melancholy appearance.

"*Bonjour, monsieur, mademoiselle.*" He rose to gather his hat and coat quietly from the bed, bowed slightly, and left the room.

When the door had shut, Roger asked Tim, "What are you doing here?" Tim was startled to hear English.

"Special mission from SOE."

"Who is your contact?"

"I don't know."

"Why not?" Tim explained to him about the broken rendezvous. "Where was the drop zone?"

"Near Ravenoville."

"When?"

"Midnight last night."

"What was your mission?"

"I can't tell you."

Roger took a drag on his cigarette. He glanced at Anne-Thérèse. "*Madamoiselle, allez-vous en, s'il vous plait. Attendez dans le café.*"

Anne-Thérèse looked quickly at Tim, then at Roger. With no sound she opened the door, slipped into the hallway, and shut the door behind her. Tim watched her go, then turned back to Roger.

Roger sat down at the table and motioned to Tim to do the same. "You're American, aren't you?"

"Yes."

"Not many Americans do what you're doing. Mostly British and French. And a few odd-lotters, like myself."

"You're . . ."

"Canadian." Roger took a sip of wine. "My friend Jean, you can tell me as little or as much of your mission as you wish. I will try and help you."

"Thanks, but I can't say much."

"When did you arrive in Sainte-Mère-Église?"

"Just now."

Roger bit his lip pensively. "I think, *monsieur,* that you are the source of our troubles."

"What troubles?"

"Last night the Germans made a roundup. There were scores of arrests along the coastal towns and in a few inland ones. Eight were arrested here in Sainte-Mère-Église, and nine or ten, I'm not yet sure which, were picked up in Saint-Sauveur-le-Vicomte. We don't know who tipped the Gestapo off. All we know is that there was talk of an airdrop."

"Perhaps."

Roger stared at him. "How much do you know about the invasion?"

"Nothing I can talk about."

"*Les sanglots longs des violons de l'automne.*"

"*Blessent mon coeur d'une langeur monotone.*"

"You know enough. We received the messages last night. Is your mission connected with the invasion?"

"Perhaps."

Roger rose and paced the room. "Okay, my friend. I believe you. You know the passwords, and you know enough to keep your mouth shut. That's good. Now the question is, what to do next? Have you run across any Germans yet?" Tim told him about the Germans at the farmhouse. As he talked Roger listened intently, standing immobile, moving only his right arm to bring the cigarette to his mouth. When Tim finished, he let out a small sigh. "It sounds like you've already had more than your share of bad luck. You're sure those were the only Germans who've seen you?"

"As far as I know."

"They won't tell anyone. That's good. The car, is it well hidden?"

"Not really. It should be easy enough to find as soon as the rain lets up a bit."

"That doesn't leave us much time. Was Anne-Thérèse there when you killed the soldiers?"

"Yes."

"That puts her in danger. We'll have to get her out of Sainte-Mère-Église for a couple of days. And her father?"

"He'd gone into town earlier."

"I'll get him out, too, just to be on the safe side."

Tim remembered the orders he had found. "One of the Germans had some written orders on him. They were searching for me, all right."

"That's very bad. Did they have a description of you?"

"No."

"That's something in our favor." Roger sat staring into his glass, thinking hard. Tim glanced out the window. The small apple trees were filled with leaves, and the first flowers were coming out in the cozy garden. It looked so tranquil and safe. He turned back when Roger spoke.

"Where do you want to go from here?"

"Sainte-Marie-du-Mont."

"What's there?"

"Someone who'll help me finish what I came for."

"Who?"

"I don't know. My broken contact knew all that."

Roger stroked his beard. "I can get you in touch with the *réseau* there. After that, you'll be on your own. The problem is getting there."

"Why's that?"

"The Germans have been putting up roadblocks all over. There's one on Route Thirteen just north of Carentan. You'll either have to go overland or risk going through the checkpoint. How good are your papers?"

Tim remembered how quickly Vuillard had discovered his cover. "I don't know."

"If you don't know, they're not good enough. Not worth the risk."

From down below in the hotel came the sounds of stamping feet and excited voices. Doors opened and slammed shut. Roger held his hand up, a signal to be quiet. Feet sounded in the hallway and then there was a knock on the door. "*Entrez,*" Roger said. The door opened and Madame Pellesier walked in.

"*Les soldats sont sur la place. C'est un contrôle de securité.*" Roger regarded her coolly. Slowly her eyes passed over Tim. Her head nodded. "*C'est vous, monsieur,*" she said, almost threateningly. "*Je crois que c'est vous qu'ils cherchent.*"

Tim's heart began to thump loudly. There was no way to find out if the Gestapo knew that he was in Sante-Mère-Église, or if this security check was routine. Roger rose swiftly and walked through the open doorway. Across the hall was a dormer window that opened onto the Place d'Église. Madame Pellesier waddled through the door and stood by Roger. Tim joined them.

Squads of two and three German soldiers were pounding on doors on both sides of the Place d'Église and ordering the occupants out into the rainy afternoon. Already some fifty Frenchmen stood in the middle of the village square, staring mutely at the Germans. A hundred yards or so from their window, Tim could see a German staff car with eight or nine soldiers standing by it. Surrounding the Frenchmen were German soldiers in ponchos, casually holding machine pistols on the crowd. Every so often one of the soldiers near the staff car would walk over to the crowd of Frenchmen and motion for twelve of them to walk over. After talking for a few minutes, they would be released.

Roger stared at the scene. "We're lucky, Jean. They are soldiers, not Gestapo." No sooner had he spoken, however, than the crowd of soldiers around the car disbanded and a black-uniformed officer emerged from it and strode over to where the crowd was

[239]

standing. Quickly and without feeling, he pointed to three of them, a young man and woman and an older man of about fifty. The German soldiers barged into the crowd and grabbed the three persons. Swiftly they were handcuffed and brought over to where the officer stood.

"*Que diable!*" Madame Pellesier said under her breath. "*Roger, ils ont pris Rudolphe!*"

"*Oui. Courage.*" The officer motioned quickly for the prisoners to be taken to the staff car. As they were led away, he addressed the crowd. He told them, in broken French, that they were looking for an Allied spy, that the spy was believed to be in the vicinity of Sainte-Mère-Église, and that if the spy was not turned over to Sipo headquarters by eight o'clock the next morning, the hostages would be shot. The crowd stared numbly at him.

Tim heard rapid steps from behind him. He turned to see Anne-Thérèse coming down the hallway. "Jean, we must go!"

Roger turned to her. "*Qu'est-ce que se passe?*"

"*J'ai vu les soldats parler avec Madame Bourquin.*"

Roger turned to Tim and spoke very softly in English. "We suspect that Madame Bourquin is a collaborator. We aren't sure, but we can take no chances. Quickly!"

The four of them descended the steps to the ground floor. As Tim and Anne-Thérèse started for the back door, they heard steps and loud voices from outside the hotel. Anne-Thérèse grabbed Tim's arm and pulled him toward the rear of the inn. Tim looked at Roger, who nodded. "Go with Anne-Thérèse. In Sainte-Marie-du-Mont you must find Henri. Good luck."

Tim and Anne-Thérèse burst out the back door just as the German soldiers knocked on the front one. Running at full speed, trying desperately not to slip on the wet grass, they plunged into the orchard, with Tim dodging to avoid low branches. Beyond the orchard was a dirt roadway. They stopped at the edge of the trees, their breath steaming in the wet afternoon.

Anne-Thérèse crept out onto the road. Seeing no one, she

motioned quickly to Tim, and together they sprinted across to the heavy woods on the other side. After running a hundred yards, they found a muddy culvert which they drove into, scrambling under the protection of a large tree trunk that hung precariously over the embankment. Huddled together, they sat back and panted until their strength was restored.

Anne-Thérèse looked up at Tim, then put her hand on his cheek. She drew it away and Tim saw that there was blood on it. The knotty branches had lacerated his face. He saw a trickle of water running down the middle of the culvert. He pulled the red handkerchief out of his pocket and crawled slowly over to the stream. Daubing the cloth into the muddy mixture, he wiped his face. Then he turned and crawled back under the log. Anne-Thérèse laughed lightly.

"*Quoi?*"

"*Vous, mon brave américain!* The Nazis will not kill you, but the trees will!"

In the distance they heard voices. After a moment Tim raised his head just above the embankment. The sounds came from the roadway in the direction of the village. He strained to hear what was being said, and whether the language was French or German. The voices echoed eerily through the fog-shrouded forest, mingling with the endless drip of water from the leaves of the trees overhead. There was the sound of men tramping through the underbrush, and the voices seemed to come nearer. They were speaking German.

Tim slid down the embankment and pulled Anne-Thérèse tightly to him underneath the log. Then he remembered that he had left his knapsack in Roger's room at the Auberge Lion d'Or. A feeling of panic hit him. The bag contained everything he needed to survive—clothes, the commando knife, the radio sets. But he still had his gun. Noiselessly he reached inside his coat for the Colt .45 and tripped the safety. Then he sat and waited.

The dripping quiet of the forest was suddenly shattered as

machine guns raked the trees. Bullets whizzed over their heads, hundreds of rounds, ricocheting into the woods, cracking limbs and branches. For nearly a minute the guns blazed as the Germans pounded the forest with lead, hoping to cut down their quarry. Then the guns stopped. The echoes of the reports filtered through the trees and mingled with the cries of birds taking wing to escape the deadly hail.

In a minute they heard the sounds of boots crunching on the wet gravel and sand. Tim guessed the Germans to be seventy-five feet away at the most. They stopped. Tim grasped the Colt and slid his finger onto the trigger.

"*Hast du was gesehen?*"
"*Nein. Nichts.*"
"*Sie sind hier nicht durchgekommen!*"

The soldiers turned and plunged back into the underbrush. Slowly the sounds of their progress through the wet forest faded. After fifteen minutes Tim and Anne-Thérèse heard nothing.

Tim flipped the safety on the pistol. Cautiously he slid out from under the log, then turned to Anne-Thérèse. He reached out to grab her outstretched hand and pulled her to her feet. Her mantle was covered with mud.

"*Eh bien, Jean.* Where do we go?"
"Sainte-Marie-du-Mont."

She smiled and brushed the wet hair back from her face. Impulsively she reached up to kiss him and then hugged him tightly. His arms held her close for a moment while they stood in the muddy culvert feeling the warmth of each other's bodies.

Then Tim looked at his watch. It was almost 1800 hours. In six hours the Allied paratroopers would start landing in France.

13

The line of SS men moved slowly across the drenched field, machine pistols poised, in an irregular pattern. Fifty meters from the hedgerow the line stopped. Two mortar teams stepped out in front of the line. The low *chunck* of rockets being delivered out of the short barrels sounded hollowly across the desolate landscape. In ten-second intervals the explosions came, moving from west to east across the line of trees. The mortar crews withdrew.

Helmut Knochen withdrew his cigarette from its ivory holder and flicked it casually into the trampled mud below. He looked up. The line of soldiers had charged the hedgerow. They clambered over the mound of dirt and bushes, pistols poised. From where he stood Knochen could hear their voices and the sound of their beating about in the underbrush only faintly. Occasionally he heard pistol shots or a short burst from a machine pistol. After a few minutes he saw the figure of the officer in charge of the search party stand up on the hedgerow and wave.

Knochen and his aides walked across the field toward the woods. Since early afternoon he had been standing in the chilly winds of the *bocage* watching detachments of SS search for the suspected Allied agent. Knochen had sent five different patrols out to comb the areas between Lion-sur-Mer and Langrune five kilometers to the west, as far inland as Douvres, and as far east as Riva Bella. The entire area had been sealed off by midday, and he felt it was only a matter of time before they would flush out the spy. If there was a spy.

Knochen reached the hedgerow. He looked across into the pine forest. In the misty afternoon he could barely make out the soldiers moving through the trees. If there was a spy, he thought. He wondered how accurate the report from General Beck was. As the captain approached him, he asked, "Did you find anything?"

"*Nichts, Herr Standartenführer.*"

Knochen nodded glumly. The wind picked up, and he felt a few drops of rain on his cheek. Thunder rolled up from the beaches and soon there was a steady drizzle. Knochen looked up. There was barely an hour of daylight left and the clouds from the west were darkening rapidly. The search would have to be called off soon.

"Regroup the men. I doubt we will find anything in this sector."

"*Jawohl, Herr Standartenführer.*"

Knochen lit another cigarette. The patrol had cut directly through the center of the sealed-off area. They had moved in a sweep a kilometer wide but had found nothing in the fields, the woods, or the farm buildings that suggested there had been an airdrop.

Yet the reports of a landing had been confirmed. Two soldiers in the 711th Wehrmacht bunkers up on the beach had reported that a plane had swept overhead around midnight the night before. They had heard the pilot cut his engines, and, rushing outside, they had seen a parachute open. Or they thought they had seen a parachute open, but it was dark and they were not sure. The drop zone would have been directly in the area which Knochen and his patrol had just searched. It was perplexing.

"What do you think, *Herr Standartenführer?*" asked his aide, Schmidt-Brümer, who had accompanied him from Paris.

"I am not sure," Knochen replied. "I'm beginning to think the Wehrmacht sees parachutes everywhere." He took a puff on his cigarette. "We will return to Caen. Perhaps we will get a report on what the other patrols have found."

They walked across the field in silence. When they reached the vehicles parked at the other end, Knochen swung into the front seat of the Opel. The rain pelted on the canvas roof. He did not appreciate having been called from Paris to crawl around in the wet fields of Normandy looking for imaginary Allied spies. Captain Schmidt-Brümer got behind the wheel. Knochen nodded to him and the car crept into life. Let Kreitzl run around in this muck, he thought. I am going to where there is some good brandy and a fire.

The last few glimmers of twilight faded over the rim of the valley. A fragrance of blossoms hung sweetly on the mountain breeze. At the center of the valley, the small houses meekly poked their roofs through the lush treeline. The night was still enough that almost every resident of Herrlingen could hear the small stream that burbled through the heart of the town.

Below the field marshal's house on the hill a phalanx of command cars waited on the highway. The evening deepened as the SS escort walked around their motorcycles, chatting and exchanging jokes. They resented having to make the entire trip to France themselves, instead of returning to District V—Southwest Headquarters in Stuttgart, but they consoled themselves jokingly with the idea that their duty was still preferable to being sent to the Eastern Front.

A light flashed at the top of the stone steps. The SS men scrambled to their motorcycles as they heard the sound of the front door slamming. Footsteps clicked down the steps. In a moment Rommel's aide, Lang, appeared and motioned to the men.

"The *Generalfeldmarschall* will be out in a minute."

The heavy BMWs rumbled to life. The light flashed again at the top of the steps. The SS men looked up in time to see the field marshal, dressed in his long field coat despite the heat, embrace his wife.

"The *Generalfeldmarschall* has forgotten he is in the *Vaterland* and not along the cold coast of France!"

"Quiet!" The SS men stopped laughing abruptly. "The *Generalfeldmarschall* is sick with fever and fatigue. The Führer has ordered him back to the Western Front, and of course he is going.

Would you expect any less of yourselves?" The reproof shamed the men, who sat on their idling motorcycles and said nothing.

The field marshal came slowly down the steps, appearing to almost stumble twice. At the bottom of the stairway, Lang rushed to him and, supporting him by the arm, led him to the second car in the procession. As the field marshal started to enter, he stood up briefly and acknowledged the SS men by waving his baton. Then he disappeared inside. Lang shut the door and walked around the car, to take his place beside his leader. One of the SS men stopped him.

"I am sorry. I did not know the *Generalfeldmarschall* was ill. He looks quite weak."

"He will be better in the morning, when we get him to La Roche-Guyon. Just keep up your speed, *Herr Scharführer.* We have little time for games!" Lang opened the door and got in the car.

From the steps appeared General Speidel. He looked into the second car, said a few words in a low voice, then walked to the first car, opened the door, and stood on the running board. *"Anfahren!"* he said, as he swung inside and shut the door. The headlights on the motorcade flashed on, and the vehicles slowly moved out.

Speidel stared at the road ahead of him. It was at least a five-hour drive back to La Roche-Guyon. It was imperative that they arrive before the Sipo could return and set some type of ambush. It was equally important, now that the contact had been broken with the Allies, to get the real Rommel back to the French castle undetected. Speidel prayed that the checkpoints would not examine the procession too hard, and that no urgent messages for Rommel would be waiting anywhere. They would make it back to La Roche-Guyon by the skin of their teeth.

Speidel sighed as he stared at the sweep second hand of his watch, each measured minute cutting down the number of options open to him. It was 2200 hours.

* * *

The radio hummed slightly as the operator swung the reception dials. Even over the noise of the water washing off the top of the car and the hum of the giant Mercedes engine, Josef Kreitzl could hear the tiny whines from the earphones on the radio operator's head. In the light of the flashlight he began to transcribe letters onto the wrinkled top sheet of the clipboard which bounced in his lap. In a minute, he stopped.

"What has happened?"

"*Augenblick, Herr Sturmbannführer.*" The young radio operator looked at the letters on the page, then patiently began to rearrange them on the other side of the page according to a code pattern he carried in his head. As he did so, Kreitzl returned his gaze to the road.

The rain danced in the headlights of the Mercedes hypnotically. The weather was deteriorating, it seemed, and Kreitzl guessed that a sweep of the encircled sector for the Allied agent was probably impossible. It would be enough to get to Bayeux for the night and stay in touch with all the outposts. Kreitzl looked at the clock mounted in the dashboard. It was 2300 hours.

"*Herr Sturmbannführer,* I have the message."

"Yes?"

"One of the patrols in the twelfth sector was found killed."

"Where?"

"Ten kilometers north of Sainte-Mère-Église."

"Are there any details?"

"Only that the men were found in their car. One had been stabbed, the other shot."

"When were they found?"

"About two hours ago, *Herr Sturmbannführer.*"

Kreitzl started thinking. His hunch had been right. The Allied agent had headed for Sainte-Mère-Église after landing near Ravenoville. There was no way to tell what time of day the murders had taken place, but they had to have been committed at least three hours before. Kreitzl tapped his fist into the palm of his hand.

The odds were strong that the Allied spy was still within the perimeter of the trap.

There remained the question of whom the spy was to have made contact with. If the hunches were correct, there would be a rendezvous with members of the Wehrmacht, and the person under greatest suspicion in the Wehrmacht was Rommel. It was impossible that Rommel could be anywhere near the beach fortifications, however, since it was known that he was in Herrlingen. Kreitzl had himself talked with the field marshal the night before, and Rommel had gone to Herrlingen under the watchful eye of a Sipo escort. It was very mysterious.

In fifteen minutes the Mercedes pulled up to the SAK checkpoint at Nonant, a few kilometers east of Bayeux. Blickensderfer parked the car alongside the small hut whose dim light peered out feebly in the stormy night. As Kreitzl alighted from the Mercedes, a brilliant flash of lightning illuminated the scene. Kreitzl held his hat and whipping coat, then yelled to be heard above the roaring winds. "No chance of invasion on a night like this, *Herr Hauptsturmführer!*"

"*Jawohl.*"

The soldier in charge of the checkpoint came to attention as Kreitzl entered. Kreitzl motioned for him to be seated and looked around. This is a cozy little retreat, he thought to himself, from the howling weather and the fortunes of war. The Normandy coast was always quiet.

"A routine check, *Herr Oberscharführer*. I am looking for any suspicious troop movements."

The soldier shuffled nervously through the sheaf of papers on his small desk. "I have my reports here, *Herr Sturmbannführer.*"

"Here? Your reports were due at my office five hours ago!"

"*Ja, Herr Sturmbannführer,* but—"

"Did you report movements to *Hauptsturmführer* Blickensderfer?"

"*Ja, Herr Sturmbannführer,* he did," Blickensderfer broke in. "Everything is under control."

Kreitzl glared at his oafish aide. "You are sure?"

"*Ja, Herr Sturmbannführer.*"

"No unusual movements?"

"*Nein, Herr Sturmbannführer.* Neither here nor at Colleville." Small drops of sweat appeared on Blickensderfer's forehead. His voice broke nervously. "There is nothing unusual, and I chastised the *Oberscharführer* here and the commanding officer at Colleville for not sending in written reports. But I decided to be lenient in view of the storm."

Kreitzl glowered at Blickensderfer and the cowering soldier. There was no point in getting angry since there was no cause for alarm. He walked to the telephone.

A weary voice answered after a few rings. "*Sturmbannführer Sammstag. Wer ist da?*"

"*Hier Sturmbannführer Kreitzl. Was gibt's Neues?*"

"Ah, *Herr Sturmbannführer,* you have heard about the patrol?"

"Yes, my headquarters radioed me the news. What can you tell me about it?"

"Little, I am afraid. They were found in their car in the woods, near a side road. They had been dead quite a while. But there is other news, *Herr Sturmbannführer.*"

"*Ja?*"

"A man and a woman escaped a patrol this afternoon in Sainte-Mère-Église. I think it was our man."

"How do you know?"

"We have a collaborator in Sainte-Mère-Église. She told us."

"Do you have a description of them?"

"A partial one. I have sent it out to all the roadblocks."

Kreitzl nodded glumly. "They are probably headed for Sainte-Marie-du-Mont."

"I guessed as much." A small laugh came over the wire. "We

will have a surprise for them there. What of the *Generalfeldmarschall?*"

"I do not know as yet. I have seen nothing."

"Where are you?"

"Nonant. I am about to return to Gestapo headquarters in Bayeux. We will put off the search until tomorrow."

"*Sehr gut, Herr Sturmbannführer.* Keep me apprised of new developments. *Auf Wiedersehen.*"

Kreitzl hung up the phone. "I am returning to Bayeux. If there are any problems, contact me there." The man looked up and nodded. "And, *Oberscharführer,* next time I will not forget your laxness so easily!"

The threat had its intended effect. The man put down the wrinkled newspaper and started going through the papers on his desk in an intent fashion.

Kreitzl put on his wet cap. "Get the reports, *Herr Hauptsturmführer.* Then meet me at the car."

As soon as the door slammed shut, the man looked up at Blickensderfer. "I told you about the *Generalfeldmarschall—!*"

"Quiet! If the *Sturmbannführer* knew that, it would go very hard on you. Feel fortunate that I spared you from discipline."

"But, *Herr Hauptsturmführer—*"

"Enough! It makes no difference tonight, because the weather means that the Allies will attempt nothing. But in the future I will not cover for you again. Do you understand?"

"*Jawohl, Herr Hauptsturmführer.*"

"*Gut.* Remember, nothing has happened, and no one has passed. It is better that way."

Blickensderfer put on his cap and walked toward the door. As he opened it, a gust of wet spring wind came rushing in. Then he turned back. "I almost forgot the reports."

"But, *Herr Hauptsturmführer,* there is a mention in them of the *Generalfeldmarschall!*"

Blickensderfer paused. The little white fib he had told was

growing steadily into a big lie. He could not dare now admit to Kreitzl that he had not mentioned the passage of an important officer. "Change them. Send them to me tomorrow. That will be soon enough." He looked at his watch. It was just past midnight. Tomorrow morning was here. It was already the sixth of June.

Tim awoke with a start when he heard the scraping of the floorboards. He sat up quickly in the darkness. There was a glimmer of light in the floor, then a small shaft, as a hand pushed aside the loose slatwork. Leaning on one arm, he rolled over and gently shook Anne-Thérèse. Her eyes fluttered open. She uttered a soft cry. He put his fingers to his lips.

The hand pushed away the rest of the floorboards. It disappeared, then returned to the opening carrying a small hurricane lamp which it set down on the floor inside of the opening. Then a head appeared.

"Ça va?"

"Bien, Jean. C'est le moment." Tim checked the time. The new day was half an hour old.

The man put both hands on the sides of the opening and with a grunt heaved himself up so that he sat in the trap. He pulled his feet up and carefully replaced the floorboards. He stood as best he could in the cramped space, then picked up the lamp and groped toward the pallet where Tim and Anne-Thérèse lay.

The flickering lamplight gleamed off the face of the man Tim knew only as Henri. He was a virile man of forty with a thick mustache and bushy eyebrows of dark auburn. His hair was matted over his forehead where beads of sweat trickled. He obviously had been exerting great energy. He smiled, and Tim noticed once again the almost toothless grin except for the two large incisors in front.

"Vous avez dormi, mes amis?"

"A little," Tim replied. "What's the news?"

"The Gestapo is all over Sainte-Marie-du-Mont. There are

patrols on every road. Two have stopped here, looking for you both."

Tim pulled the blanket off his lower body and rolled out of the pallet. On their hands and knees, the two men crawled over the floor to where Henri's radio and antenna lay.

Tim examined the crystal set. It would be a simple operation. Taking a small screwdriver from a tool kit Henri gave him, he quickly removed the back of the set, set the cover down carefully on the floor, and held the unit up against the lamp. With a jab of his thumb he popped out the crystal. Setting it on the floor, he rummaged through the kit. In a moment he withdrew another crystal. He snapped it into the radio. That would be enough to put him onto or near one of his frequencies. He replaced the cover and screwed it back on, putting the radio back on the floor.

"*Bien fait, Jean. Un moment.*" Henri took hold of the crank on the charger and slowly started turning. For three minutes he turned the coffee-grinder handle. The bearings of the magneto inside rattled as the charge built up. The sweat started pouring down Henri's face again, and Tim suddenly realized how hot and close it was in the windowless garret.

Everything was ready. Tim pulled a battered Gauloise pack from his shirt. He read the message he had written out on it and transcribed into Chelsea: CONTACT REESTABLISHED AM PROCEEDING WITH SOLSTICE. A mental image of Beauclerk's face lighting up upon reading the message danced through Tim's brain, and he chuckled.

He and Anne-Thérèse had spent an exhausting six hours in the rain following their narrow escape at Sainte-Mère-Église. They had continued through the woods to the west until they came to the railroad line that ran from Valognes to Carentan. They walked alongside the embankment, taking care to stay behind the screen of shrubbery that followed the grading. Twice they had had to scramble down the gravel and hide in the bushes when slow-moving trains had gone by. The trains creaked and groaned along the battered rail lines, sometimes going only eight or ten miles an hour. The Allied bombers had done their jobs well.

They passed through Chef du Pont by riding between two boxcars. It hadn't been difficult to jump onto the slow-moving train, but it was agonizing when the train rumbled through the tiny village and stopped and started every fifty feet. Fortunately the rain had begun again; there were few villagers out on the streets who might have observed them, and even fewer Germans.

Two miles south of Chef du Pont they had jumped off the train and struck out overland. That had been the worst part of the journey because the Germans had flooded the fields. At times they waded through water up to their waists. It was 2000 hours when they had crossed the marshlands, and darkness had begun to set in. They found a clump of trees on the edge of a pasture and crawled in to rest for twenty minutes.

Route 13, the road connecting Sainte-Mère-Église with Carentan, had been a major obstacle. It ran across open fields which provided little cover. They hid behind a hedgerow a hundred feet from the highway and waited for a clear moment. As Tim watched German cars roar up and down the road, he realized that once they crossed Route 13 they would be back where the Germans would be looking for them.

At 2100 hours they made their break. It was dark, and a large German convoy had just gone down the highway toward Carentan. Summoning their reserves of energy, Tim and Anne-Thérèse dashed the hundred feet to the road, crossed it, and forced another two hundred feet out of their tired legs and burning lungs until they collapsed over a hedgerow and lay panting.

Another hour of tramping through wet and matted grass brought them to the outskirts of Sainte-Marie-du-Mont. In the night it had been difficult to keep directions straight, but through sheer luck they had come across one of the small canals which crisscross the Cotentin Peninsula. Anne-Thérèse had given a small squeal of delight. Tim followed her as she half walked, half trotted along the small waterway north for over a mile. They soon came to a small building next to a farmhouse. The low building had been a tannery. It was owned by Henri.

The message was quickly transmitted. When he had finished, Tim again disassembled the radio and exchanged the crystals. He set the radio back on the floor and turned to Henri.

"*Et maintenant?*"

Henri rubbed his scratchy chin. "We must go to the German garrison at Pont-sur-Douve."

"What's there?"

"The German contact, *mon ami.*"

"How far is that?"

"By the road, eight or nine kilometers. By the fields, it is less: six, *peut-être.*"

Tim thought for a minute. It was nearly one o'clock now. The pathfinders were due to start landing soon, to stake out the drop zones for the paratroopers. Once the Germans realized what was happening, all hell would break loose and it would become impossible to sneak through the countryside undetected. When the Germans went to battle-alert, it would be even more difficult to penetrate their lines and get to Rommel, no matter how good a cover escort Tim might have.

"We must get there quickly, Henri. *Vitement.* Which is the best way?"

Henri shrugged. "We will go to Sainte-Marie-du-Mont."

"That's where the Germans expect us to go!"

"*Oui, monsieur.*" Henri's face broke out into a grin. "And we will get a car there." His right hand rose to his temple and he made a small circle with his right index finger. "Crazy, *non?*"

"Crazy, *oui.* Let's go."

The rain had stopped. Tim looked up at the sky. From behind a bank of clouds an incandescent moon gleamed like silver. After two days of storm and thunder, the sky was obeying its cue. Stage center was clear, ready for the final act to begin.

"Look at the sky, Anne-Thérèse." The tired French girl gazed upward. The moonlight struck her full in the face as she did, making her olive skin iridescent. She smiled.

Tim turned to Henri. "We will take her?"

"*Oui, monsieur.*"

"That's a great risk."

"There is greater risk if we do not. The Gestapo."

They scampered across the field which stretched out from the tannery. The moon seemed suddenly as bright as the sun. Out in the open they were sitting ducks for any German patrol that might happen along.

On the far side they plunged back into the forest. As they had for the last eight hours, Tim and Anne-Thérèse clawed their way through the trees, barely keeping up with Henri in the darkness, for the moonlight failed to penetrate the treetops. They reached a clearing. Anne-Thérèse slumped to her knees, then lay prostrate on the ground. Tim did the same. Henri stopped, then ran back to where they lay.

"*Qu'est-ce qui ne va pas?*"

"*Nous sommes fatigués, Henri. Un moment.*"

The carpet of pine needles felt cool against Tim's sweat-soaked shirt. The breeze refreshed him after the hours in the fetid attic. His arms and legs went limp, the muscles cramping in protest against the punishment they had received. He felt as if he would not be able to run another step for a week.

But in two minutes the three of them were running again. Plunging back into the woods, they had not gone fifty yards when Tim noticed the trees thinning ahead of them. They struggled to the edge of the timber. Fifty feet ahead of them a highway curved through the woods, cutting the dark forest in half. The moonlight bounced off the polished surface of the road. The trio stood just in back of the treeline, listening to the sound of their own heaving breathing.

"*Qu'est-ce que c'est?*"

"*Route Treize,*" Henri said quietly.
"Sainte-Marie-du-Mont?"
"*Là-bas.*" He pointed to the north. "*À deux kilomètres.*"
To the south the pine trees shimmered. A faint hum reached their ears. Through the trees at the curve of the road, first one, then two yellow lights appeared, passing along the tree trunks, causing overlapping shadows to skim along the highway in weblike patterns. Instinctively they fell to the ground, lying prone in the underbrush.

From around the curve appeared a German army truck. The lights flashed in their eyes as the giant vehicle lumbered into the turn. Then it drew parallel to them, moving very slowly. Tim could see three Germans standing in the back, holding onto the sides of the truck, machine pistols raised, scanning the woods as they rode past. Tim unconsciously sucked in his breath until the truck continued around down the road, turning out of sight. Soon the sounds of its engine died into the night.

Henri chuckled. "You must be important, Jean. Never have I seen the Germans look so hard for one man."

"*Allons-y.*"

They rose, ran across the road, and reentered the forest, to struggle in the darkness with low-hanging branches, Henri leading the way, Anne-Thérèse in the middle, Tim last. It was too dark, and Tim was too tired, even to attempt to navigate. He was thankful he had only to follow the dim shape of Anne-Thérèse in front of him.

They reached a pathway. It was quite narrow, at times only a foot wide, but it was a path nonetheless, for the branches no longer hit them in the face and the underbrush no longer tore at their clothes. The going became easier and Tim felt himself relaxing just a bit.

After they had followed the snaking path for half an hour, it opened up suddenly into a shady clearing. Beyond it Tim glimpsed a farmhouse with the usual outbuildings and barns. Henri stopped, allowing Anne-Thérèse and Tim to catch up with him. He put his fingers to his lips. Carefully he led them around the perimeter of the clearing and into the woods along another path, somewhat wider than the one they had been on before. Soon they came to another clearing with four small houses. They followed the same procedure, tracing the outside edge of the compound. Again they entered the woods, which ended after a hundred feet, revealing a tree-lined street of small houses stretched out ahead of them.

Henri turned to Tim. "Sainte-Marie-du-Mont."

They moved cautiously from house to house. Traveling through back yards, they tripped over clotheslines, rusted bicycles, and vegetable gardens. Henri would go first, peeking from the corner of a building, then almost gaily trotting the twenty feet to the next house. From the shadows he would wave, and Anne-Thérèse would dash over. Finally Tim would make the crossing. They would then pause for a moment and repeat the whole procedure.

They had passed down one whole street when Henri peered around a building and with a violent motion slammed them all back against the wall of the house. They hid in the shadows, flattened out against the mortar. In the quiet night Tim heard the clicking of boots against the cobblestones. The sound got louder. Then Tim caught a glimpse of a German patrol moving down the street. The men were spread across the width of the avenue, and each of them looked carefully up and down the houses as they passed. Tim's knees buckled giddily.

As he looked at them, he thought back to the orders he had taken from the dead German's pocket. How did they know where he would be going? He knew that Pru hadn't said anything, or he would have been captured long ago. Perhaps there had been a leak in the Resistance.

The patrol passed on, and the trio began to move again. In twenty minutes they had moved from the fringes of town into the very center, one building at a time. It was a systematic maneuver that Henri had obviously used several times before. The trees disappeared, leaving them fully exposed to the moonlight. With each succeeding house, they drew closer to the German garrison and the chance of discovery. It was a desperate game, and Henri played it with a desperate coolness. Finally, at the end of one street, he leaned back against the wall of the building and grinned at Tim as, with his right hand, he pointed around the corner. Tim took a look.

What he saw was a street leading down into a large square. No lights shone in any of the windows. From the far end of the street, perhaps fifty yards away, the moonlit square seemed to float eerily. Tim guessed that he was looking at the main square of Sainte-Marie-du-Mont.

"Where to, Henri?"

The toothy grin flashed. "Gestapo. We will visit the Gestapo, *non?*" He looked at both of them. The smile vanished. He muttered breathlessly, *"Suivez!"*

Again moving one by one, they dashed across the open avenue toward the first house. Struggling for breath, they hovered in the shadow of one of the projecting gables. Then, with Henri in the lead, they reached the rear corner of a house directly on the square.

Tim stole a look. The jagged silhouettes of the houses around the square stood boldly against the green sky. Above, the moon gleamed magically over the roofs. The gargoyles on the Hôtel de Ville, directly across the square, glimmered with silver highlights. In front of it stood a lonely Gestapo van. Tim stared at the car and stepped back into the shadows.

"Le camion. C'est ça?"

"C'est ça."

Anne-Thérèse heard it first. Tim stood against the wall next to her, steeling his courage for the dash across the square, when he noticed that her head suddenly popped up. He turned to look at her. In the darkness where they stood he saw only the flash of her eyes as she scanned the sky.

"Anne-Thérèse?"

"Sssh!" Henri turned to look at her.

The fresh wind from the sea carried the droning sound to their ears. Tim stepped out in the full moonlight. He searched the horizon over the village of Sainte-Marie-du-Mont. He found what he was looking for. "Jesus H. Christ!" he said softly.

"Qu'est-ce-que c'est?" Henri tugged Tim's sleeve to get him back into the safety of the shadows.

"Arrêtez, Henri!" He pointed up at the sky. Henri and Anne-Thérèse stepped out and followed the arc of Tim's arm. "There it is, *mes amis!* It's beginning!"

In the distance matchlike shapes appeared in the sky. Small specks trickled out from them, cascading backward from the slivers as they inched along. Every so often the moon flashed whitely off one of the shapes. In dreamlike fashion the specks blossomed like petals cast from flowers as they drifted lazily in the night. More slivers appeared. The horizon became dotted with silver flashes.

Anne-Thérèse stared at the spectacle in the sky, her mouth agape. Henri's eyes filled with tears of happiness. *"Libération!"* he exclaimed. *"C'est arrivé!"*

Tim returned to the task at hand. He feared that the planes would zoom overhead and alert the sleepy Germans. They had to get out of Sainte-Marie-du-Mont as fast as possible. He tapped Henri on the shoulder. When Henri looked down from the sky, Tim pointed over toward the police van. Henri nodded.

Tim and Henri dashed into the street and began to circle the square. They passed in and out of the moonlight as they made the long trek around the perimeter. Tim kept checking the sky and was relieved when the planes swung in a large arc to the northwest. The town remained quiet. In two minutes they had circumnavigated the square and were opposite the police van, thirty yards away. They paused. Tim saw no signs of life around the van. He clapped Henri on the shoulder. "It's quiet."

"Oui. Too quiet."

"A trap?"

Henri shrugged. *"Je ne sais pas.* I hope not. We have no choice."

They arrived at the rear of the van at the same moment. They leaned against the double doors, listening to their own furious heartbeats and waiting for any sign that the Germans had been aroused. It had seemed to Tim that their boots had made plenty of noise in the dash across the open square, but still nothing moved. Tim pulled the Colt out of his belt. He licked his dry lips and raised his left hand. He counted to three and dropped his arm to attack.

The SS man behind the wheel didn't have a chance. In a single motion Tim and Henri ripped back the doors on either side of the cab. Henri's hands, strengthened by years of pulling and scraping at hides, grabbed the driver's shoulders and neck; Tim slammed his left hand on his mouth and placed the gun nozzle up against the sweating temple. The German struggled valiantly for a moment, then went limp in their hands. Tim pushed him out of the driver's seat into the small area of the van between the seats and the steel wall which marked the front end of the prisoners' cage and leaped in after him, kneeling atop him with one knee braced against his chest and holding the gun against the man's forehead again. Henri climbed into the truck and shut the doors. He reached over the seat and deftly unfastened the German's belt. In one motion he rebuckled it tightly around the man's elbows, pinioning the arms closely to his sides. Tim pulled a rag from his pocket and stuffed it into the German's mouth. Henri moved to the driver's seat and pushed the starter button. The engine coughed and fell into a soft idle. Henri slid the van into gear and took off.

The truck circled the square. It paused at the corner, where Anne-Thérèse opened the door and slipped into the empty seat in front. Then it started up again and with a squeal of tires continued its circle until it turned a sharp right onto Route Nationale 13 and headed southwest out of town.

Sainte-Marie-du-Mont was quiet. The front door on the Hôtel

de Ville opened and the platoon leader on duty stepped out. The empty square lay before him. He looked in every direction and checked his watch. He shook his head, then looked again across the square. His body tensed. He turned and rushed back inside, slamming the heavy door behind him. He went to the night desk and sat down. He looked up and down the long sheets on the clipboard which lay on the desk, once, twice, then a third time. His head shook slowly. He set the clipboard back down and gazed out into space, a puzzled look on his face. Then he rose and walked toward the office of the commandmant.

Heinrich Sammstag slammed the phone down into the double cradle and ran to the windows. Through the wavy glass in the double French doors he could see the clear sky and the rugged silhouette of the forest. He stared intently for a full minute and exhaled slowly. Walking over to his desk, he glanced at the pile of papers and files, the records on interrogations, the endless paperwork that had occupied him for the last four hours. Then he turned his head slowly to face the map of Normandy. With a careless motion born of too much work and too little sleep, he reached over and pressed the button on his desk.

The double doors opened and an SS officer entered. Sammstag looked at him wearily. "*Untersturmführer*, there have been reports of airdrops."

"*Ja, Herr Sturmbannführer.* In Sainte-Mère-Église, Ravenoville, and Varaville."

"I have just spoken with *Standartenführer* Knochen. He is at Sipo headquarters in Caen. Reports are cascading in."

"*Ja, Herr Sturmbannführer.* But nothing has been confirmed."

Sammstag nodded and rubbed his tired face. "Have the patrols made any reports?"

"Not yet, *Herr Sturmbannführer.* They are due to arrive at any time."

"Call me when they do."

"*Jawohl, Herr Sturmbannführer.*" The officer turned and left the room, closing the doors carefully behind him.

Nervously Sammstag paced the room. His mind raced to connect the reports of the last forty-eight hours. All the pieces seemed to come from different picture puzzles: spies dropping and vanishing, mysterious codes yielding nothing but more cryptic messages, paratroopers flooding the skies. Again Sammstag looked at the map. The weather reports from the Luftwaffe station in Cherbourg had confirmed that heavy storms would continue for the next four or five days. The invasion was impossible. The airdrops therefore had to be a diversion, he thought, but a diversion for what purpose he could not decide.

Sammstag threw himself down in his chair and propped his feet up on the desk. He rested his elbows on the chair arms and sunk his head into his hands to concentrate better. What spy mission could be so strategic that the Allies had followed up this drop with further landings? And what were they after? None of the towns which had reported sightings were of any particular importance. The Resistance in each town had been suppressed and liquidated. The Sipo and the Wehrmacht together would surely arrest or annihilate small commando forces. And what, he wondered, did *Generalfeldmarschall* Rommel have to do with it all? Why had he chosen this day, if he were indeed connected with a conspiracy, to travel back to the *Vaterland?*

The telephone rang. "*Ja?*" he said into it, his voice hoarse and cracked.

"*Herr Sturmbannführer,* the patrols have come in."

"What news?"

"None, *Herr Sturmbannführer.* Everything is quiet in Sainte-Mère-Église and Sainte-Marie-du-Mont."

Sammstag replaced the phone. There were so many paths he could take, he hesitated to start on any one of them. Time was short, so the price of a mistaken direction was likely to be total failure. And if there was anything the Sipo did not appreciate, he thought, it was mistakes and failure.

The phone rang again. Sammstag looked at it in the yellow light of the table lamp. His extreme fatigue made it difficult for his eyes to focus on the black object. It seemed to be in another world, miles and miles away, connected to another set of historical circumstances. Its nagging ring, which caused the metal object to vibrate, jarred his ears but somehow did not seem urgent. He continued to stare at it, pondering what it might say if he answered it.

Then his mind snapped back. He picked up the receiver. "*Ja?*"

"*Herr Sturmbannführer,* another report has come in. A Gestapo van is missing."

"Where?"

"Sainte-Marie-du-Mont."

"When did it disappear?"

"Twenty minutes ago."

"*Danke, Untersturmführer.*" He hung up.

Then it dawned on Sammstag. A van was missing from Sainte-Marie-du-Mont! He pulled his feet off of the desk, then whirled in his chair so that he could see the map. The broken rendezvous had been near Sainte-Marie-du-Mont. The town was in the perimeter of the trap. His eyes raced back and forth across the larger paper. The spy had somehow made it from Sainte-Mère-Église to Sainte-Marie-du-Mont. It had taken him eight hours to do so, which meant he had gone overland. He probably had the assistance of the Resistance, so it was not surprising that the patrols had missed him. Having made it to Sainte-Marie-du-Mont, he could now proceed to his next destination. He was headed east with his companion. Sammstag remembered the reports of airdrops near Lion-sur-Mer, the ones which the *Standartenführer* himself had investigated. It was sixty kilometers from Lion-sur-Mer to Sainte-Marie-du-Mont. Too great a distance to walk.

Sammstag rose and went over to the map. The River Douve

cut across the probable path of the spy. There were only two bridges across the Douve, and they were both in Carentan. There was no possible way for the agent to penetrate the Sipo defenses in the town itself, no matter how excellent his papers. Besides, he was in the company of a woman, probably a French peasant. They would be too easily recognized. No, Sammstag thought, the Douve would cut off their path, unless . . .

He studied the map again. Unless he were not trying to get across the Douve. Unless the objective was on the west bank. The picture suddenly became very clear. Four kilometers from where he stood lay the locks of La Barquette, floodgates that controlled the water levels of the River Douve and its tributary canals. The gates had been ordered open by Field Marshal Rommel so that the lowlands in the Douve River valley would become flooded. The resulting marshes were perfect obstacles against airdrops. But if someone could close the gates, the flooding could be stopped, leaving hundreds of square kilometers of peaceful farmland open for Allied invasion from the air.

In five minutes, Heinrich Sammstag, in an armored personnel carrier, was speeding in the quiet night toward the locks at Pont-sur-Douve.

14

The ringing telephones jarred the normally quiet routine in the situation room at Saint-Germain-en-Laye. At 0230 hours on a Tuesday morning in this cavernous room, there would ordinarily have been no noise except for the scratching of pens and the muted tapping of typewriters. Tonight was different. At the tables lining the north wall beneath the master strategic map of France, at the desks ranged alongside the flat map table in the middle of the room, phones were ringing incessantly. A sea of voices talked into dull black receivers, and hundreds of pens and pencils dashed across paper, just as long croupier sticks moved blocks of wood across the shiny surface of the map table.

That something unusual was going on was abundantly clear to General Ludwig Beck. He stared at the flashing lights on the north wall, each one representing a Wehrmacht control station on the line reporting an incident. So many alarms, so many lights. Too many, he thought. The Allies are up to some trick.

He scanned the coastal defenses, particularly the ones near Colleville. There were alarmingly quiet. The bunker where the field marshal at the very moment awaited Beck's word to move on to the rendezvous with the Allied agent was a refuge of tranquillity. Beck wondered whether the Allies could have discovered where Rommel was hiding. He dismissed the idea. If the Sipo could not find him with their hundreds of agents, the Allies did not have a prayer of doing so.

Beck walked over to the map for a closer look. He was almost run down by a young colonel who dashed across the floor in a sprint, nearly colliding with the old general. The colonel bowed his head in apology and hurried on, as Beck returned his gaze to the map.

He found what he was looking for. Memorizing the number and letter code for the small detachment stationed near Pont-sur-Douve, the locks at La Barquette, he casually strolled past the map table, glancing at the troop dispositions as he did. They were as expected. He stopped at a desk. The captain sitting there was talking excitedly on the telephone when he looked up and saw the imposing general. He spoke a few more words, then hung up and sprang to his feet.

"*Herr Generaloberst?*"

"The locks at La Barquette, *Herr Hauptmann*. Have there been any reports?"

"*Ja, Herr Generaloberst.* A number of Allied gliders are said to have landed in the vicinity."

"How many?"

"I don't know, *Herr Generaloberst.*"

"Are the reports reliable?"

"I don't know. All the reports are confused. I believe it is happening, *Herr Generaloberst.*"

"What is happening?"

"The invasion, *Herr Generaloberst!*"

The invasion, in such weather and the night after the aborted rendezvous? Was this some sort of retribution for the mishap which caused the meeting not to occur? It was too absurd to be true. Beck smiled. "I think not. The Allies are throwing up a little smoke, but no fire."

"Do you really think so?"

"*Ja.* Our radar has not picked up any ships on the Channel. It is all part of some deception." Beck turned and walked away.

La Barquette held the key, he thought, as he went into his office to escape the din. It was there that the patrol was stationed —the patrol that was supposed to capture the spy the night before. It was from La Barquette that they were to have made their way to the secret spot near Colleville. If the Allied spy was still alive and still moving, he would sooner or later be led by the Resistance to La Barquette. If and when the word came through that the contact had been made, Beck had only to pick up the phone to set the final wheels in motion.

He sat at his desk and shut his eyes tightly. His head was swimming from lack of sleep. His hands clenched tightly for a moment, then relaxed. He opened the top drawer of his desk and, reaching far into the back of it, found a small cardboard box. Taking out a small capsule, he placed it in the left breast pocket of his uniform coat and slid the box back into the drawer. Cyanide was the traitor's closest friend.

The road stretched out in tight turns ahead of the pale headlights. Through the narrow windshield Tim started at marshy lowlands bathed in moonlight. Henri drove the vehicle like a madman, careening from one side of the road to the other as he took the turns at high speed. Tim looked down at the German, who lay on the floor beneath him. Holding the pistol in his left hand, he wiped the sweat from his right palm onto his soggy pants, then put the .45 back against the German's clammy forehead.

"How much farther?" he asked Henri.

"*Un kilomètre, Jean. C'est tout.*"

"What then?"

"I will tell you."

Henri took his foot from the accelerator, and the van began to lose speed. They hurtled through an S-curve, then glided around a lazy turn. Ahead Tim could see a crossroads. Henri shifted into third gear, and the engine whined as the van slowed, pulling up to the crossroads. A pair of roadsigns, one in French and one in German, identified it as Route Nationale 13. A weathered milepost pointed to the left: CARENTAN. 5 KM.

Henri shifted again and they took off, swinging widely to the left. Tim found it hard to believe that they were heading right into Carentan, a town that was undoubtedly swarming with Nazis. He was right. After about three quarters of a mile, they came to a small bridge.

Over the bridge, Henri turned left down a gravel road. The truck lurched in the wet ruts and came to a stop. Henri turned to Tim and Anne-Thérèse.

"Get out."

"And him?" Tim asked, pointing to the German.

"*Aussi.*"

Tim climbed into the front seat and motioned to the German to sit up. He waved his gun toward the door. The prisoner tried to climb over the seat, but with his arms tied at his side he managed only to get stuck. Tim grabbed him by the collar and pulled him free. The German tumbled head first out of the truck and into the mud. He groaned. Tim jumped out after him and pulled him to his feet.

"Over there."

Henri pointed to the tall grass which grew along the top of the riverbank. Tim looked at the German and for the first time, in the bright moonlight, saw his face clearly. He was very young, not more than seventeen. His curly blond hair was matted above his baby face, the blue eyes bewildered. Tim winced. It was like looking at a puppy. Ten weeks before, he had probably been sitting in a high school somewhere back in Germany. Then he was conscripted, given some training, and sent to the Western Front in a crash program. Now, in his first encounter with the enemy, he had failed completely. He was nothing more than a scared kid.

The German turned and stumbled toward the tall grass. Tim followed, five steps behind. He looked back and saw Henri, talking with Anne-Thérèse, leave her behind to join them. When they reached the grass, Tim could see the swollen river rushing past, the submerged grasses bent by the force of the current. A putrefying smell of swamp assailed his nostrils. Henri caught up with them.

"Kill him," Henri said.

Tim looked up quickly. "What?"

"I said, kill him! *Tout de suite.*"

"Why, for God's sake?"

"Because he knows too much."

Tim looked over at the puppy-faced blond, who showed no signs of understanding their conversation. His stomach knotted. With his left hand, he forced the German to his knees. The frightened blue eyes looked up, their expression telling Tim that the boy had guessed his fate. Tim looked at the grass and the muddy river, then at Henri. With a quick motion, he turned back, stepped forward, put the gun to the German's temple, and pulled the trigger.

There was a loud thump as the German's body landed on the grass, where it twitched violently. Henri looked briefly at the bleeding hulk and then, with a disgusted thrust, kicked it halfway into the river. With another push, the body cleared the banks and floated silently out into the water, turning this way and that as the current took hold of it. Tim stared after it. He suddenly realized how easy it had all been. No guilt, no feelings. No second thoughts. Just good-bye Germany, mother, apple strudel, and the Führer. The body continued to circle, sinking lower as the water worked into the clothing. Air pockets appeared in the cloth, then disappeared, and the body sank deeper. Tim found it impossible to care.

The three of them returned to the van, climbed back into it, and slowly lurched down the mired road. The river had overflowed in a number of places, changing the dirt road to a lumpy mass of clay and matted grass. After no more than a mile, it became hopeless. Henri pulled the van over to the side, shut it off, and motioned for them to alight. "From here, we must walk."

"Where are we going?"

"The locks. Two kilometers."

"And—?"

Henri smiled slightly. "Then we will surrender to the Germans, *mon ami.*"

"We can trust them?"

"*Oui, Jean.* It is part of the plan."

Hugging to the shoulder where the ground was firmest, they started walking. Tim couldn't feel the ground beneath him, so tired and exhausted were his nerves. He shuffled along behind Henri, stumbling through the scraggly grass, thinking only that he was in a nightmare from which he would soon awaken to find himself on silk sheets in the finest hotel in London with a piping hot breakfast waiting for him on a silver tray.

Soon the locks at La Barquette loomed before them. Against the sky Tim saw the iron wheels and chains that operated the sluice gates, which in turn controlled the flow of the River Douve. There were three gates in all, spaced in the middle of the structure. At the far end was a two-story building made from the same stone and mortar from which all the houses of Normandy were constructed. Lights gleamed from small windows in the building.

Twenty yards from the dam, on the near riverbank, was a guardhouse. A hooded light shown directly down from the iron post which jutted out of the slanting roof, illuminating the wooden barrier. Two German sentries stood by the wooden gate that blocked the road. Henri whispered to Tim as they approached the checkpoint, "We must be careful, Jean. We must get to the captain as quickly as possible. No matter what."

"*Bien. Anne-Thérèse?*"

"*Oui, Jean?*"

"*Courage. C'est le moment.*"

"*Oui, Jean. Tout va bien.*" She smiled warmly at him, then grabbed his arm and held it close to her as they walked along. Her head rested against his shoulder. It was a simple gesture, innocent and natural. Her warm body brushed his. Tim slipped his arm around her. How strange it is, he thought, that I should feel so close to this girl and she doesn't even know my real name.

"*Halt!*" The metallic click of the machine pistol being cocked brought Tim back to where he really was. "*Wohin?*"

Henri took his cue brilliantly. "*Ah, messieurs, pardon . . . mille pardons, mais nous sommes perdus."* His mimicry of drunkenness amused the guards. *"Ce soir nous sommes allés à la ferme de Monsieur Pacquelin. Vous ne le connaissez, mais c'est sa ferme qui est—"*

"Halt! Ihre Pässe, bitte!" Henri stopped. He smiled mawkishly, then reached into his coat. He fumbled as he did so, smiled even more broadly, then with an exaggerated effort withdrew his passbook. He walked up to the sentries and handed it to one of them grandly.

"Les papiers, c'est peu de chose. Ah, mes amis, venez." He motioned to Tim and Anne-Thérèse. Slowly they approached the barrier gate. One of the sentries, the one with the book, leaned back into the dim light to read. Tim saw that his uniform didn't fit, that the jacket was drawn in so tightly around the waist that it puffed comically. Even the collar was too big for his adolescent frame, so it bobbed loosely around his skinny neck.

"Ihre Papiere!" Tim and Anne-Thérèse gave him their books. He looked them over carefully. He looked up at Tim and back to the book. Then he called his fellow sentry over. Speaking in a low voice and very rapidly, he explained something about Tim's book, pointing to the picture and to Tim. The sentry glanced at Tim, then at the book, then back to Tim. The first sentry paged through the book carefully, finally returning to the picture page. Tim strained to hear what he was saying but couldn't. The first sentry opened Anne-Thérèse's book. She received the same treatment, the same once-overs, the same murmured comments.

Henri coughed. *"Messieurs, je—"*
"Ruhig!"
"Mais je connais le capitaine! Herr Schmeling!"
The machine pistols rose to cover them. *"Hände hoch!"*
Tim looked at Henri, who shrugged and raised his arms. Tim and Anne-Thérèse did the same.

"Raus!" The two Germans jerked their guns in the direction of the dam. The three prisoners started up the road as the other

sentry raised the barrier. The road was steep and the rain had turned it to a quagmire, so their feet continually slipped. Tim swore as his boots slid along the clay.

They walked across the dam. The walkway was narrow where they crossed the sluice gates. They were forced to lower their right hands and hold tightly to the cast-iron railing. As they passed over, Tim looked down at the water tumbling noisily through the cement and stone channel into the wide pond far below. The rain-swollen river cascaded through the open gates, carrying branches, twigs, and clods of earth with it. Tim thought of the German he had killed fifteen minutes before. He wondered how long it would take before his corpse crashed through the gates and tumbled out toward the sea. He wondered whether anyone would notice.

On the far side they halted by the stone building. Tim looked around while the sentry knocked on the steel door. Coils of barbed wire were strewn haphazardly around the station in a crude attempt to form defense perimeters. He looked back toward the building. Fifty feet from it sat an armored personnel carrier and a large troop transport. It was strange to see such vehicles at an isolated post. Tim noticed grimly that the troop transport was black.

The door opened and the guards motioned them inside. Tim had to crouch as he walked through the small opening. The first floor of the building had been converted to a crude barracks. Six bunks were lined against one wall, all of them filled with sleeping soldiers in half-battle dress. Desks and footlockers filled the rest of the space. The sentries pointed toward a wooden staircase. From the top of it a small beam of light glowed.

They ascended the steps, their wet boots clumping loudly as they did. At the top, the first sentry opened the door and for a moment the bright light dazzled Tim's eyes.

It was the usual command post: field telephones on a table, maps on the walls, code books and logs, desks stacked with paperwork, report forms, and pictures of the Führer. Wehrmacht soldiers sat there, quietly going about their duties. Across from the door the Wehrmacht captain stood at one of the windows, sweeping the flatlands of the Douve River valley with his binoculars. It was not at all extraordinary for a Wehrmacht post.

Except for the six SS men who grabbed Tim, Henri, and Anne-Thérèse as they entered. Tim's blood froze as strong hands dug into his arms. With wrenching force, they were handcuffed. An SS major walked over and stood directly in front of the three of them. Tim noticed the Sipo emblem on his tunic. The steel-gray eyes stared at Tim.

"*Willkommen, Herr Amerikaner,*" he said, his lips curling into a faint smile. "We have much to talk about!"

Josef Kreitzl murmured loudly, then snapped his eyes open as the hands shook him awake. He looked up into the semi-darkness of the room and saw the oafish face of Blickensderfer above him. Kreitzl yawned, then rubbed his eyes and sat upright on the chaise in his office.

"*Ja, Herr Hauptsturmführer?*"

"*Sturmbannführer* Sammstag has telephoned, *Herr Sturmbannführer.* He has captured the spy."

Kreitzl's head twisted in a new alertness. "Where?"

"Pont-sur-Douve."

"When did he call?"

"A few minutes ago, *Herr Sturmbannführer.*"

"What time is it?"

Blickensderfer looked at his watch. "Oh-three-hundred hours."

"What does the *Sturmbannführer* wish me to do?"

"He wants you to go to Pont-sur-Douve for the interrogation."

Kreitzl yawned loudly. "Now?"

"At first light, *Herr Sturmbannführer.*"

"Good enough, *Herr Hauptsturmführer.* Send orders for a car to be ready in two hours."

"*Jawohl, Herr Sturmbannführer.*"

"And bring me some schnapps, *Herr Hauptsturmführer.* It's a cold night."

"*Jawohl, Herr Sturmbannführer.*" Blickensderfer snapped a salute, turned awkwardly on his heels, and left the room.

Kreitzl lay back on the chaise in the cramped district office of the Gestapo in Bayeux. It was forty kilometers to Pont-sur-Douve. It should take no more than half an hour to reach it in the early morning, when the roads were clear. Kreitzl smiled sleepily as he stared at the ceiling. So the spy was caught! It would only be a little while before he knew the meaning of the mysterious cipher, and whether or not Wehrmacht officers were involved in a widespread conspiracy against the Führer. A good night's work, he thought. The schnapps will take the edge off the tension, so that sleep would come for another hour. It was now Tuesday, the sixth of June. It would be a busy day.

"Coffee, *bitte.* You will have some, *nicht wahr?*" The tight lips poised half open, in a mode of gentle questioning. "I have forgotten. You do not speak English. Only French."

"*Je m'appelle Jean Robichon.*"

"*Zwei Kaffee, bitte. Auch etwas Zucker.*"

The SS officer sat down in the wooden chair opposite where Tim sat handcuffed. The gray eyes stared intently at him. Tim returned the stare, his vision glazed. He barely noticed the SS soldiers seated in the background alongside the Wehrmacht captain, for the single light on the desk which had been aimed at his face left the rest of the room in darkness. Tim could count the pores on the leathery skin of his interrogator.

Tim shifted, then winced. The steel of the handcuffs bit painfully into his wrists because his arms were stretched so tightly around the back of the chair in which he sat.

"Come, *Amerikaner.* I know far too much as it is. You can please to talk."

"Je m'appelle Jean Robichon."

"You are not Jean Robichon. You are an officer in the American army."

For only an instant Tim's eyes flashed. *"Je m'appelle Jean Robichon."*

"And you are the Falcon. No?"

Tim yawned and let his head fall, so that he was looking at the floor. *"Je m'appelle Jean Robichon."*

Tim felt his head being pulled up sharply by his hair. He let out a small yell. The German officer's fist slammed across his mouth before the yell was entirely out. His jaw cracked under the blow. Tim felt a wetness about his mouth, a sticky collection of liquid which made him gag. He coughed, then turned and spat. Blood and mucus coagulated on the wooden floor.

"The Falcon, *Herr Amerikaner*. You are the Falcon!"

Tim continued to gaze at the blood. He coughed again, and the mushy syrup dribbled out of his mouth and down his chin. Unconsciously he tried to wipe it away with his hand, but the handcuffs held him firmly.

"Je m'appelle Jean Ribichon."

The fist buzzed through the air again and landed on the other side of Tim's face. His head snapped from the impact and he groaned. His mouth began to fill and he panicked. A primal fear of choking to death grabbed him. He leaned over as far as he was able and, with a wrenching gasp, spewed blood onto his lap.

"The Falcon, *Herr Amerikaner!* You are the Falcon?"

Lightheadedness hit Tim. He fell forward, his eyes shut. His stomach heaved and he vomited, again spilling blood onto his pants legs and the floor. He tried to think. Fortunately, he was so tired that there was little feeling left in his body. He can hit me all he wants, he thought. Soon I will just pass out.

The SS officer rose from his chair. He paced across the wooden floor of the guard tower, the humidity-swollen boards creaking as he walked. There was no sound in the room except for the floorboards and the gentle squeak of the leather boots. With an effort Tim sat back up in his chair and opened his eyes as far as he could. He felt the blood rolling down his cheek and dripping onto his shirt.

The boots stopped. The SS major stood in half-darkness across the room, talked to his soldiers in a quiet voice, and then turned to the Wehrmacht captain. Tim looked at him. He had sat motionless throughout the interrogation. There was no visible emotion in his face, no hint whatever that Henri's description of him as a friend and conspirator was true.

Tim closed his eyes and groaned softly. It was all over. They had been led into a trap. Solstice was a brilliant intelligence coup on the part of the Germans. Beauclerk, O'Neill-Butler—everyone had been fooled. It would be only a matter of time before they really started to work on him, before they broke him and Henri and discovered the plans for the invasion. Tim wondered how much pain he could take. He thought about the tiny pill hidden in his watch. He managed to touch the watch band with the fingers of his right hand, but there was no way he could get to the pill and swallow it with his hands bound.

"*Er sagt nichts, Herr Hauptmann.*"

"*Ja, das merk' ich wohl, Herr Sturmbannführer! Vielleicht weiss er nichts.*"

"*Unmöglich! Kann' ich nicht glauben!*"

Tim heard the exchange and wondered if indeed the captain wasn't on his side. He had suggested that Tim knew nothing. Tim had found a source of hope. Everything will be all right, he said to himself, there is an avenue of escape at hand.

The door opened. Two SS soldiers who had left the room earlier reappeared, holding Anne-Thérèse between them. Her hands also were handcuffed behind her back. They brought her to the center of the room. As the light grew stronger on her, Tim stared. Already her face was beginning to puff from where they had hit her. Her left eye was swollen completely shut, and a few dried trickles of blood traced down her cheek. As Tim looked at her, her good eye met his. It spoke to him unmistakably. *Courage.*

"*Herr Amerikaner,* look!" The SS man strode back proudly to center stage. "She is most pretty, yes? Young. What a pity to hurt her!"

"*Je m'appelle Jean Robichon.*"

For the first time the German became angry. Tim stiffened. He sensed that the SS officer had passed a threshold, that the point of patience had been reached. From here on out the questioning would become brutal.

The German walked over to Anne-Thérèse, grabbed her chin with his left hand, and with a wide swing punched her in the face. He hit her twice more. Blood gushed from her nose. She made no sound. He hit her again, and a muted cry came from her throat, although her lips did not part.

"The Falcon! Tell me you are the Falcon, and I will stop!" The sweating German glared at Tim.

"*Je m'appelle Jean Robichon.*"

In a fury the German lay back and lashed Anne-Thérèse across the face once, twice, then a third time. With a savage grunt, he grabbed at the lacing of her blouse. Seething with anger he tugged at the leather thongs, wrenching them from the wool. In a moment the blouse hung open, exposing her breasts. The German grabbed one of them and, with a violent twist, pinched the nipple so brutally that Anne-Thérèse screamed out. Satisfied, the SS man whirled around and faced Tim.

"There is more, *Herr Amerikaner.* If you do not tell me that you are the Falcon, I will give her to the soldiers!" He paused dramatically, then strode across the room and leaned over, his face mere inches from Tim's. "You are the Falcon?"

"*Je m'appelle Jean Robichon.*"

The German straightened and turned to face his men. He motioned toward the door. The two SS men who held Anne-Thérèse up dragged her away. Her knees buckled, but they still

managed to get her through the doorway and down the steps.
The other SS men followed. Tim listened as their boots sounded loudly on the wooden treads. Excited voices and yells came drifting up the steps. Through them, Tim heard soft cries and gentle sobs. Then came laughter and more yells. The sobs turned to cries and finally to screams. Tim strained in his chair. From below came the sound of boots stomping in rhythm, which was quickly followed by loud handclaps. Cheers and whistles came next. Staccato cries of pain from Anne-Thérèse filtered through the raucous noise.

"Talk and it will stop."

Tim jerked his head so that he faced the SS man. The German looked at Tim with a look of cool amusement on his face, an expression which told Tim that he knew he had finally pierced Tim's defenses. Tim pulled at his chair, lifting it off the ground, then sank back with a loud cry which was unheard over the din as the Germans began raping Anne-Thérèse in earnest.

Suddenly the world exploded with a brilliant yellow flash. Glass crashed to the floor, and Tim felt himself thrown back against his chair by a tremendous blast at the windows. Smoke streamed through the small tower room. As the smoke cleared, Tim could see the Wehrmacht captain lying prostrate on the floor. The SS major had been thrown by the force of the explosion against the wall. From the window came a whipping blast of the cool night air. Gunshots sounded dully from outside as hundreds of rounds sprayed the stone building. Whining bullets ricocheted through the room. With a grunt, Tim threw his body so that he rolled over and fell to the floor. The heavy chair pinioned him painfully, but at least he was out of the line of fire.

From down below came sounds of confusion. Tim's ear was pressed to the floor, so he could hear what was going on clearly. Boots clomped rapidly, and voices cried out in German. He heard Anne-Thérèse scream. More voices shouted, then he heard the steel door open. Through the confusion he heard someone shouting clearly, *"Sie ist weg! Sie ist weg!"* The steel door slammed shut with a heavy clang, and Tim knew that Anne-Thérèse had escaped into the night.

Suddenly a fury of gunfire exploded outside. Through the shattered window near where Tim lay came a single piercing female scream. Another burst of fire cascaded against the stone walls.

In a flash it was over. Before Tim truly comprehended that Anne-Thérèse was dead, he saw the SS major rush to the window and look out. The Wehrmacht captain rose slowly from the floor. Another series of explosions went off near the tower, then bright flashes lit the room. The SS man leaped back from the window just in time to avoid a shower of dirt. He stared at the captain incredulously.

"Die Alliierten, Herr Hauptmann!"

"Wieviele, Herr Sturmbannführer?" asked the captain as he grabbed a machine pistol from one of the tables.

"Zu viele! Wir sind umzingelt!"

To know that they were surrounded by enemy soldiers was all the captain needed. He raised the machine pistol and held the muzzle squarely on the his fellow German.

The SS man's jaw fell slack, and a look of bewilderment spread across his lined face. His voice choked, and his hands started to rise above his head.

They never made it. The volley of 7.92-mm bullets tore into the black cloth, ripping away the fabric and the flesh which lay beneath it. Blood ran red as the man twisted under the impact of the deadly fire and collapsed. His jerking body bounced off the adjacent wall, then crashed to the floor. In a final spasm, the mouth opened and coughed up blood which spilled over the chin and slowly dripped onto the black collar. After a few violent twitches, it was all over.

Mortar fire whistled through the night. The building shook as the shells exploded at the base of the structure. Guns crackled from all sides. The captain ripped off the spent magazine and tossed it on the floor. Rummaging through one of the desk drawers, he withdrew another one and rammed it into place just in time to turn and face the three SS men who tumbled in through the doorway.

They too were cut down under the spurts of the machine pistol. They fell on top of one another, yelling, crying, as the careening pieces of metal tore into them. Through the floor Tim suddenly heard another volley of fire, one which seemed almost to echo the blistering rounds which the captain was pouring into his fellow countrymen.

Then the firing, inside and out, stopped. Inside the room acrid blue powder smoke hung in filmy sheets.

Footsteps sounded on the steps. The captain held the machine pistol on the doorway long enough to see the gray of a Wehrmacht uniform before lowering the muzzle. The soldier stepped over the crowded bodies and looked sternly at his commanding officer.

"*Sie sind tot, Herr Hauptmann.*"

"*Alle?*"

The sergeant nodded. The captain laid the machine pistol on the desk. He crouched and ran over to where Tim lay, taking care to avoid becoming a target through the windows, and knelt beside him, his face solemn but not unfriendly. The sergeant, ordered to get the keys of the dead SS major, rifled the pockets, withdrew a set of keys, and tossed them deftly to the captain.

In a moment Tim's swollen wrists were free of the handcuffs. He lay back on the floor, feeling his arm and back muscles relax and uncramp while he massaged the sore joints where the handcuffs had bitten into them.

A perverse realization came over him. Before him stood the man the German leaders had picked to lead him to Field Marshal Rommel. He had finally made his contact. Yet outside, Allied soldiers were pouring down a murderous fire at them. Tim was now a prisoner of his own side. He had no sooner been rescued from one crisis than he was delivered into another.

He turned to the captain. *"Bringen Sie mich zum General-feldmarschall?"* The captain nodded. Tim shrugged. He lay back heavily on the floor and stretched his knotted muscles, which were so cramped he could not relax. Everywhere in his body nerve endings jangled. His jaw was sore, and he felt his face swelling.

The captain crawled across the room to the desk. Reaching up, he pulled down the telephone. He hit the buttons sharply, waited patiently for what seemed like several minutes as bullets whizzed around the window six inches above his head, then spoke sharply into the receiver.

"Herr Generaloberst? Hauptmann Schmeling." His eyes flickered up and fixed on Tim. *"Jawohl, Herr Generaloberst,* the Falcon has come!"

15

Helmut Knochen stared out the window toward the eastern skyline of Caen. Already small pockets of pink showed along the horizon behind the darkened silhouettes of buildings. Knochen glanced at his watch. It was 0430 hours. Sunrise would come within fifteen or twenty minutes.

He turned and puffed on his cigarette. It had been a terrible night. Reports had flooded into Saint-Germain-en-Laye about supposed airdrops. He had been on the phone with OB West almost continuously since midnight. He could make little sense out of what he had heard. The stupid Wehrmacht officers of von Rundstedt's staff! he thought. It is they who are to blame for this mess. Their outposts can't get any facts straight, and so they send along rumors. Like that one about an airdrop near Lion-sur-Mer. It had turned out to be a total fabrication.

Knochen took another puff on the cigarette, then delicately squashed it out in the ashtray on Kreitzl's desk. He wondered absently where Kreitzl was but decided not to worry about it. He removed the stub, dropped it in the ashtray, and put the ivory holder in his pocket. He sighed. The trip to Normandy had been one large false alarm. He had been up all night chasing imaginary Allied spies, thanks to the zeal of two SS majors. He remembered that there was to be a reception that night in Paris, an elegant affair at the Hotel Georges Cinq, one with champagne and courtisans. He wondered if that beautiful one with the red hair, Mademoiselle Demoreuille, whom he had met the month before at a party in the Faubourg, would be there.

He pushed the desk bell. The door opened and Schmidt-

Brümer entered. "Get the car ready. I am returning to Paris."

"But the agent?"

"There is no agent. My subordinates are seeing goblins up every tree. I have more important things to attend to."

"*Jawohl, Herr Standartenführer.*"

Knochen looked around the room to see if he had left anything lying around. Deciding he had not, he snapped his briefcase shut. Picking up the pack of cigarettes from the desk and stuffing it into his pocket, he took the case and left, shutting the door behind him.

The patches of pink turned to a pale crescent as the sun rose over the horizon through the window in the empty office on the fifth floor. Everything was quiet in the room except for the muted sounds of the rushing wind against the windowpane. Then came the jarring sound of the telephone ringing. The clanging reverberated in the empty room, the echo from each ring dying slowly. With an impatience born of emergency the phone continued to jangle in its cradle. After fifteen rings it stopped, only to recommence after a minute's silence for another fifteen measures. Then it fell silent for good.

Josef Kreitzl hung up the telephone, puzzled. He had been unable to get through to the outpost at Pont-sur-Douve and talk with Sammstag to see what developments had taken place with the Allied spy, and now he was unable to contact Knochen. Everywhere, it seemed, he was greeted with ringing telephones that no one answered. It left him very worried. This was not normal procedure.

He munched on the hard roll he had managed to find in the jumbled mess on the second floor of the Gestapo offices in Bayeux and glanced over the dispatch log. The number of radio receptions was extraordinarily high. All these reports of airdrops, Kreitzl thought, what do they mean? More nervous Wehrmacht officers, or dummies sent in by the Allies to cover the landing of the spy?

His mind returned to the unanswered phones. A curious knot formed in his stomach. Sammstag had no reason to leave Pont-sur-Douve. Indeed, his instructions had been specifically to meet him there. Perhaps it was that stupid Blickensderfer, Kreitzl thought, who had garbled up a message. Perhaps Sammstag had taken the prisoner to headquarters in order to interrogate him properly. He reached for the phone.

"The *Sturmbannführer* has not returned, *Herr Sturmbannführer*," said his aide. "I received a call from the Wehrmacht captain in charge at La Barquette. They were under siege."

"Siege?"

"*Ja, Herr Sturmbannführer*. American paratroopers had surrounded them. I heard firing in the background. I offered to send a relief detachment, but he refused."

"Why?"

"He said to wait until the situation clarified. He said the *Sturmbannführer* had agreed to wait as well."

"What did *Sturmbannführer* Sammstag say?"

"I did not talk with him, *Herr Sturmbannführer*."

"Why not?" Kreitzl felt a small tingle of suspicion.

"He was unavailable, I was told. I asked because of what we had learned."

Kreitzl stiffened. "What was that?"

"One of the Resistance prisoners confessed under heavy interrogation this morning. Pierre Deschamps from Sainte-Mère-Église. He spoke of an Henri who was leader of a *réseau* in Sainte-Marie-du-Mont. Henri was to have met last night with two men. One of them was to have been an agent, and the other was the old man from Saint-Sauveur-le-Comte."

"Which old man?"

"He was executed yesterday morning, *Herr Sturmbannführer*."

Kreitzl swore softly. "Where was the rendezvous?"

"Near Sainte-Marie-du-Mont. The prisoner said they were to

make contact with some Germans, but he did not know who they were."

"Did you press him?"

"*Ja, Herr Sturmbannführer.* His agonies were extreme."

"And he still did not know?"

"*Nein, Herr Sturmbannführer.* He knew only that Henri had a cousin with a deserted house where Allied agents had been hidden. He guessed that they would make the contact there. And he knew that Henri was friendly with several Wehrmacht officers, but he did not know their names."

"Where is this farm?"

"Vierville-sur-Mer. I do not know whether or not to believe him, *Herr Sturmbannführer.* He was hysterical."

"Can he bear further questioning?"

"*Nein, Herr Sturmbannführer.* He is unconscious."

"He is not to be executed until I can question him! Those are strict orders, *Herr Hauptsturmführer!* When the *Sturmbannführer* returns, tell him to wait for me."

"*Jawohl, Herr Sturmbannführer.*"

Kreitzl leaped to his feet, stuffing the remainder of the roll into his mouth. The other half of the broken rendezvous did not know about the capture of the Allied spy and was at this moment probably waiting for contact at Vierville. The trap waited to be sprung.

In a single moment Kreitzl pulled on his uniform tunic and burst out of the office into the anteroom. Blickensderfer was dozing in his wooden desk chair, his head lying back, his open mouth snoring. Kreitzl kicked him hard in the shin. Blickensderfer awoke with a cry.

"*Kommen Sie! Schnell!*" Kreitzl tightened the belt of his black uniform.

Blickensderfer looked at his watch. "It is only oh-four-forty-five hours, *Herr Sturmbannführer!*"

"I know, fool! Get a detachment ready! And hope that we are not too late!"

The firing diminished enough for them to make their break. Tim looked at his watch as he stood near the door to the guard tower at La Barquette. It was 0505 hours. He glanced over his shoulder and saw in the darkened room the outlines of Captain Schmeling and Henri. From upstairs came the sound of the small German garrison returning the fire of the American paratroopers who lay hidden in the grassy fields surrounding the locks.

Tim stepped quickly over to peer out of one of the small windows that faced east across the flooded river. The sky showed traces of day. In another fifteen minutes it would be light enough to make their attempt impossible. Tim listened to the firing. It came in sporadic bursts. He knew that the paratroopers were waiting until they could see clearly to make their assault. He also knew that there was no way to alert them to his presence or his mission. Even his knowledge of the passwords would not keep him from being made a prisoner of war. He walked over to Schmeling.

"Do you have mortars?"

"Mortars? *Ja, Herr Amerikaner. Zwei.*"

"Tell your men to put both of them at the north window. When I give the sign, they are to fire as many rockets as they can and spray the field with machine-gun fire. *Verstehen Sie?*"

"*Jawohl, Herr Amerikaner.*" Schmeling turned to one of his men nearby. In a low voice he spoke rapidly to the man, who then disappeared quickly up the steps. Schmeling looked back at Tim. After a few minutes, the soldier reappeared at the head of the steps. Schmeling looked at him, nodded, then turned to Tim. "*Bereit,*" he said quietly.

Tim gripped his M.P. 44 tightly and grabbed the door handle. With a mighty swing he pulled the door open so that it clanged against the stone wall. "*Anfahren!*"

From over their heads came a tremendous volley of bullets. The mortars clumped metallically as they sent their deadly charges arcing through the sky. Tim, Henri, and Captain Schmeling crouched over and dashed across the yard next to the tower toward the armored car fifty feet away. Two hundred yards from them the mortar shells exploded in bursts.

When they were halfway across the open terrain the fire was returned. Stray bullets whizzed past Tim as he struggled to keep low and run at the same time. He kept his eyes fixed on the car as he zigzagged across the ground. When he reached it, he flung himself down against the side of the vehicle. Fortunately the black SS truck which had brought the ill-fated detachment the night before stood in back of the car and shielded it from fire to the west and south. That would make it easier to climb onto the top of the car and slip down inside.

Tim looked back in horror as Henri was hit. With a single cry the Frenchman threw up his arms and fell face down onto the gravel. His rifle hit the ground next to him on its butt end and then tumbled to a resting place on one of Anne-Thérèse's legs.

In the pale morning light Tim saw her dead body for the first time. She lay on her right side, her back to Tim, so he couldn't see her face. Her auburn hair was a tangled mass, half floating in a muddy puddle. She looked as if she were sleeping peacefully, except for three circles of red on her torn russet blouse. One small corner flap of the blouse, ripped when the German officer had pulled her clothes away the night before, rippled slightly in the breeze. It was the only movement. Henri lay equally still, with arms outstretched.

Schmeling threw himself down beside Tim with a heavy grunt. *"Der Franzose. Er ist tot."*

Tim nodded. He continued to stare at the limp forms. They had been people he had known for less than a day. In that short time, he had felt a bond for them, a closeness. Yet now that they were gone his emotions were strangely vacant. There were no clenched fists, no wishes that it had been otherwise. Tim wanted to cry but found he couldn't. He turned to Schmeling. *"Kommen Sie!"*

Tim threw his machine pistol onto the ground and leaped up. The fire from the guard tower increased again. He grabbed the metal handle on the side of the car and put his foot on the front bumper. With a heave he pulled himself up onto the top of the command car. A surge of bullets struck the armor and ricocheted wildly into the night. Tim lay down on the surface and reached out to undo the lock on the hatch top. He struggled desperately with it for a minute, then managed to throw it open. As it lifted up, two bullets slammed into the cover and left it vibrating in Tim's hand. With another heave Tim pulled himself up to a kneeling position, put his hands on either side of the hatchway, and dropped inside.

The firing increased as Schmeling followed Tim and pulled the hatch cover down behind him to throw the lock. Inside it was cramped. The only light came through the two small slit windows above the driver's seat.

Schmeling sat down on the metal seat and pushed the starter button. The engine turned once slowly, then died. He tried again. Again the engine died. Tim began to panic. He guessed that the car could withstand a mortar blast, but he knew that a bazooka would blow them to pieces as they sat there. If the paratroopers had a bazooka. He searched his mind feverishly to try and remember anything about bazookas in the tactical plans. Page after page of orders and directives rolled in front of his mind's eye. He shook his head. He couldn't remember.

The engine turned and finally started. The motor belched and rattled as Schmeling raced it. Tim sat down on the other metal seat and peered out of the window. They started to move.

The car swung out from behind the tower and headed north across the fields, directly toward the ocean. When they left the gravel, the car bucked and plunged through the muddy grasslands. Every so often the wheels spun free, zinging loudly as they slipped through the surface mud at high velocity. Then they would grab again, and the awkward car would lurch forward, throwing Tim against the side.

Shots clanged harmlessly off the vehicle. Tim tried to scan the horizon through the narrow slits but could see little in the still-dim morning light. As the car crashed across the field, he caught strange glimpses of soldiers in the field hiding behind small hillocks and trees. Short bursts of fire would then hit the car. Once Tim saw a soldier lob a grenade at them, but it fell short and landed in one of the swampy pools, where it exploded and sent a tower of water twenty feet into the air.

A hundred yards north of the locks, Schmeling slammed the car sharply to the right. When it straightened out Tim saw up ahead a small bridge over the Douve. He remembered it from the aerial recons. Near the bridge was a small cluster of American troops.

"*Wieviele Soldaten, können Sie's sehen?*"

Tim tried to count, but the bumpy motion of the car made that impossible. "*Ich weiss nicht,*" he replied.

Schmeling increased their speed. The car took off, crunching through the fields until it came to the roadway that led to the bridge. The Americans, seeing the car so close, scattered and ran for cover—all except one, who knelt by the side of the road and took aim. Tim's heart leaped into his throat. That one had a flamethrower.

The armored car lumbered rapidly toward the bridge. The American ducked down, apparently expecting the machine gun on top of the car to start firing at him momentarily. When it didn't, he sat up, a bewildered expression spreading across his face. He raised the nozzle of his weapon.

With a sudden twist of the wheel Schmeling aimed the car right at the soldier. Tim saw his eyes open wide. The man froze, then let out a yell and tumbled backward down the hill. Schmeling turned the car sharply back onto the roadway and roared onto the bridge. The small causeway echoed loudly as the five-ton command car lurched over the bridge.

It was when they had reached the other side that Tim thought back to the reconnaissance maps. Ahead of them lay open farmland and back roads and, beyond that, Isigny. There would be fewer troops in that sector.

There was an eerieness to what was happening that made him uneasy. The invasion had clearly begun, but with a whimper only. Tim had seen little action except for the airdrop he had observed in Sainte-Marie-du-Mont and the soldiers at La Barquette. Otherwise nothing was happening. No air raids, no naval artillery. The roads were empty, and the guardhouse telephones had been quiet. There was only the serene silence of the dawn breaking on the coastal plains of France. It was all too easy. Something was going wrong.

Tim looked at his watch. The Allied troops were scheduled to hit the five beaches at 0630 hours. It was now 0520.

He had an hour to find Rommel.

It was ominously dark except for the small squares of light on the floor. A close silence, chilled by ocean winds, prevailed in the dense atmosphere of the concrete room. Even the roar of the ocean five hundred meters away was muffled.

Colonel von Frickstein shook the sleep from his eyes. He finished buttoning his uniform jacket as he made his way gingerly in the darkness across the plotting room, trying to avoid upsetting the tables and map stands in the semidarkness. He finished with his coat as he stopped in front of the metal door. He rapped lightly. When no sound came out, he knocked again. Surprised, he pushed the door open and peered inside. The tiny room with a single cot was empty. The bed was still made, although wrinkles in the blanket suggested that someone had lain on it not long before.

Von Frickstein left the room, shutting the door behind him.

He looked around the main room. His eyes rested on the thin ribbon of light that outlined the door leading to the observation deck. Again taking care not to stumble over anything, von Frickstein walked to the door and tried to open it. It was stuck. He pulled again, and it swung free, with a rusty groan. The wet air from the sea stung von Frickstein's face. He squinted at the spray as he crouched in the narrow passageway with six steps leading up to the deck itself.

The field marshal was there, gazing into the pale morning light. The heavy clouds filtered the sunlight, making it seem much earlier than it really was. Before him spread a deserted scene. The sand was dirty ochre, with hunks of driftwood and strips of barbed wire punctuating the level beach. Fog hovered over the shoreline, allowing only the first two or three waves to be visible from the bunker. Beyond that the fog formed an opaque curtain over the cold waters of the English Channel.

The strong winds blew at Rommel's field overcoat, but the gaunt form remained immobile. Von Frickstein held back near the passageway. After a moment Rommel slowly turned and looked at him.

"*Guten Morgen, Herr Oberst.*"

"*Guten Morgen, Herr Generalfeldmarschall. Haben Sie gut geschlafen?*"

"*Nein.*" Rommel smiled weakly. He had not slept well for months, and there was no reason why he should have gotten a good sleep on this, the most important night of the war. "You are ready?"

"*Ja, Herr Generalfeldmarschall.* The arrangements have all been made."

Rommel nodded. He looked back toward the sea. "Good. We must not waste time."

"*Ja, Herr Generalfeldmarschall.* The Sipo has been active all night."

"It is not the Sipo which worries me." Rommel stared for a

long while at the booming surf before he spoke again. "They are coming, von Frickstein."

"Who, *Herr Generalfeldmarschall?*"

"The Allies. I can feel their presence. Out there." He pointed at the fogbank. "I cannot see them, but I know they are out there, waiting for the kill."

"The invasion, *Herr Generalfeldmarschall?* That is impossible! The weather will not allow it!"

"I know that the weather will not allow it. I know many things, and one of them is that they are out there." He looked back to von Frickstein. "This single man that we are to meet?"

"The Falcon?"

"*Ja.* He is merely the first. Many more are coming right behind him." Rommel sighed deeply. "What time is it?"

"Oh-five-forty hours."

"Come. We have a most important appointment."

As Rommel turned to go, the quiet seascape erupted in a fury of artillery explosions. The *Generalfeldmarschall* whipped around so that he faced the sea. From the fog came the heavy pounding of naval guns, hundreds of them—a dull but ominous pounding from their positions far offshore. They were so far away that for a brief moment von Frickstein took them to be German destroyers attacking Allied ships in the Channel.

Then the shells whistled in on the beach. Geysers of sand and smoke shot up in the air as the projectiles began to rain their destruction along the ridge of bunkers. The air was filled with the whine of shells and the piercing sounds of explosions. Von Frickstein ran to the lip of the bunker and peered out. The cliffs to the east were shrouded in black smoke. Through it he could see flames as some of the coastal defense positions burned in the aftermath of obliteration. Through the deafening sounds came the muted cries of human voices from down the beach.

The earth trembled as the shelling continued, even though most of the shells were hitting far inland. The shaking did not let up, but instead grew. The entire bunker vibrated from the shock waves.

"It is beginning, *Herr Oberst.*"

They walked quickly back down the steps into the bunker, closing the metal door behind them. Even sheltered by two-meter concrete walls, they still felt the vibrations of the shells.

In the bunker the lights were on, and half-dressed soldiers were rushing to battle stations. Colonel Pluskat, the commandant of the four batteries on the beach, was talking hoarsely into the field telephone.

Rommel and von Frickstein crossed the bunker and opened the door that led inland just as a cascade of sand which had been shaken loose by a shell tumbled onto their heads. A Wehrmacht grenadier stood on the narrow steps which led down to the bunker, gazing skyward, his .33/40 carbine held at the ready. Startled, he turned to see Rommel, then snapped to attention.

The two German officers ran across the grass which separated the bunker from the cliffs behind it. The sound of the shells was now intolerably loud. Ducking, they ran down the twisting path between the coils of barbed wire. It was fifty meters to the outer perimeter of the coastal defense line. When they reached the car, Rommel paused to look up at the leaden sky. The explosions seemed to be concentrated inland. He guessed that the ships were aiming for Carentan and the vital railroad lines. It was only a preparatory bombardment, he concluded.

Then he glanced back at the windy coast. Petrified, he stared toward the sea.

"Von Frickstein! Look!"

They watched as the fog lifted on the new day. Where before had only been a veil of mist there now lay hundreds of ships, perhaps even thousands, four kilometers offshore. Guns blazed along the entire line of craft, a hundred thrusts of yellow flame erupting every second. Battleships and cruisers pitched majestically through the swells. Hundreds of landing craft circled near them, in large, slow sweeps.

"*Mein Gott!*" whispered von Frickstein in amazement.

Rommel continued to stare at the armada. "The Allies have tricked us. They have done brilliantly! There is no way we can stop their landings! We have now only to make our rendezvous and surrender."

"It is staggering! It is the end for Germany!" Von Frickstein looked at Rommel. "We can waste no more time, *Herr Generalfeldmarschall!*"

The two men climbed into the Mercedes. The car started with a roar. Von Frickstein let the giant engine rumble for a few moments; then he put it in gear. It lurched on the sandy terrain, swung onto the road, and lumbered slowly along toward Colleville as the shells continued to pound the fortifications at Omaha Beach.

The tired eyes gazed at the swinging pendulum on the wall clock, twitching slightly as their owner struggled to keep his lids open. The pendulum swung from side to side, marking the seconds with an agonizing slowness. Through the closed doors came the sound of voices and running feet, but Ludwig Beck's eyes didn't leave the elaborate clock face. They had scarcely left it for the half hour which had just passed.

The clock chimed, the sound of the gong almost drowned by the whirring of the strike mechanism. Six chimes, and the ancient machine fell silent again. It was too late.

The hands which shook from having had no sleep in forty-eight hours picked up the telephone. The voice of the switchboard operator came on, and the parched voice gave the necessary instructions. There was a ringing very far away. Then Speidel's voice answered.

"There has been no word," Beck told him.

There was a long silence on the other end. "What is the last you know, *Herr Generaloberst?*"

"The Falcon was at La Barquette. That was a hour ago. Since then, there has been nothing."

"There is perhaps still time," Speidel said hopefully. "Where is the *Generalfeldmarschall?*"

"*Ich weiss nicht.*" Beck breathed heavily. "I pray he is safe."

"I will stay here at La Roche-Guyon, *Herr Generaloberst.*"

"*Gut.* I hope to see you again."

Speidel paused at the implications of Beck's last sentence. "I also, *Herr Generaloberst. Auf Wiedersehen.*"

Beck stared at the wall ahead of him blankly. Unconsciously, he patted the pocket of his tunic to see if the pill was still there. Then he laid his head down on the desk, at Saint-Germain-en-Laye. In a minute he was fast asleep.

Erwin Rommel looked at the destruction which lay all around him. The sky thundered as Allied planes rolled overhead, spewing bombs. The entire earth shook as the metal canisters found their targets and exploded. From the beach and cliffs behind him Rommel could see tall pillars of smoke. Shells and rockets whistled about the car.

Vierville was nearly destroyed. Smoldering buildings greeted Rommel and von Frickstein as they passed through what had once been a sleepy little town. Flames engulfed several houses, and fire crews worked frantically to put them out. The roads were already littered with rubble from the blasted-out buildings. Two Wehrmacht detachments, busy sandbagging the streets in the center of town, stopped work and saluted as the black staff car went by them.

At the main intersection, von Frickstein turned left. The east end of the village, which was farthest from the narrow channel through the cliffs that connected Vierville with the sea, was less damaged. French families stood in front of some of the stone houses, grazing at the skies. Despite the concern on their faces, there was almost a festive air among them. Some prayed as the planes passed over, their hands crossing their breasts, while others laughed and teased their children. Others stared at the black car, their faces filled with the hate built by four years of occupation. One woman stepped forward and spat at the Mercedes as it passed by.

Just past the last house in Vierville, von Frickstein swung the car onto a heavily shaded road which led off to the south. They passed beneath the spreading limbs of somber trees for a hundred meters and then veered off to the right through a thickly wooded section bordering on a pasture. The Mercedes lurched through the rain, sheets of water shooting from her wheels, until it pulled into a clearing and stopped at a large farmhouse which to all appearances had long been deserted. Sheltered by trees, the stone structure rose two stories, roofed only by rotted timbers and dangling sections of shingles. Wooden shutters hung loosely from the windows, rocking slightly in the crisp morning wind. Tall grasses grew up at the foundations and even through the empty doorway.

Next to the house, under a stringer of camouflage netting, stood a group of Wehrmacht officers. As Rommel stepped out of the Mercedes, he recognized them all: Lieutenant Colonel Schöndienst, commandant of the 2nd Artillery Battalion of the 352nd Division; General Hellmich, commandant of the 243rd Division; Colonel von Tempelhof, operations officer for Army Group B; Major General Erdheim, commandant of the 3rd Infantry Regiment of the 711th Division; Lieutenant General Falley, the commander of the 91st Air Landing Division. Together they controlled 50,000 troops along the Normandy coastline. They watched Rommel anxiously as he walked across the wet grass and stood facing them.

Rommel exchanged salutes with the officers. *"Meine Herren!* We stand at a dangerous moment. The enemy has delivered to us the force of his might. I do not expect our shore defenses to hold for long against his assault. If these are indeed major landings, I fear that our positions will be overrun by nightfall. Even should the defenses hold and the Führer reinforce OB West, there can be nothing in the end but defeat for the *Vaterland.*"

Rommel's tired voice hung eerily in the wet glade. "I ask you to join with me in a plan to save Germany from destruction at the hands of the Bolshevik foe. By laying down our arms and seeking peace with the American and British forces, we can concentrate our might in the East and stem the tide which even now threatens our homes and our families. In defeat there can be victory." He stopped. None of the officers moved, nor did their aides, who stood behind them. The wind rippled through the leaves and netting, and the war continued on around them, but in the clearing the group of desperate German officers was motionless.

"An Allied agent will soon arrive here to arrange for our capitulation. He will carry with him plans for an expedient surrender. There will be no more bloodshed on either side. France will pass into the control of the Allies. Certain of our number of OKW . . ." He stopped. He wanted to reveal to the assembled soldiers the identities of von Stauffenberg and Beck, of von Stülpnagel and von Kluge, but he dared not. "Certain of our number will convince the Führer of the wisdom of our actions. Your honor will not be stained but will instead be glorified.

"This much you already know. I only wish now to remind you again of your highest duty to your *Vaterland.* If any of you do not wish to join us, arrangements have been made." Rommel did not have to say what the arrangements were; all assembled guessed that Colonel von Frickstein had a supply of white pills.

Lieutenant Colonel Schöndienst, a short, wiry, handsome man of thirty-four, stepped forward. *"Herr Generalfeldmarschall,* your words are comforting but they are unnecessary. Each of us has already made his choice. The radios are ready, and officers in each of our commands have been alerted."

Rommel looked around. Behind the group of officers and aides was a light truck. On the lowered lip sat two 100W transmitters and a receiving set. Taped to the radios Rommel could see two sticks of dynamite, set for destruction in the event of discovery. Next to the truck, in a line, were five staff cars. Everything was ready.

Rommel glanced at his watch. It was 0610 hours.

The heavy truck slowed down only slightly as it rounded the turn and entered the village of Vierville. It had been a harrowing journey from Tour-en-Bessin, down the partially destroyed road, dodging fleeing civilians and Wehrmacht trucks mired down in the mud or burning along the shoulder after being hit by bombs. The strafing Spitfires of the RAF had not helped matters. Josef Kreitzl was not in a good mood when they finally arrived.

"The Wehrmacht garrison, *Herr Hauptsturmführer.*" The truck rumbled down the cobblestone streets. At the central intersection, Blickensderfer turned the vehicle to the right and headed for the town center. From all directions came the sounds of gunfire, sometimes single shots, sometimes whole bursts. Kreitzl strained to see troops, friendly or otherwise, but could see only burning buildings. The Allied bombers have certainly done their work on this little town, he thought.

The truck pulled up in front of the Hôtel de Ville and Kreitzl alighted. The city hall was an unpretentious two-story building right on the central square. From just below the French windows on the second floor a flagstaff jutted out over the marketplace. From it flew a Nazi flag which had been shredded and burned. Beneath it several Werhmacht soldiers stood against the walls, machine pistols poised. Kreitzl walked briskly across the littered street to the sergeant who commanded them, a Silesian by accent, who was at least sixty years old.

"*Was gibt's?*" asked Kreitzl as he glanced sharply at the motley crew.

"*Ich weiss nicht, Herr Sturmbannführer,*" replied the old soldier in his thin, cracked voice. "All morning there have been gunshots and bombs." The old man's face trembled with fear and ignorance. Kreitzl clicked his tongue.

"What Wehrmacht officers have been here?" Blickensderfer walked up at that moment. Kreitzl noticed him out of the corner of his eye as he stood gazing at the village in apparent wonderment.

"There was a command car an hour ago, *Herr Sturmbannführer*, if that is what you mean."

"Who was in it?"

"*Ich weiss nicht, Herr Sturmbannführer.* Two officers. That's all."

Blickensderfer stiffened. "Officers? Did you recognize them?"

"*Nein, Herr Hauptsturmführer.*"

"Where did the car go?" asked Kreitzl.

"Out the road. Toward Colleville."

A small alarm bell went off in the back of Kreitzl's mind. They had just traveled the road from Colleville, but he had seen no such command car. "Are you sure, *Unterfeldwebel?*"

"*Jawohl, Herr Sturmbannführer.* Not an hour ago."

"And you have no idea where it was headed?"

The old man shook his head woefully, the helmet bouncing as he did. "*Nein, Herr Sturmbannführer.* Except perhaps the farm."

Kreitzl remembered that the officer at Carentan had mentioned a farm where Allied agents had been hidden. "Farm? Where?"

"At the end of town, *Herr Sturmbannführer.* There is a field headquarters there, I believe."

Kreitzl's blood quickened. There was no field headquarters answering that description for kilometers. The puzzle fit together. The farm must be the rendezvous point for the mysterious staff car and the Allied agent. "Quickly! How do I get there?"

"Toward Colleville, *Herr Sturmbannführer.* The first road to the south."

Kreitzl waved the old man back, then started for the truck. Blickensderfer looked up. *"Herr Sturmbannführer?"*

"Yes?"

"There is something I must tell you. There were reports yesterday from this district of a Wehrmacht officer traveling alone with his aide."

"Where?"

"Colleville, *Herr Sturmbannführer.*"

"Who was it?"

"I cannot remember, *Herr Sturmbannführer.* I believe it was a *Generalfeldmarschall.*"

Kreitzl stared at the pudgy officer, his anger rising. "Why was I not informed?"

"It was late and there was a storm, *Herr Sturmbannführer.* I thought it unnecessary to make the SAK turn in their written report."

Kreitzl was incredulous. The essential clue had been kept from him by a bumbling aide. *"Herr Hauptsturmführer,* you had best pray we are not too late! If we are, I promise you a firing squad!"

The truck took off and did a full circle in the town square of Vierville. With a squeal of tires, it headed back out of the town the way it had come. The old sergeant stared after it in bewilderment. Then he turned toward the clock tower on the Hôtel de Ville.

It was half past six.

It was 0630 hours when the armored car entered Vierville from the west. Captain Schmeling slowed down to avoid the litter and rubble in the streets. Tim looked fixedly through the narrow window of the armored vehicle. The destruction of the bombs shook him. He wondered what was happening half a mile to the north, where V Corps was supposed to be landing at Omaha Beach.

As they approached the middle of town, Tim could see the

real extent of the havoc spread by the bombers. Even as they drove through, a wave of planes passed overhead. Bombs whistled, and a trail of destruction appeared. Tim glanced up in time to see the steeple of the town church collapse in a blast of flames and smoke.

"*Augenblick, Herr Amerikaner.* We are nearly there." The car continued past the main intersection and headed east toward Colleville. As they passed the last house, Tim felt the car slowing. They turned down a shaded road which appeared to lead deep into the woods. The heavy steel car drove slowly down the rut-filled road, hidden by the cover of the oak trees. Fifty yards up the road, Schmeling stopped.

Tim looked at Schmeling, who jerked his thumb up. Tim understood and, with a deft single motion, undid the lock on the hatch cover. Schmeling threw the lid open with a resounding clang, reached behind the driver's seat, took a pair of binoculars from the case mounted there, and climbed up onto the rung welded onto the car's wall, so that he was standing halfway out of the hatch.

Tim peered at the roadway through the slit window. He felt lightheaded. He told himself over and over that he was nearly home free, that despite the setbacks and crossed signals, he was near the rendezvous. He knew his body couldn't hold out much longer. As soon as contact was made, he knew he would collapse.

"*Solch ein Pech!*" Tim turned to see Schmeling drop down into the armored car. The expression on the German's face was grim. He handed Tim the glasses. "*Sehen Sie selbst, Herr Amerikaner.*" Tim climbed up into the hatch. The cool wind of the morning felt good after the hot ride from Pont-sur-Douve.

He scanned the forest with the thick lenses. The trees moved in a dreamy procession across the wide field, the foreshortened distances causing Tim's head to swim. The glasses focused on the roadway, then passed over the trees lining the road, over the underbrush and edge of the woods and the pastureland.

It was as Tim swept them back across the vista that he saw it. A stifled cry of despair swept him as he stared through the binoculars. At the edge of the forest, banked off what appeared to be a small country lane, was a large black troop truck. And running from the truck in assault formation were men in black uniforms. Even as Tim watched, the uniforms melted into the woods. The detachment was taking up positions for an assault.

Tim dropped back down into the body of the car. He looked at Schmeling questioningly. The German stared through the slit window and exhaled slowly. *"SS, Herr Amerikaner.* They have discovered the rendezvous."

"And the field marshal?"

"He is there. He will be killed. Or he will kill himself."

Tim paused. He tried to count in his mind's eye the number of uniforms he had seen. There couldn't have been more than twenty. He looked back at Schmeling.

"Well?" Tim said.

"Das Machinengewehr, Herr Amerikaner," he said, jerking his head toward the hatch where the gun was mounted. "Can you work it?"

Josef Kreitzl withdrew his binoculars from their case and held them firmly as he circled through the forest. The damp leaves brushed against his face coldly and he batted them away, but he kept his eyes on his objective. One by one he motioned to his men to take positions. He had left three men at the truck. If the victims tried to escape down the roadway, the heavy antitank gun on the truck would blow them into pieces. Kreitzl smiled slightly. The trap was complete.

Kreitzl deployed the last of his men by assigning six of them to continue the circle behind him. When they found their spots, he guessed that he was at the middle of a semicircle which stretched some two hundred meters and was not more than a hundred meters from the farm. At a signal from him, the SS men dropped down into the brush to wait.

He could see little through the dense foliage. Quietly he

cleared away some of the leaves in front of him. Through the binoculars he could dimly make out forms walking back and forth but he was unable to make out any details. Putting the glasses down, he saw a break in the underbrush beneath one of the large chestnut trees, seven or eight meters away. He decided it was worth the risk and crawled slowly through the bushes until he reached the base of the tree. He pulled himself up against the treetrunk and took another look.

It was just by chance that he happened to fix on one of the figures in the clearing just as the graying man turned around to talk with someone. The powerful glasses zeroed in on the face of Erwin Rommel.

The field marshal began pacing nervously in the grassy clearing by the farmhouse. It was almost 0700 hours. He worried that the rendezvous had been broken again, that the SS had caught up with the Allied agent, and that the entire plan had been destroyed. He wondered if General Speidel had made it back to La Roche-Guyon from Herrlingen.

From the direction of the coast came muted explosions— sounds of a tremendous struggle. Overhead the Allied planes still crisscrossed, unloading their cargoes of bombs on the cliffs and inland towns. He could feel the earth trembling still, even though he was a full three kilometers away.

Yet he stood in a haven, a strange no-man's-land in a world being devastated by war. Birds sang in the trees. It was beautifully quiet. Rommel scanned the trees and pasturelands to the north. Perhaps it was even too quiet. Colonel von Frickstein walked over to him, his face drawn with tension. Rommel glanced at his watch.

"Oh-seven-hundred hours, von Frickstein."

"Ja, Herr Generalfeldmarschall."

Von Frickstein shook his head. He glanced back at the assembled Wehrmacht officers and shared their concern. Each one paced nervously, smoking, talking in quick, hushed sentences to one another, and, above all, looking constantly out into the pasture.

Kreitzl replaced the binoculars into their case. He thought back quickly over the long winter, the suspicions he had held, the mysterious prisoner exchanges, the codes, the airdrops. Everything. He had been right. Knochen would be properly impressed, he thought, when he found out the full story. Kreitzl reached down and pulled the Walther from its holster. Now his, Josef Kreitzl's, hour had arrived.

He stood up and fired twice into the air. From the bushes around him similar shots rang out. With a cry the SS men leaped out from their positions and rushed toward the clearing.

The Wehrmacht officers faced the woods with startled looks. Von Frickstein pulled Rommel to the ground as stray bullets zoomed over their heads.

"*Halt!*"

The explosion of the dynamite attached to the radios threw everyone who had been standing to the ground. Splintered sections of trees shot upward and a shower of dirt rained down over the fallen soldiers. As the blast echoed through the trees, von Frickstein rose to his knees. One of the SS men started running toward the roadway to cut off the escape route. Von Frickstein took aim with his Walther. The automatic barked, and the man threw up his hands and twisted with a scream to a motionless heap on the grass.

Lieutenant Colonel Schöndienst was the first of the Wehrmacht officers to reach his car. The Mercedes roared into life, and his aide wrenched the car around the farmhouse and headed for the road. As the car swung onto the dirt, a burst of machine-gun fire from the woods ripped across the engine block, hit the aide, and lifted Schöndienst nearly out of his seat. The car careened wildly over the ruts as the body of the officer fell limply into the back seat. With a screech of brakes, the aide swerved sideways into a tree. Escaping gasoline hit the hot engine block and ignited with a breathy roar.

The SS men started devastating the clearing with fire. The Wehrmacht officers returned the fire as best they could with their sidearms as they crawled toward the safety of the farmhouse. Kreitzl, running up from the rear, yelled to his men to cease firing. As they did, the smoke hung in low clouds across the clearing. The crashed automobile continued to burn in a fury of yellow flame.

"By order of the Führer, you are all under arrest!" Kreitzl yelled. "Throw down your arms! You are surrounded! In the name of the Führer, surrender!"

It was at this point that the German armored car burst through the woods with a lumbering roar, its turret machine gun pouring a murderous volley of lead into the underbrush. The startled SS men turned just in time to meet the deadly bullets. One by one they screamed and fell into the wet foliage. Others dove frantically behind trees in an effort to escape the fire. Yells of agony came from the wounded. Kreitzl turned to stare at the mechanical beast coming toward him, his jaw open, his eyes filled with confusion. The fire from the armored car continued to strafe the trees, sending bullets ricocheting in every direction.

Von Frickstein rose to his knees and grabbed Rommel's arm, pulling both of them to their feet as they stared at the armored car, this strange deliverance from the hands of Providence.

Von Frickstein beckoned toward the farmhouse, and, crouching, they dashed toward the shelter. Bullets whistled around them as they slipped on the wet grass and flung themselves through the open doorway. Inside, they continued to gaze at the car, which had almost disappeared behind a screen of smoke.

Von Frickstein turned to see several of the Wehrmacht officers rushing from the back door of the farmhouse. One by one their cars kicked into life. The first one, carrying General Erdheim, swerved past the burning wreckage of Schöndienst's car and headed down the road. Von Frickstein watched as it rounded the curve only to be met with heavy artillery fire. The Mercedes lurched, exploded, and came to rest on the shoulder of the road.

The blue smoke was so dense that Tim could barely see where he was shooting. He hung onto the handles of the gun, vibrating with it as the hot barrel spewed out its deadly rounds. His fatigued mind knew nothing but the reality of the crackling gun at his command. He became a madman, spraying bullets at everything that moved in front of him.

Then the ammunition ran out. In a fury Tim grabbed at the gun, trying to coax rounds out of it which no longer existed. He looked up in panic to see the remaining black-shirted soldiers rising from their hiding places. He uttered a stifled cry as he saw one SS man pull the pin on a grenade. As if in a slow-motion dream, he watched the man throw the projectile in his direction. Suddenly the sounds of war stopped, the world disappeared over a distant ridge, and he watched the black object fly through the air toward him. The slow arc downward triggered a reflex in him. He placed his hands on either side of the turret and, with a mighty heave, threw himself out of the hatch onto the side of the car. He heard the grenade clank against the side of the hatch as it bounced down inside the car. He rolled off onto the ground just as the muffled explosion brought to a sudden end the earthly existence of Captain Schmeling.

Tim rolled over and, still prone, looked up to see the SS detachment start its charge. He struggled desperately with his woolen shirt to free the machine pistol he had taken from the arsenal at La Barquette. The grip caught on the rough cloth, and he swore as he grabbed wildly to free it. The SS men were thirty feet away now. One of them, apparently the leader, raised his automatic and pointed it at Tim as he ran.

Tim emptied the entire clip into the advancing line. The black uniforms fell amid shrieks of pain. The officer, hit several times, stopped in his tracks and wavered hesitantly before he fell to the ground with a crash.

Then Tim saw Rommel. The aged general was unmistakable, for Tim had studied his picture a thousand times. He was running with another, younger officer toward the last staff car behind the farmhouse. A cry stopped in Tim's throat. His quarry was escaping. Across his mind flashed the last nine months of his life, months of planning, plotting, and study, of deciphering codes, of memorizing troop displacements, of Beauclerk's crusty laugh, of Hardaway's cocked eyebrows, of Pru's warm smiles. He leaped to his feet.

It was thirty yards to where the clearing merged into the dirt road. Tim started to run, his lungs bursting, his limbs aching as he slipped on the grass. The giant Mercedes lumbered over a tree limb, turned to the right, and started for the road.

"Rommel!" Tim yelled.

The car slowed down, and Tim saw the young officer at the wheel turn and look quickly out the window at him. The car stopped just as Tim tripped and fell prostrate on the ground. As he pushed himself up on his hands, he saw someone step out of the car and turn toward him.

For a flash of eternity their eyes met. Tim recognized the weathered visage of the man he had chased for such a long time. He scrambled back to his feet and started running, his mouth begging without sound, even pleading. Shells raced across the clearing from the truck parked down the road. Rommel's gaze turned from Tim to the truck, then made up his mind. In an instant he ducked back into the car, and it roared away toward the road.

"No! Stop!" Tim kept running. He tripped again over a tree branch but was on his feet in a second. Then he saw the black truck blocking the road, its three-man crew preparing to fire at Rommel's car. The Mercedes veered off to the right in an attempt to get around the vehicle. Tim yelled loudly. The soldiers on the truck looked up. One of them twisted the gun and aimed it directly at Tim. He was fifteen yards away now. He yelled again for the Mercedes to stop.

The car managed to pass the truck and pick up speed on the

road. That much Tim saw as the shell from the antitank gun exploded at his feet. The searing pain stopped him in his tracks. The second shell exploded to his right, sending scraps of hot lead ripping into his abdomen and chest. His body collapsed, caved in, and waves of shock raced through him. He opened his eyes one last time and saw the gray sky spinning dizzily above him. Then it was blackness as he tumbled headlong to the ground and lay profoundly still.

EPILOGUE

The tall soldier turned to shut the high oak door behind him and then strode down the spacious corridor beneath the soaring rotunda, his shoes clicking lightly against the patterned marble beneath his feet. A few clerks rushed across the wide space, and other people, ordinary citizens, wandered aimlessly. The soldier was at the top of the alabaster and marble staircase which swept grandly down to the first floor when the voice stopped him.

He turned slowly back toward the direction from which he had just come and watched another man in uniform approach him.

"Brigadier?"

"Yes?"

"I wanted to catch a word with you before you left."

The dour Scot eyed his companion warily. "Well?"

"I wanted you to know, sir, that I only told the jury what I thought was proper."

"I appreciate that, colonel."

"The whole affair was unfortunate, I think."

"Yes, it was." There was an awkward pause. Beauclerk thrust his hands into the pockets of his rumpled trench coat. "Most unfortunate for the husband."

"I agree, sir. Wife convicted of spying."

"No, colonel, that's not what I mean." Beauclerk stared for a moment at the shiny new brass insignias on the shoulders of the other officer's uniform. "It's grim to learn your wife's cheated. But it's worse to learn it because of a trial."

"I think the judge took that into consideration, sir."

Beauclerk started down the broad staircase of the Old Bailey. The colonel with the graying hair brushed neatly backward from the razor-sharp part extending precisely from the prominent widow's peak walked next to him.

"It was difficult for me to say what I did, sir," said Hardaway.

"I can understand that."

"We've been opposites on this from the beginning."

"There's no need for apologies, colonel. There's no rancor."

"Thank you, sir."

"I fear you were right in the long run."

"Perhaps so, sir." Hardaway nodded solemnly. There was a long pause. "Have you given up hope?"

"It's September, colonel. Four months nearly. Even Rommel's dead now."

"Rommel, sir?"

"It was Rommel we were after."

There was a pause. Hardaway's jaw slackened. "I didn't know that, brigadier. Puts things in a different light."

The two men reached the bottom of the stairs. The main lobby was more crowded as they made their way toward the front doors. Beauclerk walked with his hands still deep in his pockets. Hardaway scratched his chin. They reached the doors and went outside.

The autumn sky was gray in the wet afternoon. Clouds circled low over the bleak landscape of east London. The smoky silhouette of St. Paul's loomed starkly a few blocks away. A chilly wind bit through their clothing as they stopped on the top steps.

"What went wrong, do you know?"

"The usual things, I should think. A missed contact. Bad information." He paused. "Incorrect expectations."

"You don't think she's to blame?"

"No, colonel, I don't. She was foolish. We were all a bit foolish."

The wind blew a few strands of Hardaway's gray hair out of place. He smoothed them back with the palm of his hand. "Blasted shame, really."

"Yes, it is."

Hardaway breathed sharply. "Well, I suppose we must carry on. You have a new assignment, brigadier?"

"No. Same thing."

"Do you think they were too harsh on her?"

Beauclerk pulled out a pack of Senior Service, extracted a cigarette, and lit it. He blew out the smoke through his teeth. "I shouldn't like to spend six years at hard labor. Especially when I was only a victim of my own caring."

"No, sir, I suppose not."

A black Austin pulled up to the curb below them. The driver's door opened and a young lieutenant stepped around to the sidewalk and saluted.

Hardaway saluted back. He turned to Beauclerk. "My car's here. I'm afraid I must be off."

"Very good, colonel."

"Need a lift?"

"No, thank you. I'd rather walk, I think."

"As you wish, sir. Best of luck."

"You, too, colonel. Best of luck."

Hardaway walked down the steps to the waiting Austin. The lieutenant opened the car door for him, and he disappeared inside. Then the soldier walked around the rear of the car, got in, and drove off.

Beauclerk stared after the car for a moment, then looked back across the rooftops. A light drizzle began. The rain felt sharp and bitter against his skin. He winced slightly. Then he took another long draw on his cigarette and threw the stub across the steps.

With a sigh he replaced his hands in the trench coat, walked down the broad steps, and headed up the road toward Newgate Street. A low rumble of thunder heralded the storm.

It ended, as it had begun, in the rain.

PS
3552
.O888
S64
1979

$18.95